Technohorror:
Inventions in Terror

Also edited by James Frenkel

Bangs and Whimpers:
Stories About the End of the World

Technohorror:
Inventions in Terror

EDITED BY
JAMES FRENKEL

LOWELL HOUSE
LOS ANGELES
NTC/Contemporary Publishing Group

Published by Lowell House
A division of NTC/Contemporary Publishing Group, Inc.
4255 West Touhy Avenue, Lincolnwood (Chicago), Illinois 60646-1975 U.S.A.

A Blue Cow/Mad City Production

Lowell House books can be purchased at special discounts when ordered in bulk for premiums and special sales. Contact Department CS at the following address:
NTC/Contemporary Publishing Group
4255 West Touhy Avenue
Lincolnwood, IL 60646-1975
1-800-323-4900

ISBN: 0-7373-0298-4
Library of Congress Catalog Card Number: 99-73649

Roxbury Park is a division of NTC/Contemporary Publishing Group, Inc.

Managing Director and Publisher: Jack Artenstein
Editor in Chief, Roxbury Park Books: Michael Artenstein
Director of Publishing Services: Rena Copperman
Editorial Assistant: Nicole Monastirsky
Assistant Editors: Seth Johnson, Kristopher O'Higgins
Interior Designer: Susan H. Hartman
Cover Art: Ron Walotsky

Printed and bound in the United States of America
99 00 01 DHD 10 9 8 7 6 5 4 3 2 1

Grateful acknowledgment is made for permission to reprint the following works:

"Pretty Maggie Moneyeyes" Copyright © 1967 by Harlan Ellison. Renewed, copyright © 1995 by Harlan Ellison. Reprinted by arrangement with, and permission of, the Author and the Author's agent, Richard Curtis Associates, Inc., New York, USA. All rights reserved.

"Thinkertoy" Copyright © 1996 by John Brunner Fact & Fiction Ltd. Reprinted by permission of John Hawkins & Associates, Inc.

"Scatter My Ashes" Copyright © 1988 by *Interzone*. First published in *Interzone* #23, Spring 1988. Reprinted by permission of the author.

"Descending" Copyright © 1964 by Thomas M. Dish. First published in *Fantastic,* July 1964. Reprinted by permission of the author.

"That Hellbound Train" Copyright © 1958 by Mercury Press, Inc. First appeared in *The Magazine of Fantasy & Science Fiction,* September 1958. Reprinted by permission of the author's estate, and the agents for the estate, Ralph M. Vicinanza, Ltd.

"Survival Kit" Copyright © 1957 by Galaxy Publishing Corporation. First published in *Galaxy Science Fiction*. Reprinted by permission of the author.

"This Life and Later Ones" Copyright © 1987 by Davis Publications, Inc. First published in *Analog,* February 1987. Reprinted by permission of the author and the author's agents, Richard Curtis Associates, 171 E. 74th Street, New York, NY 10021.

"The Veldt" Copyright © 1950 by Curtis Publishing Co., renewed 1977 by Ray Bradbury. Reprinted by permission of Don Congdon Associates, Inc.

"Little Man" Copyright © 1986 by TZ Publications. First published in *Night Cry,* volume 2, number 2, Winter 1986, edited by Alan Rodgers. Reprinted by permission of the author.

Contents

Introduction
James Frenkel — xi

Pretty Maggie Moneyeyes
Harlan Ellison — 1

Thinkertoy
John Brunner — 23

Scatter My Ashes
Greg Egan — 37

Descending
Thomas M. Disch — 51

That Hellbound Train
Robert Bloch — 65

Survival Kit
Frederik Pohl — 81

This Life and Later Ones
George Zebrowski — 117

The Veldt
Ray Bradbury — 129

Little Man
Ramsey Campbell 145

Screens
John Shirley 157

Mammy Morgan Played the Organ,
Her Daddy Beat the Drum
Michael Flynn 181

Masks
Damon Knight 231

But Smile No More
Stephen Dedman 243

The Dead
Michael Swanwick 253

Patterns
Pat Cadigan 268

The Mangler
Stephen King 275

Acknowledgments

For their help in putting together *Technohorror,* I'd like to thank my editor at Lowell House, Mark Waldman; Michael Artenstein; and all the rest of the Lowell House crew. My assistant editors Seth Johnson and Kristopher O'Higgins kept track of the details, rode the front wave of letters, faxes, E-mails, and phone calls that any project like this generates, and made great contributions to making this the book it's finally become. My hard-working crew of interns help me stay afloat and suggested a couple of stories I might have otherwise overlooked. Finally, and at long last, I'd like to acknowledge all the help Marc Wolfman, Brian Ruske, and the fine folks at Insty-Prints on Park have given us over the years: Thanks, guys.

—JF

ACKNOWLEDGMENTS

Introduction

We tend to think of horror as coming to us in our nightmares. Horror is commonly associated with creepy-crawly things, things that go bump in the night. We've made a connection between the words *fear* and *unknown*. This is perfectly reasonable. We do fear the unknown. It's part of human nature. But there are other things to fear, some of them not natural at all.

Technohorror is a word that has been used for at least fifteen years by various writers and editors to describe stories in which some man-made device, in one way or another, is connected to something scary. In a world where machines are *supposed* to be helpful to people, we've found ample reasons during this century to be suspicious, if not outright fearful, of things that go *clank, whirr,* or *bzzz* in the night.

If nothing before World War II made people wary of science and technology, the explosion of the first atomic bomb was an event that terrified the entire world. Even those who previously had been advocates of technological progress had to pause and rethink their feelings about advances in science and technology.

So technohorror, while it may seem an almost oxymoronic term, isn't so far fetched after all. Hasn't everyone tried to talk to a machine to get it to work right? Why do we do that? Machines don't have minds to understand our thoughts . . . or do they?

Maybe it all started with Mary Shelley. When she wrote *Frankenstein; or, The Modern Prometheus* in 1818 (revised in 1836), technology was primitive compared with the fabulous machines we have today. Yet even then the advent of mechanical constructs was changing society in many ways. Cities were growing due to a rise in manufacturing, with all the attendant urban ills—crime, disease, pollution, overcrowding; England, which had been a farming and merchant nation, became a nation of factories as well.

The change of England from a primarily small-town nation to one with great cities created not only urban problems, but personal ones as well. Family life changed as children were pressed to work in factories alongside their parents; nor were there were any real checks on abusive practices by employers. As Ebenezer Scrooge noted in Dickens's *A Christmas Carol,* "are not the orphanages and workhouses still in operation?"

Indeed, they were. Dickens could recall, as he did in his first novel, *The Pickwick Papers,* a simpler society with a more generous and less trying spirit. But the spirit of that earlier time was fast giving way to the harder, meaner spirit of industrial England.

Dickens could feel the dark spirit of machines. In much of his work the factories, the businesses, and the encroachments of more "modern" life were enemies to be overcome or accommodated. They displaced people who weren't ready to master these new tools. Like many of the people in the stories in this anthology, they were afraid of the power and dark potentials of the machines that could help—or replace—human workers, as reflected almost a century later in Kurt Vonnegut's *Cat's Cradle.*

We've had more than a century since Dickens in which to understand and trust machines, but no matter how fast we adapt to the machines of yesterday, it seems there are always new machines or faster, better, more complex ones to keep us wary and fearful of the whole breed.

The stories we call technohorrors all have in common some element of technology, but other than that, this is a diverse group of variously scary, creepy, disquieting, unsettling, or downright horrifying tales. From the literally electrifying terror of Harlan Ellison's "Pretty Maggie Moneyeyes" to the eerie, ghostly visitations in Michael Flynn's "Mammy Morgan Played the Organ; Her Daddy Beat the Drum"; from the chilling terror of Ray Bradbury's "The Veldt" to the classically seductive devil of a conductor in Robert Bloch's "That Hellbound Train"; from the furiously homicidal menace of Stephen King's "The Mangler" to the cool, quiet horror of Thomas M. Disch's "Descending" and in all the other stories in this book, you'll find technohorrors to tickle your every taste for the scary, the deadly, the suspenseful.

At the root of horror lies the understanding that after you've put down the book, you can turn the lights up bright and feel safe, because the horror isn't in your life but in the book.

That's what they tell you, anyway.

Good luck.

Pretty Maggie Moneyeyes

Harlan Ellison

Harlan Ellison is the recipient of the Writers Guild of America most outstanding teleplay award (four times), the Horror Writers Association Bram Stoker Award (five times, including the Life Achievement Award), the Silver Pen for Journalism from PEN, the World Fantasy Award, the British Fantasy Award, the Mystery Writers of America Edgar Award, the Science Fiction Writers of America's Nebula Award (three times), the Hugo Award (eight and a half times). He is quite simply, as the *Washington Post Book World* said, "One of the great living American short story writers."

When this story was first published in 1967, it was something completely new and different. It perfectly epitomizes the concept of technohorror, melding the real and the surreal in a nightmarish tale of revenge from beyond the grave. Its depiction of Las Vegas casino gambling is as fresh today as it was then; its portrait of desperate lives all too real. Ellison's energy and vivid, incisive prose style combine to make this a brilliantly intense story of loss, longing, and redemption.

With an eight hole-card and a queen showing, with the dealer showing a four up, Kostner decided to let the house do the work. So he stood, and the dealer turned up. Six.

The dealer looked like something out of a 1935 George Raft film: Arctic diamond-chip eyes, manicured fingers long as a brain surgeon's, straight black hair slicked flat away from the pale forehead. He did not look up as he peeled them off. A three. Another three. Bam. A five. Bam. Twenty-one, and Kostner saw his last thirty dollars—six five-dollar chips—scraped on the edge of the cards, into the dealer's chip racks. Busted. Flat. Down and out in Las Vegas, Nevada. Playground of the Western World.

He slid off the comfortable stool-chair and turned his back on the blackjack table. The action was already starting again, like waves closing over a drowned man. He had been there, was gone, and no one had noticed. No one had seen a man blow the last tie with salvation. Kostner now had his choice: he could bum his way into Los Angeles and try to find something that resembled a new life . . . or he could go blow his brains out through the back of his head.

Neither choice showed much light or sense.

He thrust his hands deep into the pockets of his worn and dirty chinos, and started away down the line of the slot machines clanging and rattling on the other side of the aisle between blackjack tables.

He stopped. He felt something in his pocket. Beside him, but all-engrossed, a fiftyish matron in electric lavender capris, high heels and Ship 'n' Shore blouse was working two slots, loading and pulling one while waiting for the other to clock down. She was dumping quarters in a seemingly inexhaustible supply from a Dixie cup held in her left hand. There was a surrealistic presence to the woman. She was almost automated, not a flicker of expression on her face, the eyes fixed and unwavering. Only when the gong rang, someone down the line had pulled a jackpot, did she look up. And at that moment Kostner knew what was wrong and immoral and deadly about Vegas, about legalized gambling, about setting the traps all baited and open in front of the average human. The woman's face was gray with hatred, envy, lust and dedication to the game—in that timeless instant when she heard another drugged soul down the line winning a minuscule jackpot. A jackpot that would only lull the player with words like *luck* and *ahead of the game*. The jackpot lure; the sparkling, bobbling, many-colored wiggler in a sea of poor fish.

The thing in Kostner's pocket was a silver dollar.

He brought it out and looked at it.

The eagle was hysterical.

But Kostner pulled to an abrupt halt, only one half-footstep from the sign indicating the limits of Tap City. He was still with it. What the high-rollers called the edge, the *vigerish,* the fine hole-card. One buck. One cartwheel. Pulled out of the pocket not half as deep as the pit into which Kostner had just been about to plunge.

What the hell, he thought, and turned to the row of slot machines.

He had thought they'd all been pulled out of service, the silver dollar slots. A shortage of coinage, said the United States Mint. But right there, side by side with the nickel and quarter bandits, was one cartwheel machine. Two thousand dollar jackpot. Kostner grinned foolishly. If you're gonna go out, go out like a champ.

He thumbed the silver dollar into the coin slot and grabbed the heavy, oiled handle. Shining cast aluminum and pressed steel. Big black plastic ball, angled for arm ease, pull it all day and you won't get weary.

Without a prayer in the universe, Kostner pulled the handle.

▼

She had been born in Tucson, mother full-blooded Cherokee, father a bindlestiff on his way through. Mother had been working a truckers' stop, father had popped for spencer steak and sides. Mother had just gotten over a bad scene, indeterminate origins, unsatisfactory culminations. Mother had popped for bed. And sides. Margaret Annie Jessie had come nine months later; black of hair, fair of face, and born into a life of poverty. Twenty-three years later, a determined product of Miss Clairol and Berlitz, a dream-image formed by Vogue *and intimate association with the rat race, Margaret Annie Jessie had become a contraction.*

Maggie.

Long legs, trim and coltish; hips a trifle large, the kind that promote that *specific thought in men, about getting their hands around it; belly flat, isometrics; waist cut to the bone, a waist that works in any style from dirndl to disco-slacks; no breasts—all nipple, but no breast, like an expensive whore (the way O'Hara pinned it)—and no padding . . . forget the cans, baby, there's other, more important action; smooth, Michelangelo-sculpted neck, a pillar, proud; and all that face.*

Outthrust chin, perhaps a tot too much belligerence, but if you'd walloped as many gropers, you too, sweetheart; narrow mouth, petulant lower lip, nice to chew on, a lower lip as though filled with honey, bursting, ready for things to happen; a nose that threw the right sort of shadow, flaring nostrils, the acceptable words—aquiline, patrician, classic, allathat; cheekbones as stark and promontory as a spit of land after ten years of open ocean; cheekbones holding darkness like narrow shadows, sooty beneath the taut-fleshed bone-structure; amazing cheekbones, the whole face, really; an ancient kingdom's uptilted eyes, the touch of the Cherokee, eyes that looked out at you, as you looked in at them, like someone peering out of the keyhole as you peered in; actually, dirty eyes, they said you can get it.

Blonde hair, a great deal of it, wound and rolled and smoothed and flowing, in the old style, the pageboy thing men always admire; no tight little cap of slicked plastic; no ratted and teased Annapurna of bizarre coiffure; no ironed-flat discothèque hair like number 3 flat noodles. Hair, the way a man wants it, so he can dig his hands in at the base of the neck and pull all that face very close.

An operable woman, a working mechanism, a rigged and sudden machinery of softness and motivation.

Twenty-three, and determined as hell never to abide in that vale of poverty her mother had called purgatory for her entire life; snuffed out in a grease fire in the last trailer, somewhere in Arizona, thank God no more pleas for a little money from babygirl Maggie hustling drinks in a Los Angeles topless joint. (There ought to be some remorse in there somewhere, for a Mommy gone where all the good grease-fire victims go. Look around, you'll find it.)

Maggie.

Genetic freak. Mommy's Cherokee uptilted eye-shape, and Polack quickscrewing Daddy WithoutaNames's blue as innocence color.

Blue-eyed Maggie, dyed blonde, alla that face, alla that leg, fifty bucks a night can get it and it sounds *like it's having a climax.*

Irish-innocent blue-eyed-innocent French-legged-innocent Maggie. Polack. Cherokee. Irish. All-woman and going on the market for this month's rent on the stucco pad, eighty bucks' worth of groceries, a couple months' worth for a Mustang, three appointments with the specialist in Beverly Hills about that shortness of breath after a night on the hustle bump the sticky thigh the disco lurch the gotcha sweat: woman minutes. Increments under the meat; perspiration purchases, yeah it does.

Maggie, Maggie, Maggie, pretty Maggie Moneyeyes, who came from Tucson and trailers and rheumatic fever and a surge to live that was all kaleidoscope frenzy of clawing scabbling no-nonsense. If it took lying on one's back and making sounds like a panther in the desert, then one did it, because nothing, but nothing *was as bad as being dirt-poor, itchy-skinned, soiled-underwear, scuff-toed, hairy and ashamed lousy with the no-gots. Nothing!*

Maggie. Hooker. Hustler. Grabber. Swinger. If there's a buck in it, there's rhythm and the onomatopoeia is Maggie Maggie Maggie.

She who puts out. For a price, whatever that might be.

Maggie was dating Nuncio. He was Sicilian. He had dark eyes and an alligator-grain wallet with slip-in pockets for credit cards. He was a spender, a sport, a high-roller. They went to Vegas.

Maggie and the Sicilian. Her blue eyes and his slip-in pockets. But mostly her blue eyes.

▼

The spinning reels behind the three long glass windows blurred, and Kostner knew there wasn't a chance. Two thousand dollar jackpot. Round and round, whirring. Three bells or two bells and a jackpot bar, get 18; three plums or two plums and a jackpot bar, get 14; three oranges or two oranges and a jac—

Ten, five, two bucks for a single cherry cluster in first position. Something . . . I'm drowning . . . Something . . .

The whirring . . .

Round and round . . .

As something happened that was not considered in the pit-boss manual.

The reels whipped and snapped to a stop, clank clank clank, tight in place.

Three bars looked up at Kostner. But they did not say JACKPOT. They were three bars from which stared three blue eyes. Very blue, very immediate, very JACKPOT!!

Twenty silver dollars clattered into the payoff trough at the bottom of the machine. An orange light popped on in the casino cashier's cage, bright orange on the jackpot board. And the gong began clanging overhead.

The Slot Machine Floor Manager nodded once to the Pit Boss, who pursed his lips and started toward the seedy-looking man still standing with his hand on the slot's handle.

The token payment—twenty silver dollars—lay untouched in the payoff trough. The balance of the jackpot—one thousand nine hundred and eighty dollars—would be paid manually, by the casino cashier. And Kostner stood, dumbly as the three blue eyes stared up at him.

There was a moment of idiotic disorientation, as Kostner stared back at the three blue eyes; a moment in which the slot machine's mechanisms registered to themselves; and the gong was clanging furiously.

All through the hotel's casino people turned from their games to stare. At the roulette tables the white-on-white players from Detroit and Cleveland pulled their watery eyes away from the clattering ball and stared down the line for a second, at the ratty-looking guy in front of the slot machine. From where they sat, they could not tell it was a two grand pot, and their rheumy eyes went back into billows of cigar smoke, and that little ball.

The blackjack hustlers turned momentarily, screwing around in their seats, and smiled. They were closer to the slot-players in temperament, but they knew the slots were a dodge to keep the old ladies busy, while the players worked toward their endless twenty-ones.

And the old dealer, who could no longer cut it at the fast-action boards, who had been put out to pasture by a grateful management, standing at the Wheel of Fortune near the entrance to the casino, even he paused in his zombie-murmuring ("Annnnother winner onna Wheel of Forchun!") to no one at all, and looked toward Kostner and that incredible gong-clanging. Then, in a moment, still with no players, he called *another* nonexistent winner.

Kostner heard the gong from far away. It had to mean he had won two thousand dollars, but that was impossible. He checked the payoff chart on the face of the machine. Three bars labeled JACKPOT meant JACKPOT. Two thousand dollars.

But these three bars did not say JACKPOT. They were three gray bars, rectangular in shape, with a blue eye directly in the center of each bar.

Blue eyes?

Somewhere, a connection was made, and electricity, a billion volts of electricity, shot through Kostner. His hair stood on end, his fingertips bled raw, his eyes turned to jelly, and every fiber in his musculature became radioactive. Somewhere, out there, in a place that was not this *place, Kostner had been inextricably bound to—to someone.* Blue eyes?

The gong had faded out of his head, the constant noise level of the casino, chips chittering, people mumbling, dealers calling plays, it had all gone, and he was embedded in silence.

Tied to that someone else, out there somewhere, through those three blue eyes.

Then in an instant, it had passed, and he was alone again, as though released by a giant hand, the breath crushed out of him. He staggered up against the slot machine.

"You all right, fellah?"

A hand gripped him by the arm, steadied him. The gong was still clanging overhead somewhere, and he was breathless from a journey he had just taken. His eyes focused and he found himself looking at the stocky Pit Boss who had been on duty while he had been playing blackjack.

"Yeah . . . I'm okay, just a little dizzy is all."

"Sounds like you got yourself a big jackpot, fellah." The Pit Boss grinned; it was a leathery grin; something composed of stretched muscles and conditioned reflexes, totally mirthless.

"Yeah . . . great . . . " Kostner tried to grin back. But he was still shaking from that electrical absorption that had kidnapped him.

"Let me check it out," the Pit Boss was saying, edging around Kostner, and staring at the face of the slot machine. "Yeah, three jackpot bars, all right. You're a winner."

Then it dawned on Kostner! Two thousand dollars! He looked down at the slot machine and saw—

Three bars with the word JACKPOT on them. No blue eyes, just words that meant money. Kostner looked around frantically, was he losing his mind? *From somewhere, not in the casino, he heard a tinkle of rhodium-plated laughter.*

He scooped up the twenty silver dollars. The Pit Boss dropped another cartwheel into the Chief, and pulled the jackpot off. Then the Pit Boss walked him to the rear of the casino, talking to him in a muted, extremely polite tone of voice. At the cashier's window, the Pit Boss nodded to a weary-looking man at a huge Rolodex cardfile, checking credit ratings.

"Barney, jackpot on the cartwheel Chief; slot five-oh-oh-one-five." He grinned at Kostner, who tried to smile back. It was difficult. He felt stunned.

The cashier checked a payoff book for the correct amount to be drawn and leaned over the counter toward Kostner. "Check or cash, sir?"

Kostner felt buoyancy coming back to him. "Is the casino's check good?" They all three laughed at that. "A check's fine," Kostner said. The check was drawn, and the Check-Riter punched out the little bumps that said two thousand. "The twenty cartwheels are a gift," the cashier said, sliding the check through to Kostner.

He held it, looked at it, and still found it difficult to believe. Two grand, back on the golden road.

As he walked back through the casino with the Pit Boss, the stocky man asked pleasantly, "Well, what are you going to do with it?" Kostner had to think a moment. He didn't really have any plans. But the sudden realization came to him: "I'm going to play that slot machine again." The Pit Boss smiled: a congenital sucker. He would put all twenty of those silver dollars back into the Chief, and then turn to the other games. Blackjack, roulette, faro, baccarat . . . in a few hours he would have redeposited the two grand with the hotel casino. It always happened.

He walked Kostner back to the slot machine, and patted him on the shoulder. "Lotsa luck, fellah."

As he turned away, Kostner slipped a silver dollar into the machine, and pulled the handle.

The Pit Boss had only taken five steps when he heard the incredible sound of the reels clicking to a stop, the clash of twenty token silver dollars hitting the payoff trough, and that goddamned gong went out of its mind again.

▼

She had known that sonofabitch Nuncio was a perverted swine. A walking filth. A dungheap between his ears. Some kind of monster in nylon undershorts. There weren't many kinds of games Maggie hadn't played, but what that Sicilian de Sade wanted to do was outright vomity!

She nearly fainted when he suggested it. Her heart—which the Beverly Hills specialist had said she should not tax—began whumping frantically. "You pig!" she screamed. "You filthy dirty ugly pig you, Nuncio you pig!" She had bounded out of the bed and started to throw on clothes. She didn't even bother with a brassiere, pulling the poorboy sweater on over her thin breasts, still crimson with the touches of love-bites Nuncio had showered on them.

He sat up in the bed, a pathetic-looking little man, gray hair at the temples and no hair atall on top, and his eyes were moist. He was porcine, was indeed the swine she had called him, but he was helpless before her. He was in love with his hooker, with the tart whom he was supporting. It had been the first time for the swine Nuncio, and he was helpless. Back in Detroit, had it been a floozy, a bimbo, a chippy broad, he would have gotten out of the double bed and rapped her around pretty good. But this Maggie, she tied him in knots. He had suggested . . . that, *what they should do together . . . because he was so consumed with her. But she was furious with* him. *It wasn't* that *bizarre an idea!*

"Gimme a chanct'a talk t'ya, honey . . . Maggie . . . "

"You filthy pig, Nuncio! Give me some money, I'm going down to the casino, and I don't want to see your filthy pig face for the rest of the day, remember that!"

And she had gone in his wallet and pants, and taken eight hundred and sixteen dollars, while he watched. He was helpless before her. She was something stolen from a world he knew only as "class" and she could do what she wanted with him.

Genetic freak Maggie, blue-eyed posing mannequin Maggie, pretty Maggie Moneyeyes, who was one-half Cherokee and one-half a buncha other things, had absorbed her lessons well. She was the very model of a "class broad."

"Not for the rest of the day, do you understand?" She stared at him till he nodded; then she went downstairs, furious, to fret and gamble and wonder about nothing but years of herself.

Men stared after her as she walked. She carried herself like a challenge, the way a squire carried a pennon, the way a prize bitch carried herself in the judge's ring. Born to the blue. The wonders of mimicry and desire.

Maggie had no lust for gambling, none whatever. She merely wanted to taste the fury of her relationship with the swine Sicilian, her need for solidity in a life built on the edge of the slide area, the senselessness of being here in Las Vegas when she could be back in Beverly Hills. She grew angrier and more ill at the thought of Nuncio upstairs in the room, taking another shower. She bathed three times a day. But it was different with him. He knew she resented his smell; he had the soft odor of wet fur sometimes, and she had told him about it. Now he bathed constantly, and hated it. He was a foreigner to the bath. His life had been marked by various kinds of filths, and baths for him now were more of an obscenity than dirt could ever have been. For her, bathing was different. It was a necessity. She had to keep the patina of the world off her, had to remain clean and smooth and white. A presentation, not an object of flesh and hair. A chromium instrument, something never pitted by rust and corrosion.

When she was touched by them, by any one of them, by the men, by all the Nuncios, they left little pitholes of bloody rust on her white, permanent flesh; cobwebs, sooty stains. She had *to bathe. Often.*

She strolled down between the tables and the slots, carrying eight hundred and sixteen dollars. Eight one hundred dollar bills and sixteen dollars in ones.

At the change booth she got cartwheels for the sixteen ones. The Chief waited. It was her baby. She played it to infuriate the Sicilian. He had told her to play the nickel slots, the quarter or dime slots, but she always infuriated him by blowing fifty or a hundred dollars in ten minutes, one coin after another, in the big Chief.

She faced the machine squarely, and put in the first silver dollar. She pulled the handle that swine Nuncio. Another dollar, pulled the handle how long does this go on? The reels cycled and spun and whirled and whipped in a blurringspinning metalhumming overandoverandoverandover as Maggie blue-eyed Maggie hated and hated and thought of hate and all the days and nights of swine behind her and ahead of her and if only she had all the money in this room in this casino in this hotel in this town right now this very instant just aninstant thisinstant it would be enough to whirring and humming and spinning and overandoverandover and she would be free free free free free and all the world would never touch her body again the swine would never touch her white flesh again and then suddenly as dollarafterdollarafterdollar went aroundaroundaround hummmmming in reels of cherries and bells and bars and plums and oranges there was suddenly painpainpain a SHARP pain!pain!pain! in her chest, her heart , her center, a needle, a lancet, a burning, a pillar of flame that was purest pure purer PAIN!

Maggie, pretty Maggie Moneyeyes, who wanted all that money in that cartwheel Chief slot machine, Maggie who had come from filth and rheumatic fever, who had come all the way to three baths a day and a specialist in Very Expensive Beverly Hills, that *Maggie suddenly had a seizure, a flutter, a slam of a coronary thrombosis and fell instantly dead on the floor of the casino. Dead.*

One instant she had been holding the handle of the slot machine, willing her entire being, all that hatred for all the swine she had ever rolled with, willing every fiber of every cell of every chromosome into that machine, wanting to suck out every silver vapor within its belly, and the next instant—so close they might have been the same—her heart exploded and killed her and she slipped to the floor . . . still touching the Chief.

On the floor.
Dead.
Struck dead.
Liar. All the lies that were her life.
Dead on a floor.

[A moment out of time ■ lights whirling and spinning in a cotton candy universe ■ down a bottomless funnel roundly sectioned like a goat's horn ■ a cornucopia that rose up cuculiform smooth and slick as a worm's belly ■ endless nights that pealed ebony funeral bells ■ out of fog ■ out of weightlessness ■ suddenly total cellular knowledge ■ memory running backward ■ gibbering spastic blindness ■ a soundless owl of frenzy trapped in a cave of prisms ■ sand endlessly draining down ■ billows of forever ■ edges of the world as they splintered ■ foam rising drowning from inside ■ the smell of rust ■ rough green corners that burn ■ memory the gibbering spastic blind memory ■ seven rushing vacuums of nothing ■ yellow ■ pinpoints cast in amber straining and elongating running like live wax ■ chill fevers ■ overhead the odor of stop ■ this is the stopover before hell or heaven ■ this is limbo ■ trapped and doomed alone in a mist-eaten nowhere ■ a soundless screaming a soundless whirring a soundless spinning spinning spinning ■ spinning ■ spinninggggggggggg]

Maggie had wanted all the silver in the machine. She had died, willing herself into the machine. Now, looking out from within, from inside the limbo that had become her own purgatory, Maggie was trapped, in the oiled and anodized interior of the silver dollar slot machine. The prison of her final desires, where she had wanted to be, completely trapped in that last instant of life between life/death. Maggie, gone inside, all soul now, trapped for all eternity in the cage soul of the machine. Limbo. Trapped. Trapped.

▼

"I hope you don't mind if I call over one of the slot men," the Slot Machine Floor Manager was saying, from a far distance. He was in his late fifties, a velvet-voiced man whose eyes held nothing of light and certainly nothing of kindness. He had stopped the Pit Boss as the stocky man had turned in mid-step to return to Kostner and the jack-potted machine; he had taken the walk himself. "We have to make sure, you know how it is: somebody didn't fool with the slot, you know, maybe it's outta whack or something, you know."

He lifted his left hand and there was a clicker in it, the kind children use at Halloween. He clicked half a dozen times, like a rabid cricket, and there was a scurrying in the pit between the tables.

Kostner was only faintly aware of what was happening. Instead of being totally awake, feeling the surge of adrenaline through his veins, the feeling any gambler gets when he is ahead of the game, a kind of desperate urgency when he has hit it for a boodle, he was numb, partaking of the action around him only as much as a drinking glass involves itself in the alcoholic's drunken binge.

All color and sound had been leached out of him.

A tired-looking, resigned-weary man wearing a gray porter's jacket, as gray as his hair, as gray as his indoor skin, came to them, carrying a leather wrap-up of tools. The slot repairman studied the machine, turning the pressed steel body around on its stand, studying the back. He used a key on the back door and for an instant Kostner had a view of gears, springs, armatures and the clock that ran the slot mechanism. The repairman nodded silently over it, closed and relocked it, turned it around again and studied the face of the machine.

"Nobody's been spooning it," he said, and went away.

Kostner stared at the Floor Manager.

"Gaffing. That's what he meant. Spooning's another word for it. Some guys use a little piece of plastic, or a wire, shove it down through the escalator, it kicks the machine. Nobody thought that's what happened here, but you know, we have to make sure, two grand is a big payoff, and twice . . . well, you know, I'm sure you'll understand. If a guy was doing it with a boomerang—"

Kostner raised an eyebrow.

"—uh, yeah, a boomerang, it's another way to spoon the machine. But we just wanted to make a little check, and now everybody's satisfied, so if you'll just come back to the casino cashier with me—"

And they paid him off again.

So he went back to the slot machine, and stood before it for a long time, staring at it. The change girls and the dealers going off-duty; the little old ladies with their canvas work gloves worn to avoid calluses when pulling the slot handles; the men's room attendant on his way up front to get more matchbooks; the floral tourists, the idle observers, the hard drinkers, the sweepers, the busboys; the gamblers with poached-egg eyes who had been up all night; the showgirls with massive breasts and diminutive sugar daddies; all of them conjectured mentally about the beat-up walker who was staring at the silver dollar Chief. He did not move, merely stared at the machine . . . and they wondered.

The machine was staring back at Kostner.

Three blue eyes.

The electric current has sparked through him again, as the machine had clocked down and the eyes turned up a second time, as he had *won* a second time. But this time he knew there was something more than luck involved, for no one else had seen those three blue eyes.

So now he stood before the machine, waiting. It spoke to him. Inside his skull, where no one had ever lived but himself, now someone else moved and spoke to him. A girl. A beautiful girl. Her name was Maggie, and she spoke to him.

I've been waiting for you. A long time, I've been waiting for you, Kostner. Why do you think you hit the jackpot? Because I've been waiting for you, and I want you. You'll win all the jackpots. Because I want you, I need you. Love me, I'm Maggie, I'm so alone, love me.

Kostner had been staring at the slot machine for a very long time, and his weary brown eyes had seemed to be locked to the blue eyes on the jackpot bars. But he knew no one else could see the blue eyes, and no one else could hear the voice, and no one else knew about Maggie.

He was the universe to her. Everything to her.

He thumbed in another silver dollar, and the Pit Boss watched, the slot machine repairman watched, the Slot Machine Floor Manager watched, three change girls watched, and a pack of unidentified players watched, some from their seats.

The reels whirled, the handle snapped back, and in a second they flipped down to a halt, twenty silver dollars tokened themselves into the payoff trough and a woman at one of the crap tables belched a fragment of hysterical laughter.

And the gong went insane again.

The Floor Manager came over and said, very softly, "Mr. Kostner, it'll take us about fifteen minutes to pull this machine and check it out. I'm sure you understand." As two slot repairmen came out of the back, hauled the Chief off its stand, and took it into the repair room at the rear of the casino.

While they waited, the Floor Manager regaled Kostner with stories of spooners who had used intricate magnets inside their clothes, of boomerang men who attached their plastic implements under their sleeves so they could be extended on spring-loaded clips, of cheaters who had come equipped with tiny electric drills in their hands and wires that slipped into the tiny drilled holes. And he kept saying he knew Kostner would understand.

But Kostner knew the Floor Manager would not understand.

When they brought the Chief back, one of the repairmen nodded assuredly. "Nothing wrong with it. Works perfectly. Nobody's been boomin' it."

But the blue eyes were gone on the jackpot bars.

Kostner knew they would return.

They paid him off again.

He returned and played again. And again. And again. They put a "spotter" on him. He won again. And again. And again. The crowd had grown to massive proportions. Word had spread like the silent communications of the telegraph vine, up and down the Strip, all the way to downtown Vegas and the sidewalk casinos where they played night and day every day of the year, and the crowd surged in a tide toward the hotel, and the casino, and the seedy-looking walker with his weary brown eyes. The crowd moved to him inexorably, drawn like lemmings by the odor of the luck that rose from him like musky electrical cracklings. And he won. Again and again. Thirty-eight thousand dollars. And the three blue eyes continued to stare up at him. Her lover was winning. Maggie and her Moneyeyes.

Finally, the casino decided to speak to Kostner. They pulled the Chief for fifteen minutes, for a supplemental check by experts from the slot machine company in downtown Vegas, and while they were checking it, they asked Kostner to come to the main office of the hotel.

The owner was there. His face seemed faintly familiar to Kostner. Had he seen it on television? The newspapers?

"Mr. Kostner, my name is Jules Hartshorn."

"I'm pleased to meet you."

"Quite a string of luck you're having out there."

"It's been a long time coming."

"You realize, this sort of luck is impossible."

"I'm compelled to believe it, Mr. Hartshorn."

"Um. As am I. It's happening to my casino. But we're thoroughly convinced of one of two possibilities, Mr. Kostner; one, either the machine is inoperable in a way we can't detect; or two, you are the cleverest spooner we've ever had in here."

"I'm not cheating."

"As you can see, Mr. Kostner, I'm smiling. The reason I'm smiling is at your naïveté in believing I would take your word for it. I'm perfectly happy to nod politely and say of course you aren't cheating. But no one can win thirty-eight thousand dollars on nineteen straight jackpots off one slot machine; it doesn't even have mathematical odds against its happening, Mr. Kostner. It's on a cosmic scale of improbability with three dark planets crashing into our sun within the next twenty minutes. It's on a par with the Pentagon, the Forbidden City and the Kremlin all three pushing the red button at the same microsecond. It's an impossibility, Mr. Kostner. An impossibility that's happening to me."

"I'm sorry."

"Not really."

"No, not really. I can use the money."

"For what, exactly, Mr. Kostner?"

"I hadn't thought about it, really."

"I see. Well, Mr. Kostner let's look at it this way. I can't stop you from playing, and if you continue to win, I'll be required to pay off. And no stubble-chinned thugs will be waiting in an alley to jack-roll you and take the money. The checks will be honored. The best I can hope for, Mr. Kostner, is the attendant publicity. Right now, every high-roller in Vegas is in that casino, waiting for you to drop cartwheels into that machine. It won't make up for what I'm losing, if you continue the way you've been; but it'll help. Every sucker in town likes to rub up next to luck. All I ask is that you cooperate a little."

"The least I can do, considering your generosity."

"An attempt at humor."

"I'm sorry. What is it you'd like me to do?"

"Get about ten hours' sleep."

"While you pull the slot and have it worked over thoroughly?"

"Yes."

"If I wanted to keep winning, that might be a pretty stupid move on my part. You might change the thingamajig inside so I couldn't win if I put back every dollar of that thirty-eight grand."

"We're licensed by the state of Nevada, Mr. Kostner."

"I come from a good family, too, and take a look at me. I'm a bum with thirty-eight thousand dollars in my pocket."

"Nothing will be done to that slot machine, Kostner."

"Then why pull it for ten hours?"

"To work it over thoroughly in the shop. If something as undetectable as metal fatigue or a worn escalator tooth or—we want to make sure this doesn't happen with other machines. And the extra time will get the word around town; we can use the crowd. Some of those tourists will stick to our fingers, and it'll help defray the expense of having you break the bank at this casino—on a slot machine."

"I have to take your word."

"This hotel will be in business long after you're gone, Kostner."

"Not if I keep winning."

Hartshorn's smile was a stricture. "A good point."

"So it isn't much of an argument."

"It's the only one I have. If you want to get back out on that floor, I can't stop you."

"No Mafia hoods ventilate me later?"

"I beg your pardon?"

"I said: no Maf—"

"You have a picturesque manner of speaking. In point of fact, I haven't the faintest idea what you're talking about."

"I'm sure you haven't."

"You've got to stop reading *The National Enquirer.* This is a legally run business. I'm merely asking a favor."

"Okay, Mr. Hartshorn, I've been three days without any sleep. Ten hours will do me a world of good."

"I'll have the desk clerk find you a quiet room on the top floor. And thank you, Mr. Kostner."

"Think nothing of it."

"I'm afraid that will be impossible."

"A lot of impossible things are happening lately."

He turned to go, as Hartshorn lit a cigarette.

"Oh, by the way, Mr. Kostner?"

Kostner stopped and half-turned. "Yes?"

His eyes were getting difficult to focus. There was a ringing in his ears. Hartshorn seemed to waver at the edge of his vision like heat lightning across a prairie. Like memories of things Kostner had come across the country to forget. Like the whimpering and pleading that kept tugging at the cells of his brain. The voice of Maggie. Still back there, saying . . . things . . .

They'll try to keep you from me.

All he could think about was the ten hours of sleep he had been promised. Suddenly it was more important than the money, than forgetting, than anything. Hartshorn was talking, was saying things, but Kostner could not hear him. It was as if he had turned off the sound and saw only the silent rubbery movement of Hartshorn's lips. He shook his head trying to clear it.

There were half a dozen Hartshorns all melting into and out of one another. And the voice of Maggie.

I'm warm here, and alone. I could be good to you, if you can come to me. Please come, please hurry.

"Mr. Kostner?"

Hartshorn's voice came draining down through exhaustion as thick as velvet flocking. Kostner tried to focus again. His extremely weary brown eyes began to track.

"Did you know about that slot machine?" Hartshorn was saying. "A peculiar thing happened with it about six weeks ago."

"What was that?"

"A girl died playing it. She had a heart attack, a seizure while she was pulling the handle, and died right out there on the floor."

Kostner was silent for a moment. He wanted desperately to ask Hartshorn what color the dead girl's eyes had been, but he was afraid the owner would say blue.

He paused with his hand on the office door. "Seems as though you've had nothing but a streak of bad luck on that machine."

Hartshorn smiled an enigmatic smile. "It might not change for a while, either."

Kostner felt his jaw muscles tighten. "Meaning I might die, too, and wouldn't *that* be bad luck."

Hartshorn's smile became hieroglyphic, permanent, stamped on him forever. "Sleep tight, Mr. Kostner."

▼

In a dream, she came to him. Long, smooth thighs and soft golden down on her arms; blue eyes deep as the past, misted with a fine scintillance like lavender spiderwebs; taut body that was the only body Woman had ever had, from the very first. Maggie came to him.

Hello, I've been traveling a long time.

"Who are you?" Kostner asked, wonderingly. He was standing on a chilly plain, or was it a plateau? The wind curled around them both, or was it only around him? She was exquisite, and he saw her clearly, or was it through a mist? Her voice was deep and resonant, or was it light and warm as night-blooming jasmine?

I'm Maggie. I love you. I've waited for you.

"You have blue eyes."

Yes. *With love.*

"You're very beautiful."

Thank you. *With female amusement.*

"But why me? Why let it happen to me? Are you the girl who—are you the one that was sick—the one who—?"

I'm Maggie. And you, I picked you, because you need me. You've needed someone for a long long time.

Then it unrolled for Kostner. The past unrolled and he saw who he was. He saw himself alone. Always alone. As a child, born to kind and warm parents who hadn't the vaguest notion of who he was, what he wanted to be, where his talents lay. So he had run off, when he was in his teens, and alone always alone on the road. For years and months and days and hours, with no one. Casual friendships, based on food, or sex, or artificial similarities. But no one to whom he could cleave, and cling, and belong. It was that way till Susie, and with her he had found light. He had discovered the scents and aromas of a spring that was eternally one day away. He had laughed, really laughed, and known with her it would at last be all right. So he had poured all of himself into her, giving her everything; all his hopes, his secret thoughts, his tender dreams; and she had taken them, taken him, all of him, and he had known for the first time what it was to have a place to live, to have a home in someone's heart. It was all the silly and gentle things he laughed at in other people, but for him it was breathing deeply of wonder.

He had stayed with her for a long time, and had supported her, supported her son from the first marriage; the marriage Susie never talked about. And then one day, he *had come back, as Susie had always known he would. He was a dark creature of ruthless habits and vicious nature, but she had been his woman, all along, and Kostner realized he had been used as a stop-gap, as a bill-payer till her wandering terror came home to nest. Then she had asked him to leave. Broke, and tapped out in all the silent inner ways a man can be drained, he had left, without even a fight, for all the fight had been leached out of him. He had left, and wandered west, and finally come to Las Vegas, where he had hit bottom. And found Maggie. In a dream, with blue eyes, he had found Maggie.*

I want you to belong to me. I love you. *Her truth was vibrant in Kostner's mind. She was his, at last someone who was special, was his.*

"Can I trust you? I've never been able to trust anyone before. Women, never. But I need someone. I really need someone."

It's me, always. Forever. You can trust me.

And she came to him, fully. Her body was a declaration of truth and trust such as no other Kostner had ever known before. She met him on a windswept plain of thought, and he made love to her more completely than he had known any passion before. She joined with him, entered him, mingled with his blood and his thought and his frustration, and he came away clean, filled with glory.

"Yes, I can trust you, I want you, I'm yours," he whispered to her, when they lay side by side in a dream nowhere of mist and soundlessness. "I'm yours."

She smiled, a woman's smile of belief in her man; a smile of trust and deliverance. And Kostner woke up.

The Chief was back on its stand, and the crowd had been penned back by velvet ropes. Several people had played the machine, but there had been no jackpots.

Now Kostner came into the casino, and the "spotters" got themselves ready. While Kostner had slept, they had gone through his clothes, searching for wires, for gaffs, for spoons and boomerangs. Nothing.

Now he walked straight to the Chief, and stared at it.

Hartshorn was there. "You look tired," he said gently to Kostner, studying the man's weary brown eyes.

"I am, a little." Kostner tried a smile; it didn't work. "I had a funny dream."

"Oh?"

"Yeah . . . about a girl . . . " He let it die off.

Hartshorn's smile was understanding. Pitying, empathic and understanding. "There are lots of girls in this town. You shouldn't have any trouble finding one with your winnings."

Kostner nodded, and slipped his first silver dollar into the slot. He pulled the handle. The reels spun with a ferocity Kostner had not heard before and suddenly everything went whipping slantwise as he felt a wrenching of pure flame in his stomach, as his head was snapped on its spindly neck, as the lining behind his eyes was burned out. There was a terrible shriek, of tortured metal, of an express train ripping through the air with is passage, of a hundred small animals being gutted and torn to shreds, of incredible pain, of night winds that tore the tops off mountains of lava. And a keening whine of a voice that wailed and wailed and wailed as it went away from there in blinding light—

Free! Free! Heaven or Hell it doesn't matter! Free!

The sound of a soul released from an eternal prison, a genie freed from a dark bottle. And in that instant of damp soundless nothingness, Kostner saw the reels snap and clock down for the final time:

One, two, three. Blue eyes.

But he would never cash his checks.

The crowd screamed through one voice as he fell sidewise and lay on his face. The final loneliness . . .

▼

The Chief was pulled. Bad luck. Too many gamblers resented its very presence in the casino. So it was pulled. And returned to the company, with explicit instructions it was to be melted down to slag. And not till it was in the hands of the ladle foreman, who was ready to dump it into the slag furnace, did anyone remark on the final tally the Chief had clocked.

"Look at that, ain't that weird," said the ladle foreman to his bucket man. He pointed to the three glass windows.

"Never saw jackpot bars like that before," the bucket man agreed. "Three eyes. Must be an old machine."

"Yeah, some of these old games go way back," the foreman said, hoisting the slot machine onto the conveyor track leading to the slag furnace. "Three eyes, huh? How about that. Three brown eyes."

And he threw the knife-switch that sent the Chief down the track, to puddle in the roaring inferno of the furnace.

Three brown *eyes.*

Three brown eyes that looked very very weary. That looked very very trapped. That looked very very betrayed. Some of these old games go way back.

Thinkertoy

JOHN BRUNNER

The late John Brunner was one of the most brilliantly eclectic SF writers of our time. His novel *Stand on Zanzibar* is a landmark of the "New Wave" of science fiction that blew in from England like a fresh sea breeze during the mid-1960s. Experimental in style and explosive in impact, that novel is but one of the outstanding works by this innovative, powerful British author.

"Thinkertoy," first published in 1996, takes a common science fiction device and places it in the hands of children. As we've learned from the carnage of chain saws, machines can be tools for good or evil, magnifying the powers of human beings to execute their desires, however dark. The children in this straightforward yet chilling tale are all too real, and their desires quite dark indeed.

Paul Walker was afraid of his children. For months now he had been afraid for them, ever since the fatal accident, but this was different—not a rapid change, but the gradual kind that is recognized one morning as having happened.

And he and Lisa had been so proud of their outstanding intelligence. . . .

He could not tell which of them he found the more disturbing. Logically it should have been Rick because of the way the crash had altered him. He bore no visible scars, but it had done incontestable damage. Whether directly, as the result of trauma, or indirectly, through showing him his mother hideously dead, had proved impossible to establish.

Yes in many ways Kelly, two years the older, affected him worse. There was something unnerving about the composure she maintained: in particular, the way she cared for Rick now that he showed so little interest in the world. It wasn't right for a child barely in her teens to be so organized, so self-possessed: to rouse her brother in the mornings, make sure he was neatly dressed and came to breakfast on time, arrange their return home because though Paul could drop them at school on his way to the office he was still at work when classes finished. Most days they came back by bus, now and then in the car of one of the numerous other parents living nearby who had been shocked by Lisa's death. . . . It was in principle a great arrangement; as his friends kept reminding him, it meant he could keep his job and even work overtime now and then, without worrying.

But he had worried all along. Now he had progressed beyond that. He had grown used to the sense of Rick not being wholly present anymore, yet not resigned to it. The boy went to school without protest, and endured his classes and maybe soaked up the odd droplet of information. But on regaining his room he would sit, both before and after supper unless Kelly coaxed him to watch TV, in front of his computer or his games console, perhaps with a game loaded, more often watching a net display scrolling of its own accord, looking—this had crossed Paul's mind weeks ago though he was tired of being able to remember that he had used to operate these expensive gadgets, without recalling what he had actually done to make them work. For a while Paul had offered to partner him, but was defeated by his frustrating wall of indifference.

Every weekend he sought some stimulus that might reawaken his son's dormant personality, making a trip to a game or a show or some place of interest out of town. This time, though, Kelly had asked to visit a shopping mall, to which he gladly consented because he felt she ought to let him buy her new and more stylish clothes to keep up with her school friends. It was fruitless; she insisted on the same kind of items as usual, inexpensive, practical, plain.

However, there proved to be a compensation. He was double-checking his grocery list for the coming week before continuing to the supermarket when Kelly—in T-shirt, jeans, and trainers as she would remain until it was time for sweater, jeans, and boots—returned to him with a thoughtful air.

"Dad, I think you ought to see this."

Instantly: "Where's Rick? Why isn't he with you?"

"That's what I want you to see. Look."

And there the boy was, standing riveted before a display in a section of the mall it had not crossed Paul's mind to make for.

But why did I not think of toys? After all, in some ways he has become a child again. . . .

Hastening in Kelly's wake, he wondered what could have broken through that armor of remoteness. It must be something special, for there were as many adults and even teenagers, normally contemptuous of childish things, as there were children gathered here. A smiling salesman was putting his wares through their paces.

And quite some paces they were.

They were performing under an arch bearing the name THINKERTOY in brightly colored letters, on a display one part of which modeled a modern city block with buildings of various heights; another, a medieval castle with donjon, moat, and curtain wall; another, an icebound coastline lapped by miniature waves. All over these were roaming little machines, some with wheels, some arms and/or legs, some tentacles, some hooks and suckers for hauling themselves up cliffs or trees or vertical walls. Occasionally they came to an obstacle they could neither surmount nor traverse, whereupon, seemingly of their own volition, they repaired to a heap of miscellaneous parts at the side of the display, disconnected part of their or another's current fitments, plugged in replacements and renewed their progress. Now and then the onlookers clapped and laughed at some particularly ingenious configuration, such as a scaling-ladder. Also there were a pair of video screens showing other actions they were capable of. Paul found himself fascinated along with all the rest.

"Excuse me."

A tentative voice. The salesman deployed his broadest beam.

"Suppose you change things around."

Rick? Could it be . . . ? Yes, it was Rick who had spoken! This was fantastic!

"You mean like shifting things to new places? They keep right on going. They learn in moments. For instance—" He reached for a handful of the spare parts, then checked.

"No kid, you can do it. Dump 'em wherever you like. When they bump into one of these bits they'll recognize it, remember it's in the wrong place, collect it, and return it to store. You'll see."

The little machines performed as predicted, watched by Rick with total attention. Meantime the man continued his spiel, while two pretty girls took station beside a credit-card reader in anticipation of impending sales.

"But you haven't seen a fraction of what Thinkertoys can do! You can find out more from the screens here, and our full-color literature." On cue, the girls fanned brilliant leaflets like oversize poker hands. "You can discover how much more fun, how much more fulfilling for adults too is life with Thinkertoys around! Want your Thinkertoy to answer your phone, and that includes videophones by the way, with any of a hundred voices and identities? Make 'em up yourself or use the ones supplied. Want your games console or computer to play against you in exactly the style of your favorite partner, only he or she is not available? Easy! Just record a sample of the games you've played together. Your Thinkertoy will analyze and duplicate anybody's style to grandmaster level and beyond. Want to integrate your computer with your stereo, your stereo with your TV, your TV with your phone—so you can call home and tell the VCR to record a program you only just found out about? Your phone with your cooker, your microwave, your refrigerator? It's done for you! And as for what two or more of these little pals can do, it's astonishing! Two Thinkertoys working together can open an icebox or freezer, read the labels on stored food, or if unlabeled show it to a videophone for you to identify, then locate the recipe you name and prepare it against your return home, substituting if need be alternative ingredients of equal or superior quality. Thinkertoys retrieve from awkward places. They clean tirelessly and unobtrusively. They hide in corners when not required and reactivate instantly on hearing their names. No need to connect them to wires or cables, though that is an option. They communicate like portable phones, and with ultrasound, and with infrared—"

"Say!" one of the listeners burst out. "If they do all these things why call them toys?"

"They're for playing with," was the suave rejoinder. "Most people don't have enough fun in their lives. Thinkertoys are designed to put the fun back in living! And . . . " His voice dropped to a confidential level, though everyone in the small crowd still heard every syllable. "To be absolutely frank, our company was intending to introduce a family model, what you might call a more sober design, just to do dull things like help out around the house. But then this new chip came out, the very latest most sophisticated kind, and we found we could pack all these features in as well, and . . . okay, I'll let you in on the secret. Thinkertoys work so well, people buy them for their kids and wind up using them themselves, so they have to come back and buy another, catch?"

He flashed a mouthful of excellently cared-for teeth, and several people chuckled at his engaging blatancy.

"Of course," he added, "it makes sense to save yourself the second trip, and these young ladies will be pleased to show you our double packs at a net savings of fifteen percent. And of course all Thinkertoys are fully guaranteed."

"Dad," Kelly whispered, "are you going to buy one for Rick?"

The things weren't cheap, especially with the full kit of parts warranted to permit access anywhere in any house or apartment. However, the sight of Rick showing animation for the first time since he came home from the hospital. . . .

He hadn't spent the insurance he had had on Lisa, meaning to invest it until the kids were of college age. But this was a special case. Just how special became plain when, instead of showing his customary indifference, Rick made a careful selection of the optional extras. As he put his credit card away Paul's heart felt light for the first time since his wife's death.

"What's got into you?" demanded Carlos Gomez when they met during lunch break. Carlos was the firm's computer manager, and as personnel supervisor Paul worked closely with him, but they had been drawn together most of all because Belita Gomez had been a good friend of Lisa, and immensely supportive since the tragedy. It was she who most often gave Rick and Kelly a ride home from school.

"What do you mean?"

"You're looking cheerful for a change."

Paul explained, with the aid of some of Thinkertoys's promotional literature that he had in his pocket. Studying it, Carlos gave a soft whistle.

"I'd heard they were working on stuff like this, but I didn't know it was on the market. And for kids, yet! There must be something wrong with it."

Paul blinked. "What makes you so sure? I haven't noticed anything wrong. In fact the opposite. Kelly has been so anxious to help Rick get better, and this is the first real chance she's had. First thing they had to do when they switched the gizmo on was choose a name for it, and they settled on Marmaduke and that was the first time I've heard Rick show any sign of amusement since . . . Well, recently. But I swear I heard him chuckle.

"Then they settled down to try out everything in the manual, and I had to take supper to Rick's room for them and eventually become the heavy father at midnight. And today I've let them stay home from school, just for once, because . . . well, because of the change it's worked on my son." He sounded almost belligerent. "And you immediately conclude something is wrong? I think it's all extremely right!"

"Cool it," Carlos sighed. "I didn't mean wrong from your kids' point of view. I meant from the point of view of what they originally intended the things to do. Maybe they're fine for home use but no good for autopiloting an airliner or controlling an industrial plant."

"You ever heard of this operation before? No? Then what makes you so positive?"

"Just the sort of things a Thinkertoy is capable of, on its own or in conjunction with others. Paul, a chip like that simply isn't the sort you develop for the toy market."

"During the Cold War, didn't the Soviets buy gaming machines intended for Las Vegas because that way they got their hands on electronics that were otherwise under ban?"

"Sure, but those aren't exactly toys. The gambling market operates in the billion-dollar league. Even the biggest hits in the toy market arrive one season, thrive for another, and fade away the next. Exceptions exist, like Barbie dolls, but have you seen a Peppervine doll lately? Or a Captain Carapace? So I can't help wondering what the intended application was for these things. I guess I'll ask around. Mind if I keep this?" He tapped the stiff polychrome paper of the advertising flyer.

Paul shrugged and nodded. But he felt annoyed with Carlos. He had spent months in a nonstop condition of worry; thought it was ended; and now found himself given a reason to start worrying all over again.

He was still further alarmed when he arrived home to find Kelly alone in the kitchen defrosting food for supper.

"What's Rick doing?" he demanded. "Never tell me he's bored with Marmaduke already!"

Wrestling with a too-tough plastic cover, she shook her head. "No, it's just that we've done everything in the manual that we can—you need some extra connectors to wire up the kitchen, like the oven and broiler, and he didn't pick them up—and . . . Well you'd better ask him yourself. He lost me halfway. Ah!"—as the obstinate cover finally peeled back.

"He'll lose me sooner than that," Paul sighed, and headed for his son's room.

The boy was seated contemplatively before his computer. Marmaduke squatted beside the keyboard, or rather its torso, devoid of the attachments. The screen showed mazy lines.

"Circuit diagram?" Paul hazarded.

"Mm-hm"—without looking around.

"Something wrong? Kelly said you can do everything in the manual except jobs you need special parts for."

"Mm-hm."

"So—uh—are you running an autodiagnostic?"

"Trying to. I can't get it to run properly."

"I was talking to Carlos Gomez over lunch. You know, our computer manager. He seemed very interested in these Thinkertoys. How about downloading it to him and seeing if he can help?"

"Nope." The boy's tone held the first hint of determination his father could recall since the crash. "I think I know what's wrong and I'd rather fix it myself."

He rose stiffly from his chair, as though he had been there all day.

"I'm hungry," he added. "What's Kelly fixing? Smells good."

Paul had to wait a moment before following him downstairs. His eyes were blurred with tears.

▼

The following day Kelly said she wanted to go to school. Rick didn't. He wanted to finish solving his problem and thought he could. Unwilling to risk an argument that might make him late for work, Paul exacted a promise that he would certainly attend the next day, and was astonished and delighted when the Thinkertoy appeared unexpectedly on the breakfast counter in a quasi-humanoid configuration with two arms, two legs, and one head, threw up a smart salute and shouted, "You got it, Mister Admiral, sir!"

His son had often made jokes like that, way back when . . .

In the car, he hoped Kelly's detachment might thaw, but it didn't. Drawing up before her school, he ventured, "Buying Marmaduke seems to have been a bright idea, hm?"

With her customary abnormal gravity she shrugged. "Too soon to say."

And was gone, not pausing to kiss him goodbye.

That, though, had become the pattern.

Carlos was not in the office today—on a trip, Paul learned, to inspect a batch of expensive gear being offered second-hand at a bargain price. The seller, a bankrupt arms company, had been a casualty of the end of the Cold War. He resolved to phone him at home tonight if Rick hadn't sorted out his problem. Two days off school were enough.

And of course if there really was something wrong with Marmaduke they could always return him—it—on Saturday, under guarantee.

But, Kelly declared as soon as he entered the house, that wasn't going to be necessary. Pleased, more than a little proud of his son, who had been a real computer whiz before the accident and seemed to be recovering at last, he headed upstairs.

"Rick! Kelly tells me you figured it out," he said heartily.

"Mm-hm." The screen was acrawl with lines like yesterday, but this time the boy was using his mouse rather as though he was in Draw mode, marking a dot here and a dot there and leaving the computer to connect them.

Paul hesitated, aware that he understood far less about computers than his son, but finally ventured, "Are you repairing Marmaduke?"

"Yup."

"I didn't know you could. I mean, not on the sort of gear you have."

"He's designed that way. To be fixed in the field."

"Field?"

"Away from the shop. It's a really dense chip in there. You can write to it with real tiny currents. Amazing stuff. 'Course, reprogramming it would be a different matter."

"You're not—uh—doing that?"

"Nah. Just cleaning it up. Getting rid of some junk."

"So what exactly did you find wrong?"

Rick leaned back and stretched.

"It got damaged. Like my brain . . . Say, I'm hungry."

And after they'd eaten, he carried his plate to the sink, announcing, "Okay, well, if I got to go to school in the morning I better make sure Marmaduke is one hundred percent. See you later."

After a pause, Kelly's mood softened enough for her to concede, "I guess you were right, what you said about Marmaduke."

That was as far as she was prepared to go, but Paul passed his most relaxed evening in a long, long while.

Around ten-thirty Rick decided he was satisfied, emerged yawning from his room, took a shower, and retired peacefully to bed. Kelly decided to do the same. As she headed for the stairs there was a soft scuttling noise.

"What's that?" Paul exclaimed.

"Marmaduke, of course, this time with all his wits about him. You turning in too?"

"In a little while. I want to call Carlos, see if he's home yet—Just a moment! Do I need to set the answering machine as usual or has Marmaduke been programmed to switch it on?"

"Better than that," the Thinkertoy replied. It was perching on the newel post of the banister. "I can act as one, using whichever phone is nearest and adjusting the outgoing message to correspond with the current station. I shall memorize your usual bedtime and rising time with allowance for weekends, but in addition I can take calls whenever the house is unoccupied and give the other party your estimated time of return. Let me know if ever you would like these parameters changed. By the way, I can also control a modem and a fax and reprogram your VCR in response to a phone call—but you've read the brochure. At least I hope you have."

"You forgot to mention," Kelly murmured, "that we've fixed you to sound like me, or Rick, or Dad, or Donald Duck, according to who the caller wants to talk to. The Donald Duck one is for telephone solicitors. In case you're interested, Dad, the voice he's using right now is a three-way mix of all of us. I told Rick it would be kind of suitable."

For a second Paul was stunned. Then he chuckled.

"Marmaduke, I think you are going to be a distinct asset to the Walker household. Good night!"

He reached for the phone. They only had the regular kind. Videophones were still very expensive, even though it was clear from the Thinkertoy literature the manufacturers took it for granted that if you could afford one you could afford the other.

Moments later Belita Gomez's drowsy voice sounded in his ear.

"No, Paul, Carlos isn't home yet. He called to say he'd closed the deal and they were all going to a restaurant. Want him to call back?"

"Don't even give him a message. It can wait until morning. The kids are in bed and I'm about to follow their example. *Buenas noches.*"

"I'm *in* bed. G'night."

Later there was the faintest beep from the phone bell, cut off so quickly it was barely audible.

Whereafter, to the accompaniment of a yawning noise: "Hello."

In a whisper: "Paul, this is Carlos. Sorry to call so late. I'll try and keep it short but you need to hear this. 'Fraid I got to keep my voice down. Belita's asleep and I don't want to disturb her."

A deep breath.

"At this company where I went today, after we agreed on a figure, I stuck around for dinner with the guys I was mainly dealing with. I happened to ask whether they knew anything about Thinkertoys. I hit pay dirt. Remember I said those chips weren't developed for the toy market even if the toys do double as home appliances? Well this company I was at used to be in arms back in the Cold War period, and this guy says yes, he knows who made them, though he wouldn't give me a name, but he did tell me what they were intended for. Sabotage! Plant 'em behind enemy lines, or leave 'em during a retreat, and they activate and start wrecking everything in reach. Electronics first, naturally—they have built-in jamming capacity. But they can start fires and foul up bearings and unscrew closed valves in chemical plants, even loosen tacks in stair carpet so people break their necks. . . . They're supposed to have been rendered harmless. Some kind of inactivation program. But this guy I was talking to: he says the security is lousy and you can get around it in an hour, or sooner if you automate the job, and the word's out on the net and you want to guess who's buying? The Sword Arm of the Lord, that's who, hoping to destroy black-owned businesses, and the Islamic League for Female Decency, and the Choosers of the Slain, and—Shit, I think I woke Belita after all. Talk to you in the morning. 'Bye."

The connection broke.

Whereupon Marmaduke went on about its proper business, the liberty for which Rick had restored.

▼

"Sorry, *querida*—didn't mean to wake you."

"It's okay, I wasn't really asleep. . . . Who were you talking to at this hour?"

Sitting on the edge of the bed to remove his shoes: "Paul. Paul Walker. I learned something about those Thinkertoys that couldn't wait for morning."

"If it was that urgent why didn't you call from the car?"

"His home number is unlisted and I don't have it in the car memory."

"Ah-yah. . . . " Belita was struggling to keep her eyes open. Then, with a sudden start: "What do you mean, it couldn't wait until morning? It'll have to anyway, won't it?"

Carlos, unfastening his tie, checked and glanced at his wife. "I don't get you," he said after a pause.

She forced herself to sit up against the pillows. "You got his answering machine, right?"

"No! I talked to Paul—"

"But he called here about ten-thirty to ask if you were home yet. When I told him no he said the kids where in bed and he was going to turn in as well. Ever know him to set his answering machine?"

Carlos was staring. "But I know his message! He never changes it. I must have heard it a hundred times. . . . Oh my God."

"What is it?" Belita was alarmed into full wakefulness now.

Feverishly he retrieved the Thinkertoy advertisement from his jacket. "Yes, I'm right," he muttered. "One of the things they can do is impersonate their owner on the phone."

"You mean carry on a conversation that can fool the caller?"

"No, that's the Turing test and no machine has passed it yet. But it could exploit the Eliza principle. That goes right back to the early days, but it's still used and it can sure as hell fool people, especially if they're under stress and their guard is down. . . . 'Lita, I got to go check that the Walkers are okay."

"But why should they not be?"

He told her. Before he finished she was out of bed and scrambling into whatever clothes she could reach.

▼

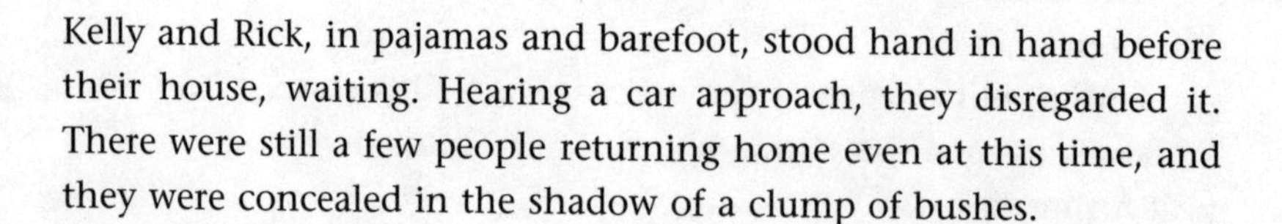

Kelly and Rick, in pajamas and barefoot, stood hand in hand before their house, waiting. Hearing a car approach, they disregarded it. There were still a few people returning home even at this time, and they were concealed in the shadow of a clump of bushes.

Just as Carlos braked, there came a faint whooshing sound from the kitchen, which lay partly below the bathroom but mainly below Paul's room, the one that had been his and Lisa's. An orange glow followed, and a crackling noise. The house was largely timber-built. Later it was established that Marmaduke had loosened the valve on a cylinder of propane and ignited the leak, as it was designed to, by short-circuiting its powerpack.

The glow revealed the children.

"Madre de dios!" Belita exclaimed. "But what are Rick and Kelly doing out here? And where's Paul?"

"Save your breath!" Carlos was frantically escaping his safety belt. "Blast away on the horn! Rouse everyone you can! Call 911!"

"Carlos, don't do anything foolish—"

But he was already rushing towards the porch. Kelly and Rick recognized him and seemed to scowl and mutter. Suspicion burgeoned but he had no time. He reached the door.

It was locked. Suspicion grew brighter and fiercer like the fire within. But he still had no time. In the car he kept a baseball bat for security. He ran back for it. Thus armed, he smashed a glass panel alongside the door and managed to reach the inside lock.

By now lights were coming on, windows being flung open as the car horn shattered the night silence. Slamming shut the kitchen door, which he found open, gained Carlos a few more precious moments before heat and smoke made the stairway impassable. Three at a time he dashed up it.

The front door was not the only one that was locked.

Suspicion approached certainty, but still he had not time. He smashed the flimsy jamb, found Paul sleepily approaching the window, aroused by the horn, dragged him down the stairs and staggering into the garden. . . .

With seconds to spare. Like a puff of breath from a dragon, the gas cylinder burst and blew out all the house's doors and windows. Flame erupted through the ceiling under Paul's room.

Distant but closing fast, sirens wailed.

Paul collapsed, choking from a lungful of smoke, but Carlos managed to retain his feet. Gasping, he found himself confronting Rick and Kelly. Their faces were stony and frustrated. He whispered, "You knew, didn't you?"

Impassivity.

"Paul said you spent most of your time scrolling around the net. That must be how you found out. I guess the Thinkertoy display at the mall must have been pretty widely advertised. And like the guy said, the protection that was supposed to make the chips harmless could be easily erased."

He stood back, hands on hips, ignoring Belita, who clearly wanted to fuss over the children. He barely registered that Paul was albeit unsteadily regaining his feet. Before his friend could speak:

"But why?" Carlos pleaded.

The children exchanged glances. At length Rick gave a shrug.

"He was driving."

After which Belita's importunities could no longer be ignored.

▼

Paul Walker was afraid of his children.

As those three words made clear, he had good reason.

Scatter My Ashes

GREG EGAN

By now we've been exposed to so much graphic violence on television, in films, and in other media that we may have become somewhat inured to the true horror of violent acts. No matter how often it is seen, however, such violence never becomes less terrible.

Greg Egan, one of the most talented young writers to come out of Australia over the past fifteen years, wrote "Scatter My Ashes" in 1987. It remains a truly disturbing story about not only the hideousness of violence committed by sick individuals, but also about the obsession that one man develops for catching the act on film.

Egan poses questions about responsibility and culpability, exposing the voyeurism that the media have encouraged and exploited. All too often, we stop asking questions about a crime once we know who did it and who the victims were. Do the sick people who kill for some bizarre pleasure commit these acts alone? Or do we also participate, by acknowledging their acts and splashing lurid photos throughout the media? Tough questions, great story.

Every night, at exactly a quarter past three, something dreadful happens on the street outside our bedroom window. We peek through the curtains, yawning and shivering in the life-draining chill, and then we clamber back beneath the blankets without exchanging a word, to hug each other tightly and hope for sound sleep before it's time to rise.

Usually what we witness verges on the mundane. Drunken young men fighting, swaying about with outstretched knives, cursing incoherently. Robbery, bashings, rape. We wince to see such violence, but we can hardly be shocked or surprised any more, and we're never tempted to intervene: it's always far too cold, for a start! A single warm exhalation can coat the window pane with mist, transforming the most stomach-wrenching assault into a safely cryptic ballet for abstract blobs of light.

On some nights, though, when the shadows in the room are subtly wrong, when the familiar street looks like an abandoned film set, or a painting of itself perversely comes to life, we are confronted by truly disturbing sights, oppressive apparitions which almost make us doubt we're awake, or, if awake, sane. I can't catalogue these visions, for most, mercifully, are blurred by morning, leaving only a vague uneasiness and a reluctance to be alone even in the brightest sunshine.

One image, though, has never faded.

In the middle of the road was a giant human skull. How big was it? Big enough for a child, perhaps six or seven years old, to stand trapped between the jaws, bracing them apart with outstretched arms and legs, trembling with the effort but somehow, miraculously, keeping the massive teeth from closing in.

As we watched I felt, strange as it may sound, inspired, uplifted, filled with hope by the sight of that tiny figure holding out against the blind, brutal creature of evil. Wouldn't we all like to think of innocence as a tangible force to be reckoned with? Despite all evidence to the contrary.

Then the four huge, blunt teeth against which the child was straining began to reform, tapering to needle-fine points. A drop of blood fell from the back of each upraised hand. I cried out something, angry and horrified. But I didn't move.

A gash appeared in the back of the child's neck. Not a wound: a mouth, the child's new and special mouth, violently writhing, stretched open ever wider by four sharp, slender fangs growing in perfect mimicry of the larger fangs impaling the child's palms and feet.

The new mouth began to scream, at first a clumsy, choking sound, made without a tongue; but then a torn, bloody scrap of flesh appeared in place, the tongue of the old mouth uprooted and inverted, and the cries gave full voice to an intensity of suffering and fear that threatened to melt the glass of the window, sear away the walls of the room, and drag us into a pit of darkness where one final scream would echo forever.

When it was over, we climbed into bed and snuggled up together.

I dreamt that I found a jigsaw puzzle, hidden in a dark, lost corner of the house. The pieces were in a plain cardboard box, unaccompanied by any illustration of what the assembled puzzle portrayed. Wendy laughed and told me not to waste my time, but I sat frowning over it for an hour every evening, until after many weeks only a handful of pieces remained unplaced.

Somehow, even then, I didn't know what the picture was but as I lazily filled in the very last gap, I felt a sudden overpowering conviction that whatever the jigsaw showed, *I did not want to see it.*

I woke a little before dawn. I kissed Wendy very softly, I gently stroked her shoulders and breasts with my fingertips. She rearranged herself, pulled a face, but didn't wake. I was about to brush her forehead with one hand, which I knew would make her open her eyes and give me a sleepy smile, when it occurred to me that if she did, there might be small, fanged mouths behind her eyelids.

▼

When I woke again it was half past seven, and she was already up. I hate that, I hate waking in an empty bed. She was reading the paper as I sat down to breakfast.

"So, what's happening in the world?"

"A fifth child's gone missing."

"Shit. Don't they have any suspects yet? Any evidence, any clues?"

"A fisherman reported something floating on the lake. The police went out in a boat to have a look."

"And?"

"It turned out to be a calf fetus."

I gulped coffee. I hate the taste of coffee, and if sets my stomach squirming, but I simply have to drink it.

"It says police will be diving all day today, searching the lake."

"I might go out there, then. The lake looks fantastic in this weather."

"When I'm snug in my office with the heater on full blast, I'll think of you."

"Think of the divers. They'll have the worst of it."

"At least they know they'll get paid. You could spend the whole day there for nothing."

"I'd rather take my kind of risk than theirs."

Once she was gone, I cut out the article on the vanished child. The walls of my study are papered with newsprint, ragged grey odd-shaped pieces affixed only at their top corners, free to rustle when the door is opened or closed. Sometimes, when I'm sitting at my desk for a moment after I've switched off the lamp, I get a strong impression of diseased skin.

"Put them in a scrap book!" says Wendy, whenever she ventures in to grimace at the state of the room. "Or better still, put them in a filing cabinet and see if you can lose the key!" But I need to keep them this way, I need to see them all at once, spread out before me like a satellite photograph, an aerial view of this age of violence. I'm looking for a pattern. My gaze darts from headline to headline, from STRANGLER to STALKER to RIPPER to SLASHER, hunting for a clue to the terrible unity, hunting for the nature of the single dark force which I know lies behind all the different nightmare stories, all the different fearful names.

I have books, too, of course, I have shelves stuffed with volumes, some learned, some hysterical, from treatises on Vlad the Impaler to discussions of the entrails of London prostitutes to heavy psychoanalysis of the Manson gang. I have skimmed these works, read a page here and a page there only, for to clutter my mind with details can only distract me from the whole.

I recall precisely when my obsession began. I was ten. A convict, a murderer, had escaped from a nearby prison, and warnings were broadcast urging us to barricade our homes. My parents, naturally tried not to alarm me, but we all slept together that night, in the room with the smallest window, and when the poor cat mewed to be let in the back door, my mother would let nobody, not even my father, budge.

I dozed and woke, dozed and woke, and each time dreamt that I was not sleeping buy lying awake, waiting for the utter certainty of the unstoppable, bloodthirsty creature through the door and slicing us all in two.

They caught him the next morning. They caught him too late. A service station attendant was dead, cut up beyond belief by an implement that was never found.

They showed the killer on TV that night, and he looked nothing like the stuff of nightmares: thin, awkward, squinting, dwarfed between two massive, smug policemen. Yet for all his apparent weakness and shyness, he seemed to know something, he seemed to be holding a secret, not so much about murder itself as about the cameras, the viewers, about exactly what he meant to us. He averted his eyes from the lenses, but the hint of a smile on his lips declared that everything was, and always would be, just the way he wanted it, just the way he'd planned it from the start.

▼

I drove to the lake and set up my camera with its longest lens, but after peering through the viewfinder for ten minutes, keeping the police boat perfectly framed, following its every tiny drift, I switched to binoculars to save my eyes and neck. Nothing was happening. Faint shouts reached me now and then, but the tones were always of boredom, discomfort, irritation. Soon I put down the binoculars. If they found something, I'd hear the change at once.

I drank coffee from a flask, I paced. I took a few shots of divers backflipping into the water, but none seemed special, none captured the mood. I watched the water birds and felt somehow guilty for not knowing their names.

The sky and the water were pale grey, the colour of soggy newsprint. Thick smoke rose from a factory on the far shore, but seemed to fall back down again on almost the same spot. The chill, the bleakness, and the morbid nature of my vigil worked together to fill me with an oppressive sense of gloom, but cutting through that dullness and despair was the acid taste of anticipation.

My back was turned when I heard the shouts of panic. It took me seconds to spot the boat again, forever to point the camera. An inert diver was being hauled on board, to the sound of much angry swearing. Someone ripped off his face mask and began resuscitation. Each time I fired the shutter, I thought: what if he dies? If he dies it will be my fault, because if he dies I'll have a sale for sure.

I packed up my gear and fled before the boat reached the shore, but not before the ambulance arrived. I glanced at the driver, who looked about my age, and thought: why am I doing my job, and not his? Why am I voyeur, a parasite, a vulture, a leech, when I could be saving people's lives and sleeping the sleep of the just every night?

Later, I discovered that the cop was in a coma. Evidently there'd been a malfunction of his air supply. I sold one of the pictures, which appeared with the caption, KISS OF LIFE! The editor said, "That could easily win you a prize." I smiled immodestly and mumbled about luck.

Wendy is a literary agent. We went out to dinner that night with one of her clients, to celebrate the signing of a contract. The writer was a quiet, thoughtful, attractive woman. Her husband worked in a bank, but played football for some team or other on weekends, and was built like a vault.

"So, what do you do for a crust?" he asked.

"I'm a freelance photographer."

"What's that mean? Fashion models for the front of *Vogue* or centrefolds for *Playboy?"*

"Neither. Most of my work is for newspapers, or news magazines. I had a picture in *Time* last year."

"What of?"

"Flood victims trapped on the roof of their farm."

"Yeah? Did you pay them some of what you got for it?"

Wendy broke in and described my day's achievement, and the topic switched naturally to that of the missing children.

"If they ever catch the bloke who's doing it," said the footballer, "he shouldn't be killed. He should be tortured for a couple of days, and then crippled. Say they cut off both legs. Then there's no chance he'll escape from prison on his own steam, and when they let him free in a year or two from prison, like they always end up doing, who's he going to hurt?"

I said, "Why does everyone assume there's a killer? Nobody's yet found a single drop of blood, or a fingerprint, or a footprint. Nobody knows for sure that the children are dead, nobody's proved that at all."

The writer said, "Maybe the Innocents are ascending into Heaven."

For a moment I thought she was serious, but then she smirked at the cleverness of her sarcasm. I kept my mouth shut for the rest of the evening.

In the taxi home, though, I couldn't help muttering a vague, clumsy insult about Neanderthal fascists who reveled in torture. Wendy laughed and put an arm around my waist.

"Jealousy really becomes you," she said. I couldn't think of an intelligent reply.

That night, we witnessed a particularly brutal robbery. A taxi pulled up across the road, and the passengers dragged the driver out and kicked him in the head until he was motionless. They virtually stripped him naked searching for the key to his cashbox, then they smashed his radio, slashed his tyres, and stabbed him in the stomach before walking off, whistling Rossini.

Once Wendy had drifted back to sleep, I crept out of the bedroom and phoned for an ambulance. I nearly went outside to see what I could do, but thought: if I move him, if I even just try to stop the bleeding, I'll probably do more harm than good, maybe mange to kill him with my well-intentioned incompetence. End up in court. I'd be crazy to take the risk.

I fell asleep before the ambulance arrived. By morning there wasn't a trace of the incident. The taxi must have been towed away, the blood washed off the road by the water truck.

A sixth child had vanished. I returned to the lake, but found it was deserted. I dipped my hand in the water: it was oily, and surprisingly warm. Then I drove back home, cut out the relevant articles, and taped them into place on the wall.

As I did so, the jigsaw puzzle dream flooded my mind, with the dizzying power of *déjà vu*. I stared at the huge grey mosaic, almost expecting it to change before my eyes, but then the mood passed and I shook my head and laughed weakly.

The door opened. I didn't turn. Someone coughed. I still didn't turn.

"Excuse me."

It was a man in his mid-thirties, I'd say. Balding slightly, but with a young, open face. He was dressed like an office worker, in a white shirt with the cuffs rolled up, neatly pressed black trousers, a plain blue tie.

"What do you want?"

"I'm sorry. I knocked on the front door, and it was ajar. Then I called out twice."

"I didn't hear you."

"I'm sorry."

"What do you want?"

"Can I look? At your walls? Oh there! The Marsden Mangler! I wonder how many people remember him today. Five years ago there were two thousand police working full time on that case, and probably a hundred reporters scurrying back and forth between the morgue and the nightclub belt. You know, half the jury fainted when they showed slides at the trial, including an abattoir worker."

"Nobody *fainted*. A few people closed their eyes, that's all. I was there."

"Watching the jury and not the slides apparently."

"Watching both. Were you there?"

"Oh, yes! Everyday without fail."

"Well I don't remember you. And I got to know most of the regular faces in the public gallery."

"I was never in the public gallery." He crossed the room to peer closely at a Sunday paper's diagram detailing the *modus operandi* of the Knightsbridge Knifeman. "This is pretty coy, isn't it? I mean, anybody would think that the female genitalia—" I glared at him, and he turned his attention to something else, smiling a slight smile of tolerant amusement.

"How did you find out about my collection of clippings?" It wasn't something that I boasted about, and Wendy found it a bit embarrassing, perhaps a bit sick.

"Collection of clippings! You mustn't call it that! I'll tell you what this room is: it's a shrine. No lesser word will do. A shrine."

I glanced behind me. The door was closed. I watched him as he read a two-page spread on a series of unsolved axe murders, and although his gaze was clearly directed at the print, I felt as if he was staring straight back at me.

Then I knew that I *had* seen him before. Twenty years before, on television, smiling shyly as they hustled him along, never quite looking at the camera, but never quite turning away. My eyes began to water, and a crazy thought filled my head: hadn't I known then, hadn't I been certain, that the killer would come and get me, that nothing would stand in his way? That the man had not aged was unremarkable, no it was *necessary,* because if he had aged I would never have recognized him, and recognition was exactly what he wanted. Recognition was the start of my fear.

I said, "You might tell me your name."

He looked up. "I'm sorry. I have been discourteous, haven't I? But—" (he shrugged) "—I have so many nicknames." He gestured widely with both hands, taking in all the walls, all the headlines. I pictured the door handle, wondering how quickly I could turn it with palms stinking wet, with numb, clumsy fingers. "My friends, though, call me Jack."

He easily lifted me over his head, and then somehow (did he float up off the floor, or did he stretch up, impossibly doubling his height?) pinned me facedown against the ceiling. Four fangs grew to fill his mouth, and his mouth opened to fill my vision. It was like hanging over a living well, and as his distorted words echoed up from the depths, I thought: if I fall, nobody will ever find me.

"Tonight you will take my photograph. Catch me in the act with your brightest flashgun. That's what you want, isn't it?" He shook me.

"Isn't it?" I closed my eyes, but that brought visions of a tumbling descent. I whispered, "Yes."

"You invoke me and invoke me and invoke me!" he roared. "Aren't you ever sick of blood? Aren't you ever sick of the taste of blood? Today it's the blood of tiny children, tomorrow the blood of old women, next the blood of . . . who? Dark-haired prostitutes? Teenaged baby sitters? Blue-eyed homosexuals? And each time simply leaves you more jaded, longing for something crueller and more bizarre. Can't you sweeten your long, bland lives with anything but blood?

"Colour film. Bring plenty of colour film. Kodachrome, I want saturated hues. Understand?" I nodded. He told me where and when: a nearby street corner, at three fifteen.

I hit the floor with my hands out in front of me, jarring one wrist but not breaking it. I was alone. I ran through the house, I searched every room, then I locked the doors and sat on the bed, shaking, emitting small, unhappy noises every few minutes.

When I'd calmed down, I went out and bought ten rolls of Kodachrome.

We ate at home that night. I was supposed to cook something, but I ended up making do with frozen pizzas. Wendy talked about her tax problems, and I nodded.

"And what did you do with yourself today?"

"Research."

"For what?"

"I'll tell you tomorrow."

We made love. For a while it seemed like some sort of ritual, some kind of magic: Wendy was giving me strength, yes, she was fortifying me with mystical energy and spiritual power. Afterwards, I couldn't laugh at such a ludicrous idea, I could only despise myself for being able to take it seriously for a moment.

I dreamt that she gave me a shining silver sword.

"What's it for?" I asked her.

"When you feel like running away, stab yourself in the foot."

I climbed out of bed at two. It was utterly freezing, even once I was fully dressed. I sat in the kitchen with the light off, drinking coffee until I was so bloated that I could hardly breathe. Then I staggered to the toilet and threw it all up. My throat and lungs stung, I wanted to curl up and dissolve, or crawl back to the warm blankets, back to Wendy to stay hidden under the covers until morning.

As I clicked the front door shut, it was like diving into a moonlit pool. Being safe indoors was at once a distant memory, lying warm in bed was a near-forgotten dream. No cars, no distant traffic noises, no clouds, just a huge night sky and empty, endless streets.

It was five to three when I reached the place. I paced for a while, then walked around the block, but that only killed three minutes. I chose a direction and resolved to walk a straight line for seven minutes, then turn around and come back.

If I didn't turn around, if I kept walking, would he catch me? Would he return to the house and punish me? What if we moved, to another city, another state?

I passed a phone box, an almost blinding slab of solid light. I jingled my pockets, then remembered that I'd need no coin. I stood outside the booth for two minutes, I lingered in the half-open doorway for three, and then I lifted and replaced the handset a dozen times before I finally dialled.

When the operator answered, I slammed the phone down. I needed to defecate, I needed to lie down. I dialled again, and asked for the police. It was so easy. I even gave them my true name and address when they asked, without the least hesitation. I said "thank you" about six thousand times.

I looked at my watch: thirteen past three. I ran for the corner, camera swinging by the carrying strap, and made it back in ninety seconds.

Someone was climbing out through a dark window, holding a gagged, struggling child. It wasn't the man who'd called himself Jack, it wasn't the killer I'd seen on TV when I was ten.

I raised my camera.

Drop it and do something, drop it and save the child, you fool! Me against him? Against that? I'd be slaughtered! The police are coming. It's their job, isn't it? Just take the pictures. It's what you really want, it's what you're here to do.

Once I'd fired the shutter, once I'd taken the first shot, it was like flicking through the pages of a magazine. I was sickened, I was horrified, I was angry, but I wasn't there, sow what could I do? The child was tortured. The child was raped. The child was mutilated. The child suffered but I heard no cries, and I saw only the flashgun's frozen tableaux, a sequence of badly-made waxworks.

The killer and I arranged each shot with care. He waited patiently while the flash recharged, and while I changed rolls. He was a consummate model: each pose he struck appeared completely natural, utterly spontaneous.

I didn't notice just when the child actually died. I only noticed when I ran out of film. It was then that I looked around at the houses on the street and saw half a dozen couples, peeking through their bedroom windows and stifling yawns.

He sprinted away when the police arrived. They didn't pursue him in the car; one officer loped off after him, the other knelt to examine the remains, then walked up to me. He tipped his head at my camera.

"Got it all, did you?"

I nodded. Accomplice, accomplice, accomplice. How could I ever explain, let alone try to excuse, my inaction?

"Fantastic. Well done."

Two more police cars appeared, and then the officer who'd gone in pursuit came marching up the street, pushing the hand-cuffed killer ahead of him.

▼

The best of the photographs were published widely, even shown on TV ("the following scenes may disturb some viewers"). A thousand law-abiding citizens rioted outside the courthouse, burning and slashing effigies, when he appeared to be placed on remand.

He was killed in his cell a week before the trial was due to start. He was tortured, raped and mutilated first. He must have been expecting to die, because he had written out *a will:*

Burn my body and scatter my ashes from a high place.

Only then will I be happy. Only then will I find peace.

They did it for him, too.

He has a special place on my wall now, and I never tire of reviewing it. The whole process can be seen at a glance. How the tabloids cheered him on, rewarding each presumed death with ever larger headlines, ever grislier speculations. How the serious papers strove so earnestly to understand him, with scholarly dissertations on the formative years of the great modern killers. How all the well-oiled mechanisms slipped into gear, how everybody knew their role. Quotes from politicians: "The community is outraged." But the outrage was bottled, recycled, flat and insincere.

What would-be killer could hesitate, could resist for even a second, such a cosy niche so lovingly prepared?

And I understand now why he wanted me there that night. He must have believed that if people could see, in colour, in close-up, the kind of atrocities that we treat as an industry, an entertainment, a thrilling diversion from the pettiness and banality of our empty lives, then we would at last recoil, we would at last feel some genuine shock, some genuine sadness, we would at last be cured, and he would be free.

He was wrong.

So they've burnt his corpse and scattered his ashes. So what? Did he really believe that could possibly help him, did he really hope to end the interminable cycle of his incarnations?

I dream of fine black cinders borne by the wind, floating down to anoint ten thousand feverish brows. The sight of the tortured child, you see, has exerted an awful fascination upon people around the world.

The first wave of imitators copied the murder exactly as portrayed by my slides.

The second wave embellished and improvised.

The current fashion is for live broadcasts, and the change of medium has, of course, had some influence upon the technical details of the act.

I often sit in my study these days, just staring at the walls. Now and then I suffer moments of blind panic, when I am convinced for no reason that Jack has returned, and is standing right behind me with his mouth stretched open. But when I turn and look, I am always still alone. Alone with the headlines, alone with the photographs, alone with my obsession. And that, somehow, is far more frightening.

Descending

THOMAS M. DISCH

Horror can be evoked in many ways, and can come in a wide variety of guises. There have been stories that take what we generally consider harmless, ordinary things, only to make of them objects of sheer terror.

Thomas M. Disch's story "Descending," first published in 1964, makes a simple ride on an escalator a journey unlike any you're ever likely to experience. Disch, who has mesmerized readers for more than thirty years with stories and novels of brilliant clarity and elegance such as *The M.D.: A Horror Story, 334,* and *Camp Concentration,* subtly weaves a marvelously effective tale of crushing anomie.

Part of Disch's genius is in his acute observation of the everyday, using apparently innocuous details to build a crescendo of unease and doubt, bringing us into the mind of his narrator, until we have no escape from the disturbing scenario in which he is trapped.

Unlikely though it may seem, "Descending," is a story of memorable disquietude.

Catsup, mustard, pickle relish, mayonnaise, two kinds of salad dressing, bacon grease, and a lemon. Oh yes, two trays of ice cubes. In the cupboard it wasn't much better: jars and boxes of spice, flour, sugar, salt—and a box of raisins!

An empty box of raisins.

Not even any coffee. Not even tea, which he hated. Nothing in the mailbox but a bill from Underwood's: *Unless we receive the arrears on your account . . .*

$4.75 in change jingled in his coat pocket—the plunder of the Chianti bottle he had promised himself never to break open. He was spared the unpleasantness of having to sell his books. They had all been sold. The letter to Graham had gone out a week ago. If his brother intended to send something this time, it would have come by now.

—I should be desperate, he thought. —Perhaps I am.

He might have looked in the *Times*. But, no, that was too depressing applying for jobs at $50 a week and being turned down. Not that he blamed them; he wouldn't have hired himself himself. He had been a grasshopper for years. The ants were on to his tricks.

He shaved without soap and brushed his shoes to a high polish. He whitened the sepulchre of his unwashed torso with a fresh, starched shirt and chose his somberest tie from the rack. He began to feet excited and expressed it, characteristically, by appearing statuesquely, icily calm. Descending the stairway to the first floor, he encountered Mrs. Beale, who was pretending to sweep the well-swept floor of the entrance.

"Good afternoon—or I s'pose it's good morning for you, eh?"

"Good afternoon, Mrs. Beale."

"Your letter come?"

"Not yet."

"The first of the month isn't far off."

"Yes indeed, Mrs. Beale."

At the subway station he considered a moment before answering the attendant: One token or two? Two, he decided. After all, he had no choice, but to return to his apartment. The first of the month was still a long way off.

—If Jean Valjean had had a charge account, he would have never gone to prison.

Having thus cheered himself, he settled down to enjoy the ads in the subway car. *Smoke. Try. Eat. Give. See. Drink. Use. Buy.* He thought of Alice with her mushrooms: Eat me.

At 34th Street he got off and entered Underwood's Department Store directly from the train platform. On the main floor he stopped at the cigar stand and bought a carton of cigarettes. "Cash or charge?"

"Charge." He handed the clerk the laminated plastic card. The charge was rung up.

▼

Fancy groceries was on 5. He made his selection judiciously. A jar of instant and a 2-pound can of drip-ground coffee, a large tin of corned beef, packaged soups and boxes of pancake mix and condensed milk. Jam, peanut butter, and honey. Six cans of tuna fish. Then, he indulged himself in perishables: English cookies, and Edam cheese, a small frozen pheasant—even fruitcake. He never ate so well as when he was broke. He couldn't afford to.

"$14.87."

This time after ringing up his charge, the clerk checked the number on his card against her list of closed or doubtful accounts. She smiled apologetically and handed the card back.

"Sorry, but we have to check."

"I understand."

The bag of groceries weighed a good twenty pounds. Carrying it with the exquisite casualness of a burglar passing before a policeman with his loot, he took the escalator to the bookshop on 8. His choice of boos was determined by the same principle as his choice of groceries. First, the staples: two Victorian novels he had never read, *Vanity Fair* and *Middlemarch*; the Sayers' translation of Dante, and a two-volume anthology of German plays none of which he had read and few he had even heard of. Then the perishables: a sensational novel that had reached the best seller list via the Supreme Court, and two mysteries.

He had begun to feel giddy with self-indulgence. He reached into his jacket pocket for a coin.

—Heads a new suit; tails the Sky Room.

Tails.

The Sky Room on 15 was empty of all but a few women chatting over coffee and cakes. He was able to get a seat by a window. He ordered from the à la Carte side of the menu and finished his meal with Espresso and baklava. He handed the waitress his credit card and tipped her fifty cents.

Dawdling over his second cup of coffee, he began *Vanity Fair.* Rather to his surprise, he found himself enjoying it. The waitress returned with his card and a receipt for the meal.

Since the Sky Room was on the top floor of Underwood's there was only one escalator to take now—Descending. Riding down, he continued to read *Vanity Fair.* He could read anywhere—in restaurants, on subways, even walking down the street. At each landing he made his way from the foot of one escalator to the head of the next without lifting his eyes from the book. When he came to the Bargain Basement, he would be only a few steps from the subway turnstile. He was halfway through Chapter VI (on page 55, to be exact) when he began to feel something amiss.

—How long does this damn thing take to reach the basement?

He stopped at the next landing, but there was no sign to indicate on what floor he was nor any door by which he might re-enter the store. Deducing from this that he was between floors, he took the escalator down one more flight only to find the same perplexing absence of landmarks.

There was, however, a water fountain, and he stooped to take a drink.

—I must have gone to a sub-basement. But this was not too likely after all. Escalators were seldom provided for janitors and stockboys.

He waited on the landing watching the steps of the escalators slowly descend toward him and, at the end of their journey, telescope in upon themselves and disappear. He waited a long while, and no one else came down the moving steps.

—Perhaps the store has closed. Having no wristwatch and having rather lost track of the time, he had no way of knowing. At last, he reasoned that he had become so engrossed in the Thackeray novel that he had simply stopped on one of the upper landings—say, on 8—to finish a chapter and had read on to page 55 without realizing that he was making no progress on the escalators.

When he read, he could forget everything else.

He must, therefore, still be somewhere above the main floor. The absence of exits, though disconcerting, could be explained by some quirk in the floor plan. The absence of signs was merely a carelessness on the part of the management.

▼

He tucked *Vanity Fair* into his shopping bag and stepped onto the grilled lip of the down-going escalator not, it must be admitted, without a certain degree of reluctance. At each landing, he marked his progress by a number spoken aloud. By *eight* he was uneasy; by *fifteen* he was desperate.

It was, of course, possible that he had to descend two flights of stairs for every floor of the department store. With this possibility in mind, he counted off fifteen more landings.

—No.

Dazedly and as though to deny the reality of this seemingly interminable stairwell, he continued his descent. When he stopped again at the forty-fifth landing, he was trembling. He was afraid.

He rested the shopping bag on the bare concrete floor of the landing, realizing that his arm had gone quite sore from supporting the twenty pounds and more of groceries and books. He discounted the enticing possibility that "it was all a dream," for the dream-world is the reality of the dreamer, to which he could not weakly surrender, no more than one could surrender to the realities of life. Besides, he was not dreaming; of that he was quite sure.

He checked his pulse. It was fast—say, eighty a minute. He rode down two more flights, counting his pulse. Eighty almost exactly. Two flights took only one minute.

He could read approximately one page a minute, a little less on an escalator. Suppose he had spent one hour on the escalators while he had read: sixty minutes—one hundred and twenty floors. Plus forty-seven that he had counted. One hundred sixty-seven. The Sky Room was on 15.

167-15=152.

He was in the one-hundred-fifty-second sub-basement. That was impossible.

The appropriate response to an impossible situation was to deal with it as though it were commonplace—like Alice in Wonderland.

Ergo, he would return to Underwood's the same way he had (apparently) left it. He would walk up one hundred fifty-two flights of downgoing escalators. Taking the steps three at a time and running, it was almost like going up a regular staircase. But after ascending the second escalator in this manner, he found himself already out of breath.

There was no hurry. He would not allow himself to be overtaken by panic.

No.

He picked up the bag of groceries and books he had left on that landing, waiting for his breath to return, and darted up a third and fourth flight. While he rested on the landing, he tried to count the steps between floors, but this count differed depending on whether he counted with the current or against it, down or up. The average was roughly eighteen steps, and the steps appeared to be eight or nine inches deep. Each flight was, therefore, about twelve feet.

It was one-third of a mile, as the plumb drops, to Underwood's main floor.

Dashing up the ninth escalator, the bag of groceries broke open at the bottom, where the thawing pheasant had dampened the paper. Groceries and books tumbled onto the steps, some rolling of their own accord to the landing below, others being transported there by the moving stairs and forming a neat little pile. Only the jam jar had been broken.

He stacked the groceries in the corner of the landing, except for the half-thawed pheasant, which he stuffed into his coat pocket, anticipating that his ascent would take him well past his dinner hour.

Physical exertion had dulled his finer feelings—to be precise, his capacity for fear. Like a cross-country runner in his last laps, he thought single-mindedly of the task at hand and made no effort to understand what he had in any case already decided was not to be understood. He mounted one flight, rested, mounted and rested again. Each mount was wearier; each rest longer. He stopped counting the landings after the twenty-eighth, and some time after that—how long he had no idea—his legs gave out and he collapsed to the concrete floor of the landing. His calves were hard aching knots of muscle; his thighs quivered erratically. He tried to do knee-bends and fell backward.

Despite his recent dinner (assuming that it had been recent), he was hungry and he devoured the entire pheasant, completely thawed now, without being able to tell if it were raw or had been pre-cooked.

—This is what it's like to be a cannibal, he thought as he fell asleep.

Sleeping, he dreamed he was falling down a bottomless pit. Waking, he discovered nothing had changed, except the dull ache in his legs, which had become a sharp pain.

Overhead, a single strip of fluorescent lighting snaked down the stairwell. The mechanical purr of the escalators seemed to have heightened to the roar of a Niagara, and their rate of descent seemed to have increased proportionately.

Fever, he decided. He stood up stiffly and flexed some of the soreness from his muscles.

Halfway up the third escalator, his legs gave way under him. He attempted the climb again and succeeded. He collapsed again on the next flight. Lying on the landing where the escalator had deposited him, he realized that his hunger had returned. He also needed to have water—and to let it.

The latter necessity he could easily—and without false modesty—satisfy. Also he remembered the water fountain he had drunk from yesterday, and he found another three floors below.

—It's so much easier going down.

His groceries were down there. To go after them now, he would erase whatever progress he had made in his ascent. Perhaps Underwood's main floor was only a few more flights up. Or a hundred. There was no way to know.

Because he was hungry and because he was tired and because the futility of mounting endless flights of descending escalators was, as he now considered it, a labor of Sisyphus, he returned, descended, gave in.

At first, he allowed the escalator to take him along at its own mild pace, but soon grew impatient of this. He found that the exercise of running down the steps three at a time was not so exhausting as running *up*. It was refreshing, almost. And, by swimming with the current instead of against it, his progress, if such it can be called, was appreciable. In only minutes he was back at his cache of groceries.

After eating half the fruitcake and a little cheese, he fashioned his coat into a sort of sling for the groceries, knotting the sleeves together and buttoning it closed. With one hand at the collar and the other about the hem, he could carry all his food with him.

He looked up the descending staircase with a scornful smile, for he had decided with the wisdom of failure to abandon *that* venture. If the stairs wished to take him down, then down, giddily, he would go.

Then, down he did go, down dizzily, down, down and always, it seemed, faster, spinning about lightly on his heels at each landing so that there was hardly any break in the wild speed of his descent. He whooped and halooed and laughed to hear his whoopings echo in the narrow, low-vaulted corridors, following him as though they could not keep up his pace.

Down, ever deeper down.

Twice he slipped at the landings and once he missed his footing in mid-leap on the escalator, hurtled forward, letting go of the sling of groceries and falling, hands stretched out to cushion him, onto the steps, which, imperturbably, continued their descent.

He must have been unconscious then, for he woke up in a pile of groceries with a split check and a splitting headache. The telescoping steps of the escalator gently grazed his heels.

He knew then his first moment of terror—a premonition that there was no end to his descent, but this feeling gave way quickly to a laughing fit.

"I'm going to hell!" he shouted, though he could not drown with his voice the steady purr of the escalators. "This is the way to hell. Abandon hope all ye who enter here."

—If only I were, he reflected. —If that were the case, it would make sense. Not quite orthodox sense, but some sense, a little.

Sanity, however, was so integral to his character that neither hysteria nor horror could long have their way with him. He gathered up his groceries again, relieved to find that only the jar of instant coffee had been broken this time. After reflection be also discarded the can of drip-ground coffee, for which he could conceive no use—under the present circumstances. And he would allow himself, for the sake of sanity, to conceive of no other circumstances than those.

He began a more deliberate descent. He returned to *Vanity Fair*, reading it as he paced down the down-going steps. He did not let himself consider the extent of the abyss into which he was plunging, and the vicarious excitement of the novel helped him keep his thoughts from his own situation. At page 235, he lunched (that is, he took his second meal of the day) on the remainder of the cheese and fruitcake; at 523 he rested and dined on the English cookies dipped in peanut butter.

—Perhaps I had better ration my food.

If he could regard this absurd dilemma merely as a struggle for survival, another chapter in his own Robinson Crusoe Story, he might get to the bottom of this mechanized vortex alive and sane. He thought proudly that many people in his position could not have adjusted, would have gone mad.

Of course, he *was* descending . . .

But he was still sane. He had chosen his course and now he was following it.

There was no night in the stairwell, and scarcely any shadows. He slept when his legs could no longer bear his weight and his eyes were tearful from reading. Sleeping, he dreamed that he was continuing his descent on the escalators. Waking, his hand resting on the rubber railing that moved along at the same rate as the steps he discovered this to be the case.

Somnambulistically, he had ridden the escalators further down into this mild, interminable hell, leaving behind his bundle of food and even the still-unfinished Thackeray novel.

Stumbling up the escalators, he began, for the first time, to cry. Without the novel, there was nothing to *think* of but this, this . . .

—How far? How long did I sleep?

His legs, which had only been slightly wearied by his descent, gave out twenty flights up. His spirit gave out soon after. Again he turned around, allowed himself to be swept up by current—or, more exactly, swept down.

The escalator seemed to be traveling more rapidly, the pitch of the steps to be more pronounced. But he no longer trusted the evidence of his senses.

—I am, perhaps, insane—or sick from hunger. Yet, I would have run out of food eventually. This will bring the crisis to a head. Optimism, that's the spirit!

Continuing his descent, he occupied himself with a closer analysis of his environment, not undertaken with any hope of bettering his condition but only for lack of other diversions. The walls and ceilings were hard, smooth, and off-white. The escalator steps were a dull nickel color, the treads being somewhat shinier, the crevices darker. Did that mean that the treads were polished from use? Or were they designed in that fashion? The treads were half an inch wide and spaced apart from each other by the same width. They projected slightly over the edge of each step, resembling somewhat the head of a barber's shears. Whenever he stopped at a landing, his attention would become fixed on the illusory "disappearance" of the steps, as they sank flush to the floor and slid, tread in groove, into the grilled baseplate.

Less and less would he run, or even walk, down the stairs, content merely to ride his chosen step from top to bottom of each flight and, at the landing, step (left foot, right, and left again) onto the escalator that would transport him to the floor below. The stairwell now had tunneled, by his calculations, miles beneath the department store—so many miles that he began to congratulate himself upon his unsought adventure, wondering if he had established some sort of record. Just so, a criminal will stand in awe of his own baseness and be most proud of his vilest crime, which he believes unparalleled.

In the days that followed, when his only nourishment was the water from the fountains provided at every tenth landing, he thought frequently of food, preparing imaginary meals from the store of groceries he had left behind, savoring the ideal sweetness of the honey, the richness of the soup which he would prepare by soaking the powder in the emptied cookie tin, licking the film of gelatin lining the opened can of corned beef. When he thought of the six cans of tuna fish, his anxiety became intolerable, for he had (would have had) no way to open them. Merely to stamp on them would not be enough. What, then? He turned the question over and over in his head, like a squirrel spinning the wheel in its cage, to no avail.

Then a curious thing happened. He quickened again the speed of his descent, faster now than when first he had done this, eagerly, headlong, absolutely heedless. The several landings seemed to flash by like a montage of Flight, each scarcely perceived before the next was before him. A demonic, pointless race—and why? He was running, so he thought, toward his store of groceries, either believing that they had been left *below* or thinking that he was running *up*. Clearly, he was delirious.

It did not last. His weakened body could not maintain the frantic pace, and he awoke from his delirium confused and utterly spent. Now began another, more rational delirium, a madness fired by logic. Lying on the landing, rubbing a torn muscle in his ankle, he speculated on the nature, origin and purpose of the escalators. Reasoned thought was of no more use to him, however, than unreasoning action. Ingenuity was helpless to solve a riddle that had no answer, which was its own reason, self-contained and whole. He—not the escalators—needed an answer.

▼

Perhaps his most interesting theory was the notion that these escalators were a kind of exercise wheel, like those found in a squirrel cage, from which, because it was a closed system, there could be no escape. This theory required some minor alterations in his conception of the physical universe, which had always appeared highly Euclidean to him before, a universe in which his descent seemingly along a plumb-line was, in fact, describing a loop. This theory cheered him, for he might hope, coming full circle, to return to his store of groceries again, if not to Underwood's. Perhaps in his abstracted state he had passed one or the other already several times without observing.

There was another, and related, theory concerning the measures taken by Underwood's Credit Department against delinquent accounts. This was mere paranoia.

—Theories! I don't need theories. I must get on with it.

So, favoring his good leg, he continued his descent, although his speculations did not immediately cease. They became, if anything, more metaphysical. They became vague. Eventually, he could regard the escalators as being entirely matter-of-fact, requiring no more explanation than, by their sheer existence, they offered him.

He discovered that he was losing weight. Being so long without food (by the evidence of his beard, he estimated that more than a week had gone by), this was only to be expected. Yet, there was another possibility that he could not exclude: that he was approaching the center of the earth where, as he understood, all things were weightless.

—Now *that*, he thought, is something worth striving for.

He had discovered a goal. On the other hand, he was dying, a process he did not give all the attention it deserved. Unwilling to admit this eventuality and yet not so foolish as to admit any other, he side-stepped the issue by pretending to hope.

—Maybe someone will rescue me, he hoped.

But his hope was as mechanical as the escalators he rode and tended, in much the same way, to sink.

Waking and sleeping were no longer distinct states of which he could say: "Now I am sleeping," or "Now I am awake." Sometimes he would discover himself descending and be unable to tell whether he had been waked from sleep or roused from inattention.

He hallucinated.

A woman, loaded with packages from Underwood's and wearing a trim, pillbox-style hat, came down the escalator toward him, turned around on the landing, high heels clicking smartly, and rode away without even nodding to him.

More and more, when he awoke or was roused from his stupor, he found himself, instead of hurrying to his goal, lying on a landing, weak, dazed, and beyond hunger. Then he would crawl to the down-going escalator and pull himself onto one of the steps, which he would ride to the bottom, sprawled head foremost, hands and shoulders braced against the treads to keep from skittering bumpily down.

—At the bottom, be thought—at the bottom . . . I will . . . when I get there . . .

From the bottom, which he conceived of as the center of the earth, there would be literally nowhere to go but up. Probably another chain of escalators, ascending escalators, but preferably by an elevator. It was important to believe in a bottom.

Thought was becoming as difficult, as demanding and painful, as once his struggle to ascend had been. His perceptions were fuzzy. He did not know what was real and what imaginary. He thought he was eating and discovered he was gnawing at his hands.

He thought he had come to the bottom. It was a large, high-ceilinged room. Signs pointed to another escalator: *Ascending.* But there was a chain across it and a small typed announcement. "Out of order. Please bear with us while the escalators are being repaired. Thank you. The Management."

He laughed weakly.

He devised a way to open the tuna fish cans. He would slip the can sideways beneath the protecting treads of the escalator, just at the point where the steps were sinking flush to the floor. Either the escalator would split the can open or the can would jam the escalator. Perhaps if one escalator were jammed the whole chain of them would stop. He should have thought of that before, but he was, nevertheless, quite pleased to have thought of it at all.

—I might have escaped.

His body seemed to weigh so little now. He must have come hundreds of miles. Thousands.

Again, he descended.

Then, he was lying at the foot of the escalator. His head rested on the cold metal of the baseplate and he was looking at his hand, the fingers of which were pressed into the creviced grille. One after another, in perfect order, the steps of the escalator slipped into these crevices, tread in groove, rasping at his fingertips, occasionally tearing away a sliver of his flesh.

That was the last thing he remembered.

That Hellbound Train

Robert Bloch

Best known for his novel *Psycho* and its adaptation for the screen by Alfred Hitchcock, Robert Bloch was a writer whose work is well known in both the science fiction and suspense fields. His novels and stories that are classified as horror tend to focus not so much on supernatural evil, but rather on the evil to be found in people.

"That Hellbound Train," winner of the 1958 Hugo Award for Best Science Fiction Short Story, is no exception. Yes, you'll find the Devil here without looking too hard, but the crux of the story lies in Bloch's superb storytelling skill and his keen understanding of human nature.

When he was growing up in Milwaukee, Bloch corresponded with the great horror and fantasy writer H.P. Lovecraft, who encouraged him in his writing. But while Lovecraft created an even odder mythos of dread and madness, Bloch's work was usually set in the ordinary world of people with petty greeds and fallible natures.

"That Hellbound Train" shows his easy skill at setting and narrative drive, as we follow the tracks of this story through the eyes of its unfortunate protagonist. What Bloch does all too well is make each reader feel that his doom could all too easily be your own.

When Martin was a little boy, his Daddy was a Railroad Man. Daddy never rode the high iron, but he walked the tracks for the *CB&Q*, and he was proud of his job. And every night when he got drunk, he sang this old song about *That Hell-Bound Train*.

Martin didn't quite remember any of the words, but he couldn't forget the way his Daddy sang them out. And when Daddy made the mistake of getting drunk in the afternoon and got squeezed between a Pennsy tank-car and an *AT&SF* gondola, Martin sort of wondered why the Brotherhood didn't sing the song at his funeral.

After that, things didn't go so good for Martin, but somehow he always recalled Daddy's song. When Mom up and ran off with a traveling salesman from Keokuk (Daddy must have turned over in his grave, knowing she'd done such a thing, and with a *passenger*, too!) Martin hummed the tune to himself every night in the Orphan Home. And after Martin himself ran away, he used to whistle the song softly at night in the jungles, after the other bindlestiffs were asleep.

Martin was on the road for four-five years before he realized he wasn't getting anyplace. Of course he's tried his hand at a lot of things—picking fruit in Oregon, washing dishes in a Montana hash-house, stealing hub-caps in Denver and tires in Oklahoma City—but by the time he'd put in six months on the chain-gang in Alabama he knew he had no future drifting around this way on his own.

So he tried to get on the railroad like his Daddy had and they told him that times were bad.

But Martin couldn't keep away from the railroads. Wherever he traveled, he rode the rods; he'd rather hop a freight heading north in sub-zero weather than lift his thumb to hitch a ride with a Cadillac headed for Florida. Whenever he managed to get hold of a can of Sterno, he'd sit there under a nice warm culvert, think about the old days, and often as not he'd hum the song about *That Hell-Bound Train*. That was the train the drunks and the sinners rode—the gambling men and the grifters, the big-time spenders, the skirt-chasers, and all the jolly crew. It would be really fine to take a trip in such good company, but Martin didn't like to think of what happened when that train finally pulled into the Depot Way Down Yonder. He didn't figure on spending eternity stoking boilers in Hell, without even a Company Union to protect him. Still, it would be a lovely ride. If there was *such* a thing as a Hell-Bound Train. Which, of course, there wasn't.

At least Martin didn't *think* there was, until that evening when he found himself walking the tracks heading south, just outside of Appleton Junction. The night was cold and dark, the way November nights are in the Fox River Valley, and he knew he'd have to work his way down to New Orleans for the winter, or maybe even Texas. Somehow he didn't much feel like going, even though he'd heard tell that a lot of those Texas automobiles had solid gold hub-caps.

No sir, he just wasn't cut out for petty larceny. It was worse than a sin—it was unprofitable, too. Bad enough to do the Devil's work, but then to get such miserable pay on top of it! Maybe he'd better let the Salvation Army convert him.

Martin trudged along humming Daddy's song, waiting for a rattler to pull out of the Junction behind him. He'd have to catch it—there was nothing else for him to do.

But the first train to come along came from the other direction, roaring towards him along the track from the south.

Martin peered ahead, but his eyes couldn't match his ears, and so far all he could recognize was the sound. It was a train, though; he felt the steel shudder and sing beneath his feet.

And yet, how could it be? The next station south was Neenah-Menasha, and there was nothing due out there for hours.

The clouds were thick overhead, and the field-mists rolled like a cold fog in a November midnight. Even so, Martin should have been able to see the headlight as the train rushed on. But there was only the whistle, screaming out of the black throat of the night. Martin could recognize the equipment of just about any locomotive ever built, but he'd never heard a whistle that sounded like this one. It wasn't signalling; it was screaming like a lost soul.

He stepped to one side, for the train was almost on top of him now. And suddenly there it was, looming along the tracks and grinding to a stop in less than he'd believed possible. The wheels hadn't been oiled, because they screamed too, screamed like the damned. But the train slid to a halt and the screams died away into a series of low, groaning sounds, and Martin looked up and saw that this was a passenger train. It was big and black, without a single light shining in the engine cab or any of the long string of cars; Martin couldn't read any lettering on the sides, but he was pretty sure this train didn't belong on the Northwestern Road.

He was even more sure when he saw the man clamber down out of the forward car. There was something wrong about the way he walked, as though one of his feet dragged, and about the lantern he carried. The lantern was dark, and the man held it up to his mouth and blew, and instantly it glowed redly. You don't have to be a member of the Railway Brotherhood to know that this is a mighty peculiar way of lighting a lantern.

As the figure approached, Martin recognized the conductor's cap perched on his head, and this made him feel a little better for a moment—until he noticed that it was worn a bit too high, as though there night be something sticking up on the forehead underneath it.

Still, Martin knew his manners, and when the man smiled at him, he said, "Good evening, Mr. Conductor."

"Good evening, Martin."

"How did you know my name?"

The man shrugged. "How did you know I was the Conductor?"

"You *are*, aren't you?"

"To you, yes. Although other people, in other walks of life, may recognize me in different roles. For instance, you ought to see what I look like to the folks out in Hollywood." The man grinned. "I travel a great deal," he explained.

"What brings you here?" Martin asked.

"Why, you ought to know the answer to that, Martin. I came because you needed me. Tonight, I suddenly realized you were backsliding. Thinking of joining the Salvation Army, weren't you?"

"Well—" Martin hesitated.

"Don't be ashamed. To err is human, as somebody-or-other once said. *Reader's Digest,* wasn't it? Never mind. The point is, I felt you needed me. So I switched over and came your way."

"What for?"

"Why, to offer you a ride, of course. Isn't it better to travel comfortably by train than to march along the cold streets behind a Salvation Army band? Hard on the feet, they tell me, and even harder on the eardrums."

"I'm not sure I'd care to ride on your train, sir," Martin said. "Considering where I'm likely to end up."

"Ah, yes. The old argument." The Conductor sighed. "I suppose you'd prefer some sort of bargain, is that it?"

"Exactly," Martin answered.

"Well, I'm afraid I'm all through with that sort of thing. There's no shortage of prospective passengers any more. Why should I offer you any special inducements?"

"You must want me, or else you wouldn't have bothered to go out of your way to find me."

The Conductor sighed again. "There you have a point. Pride was always my besetting weakness, I admit. And somehow I'd hate to lose you to the competition, after thinking of you as my own all these years." He hesitated. "Yes, I'm prepared to deal with you on your own terms, if you insist."

"The terms?" Martin asked.

"Standard proposition. Anything you want."

"Ah," said Martin.

"But I warn you in advance, there'll be no tricks. I'll grant you any wish you can name—but in return, you must promise to ride the train when the time comes."

"Suppose it never comes?"

"It will."

"Suppose I've got the kind of a wish that will keep me off forever?"

"There is no such wish."

"Don't be too sure."

"Let me worry about that," the Conductor told him. "No matter what you have in mind, I warn you that I'll collect in the end. And there'll be none of this last-minute hocus-pocus, either. No last-hour repentances, no blonde *frauleins* or fancy lawyers showing up to get you off. I offer a clean deal. That is to say, you'll get what you want, and I'll get what I want."

"I've heard you trick people. They say you're worse than a used-car salesman."

"Now, wait a minute—"

"I apologize," Martin said, hastily. "But it is supposed to be a fact that you can't be trusted."

"I admit it. On the other hand, you seem to think you have found a way out."

"A sure-fire proposition."

"Sure-fire? Very funny!" The man began to chuckle, then halted. "But we waste valuable time, Martin. Let's get down to cases. What do you want from me?"

Martin took a deep breath. "I want to be able to stop Time."

"Right now?"

"No. Not yet. And not for everybody. I realize that would be impossible, of course. But I want to be able to stop Time for myself. Just once, in the future. Whenever I get to a point where I know I'm happy and contented, that's where I'd like to stop. So I can just keep on being happy forever."

"That's quite a proposition," the Conductor mused. "I've got to admit I've never heard anything just like it before—and believe me, I've listened to some lulus in my day." He grinned at Martin. "You've really been thinking about this, haven't you?"

"For years," Martin admitted. Then he coughed. "Well, what do you say?"

"It's not impossible, in terms of your own *subjective* time-sense," the Conductor murmured. "Yes, I think it could be arranged."

"But I mean *really* to stop. Not for me just to *imagine* it."

"I understand. And it can be done."

"Then you'll agree?"

"Why not? I promised you, didn't I? Give me your hand."

Martin hesitated. "Will it hurt very much? I mean, I don't like the sight of blood, and—"

"Nonsense! You've been listening to a lot of poppycock. We already have made our bargain, my boy. I merely intend to put something into your hand. The ways and means of fulfilling your wish. After all, there's no telling at just what moment you may decide to exercise the agreement, and I can't drop everything and come running. So it's better if you can regulate matters for yourself."

"You're going to give me a Time-stopper?"

"That's the general idea. As soon as I can decide what would be practical." The Conductor hesitated. "Ah, the very thing! Here, take my watch."

He pulled it out of his vest-pocket; a railroad watch in a silver case. He opened the back and made a delicate adjustment; Martin tried to see just exactly what he was doing, but the fingers moved in a blinding blur.

"There we are," the Conductor smiled. "It's all set, now. When you finally decide where you'd like to call a halt, merely turn the stem in reverse and unwind the watch until it stops. When it stops, Time stops, for you. Simple enough?" And the Conductor dropped the watch into Martin's hand.

The young man closed his fingers tightly around the case. "That's all there is to it, eh?"

"Absolutely. But remember—you can stop the watch only once. So you'd better make sure that you're satisfied with the moment you choose to prolong. I caution you in all fairness; make very certain of your choice."

"I will." Martin grinned. "And since you've been so fair about it, I'll be fair too. There's one thing you seem to have forgotten. It doesn't really matter *what* moment I choose. Because once I stop Time for myself, that means I stay where I am forever. I'll never have to get any older. And if I don't get any older, I'll never die. And if I never die, then I'll never have to take a ride on your train."

The Conductor turned away. His shoulders shook convulsively, and he may have been crying. "And you said *I* was worse than a used-car salesman," he gasped, in a strangled voice.

Then he wandered off into the fog, and the train-whistle gave an impatient shriek, and all at once it was moving swiftly down the track, rumbling out of sight in the darkness

Martin stood there, blinking down at the silver watch in his hand. If it wasn't that he could actually see it and feel it there, and if he couldn't smell that peculiar odor, he might have thought he'd imagined the whole thing from start to finish—train, Conductor, bargain, and all.

But he had the watch, and he could recognize the scent left by the train as it departed, even though there aren't many locomotives around that use sulphur and brimstone as fuel.

And he had no doubts about his bargain. That's what came of thinking things through to a logical conclusion. Some fools would have settled for wealth, or power, or Kim Novak. Daddy might have sold out for a fifth of whiskey.

Martin knew that he'd made a better deal. Better? It was foolproof. All he needed to do now was choose his moment.

He put the watch in his pocket and started back down the railroad track. He hadn't really had a destination in mind before, but he did now. He was going to find a moment of happiness. . . .

▼

Now young Martin wasn't altogether a ninny. He realized perfectly well that happiness is a relative thing; there are conditions and degrees of contentment, and they vary with one's lot in life. As a hobo, he was often satisfied with a warm handout, a double-length bench in the park, or a can of Sterno made in 1957 (a vintage year). Many a time he had reached a state of momentary bliss through such simple agencies, but he was aware that there were better things. Martin determined to seek them out.

Within two days he was in the great city of Chicago. Quite naturally, he drifted over to West Madison Street, and there he took steps to elevate his role in life. He became a city bum, a panhandler, a moocher. Within a week he had risen to the point where happiness was a meal in a regular one-arm luncheon joint, a two-bit flop on a real army cot in a real flophouse, and a full fifth of muscatel.

There was a night, after enjoying all three of these luxuries to the full, when Martin thought of unwinding his watch at the pinnacle of intoxication. But he also thought of the faces of the honest johns he'd braced for a handout today. Sure, they were squares, but they were prosperous. They wore good clothes, held good jobs, drove nice cars. And for them, happiness was even more ecstatic—they ate dinner in fine hotels, they slept on inner-spring mattresses, they drank blended whiskey.

Squares or no, they had something there. Martin fingered his watch, put aside the temptation to hock it for another bottle of muscatel, and went to sleep determined to get himself a job and improve his happiness-quotient.

When he awoke he had a hangover, but the determination was still with him. Before the month was out Martin was working for a general contractor over on the South Side, at one of the big rehabilitation projects. He hated the grind, but the pay was good, and pretty soon he got himself a one-room apartment out on Blue Island Avenue. He was accustomed to eating in decent restaurants now, and he bought himself a comfortable bed, and every Saturday night he went down to the corner tavern. It was all very pleasant, but—

The foreman liked his work and promised him a raise in a month. If he waited around, the raise would mean that he could afford a second-hand car. With a car, he could even start picking up a girl for a date now and then. Other fellows on the job did, and they seemed pretty happy.

So Martin kept on working, and the raise came through and the car came through and pretty soon a couple of girls came through.

The first time it happened, he wanted to unwind his watch immediately. Until he got to thinking about what some of the older men always said. There was a guy named Charlie, for example, who worked alongside him on the hoist. "When you're young and don't know the score, maybe you get a kick out of running around with those pigs. But after a while, you want something better. A nice girl of your own. That's the ticket."

Martin felt he owed it to himself to find out. If he didn't like it better, he could always go back to what he had.

Almost six months went by before Martin met Lillian Gillis. By that time he'd had another promotion and was working inside, in the office. They made him go to night school to learn how to do simple book-keeping, but it meant another fifteen bucks extra a week, and it was nicer working indoors.

And Lillian *was* a lot of fun. When she told him she'd marry him, Martin was almost sure that the time was now. Except that she was sort of—well, she was a *nice* girl, and she said they'd have to wait until they were married. Of course, Martin couldn't expect to marry her until he had a little more money saved up, and another raise would help, too.

That took a year. Martin was patient, because he knew it was going to be worth it. Every time he had any doubts, he took out his watch and looked at it. But he never showed it to Lillian, or anybody else. Most of the other men wore expensive wristwatches and the old silver railroad watch looked just a little cheap.

Martin smiled as he gazed at the stem. Just a few twists and he'd have something none of these other poor working slobs would ever have. Permanent satisfaction, with his blushing bride—

Only getting married turned out to be just the beginning. Sure, it was wonderful, but Lillian told him how much better things would be if they could move into a new place and fix it up. Martin wanted decent furniture, a TV set, a nice car.

So he started taking night courses and got a promotion to the front office. With the baby coming, he wanted to stick around and see his son arrive. And when it came, he realized he'd have to wait until it got a little older, started to walk and talk and develop a personality of its own.

About this time the company sent him out on the road as a trouble-shooter on those other jobs, and now he *was* eating at those good hotels, living high on the hog and the expense-account. More than once he was tempted to unwind his watch. This was the good life. . . . Of course, it would be even better if he just didn't have to *work*. Sooner or later, if he could cut in on one of the company deals, he could make a pile and retire. Then everything would be ideal.

It happened, but it took time. Martin's son was going to high school before he really got up there into the chips. Martin got a strong hunch that it was now or never, because he wasn't exactly a kid any more.

But right about then he met Sherry Westcott, and she didn't seem to think he was middle-aged at all, in spite of the way he was losing hair and adding stomach. She taught him that a *toupee* could cover the bald spot and a cummerbund could cover the potgut. In fact, she taught him quite a lot and he so enjoyed learning that he actually took out his watch and prepared to unwind it.

Unfortunately, he chose the very moment that the private detectives broke down the door of the hotel room, and then there was a long stretch of time when Martin was so busy fighting the divorce action that he couldn't honestly say he was enjoying any given moment.

When he made the final settlement with Lil he was broke again, and Sherry didn't seem to think he was so young, after all. So he squared his shoulders and went back to work.

He made his pile, eventually, but it took longer this time, and there wasn't much chance to have fun along the way. The fancy dames in the fancy cocktail lounges didn't seen to interest him any more, and neither did the liquor. Besides, the Doc had warned him off that.

But there were other pleasures for a rich man to investigate. Travel, for instance—and not riding the rods from one hick burg to another, either. Martin went around the world by plane and luxury liner. For a while it seemed as though he would find his moment after all, visiting the Taj Mahal by moonlight. Martin pulled out the battered old watchcase, and got ready to unwind it. Nobody else was there to watch him—

And that's why he hesitated. Sure, this was an enjoyable moment, but he was alone. Lil and the kid were gone, Sherry was gone, and somehow he'd never had time to make any friends. Maybe if he found new congenial people, he'd have the ultimate happiness. That must be the answer—it wasn't just money or power or sex or seeing beautiful things. The real satisfaction lay in friendship.

So on the boat trip home, Martin tried to strike up a few acquaintances at the ship's bar. But all these people were much younger, and Martin had nothing in common with them. Also, they wanted to dance and drink, and Martin wasn't in condition to appreciate such pastimes. Nevertheless, he tried.

Perhaps that's why he had the little accident the day before they docked in San Francisco. "Little accident" was the ship's doctor's way of describing it, but Martin noticed he looked very grave when he told him to stay in bed, and he'd called an ambulance to meet the liner at the dock and take the patient right to the hospital.

At the hospital, all the expensive treatment and the expensive smiles and the expensive words didn't fool Martin any. He was an old man with a bad heart, and they thought he was going to die.

But he could fool them. He still had the watch. He found it in his coat when he put on his clothes and sneaked out of the hospital.

He didn't have to die. He could cheat death with a single gesture—and he intended to do it as a free man, out there under a free sky.

That was the real secret of happiness. He understood it now. Not even friendship meant as much as freedom. This was the best thing of all—to be free of friends or family or the furies of the flesh.

Martin walked slowly beside the embankment under the night sky. Come to think of it, he was just about back where he'd started, so many years ago. But the moment was good, good enough to prolong forever. Once a bum, always a bum.

He smiled as he thought about it, and then the smile twisted sharply and suddenly, like the pain twisting sharply and suddenly in his chest. The world began to spin and he fell down on the side of the embankment.

He couldn't see very well, but he was still conscious, and he knew what had happened. Another stroke, and a bad one. Maybe this was it. Except that he wouldn't be a fool any longer. He wouldn't wait to see what was still around the corner.

Right now was his chance to use his power and save his life. And he was going to do it. He could still move, nothing could stop him.

He groped in his pocket and pulled out the old silver watch, fumbling with the stem. A few twists and he'd cheat death, he'd never have to ride that Hell-Bound Train. He could go on forever.

Forever.

Martin had never really considered the word before. To go on forever—but *how?* Did he want to go on forever, like this; a sick old man, lying helplessly here in the grass?

No. He couldn't do it. He wouldn't do it. And suddenly he wanted very much to cry, because he knew that somewhere along the line he'd outsmarted himself. And now it was too late. His eye dimmed, there was a roaring in his ears . . .

He recognized the roaring, of course, and he wasn't at all surprised to see the train come rushing out of the fog up there on the embankment. He wasn't surprised when it stopped, either, or when the Conductor climbed off and walked slowly towards him.

The Conductor hadn't changed a bit. Even his grin was still the same.

"Hello, Martin," he said. "All aboard."

"I know," Martin whispered. "But you'll have to carry me. I can't walk. I'm not even really talking any more, am I?"

"Yes you are," the Conductor said. "I can hear you fine. And you can walk, too." He leaned down and placed his hand on Martin's chest. There was a moment of icy numbness, and then, sure enough, Martin could walk after all.

He got up and followed the Conductor along the slope, moving to the side of the train.

"In here?" he asked.

"No, the next car," the Conductor murmured. "I guess you're entitled to ride Pullman. After all, you're quite a successful man. You've tasted the joys of wealth and position and prestige. You've known the pleasures of marriage and fatherhood. You've sampled the delights of dining and drinking and debauchery, too, and you traveled high, wide and handsome. So let's not have any last-minute recriminations."

"All right," Martin sighed. "I can't blame you for my mistakes. On the other hand, you can't take credit for what happened, either. I worked for everything I got. I did it all on my own. I didn't even need your watch."

"So you didn't," the Conductor said, smiling. "But would you mind giving it back to me now?"

"Need it for the next sucker, eh?" Martin muttered.

"Perhaps."

Something about the way he said it made Martin look up. He tried to see the Conductor's eyes, but the brim of his cap cast a shadow. So Martin looked down at the watch instead.

"Tell me something," he said, softly. "If I give you the watch, what will you do with it?"

"Why, throw it into the ditch," the Conductor told him. "That's what I'll do with it." And he held out his hand.

"What if somebody comes along and finds it? And twists the stem backwards, and stops Time?"

"Nobody would do that," the Conductor murmured. "Even if they knew."

"You mean, it was all a trick? This is only an ordinary, cheap watch?"

"I didn't say that," whispered the Conductor. "I only said that no one has ever twisted the stem backwards. They've all been like you, Martin—looking ahead to find that perfect happiness. Waiting for the moment that never comes."

The Conductor held out his hand again.

Martin sighed and shook his head. "You cheated me after all."

"You cheated yourself, Martin. And now you're going to ride that Hell-Bound Train."

He pushed Martin up the steps and into the car ahead. As he entered, the train began to move and the whistle screamed. And Martin stood there in the swaying Pullmann, gazing down the aisle at the other passengers. He could see them sitting there, and somehow it didn't seem strange at all.

Here they were; the drunks and the sinners, the gambling men and the grifters, the big-time spenders, the skirt-chasers, and all the jolly crew. They knew where they were going, of course, but they didn't seem to give a damn. The blinds where drawn on the windows, yet it was light inside, and they were all living it up—singing and passing the bottle and roaring with laughter, throwing the dice and telling their jokes and bragging their big brags, just the way Daddy used to sing about them in the old song.

"Mighty nice traveling companions," Martin said. "Why, I've never seen such a pleasant bunch of people. I mean, they seem to be really enjoying themselves!"

The Conductor shrugged. "I'm afraid things won't be quite so jazzy when we pull into that Depot Way Down Yonder."

For the third time, he held out his hand. "Now, before you sit down, if you'll just give me that watch. A bargain's a bargain—"

Martin smiled. "A bargain's a bargain," he echoed. "I agreed to ride your train if I could stop Time when I found the right moment of happiness. And I think I'm about as happy right here as I've ever been."

Very slowly, Martin took hold of the silver watch-stem.

"No!" gasped the Conductor. "No!"

But the watch-stem turned.

"Do you realize what you've done?" the Conductor yelled. "Now we'll never reach the Depot! We'll just go on riding, all of us—forever!"

Martin grinned. "I know," he said. "But the fun is in the trip, not the destination. You taught me that. And I'm looking forward to a wonderful trip. Look, maybe I can even help. If you were to find me another one of those caps, now, and let me keep this watch—"

And that's the way it finally worked out. Wearing his cap and carrying his battered old silver watch, there's no happier person in or out of this world—now and forever—than Martin. Martin the new Brakeman on That Hell-Bound Train.

Survival Kit

Frederik Pohl

Life throws us curves, and how we deal with those unexpected turns of fate sometimes makes the difference between comedy and tragedy. Science fiction is full of first-contact stories—humans coming face to face with aliens for the first time; usually it's an encounter with great consequences, either good or bad.

But occasionally, it's just plain sleazy. Frederik Pohl, who has done just about everything a writer and editor can do in science fiction, spins an offbeat first-contact story in "Survival Kit." Writing in 1957, Pohl offers as protagonist one Mr. Mooney, who isn't exactly a hero. He's a petty criminal, trying to get ahead with a minimum of effort and maximum of other people's money.

When Mooney meets the silver-clad, tall figure known only as Harse, he's sure his fortune is made. If he knew what awaited him at the end of his little adventure, he probably would have run, fast. . . . Then again, maybe he wouldn't have run. Mooney, unlike his creator, isn't very bright.

Mooney looked out of his window, and the sky was white. It was a sudden, bright, cold flare and it was gone again. It had no more features than a fog, at least not through the window that was showered with snow and patterned with spray from the windy sea.

Mooney blew on his hands and frowned at the window.

"Son of a gun," he said, and thought for a moment about phoning the Coast Guard station. Of course, that meant going a quarter of a mile in the storm to reach the only other house nearby that was occupied; the Hansons had a phone that worked, but a quarter of a mile was a long way in the face of December gale. And it was all dark out there now. Less than twenty miles across the bay was New York, but this Jersey shore coast was harsh as the face of the Moon.

Mooney decided it was none of his business.

He shook the kettle, holding it with an old dish towel because it was sizzling hot. It was nearly empty, so he filled it again and put it back on the stove. He had all four top burners and the oven going , which made the kitchen tolerably warm—as long as he wore the scarf and the heavy quilted jacket and kept his hand in his pockets. And there was plenty of tea.

Uncle Lester had left that much behind him—plenty of tea, nearly a dozen boxes of assorted cookies and a few odds and ends of canned goods. And God's own quantity of sugar.

It wasn't exactly a balanced diet, but Mooney had lived on it for three weeks now—smoked turkey sausages for breakfast, and oatmeal cookies for lunch, and canned black olives for dinner. And always plenty of tea.

▼

The wind screamed at him as he poured the dregs of his last cup of tea into the sink and spooned sugar into the cup for the next one. It was, he calculated, close to midnight. If the damn wind hadn't blown down the TV antenna, he could be watching the late movies now. It helped to pass the time; the last movie was off the air at two or three o'clock, and then he could go to bed and, with any luck, sleep till past noon.

And uncle Lester had left a couple of decks of sticky child-handled cards behind him, too, when the family went back to the city at the end of the summer. So what with four kinds of solitaire, and solo bridge, and television, and a few more naps, Mooney could get through to the next two or three A.M. again. If only the wind hadn't blown down the antenna!

But as it was, all he could get on the cheap little set his uncle had left behind was a faint gray herringbone pattern—

He straightened up with the kettle in his hand, listening.

It was almost as though somebody was knocking at the door.

"That's crazy," Mooney said out loud after a moment. He poured the water over the tea bag, tearing a little corner off the paper tag on the end of the string to mark the fact that this was the second cup he had made with the bag. He had found he could get three cups out of a single bag, but even loaded with sugar, the fourth cup was no longer very good. Still, he had carefully saved all the used, dried-out bags against the difficult future day when even the tea would be gone.

That was going to be one bad day for Howard Mooney.

Rap, tap. It really was someone at the door! Not knocking, exactly, but either kicking at it or striking it with a stick.

Mooney pulled his jacket tight around him and walked out into the frigid living room, not quite so frigid as his heart.

"Damn!" he said. "Damn, damn!"

What Mooney knew for sure was that nothing good could be coming in that door for him. It might be a policeman from Sea Bright, wondering about the light in the house; it might be a member of his uncle's family. It was even possible that one of the stockholders who had put up the money for that unfortunate venture into frozen-food club management had tracked him down as far as the Jersey shore. It could be almost anything or anybody, but it couldn't be good.

All the same, Mooney hadn't expected it to turn out to be a tall, lean man with angry pale eyes, wearing a silvery sort of leotard.

"I come in," said the angry man, and did.

Mooney slammed the door behind him. Too bad, but he couldn't keep it open, even if it was conceding a sort of moral right to enter to the stranger; he couldn't have all that cold air coming in to dilute his little bubble of warmth.

"What the devil do you want?" Mooney demanded.

The angry man looked about him with an expression of revulsion. He pointed to the kitchen. "It is warmer. In there?"

"I suppose so. What do—" But the stranger was already walking into the kitchen. Mooney scowled and started to follow, and stopped, and scowled even more. The stranger was leaving footprints behind him, or anyway some kind of marks that showed black on the faded summer rug. True, he was speckled with snow, but that much snow? The man was drenched. It looked as though he had just come out of the ocean.

The stranger stood by the stove and glanced at Mooney warily. Mooney stood six feet, but this man was bigger. The silvery sort of thing he had on covered his legs as far as the feet, and he wore no shoes. It covered his body and his arms, and he had silvery gloves on his hands. It stopped at the neck, in a collar of what looked like pure silver, but could not have been because it gave with every breath the man took and every tensed muscle or tendon in his neck. His head was bare and his hair was black, cut very short.

He was carrying something flat and shiny by a molded handle. If it had been made of pigskin, it would have resembled a junior executive's briefcase.

The man said explosively: "You will help me"

Mooney cleared his throat. "Listen, I don't know what you want, but this is my house and—"

"You will help me," the man said positively. "I will pay you. Very well?"

He had a peculiar way of parting his sentences in the middle, but Mooney didn't care about that. He suddenly cared about one thing and that was the word "pay."

"What do you want me to do?"

The angry-eyed man ran his gloved hands across his head and sluiced drops of water onto the scuffed linoleum and the bedding of the cot Mooney had dragged into the kitchen. He said irritably: "I am a wayfarer who needs a. Guide? I will pay you for your assistance."

The question that rose to Mooney's lips was "How much?" but he fought it back. Instead, he asked, "Where do you want to go?"

"One moment." The stranger sat damply on the edge of Mooney's cot and, click-snap, the shiny sort of briefcase opened itself in his hands. He took out a flat round thing like a mirror and looked into it, squeezing it by the edges, and holding it this way and that.

Finally he said: "I must go to Wednesday, the twenty-sixth of December, at—" He tilted the little round thing again. "Brooklyn?" he finished triumphantly.

Mooney said, after a second: "That's a funny way to put it."

"Question?"

"I mean," said Mooney, "I know where Brooklyn is and I know *when* the twenty-sixth of December is—it's next week—but you have to admit that that's an odd way of putting it. I mean you don't go anywhere in time."

The wet man turned his pale eyes on Mooney. "Perhaps you are. Wrong?"

▼

Mooney stared at his napping guest in a mood of wonder and fear and delight.

Time traveler! But it was hard to doubt the pale-eyed man. He had said he was from the future and he mentioned a date that made Mooney gasp. He had said: "When you speak to me, you must know that my. Name? Is Harse." And then he had curled up on the floor, surrounding his shiny briefcase like a mother cat around a kitten, and begun dozing alertly.

But not before he showed Mooney just what it was he proposed to pay him with.

Mooney sipped his cooling tea and forgot to shiver, though the drafts were fiercer and more biting than ever, now just before dawn. He was playing with what had looked at first like a string of steel ball-bearings, a child's necklace, half-inch spheres linked together in a strand a yard long.

Wampum! That was what Harse had called the spheres when he picked the string out of his little kit, and that was what they were.

Each ball-bearing was hollow. Open them up an out come the treasures of the crown. Pop, and one of the spheres splits neatly in half, and out spills a star sapphire, as big as the ball of your finger, glittering like the muted lights of hell. Pop, and another sphere drops a ball of yellow gold into your palm. Pop for a narwhal's tooth, pop for a cube of sugar; pop, pop, and there on the table before Harse sparkled diamonds and lumps of coal, a packet of heroin, a sphere of silver, pearls, beads of glass, machined pellets of tungsten, lumps of saffron and lumps of salt.

"It is," said Harse, "for your. Pay? No, *no!*" And he headed off Mooney's greedy fingers.

Click, click, click, and the little pellets of treasure and trash were back in the steel balls.

"No, *no!*" said Harse again, grinning, snapping the balls together like poppets in a string. "After you have guided me to Brooklyn and the December twenty-sixth. But I must say to you. This? That some of the balls contain plutonium and some radium. And I do not think that you can get them. Open? But if you did, you perhaps would die. Oh, Ho?" And, laughing, he began his taut nap.

Mooney swallowed the last of his icy tea. It was full daylight outside.

Very well, castaway, he said silently to the dozing pale-eyed man, I will guide you. Oh, there never was a guide like Mooney—not when a guide's fee can run so high. But when you are where you want to go, then we'll discuss the price . . .

A hacksaw, he schemed, and a Geiger counter. He had worn his fingers raw trying to find the little button or knob that Harse had used to open them. All right, he was licked there. But there were more ways than one to open a cat's eye.

A hacksaw. A Geiger counter. And, Mooney speculated drowsily, maybe a gun, if the pale-eyed man got tough.

Mooney fell asleep in joy and anticipation for the first time in more than a dozen years.

It was bright the next morning. Bright and very cold.

"Look alive!" Mooney said to the pale-eyed man, shivering. It had been a long walk from Uncle Lester's house to the bridge, in that ripping, shuddering wind that came in off the Atlantic.

Harse got up off his knees, from where he had been examining the asphalt pavement under the snow. He stood erect beside Mooney, while Mooney put on an egg-sucking smile and aimed his thumb down the road.

The station wagon he had spotted seemed to snarl and pick up speed as it whirled past them onto the bridge.

"I hope you skid into a ditch!" Mooney bawled into the icy air. He was in a fury. There was a bus line that went where they wanted to go. A warm, comfortable bus that would stop for them if they signaled, that would drop them just where they wanted to be, to convert one of Harse's ball-bearings into money. The gold one, Mooney planned. Not the diamond, not the pearl. Just a few dollars was all they wanted, in this Jersey shore area where the towns were small and the gossip big. Just the price of fare into New York where they could make their way to Tiffany's.

But the bus cost thirty-five cents apiece. Total, seventy cents. Which they didn't have.

"Here comes another. Car?"

Mooney dragged back the corners of his lips into another smile and held out his thumb.

It was a panel truck, light blue, with the sides lettered: *Chris's Delicatessen. Free Deliveries*. The driver slowed up, looked them over and stopped. He leaned toward the right-hand window.

He called: "I can take you far's Red Ba—"

He got a good look at Mooney's companion then and swallowed. Harse had put on an overcoat because Mooney insisted on it and he wore a hat because Mooney had told him flatly there would be trouble and questions if he didn't. But he hadn't taken off his own silvery leotard, which peeped through between neck and hat where the coat flapped open.

"—ank," finished the driver thoughtfully.

Mooney didn't give him a chance to change his mind. "Red Bank is just where we want to go. Come on!" Already he had his hand on the door. He jumped in, made room for Harse, reached over him and slammed the door.

"Thank you very much," he said chattily to the driver. "Cold morning, isn't it? And that was some storm last night. Say, we really do appreciate this. Anywhere in Red Bank will be all right to drop us, anywhere at all."

He leaned forward slightly, just enough to keep the driver from being able to get a really good look at his other passenger.

It would have gone all right, it really would, except that just past Fair Haven, Harse suddenly announced: "It is the time for me to. Eat?"

▼

He snip-snapped something around the edges of the gleaming sort of dispatch case, which opened. Mooney, peering over his shoulder, caught glimpses of shiny things and spinning things and things that seemed to glow. So did the driver.

"Hey," he said, interested, "what've you got there?"

"My business," said Harse, calmly and crushingly.

The driver blinked. He opened his mouth, and then he shut it again, and his neck became rather red.

Mooney said rapidly: "Say, isn't there—uh—isn't there a lot of snow?" He feigned fascination with the snow on the road, leaning forward until his face was nearly at the frosty windshield. "My gosh, I've never seen the road so snowy!"

Beside him, Harse was methodically taking things out of other things. A little cylinder popped open and began to steam; he put it to his lips and drank. A cube the size of a fist opened up at one end and little pellets dropped out into a cup. Harse picked a couple up and began to chew them. A flat, round object the shape of a cafeteria pie flipped open and something gray and doughy appeared—

"Holy heaven!"

Mooney's face slammed into the windshield as the driver tramped on his brakes. Not that Mooney could really blame him. The smell from that doughy mass could hardly be believed; and what made it retchingly worse was that Harse was eating it with a pearly small spoon.

The driver said complainingly: "Out! Out, you guys! I don't mind giving you a lift, but I've got hard rolls in the back of the truck and that smell's going to— Out! You heard me!"

"Oh," said Harse, tasting happily. "No."

"No?" roared the driver. "Now listen! I don't have to take any lip from hitchhikers! I don't have to—"

"One moment," said Harse. "Please." Without hurry and without delay, beaming absently at the driver, he reached into the silvery case again. Snip, snippety-snap; a jointed metal thing wriggled and snicked into place. And Harse, still beaming, pointed it at the driver.

Pale blue light and a faint whine.

It was a good thing the truck was halted, because the whining blue light reached diffidently out and embraced the driver; and then there was no driver. There was nothing. He was gone, beyond the reach of any further lip from hitchhikers.

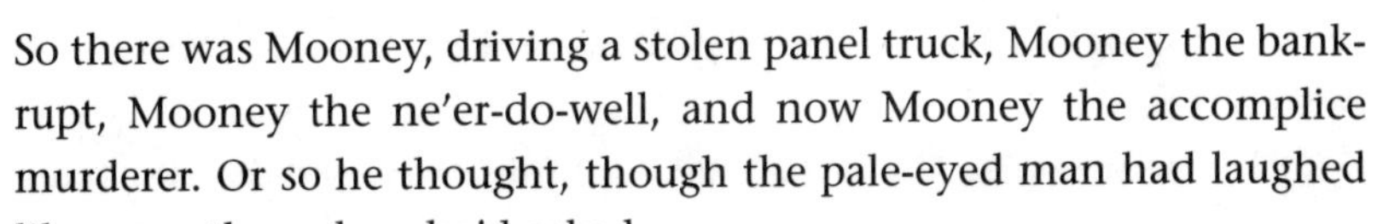

So there was Mooney, driving a stolen panel truck, Mooney the bankrupt, Mooney the ne'er-do-well, and now Mooney the accomplice murderer. Or so he thought, though the pale-eyed man had laughed like a panther when he'd asked.

He rehearsed little speeches all the day down U.S. One, Mooney did, and they all began: "Your Honor, I didn't know—"

Well, he hadn't. How could a man like Mooney know that Harse was so bereft of human compassion as to snuff out a life for the sake of finishing his lunch in peace? And what could Mooney have done about it, without drawing the diffident blue glow to himself? No, Your Honor, really, Your Honor, he took me by surprise . . .

But by the time they ditched the stolen car, nearly dry of gas, at the Hoboken ferry, Mooney had begun to get his nerve back. In fact, he was beginning to perceive that in that glittering silvery dispatch case that Harse hugged to him were treasures that might do wonders for a smart man unjustly dogged by hard times. The wampum alone! But beyond the wampum, the other good things that might in time be worth more than any amount of mere money.

There was that weapon. Mooney cast a glance at Harse, blank-eyed and relaxed, very much disinterested in the crowds of commuters on the ferry.

Nobody in all that crowd would believe that Harse could pull out a little jointed metal thing and push a button and make any one of them cease to exist. Nobody would believe it—not even a jury. Corpus delicti, body of evidence—why, there would *be* no evidence! It was a simple, workable, foolproof way of getting any desired number of people out of the way without fuss, muss or bother—and couldn't a smart but misfortunate man like Mooney do wonders by selectively removing those persons who stood as obstacles in his path?

And there would be more, much, much more. The thing to do, Mooney schemed, was to find out just what Harse had in that kit and how to work it; and then—who could know, perhaps Harse would himself find the diffident blue light reaching out for him before the intersection of Brooklyn and December twenty-sixth?

Mooney probed.

"Ah," laughed Harse. "Ho! I perceive what you want. You think perhaps there is something you can use in my survival kit."

"All right, Harse," Mooney said submissively, but he did have reservations.

First, it was important to find out just what was in the kit. After that—

Well, even a man from the future had to sleep.

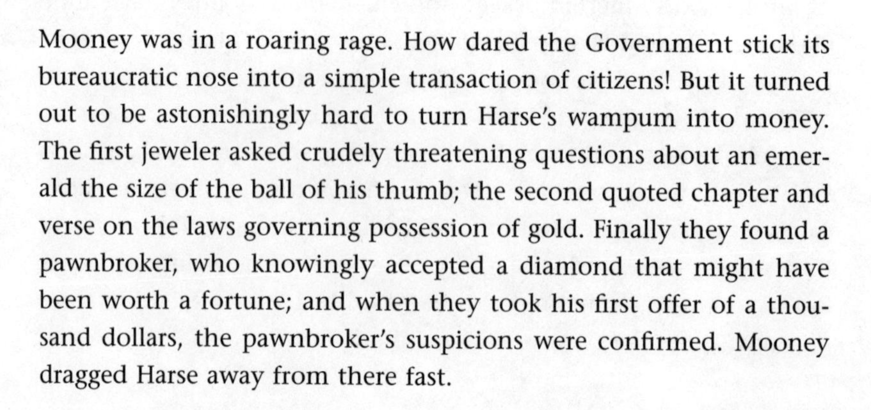

Mooney was in a roaring rage. How dared the Government stick its bureaucratic nose into a simple transaction of citizens! But it turned out to be astonishingly hard to turn Harse's wampum into money. The first jeweler asked crudely threatening questions about an emerald the size of the ball of his thumb; the second quoted chapter and verse on the laws governing possession of gold. Finally they found a pawnbroker, who knowingly accepted a diamond that might have been worth a fortune; and when they took his first offer of a thousand dollars, the pawnbroker's suspicions were confirmed. Mooney dragged Harse away from there fast.

But they did have a thousand dollars.

As the cab took them across town, Mooney simmered down; and by the time they reached the other side, he was entirely content. What was a fortune more or less to a man who very nearly owned some of the secrets of the future?

He sat up, lit a cigarette, waved an arm and said expansively to Harse: "Our new home."

The pale-eyed man took a glowing little affair with eye-pieces away from in front of his eyes.

"Ah," he said. "So."

It was quite an attractive hotel, Mooney thought judiciously. It did a lot to take away the sting of those sordidly avaricious jewelers. The lobby was an impressively close approximation of a cathedral and the bellboys looked smart and able.

Harse made an asthmatic sound. "What is. That?" He was pointing at a group of men standing in jovial amusement around the entrance to the hotel's grand ballroom, just off the lobby. They wore purple harem pants and floppy green hats, and every one of them carried a silver-paper imitation of a scimitar.

Mooney chuckled in a superior way. "You aren't up on our local customs, are you? That's a convention, Harse. They dress up that way because they belong to a lodge. A lodge is a kind of fraternal organization. A fraternal organization is—"

Harse said abruptly: "I want."

Mooney began to feel alarm. "What?"

"I want one for a. Specimen? Wait, I think I take the big one there."

"Harse! Wait a minute!" Mooney clutched at him. "Hold everything, man! You can't do that."

Harse stared at him. "Why?"

"Because it would upset everything, that's why! You want to get to your rendezvous, don't you? Well, if you do anything like that, we'll *never* get there!"

"Why not?"

"Please," Mooney said, "please take my word for it. You hear me? I'll explain later!"

Harse looked by no means convinced, but he stopped opening the silvery metal case. Mooney kept an eye on him while registering. Harse continued to watch the conventioneers, but he went no further. Mooney began to breathe again.

"Thank *you* sir," said the desk clerk—not every guest, even in this hotel, went for a corner suite with two baths. "Front!"

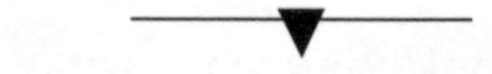

A smart-looking bellboy stepped forward, briskly took the key from the clerk, briskly nodded at Mooney and Harse. With the automatic reflex of any hotel bellhop, he reached for Harse's silvery case. Baggage was baggage, however funny it looked.

But Harse was not just any old guest. The bellboy got the bag away from him, all right, but his victory was purely transitory. He yelled, dropped the bag, grabbed his fist with the other hand.

"Hey! It shocked me! What kind of tricks are you trying to do with electric suitcases?"

Mooney moaned softly. The whole lobby was looking at them—even the conventioneers at the entrance to the ballroom; even the men in mufti mingling with the conventioneers, carrying cameras and flash guns; even the very doorman, the whole lobby away. That was bad. What was worse was that Harse was obviously getting angry.

"Wait, wait!" Mooney stepped between them in a hurry. "I can explain everything. My friend is, uh, an inventor. There's some very important material in that briefcase, believe me!"

He winked, patted the bellhop on the shoulder, took his hand with friendly concern and left in it a folded bill.

"Now," he said confidentially, "we don't want any disturbance. I'm sure you understand how it is, son. Don't you? My friend can't take any chances with his, uh, confidential material, you see? Right. Well, let's say no more about it. Now if you'll show us to our room—"

The bellhop, still stiff-backed, glanced down at the bill and the stiffness disappeared as fast as any truckdriver bathed in Harse's pale blue haze. He looked up again and grinned.

"Sorry, sir—" he began.

But he didn't finish. Mooney had let Harse get out of his sight a moment too long.

The first warning he had was when there was a sudden commotion among the lodge brothers. Mooney turned, much too late. There was Harse; he had wandered over there, curious and interested—and Harse. He had stared them up and down, but he hadn't been content to stare. He had opened the little silvery dispatch-case and taken out of it the thing that looked like a film viewer; and maybe it was a camera, too, because he was looking through it at the conventioneers. He was covering them as Dixie is covered by the dew, up and down, back and forth, heels to head.

And it was causing a certain amount of attention. Even one of the photographers thought maybe this funny-looking guy with the funny-looking opera glasses was curious enough to be worth a shot. After all, that was what the photographer was there for. He aimed and popped a flash gun.

There was an abrupt thin squeal from the box. Black fog sprayed out of it in a greasy jet. It billowed toward Harse. It collected around him, swirled high. Now all the flashguns were popping . . .

It was a clear waste of a twenty-dollar bill, Mooney told himself aggrievedly out on the sidewalk. There had been no point in buttering up the bellhop as long as Harse was going to get them thrown out anyway.

▼

On the other side of the East River, in a hotel that fell considerably below Mooney's recent, brief standards of excellence, Mooney cautiously tipped a bellboy, ushered him out, locked the door behind him and, utterly exhausted, flopped on one of the twin beds.

Harse glanced at him briefly, then wandered over to the window and stared incuriously at the soiled snow outside.

"You were fine, Harse," said Mooney without spirit. "You didn't do anything wrong at all."

"Ah," said Harse without turning. "So?"

Mooney sat up, reached for the phone, demanded setups and a bottle from room service and hung up.

"Oh, well," he said, beginning to revive, "at least we're in Brooklyn now. Maybe it's just as well."

"As well. What?"

"I mean this is where you wanted to be. Now we just have to wait four days, until the twenty-sixth. We'll have to raise some more money, of course," he added experimentally.

Harse turned and looked at him with the pale eyes. "One thousand dollars you have. Is not enough?"

"Oh, no, Harse," Mooney assured him. "Why, that won't be nearly enough. The room rent in this hotel alone is likely to use that up. Besides all the extras, of course."

"Ah." Harse, looking bored, sat down in the chair near Mooney, opened his kit, took out the thing that looked like a film viewer and put it to his eyes.

"We'll have to sell some more of those things. After all—" Mooney winked and dug at the pale-eyed man's ribs with his elbow— "we'll be needing some, well, entertainment."

Harse took the viewer away from his eyes. He glanced thoughtfully at the elbow and then at Mooney. "So," he said.

Mooney coughed and changed the subject. "One thing, though," he begged. "Don't get me in any more trouble like you did in that hotel lobby—or with that guy in the truck. Please? I mean, after all, you're making it hard for me to carry out my job."

Harse was thoughtfully silent.

"Promise?" Mooney urged.

Harse said, after some more consideration: "It is not altogether me. That is to say, it is a matter of defense. My picture should not be. Photographed? So the survival kit insures that it is not. You understand?"

Mooney leaned back. "You mean—" The bellboy with the drinks interrupted him; he took the bottle, signed the chit, tipped the boy and mixed himself a reasonably stiff but not quite stupefying highball, thinking hard.

"Did you say 'survival kit'?" he asked at last.

Harse was deep in the viewer again, but he looked away from it irritably. "Naturally, survival kit. So that I can. Survive?" He went back to the viewer.

Mooney took a long, thoughtful slug of the drink.

Survival kit. Why, that made sense. When the Air Force boys went out and raided the islands in the Pacific during the war, sometimes they got shot down—and it was enemy territory, or what passed for it. Those islands were mostly held by Japanese, though their populations hardly knew it. All the aboriginals knew was that strange birds crossed the sky and sometimes men came from them. The politics of the situation didn't interest the headhunters. What really interested them was heads.

But for a palatable second choice, they would settle for trade goods—cloth, mirrors, beads. And so the bomber pilots were equipped with survival kits—maps, trade goods, rations, weapons, instructions for proceeding to a point where, God willing, a friendly submarine might put ashore a rubber dingy to take them off.

Mooney said persuasively: "Harse. I'm sorry to bother you, but we have to talk." The man with the pale eyes took them away from the viewer again and stared at Mooney. "Harse, were you shot down like an airplane pilot?"

Harse frowned—not in anger, or at least not at Mooney. It was the effort to make himself understood. He said at last: "Yes. Call it that."

"And—and this place you want to go—is that where you will be rescued?"

"Yes."

Aha, thought Mooney, and the glimmerings of a new idea began to kick and stretch its fetal limbs inside him. He put it aside, to bear and coddle in private. He said: "Tell me more. Is there any particular part of Brooklyn you have to go to?"

"Ah. The Nexus Point?" Harse put down the viewer and, snap-snap, opened the gleaming kit. He took out the little round thing he had consulted in the house by the cold Jersey sea. He tilted it this way and that, frowned, consulted a small square sparkly thing that came from another part of the case, tilted the round gadget again.

"Correcting for local time," he said, "the Nexus Point is one hour and one minute after midnight at what is called. The Vale of Cashmere?"

Mooney scratched his ear. "The Vale of Cashmere? Where the devil is that—somewhere in Pakistan?"

"Brooklyn," said Harse with an imp's grimace. "You are the guide and you do not know where you are guiding me to?"

Mooney said hastily: "All right, Harse, all right. I'll find it. But tell me one thing, will you? Just suppose—suppose, I said—that for some reason or other, we don't make it to the what-you-call, Nexus Point. Then what happens?"

Harse for once neither laughed nor scowled. The pale eyes opened wide and glanced around the room, at the machine-made candlewick spreads on the beds, at the dusty red curtains that made a "suite" out of a long room, at the dog-eared Bible that lay on the night table.

"Suh," he stammered, "suh—suh—seventeen years until there is another Nexus Point!"

▼

Mooney dreamed miraculous dreams and not entirely because of the empty bottle that had been full that afternoon. There never was a time, never will be a time, like the future Mooney dreamed of—Mooney owned, houri-inhabited, a fair domain for a live-wire Emperor of the Eons . . .

He woke up with a splitting head.

Even a man from the future had to sleep, so Mooney had thought, and it had been in his mind that, even this first night, it might pay to stay awake a little longer than Harse, just in case it might then seem like a good idea to—well, to bash him over the head and grab the bag. But the whiskey had played him dirty and he had passed out—drunk, blind drunk, or at least he hoped so. He hoped that he hadn't seen what he thought he had seen *sober*.

He woke up and wondered what was wrong. Little tinkling ice spiders were moving around him. He could hear their tiny crystal sounds and feel their chill legs, so lightly, on him. It was still a dream—wasn't it?

Or was he awake? The thing was, he couldn't tell. If he was awake, it was the middle of the night, because there was no light whatever; and besides, he didn't seem to be able to move.

Thought Mooney with anger and desperation: I'm dead. And: What a time to die!

But second thoughts changed his mind: there was no heaven and no hell, in all the theologies he had investigated, that included being walked over by tiny spiders of ice. He *felt* them. There was no doubt about it.

It was Harse, of course—had to be. Whatever he was up to, Mooney couldn't say, but as he lay there sweating cold sweat and feeling the crawling little feet, he knew that it was something Harse had made happen.

Little by little, he began to be able to see—not much, but enough to see that there really was something crawling. Whatever the things were, they had a faint tenuous glow, like the face of a watch just before dawn. He couldn't make out shapes, but he could tell the size—not much bigger than a man's hand—and he could tell the number, and there were dozens of them.

He couldn't turn his head, but on the walls, on his chest, on his face, even on the ceiling, he could see faint moving patches of foxfire light.

He took a deep breath. "Harse!" he started to call; wake him up, make him stop this! But he couldn't. He got no further than the first huff of the aspirate when the scurrying cold feet were on his lips. Something cold and damp lay across them and it stuck. Like spider silk, but stronger—he couldn't speak, couldn't move his lips, though he almost tore the flesh.

Oh, he could make a noise, all right. He started to do so, to snort and hum through his nose. But Mooney was not slow of thought and he had a sudden clear picture of that same cold ribbon crossing his nostrils, and what would be the use of all of time's treasures then, when it was no longer possible to breathe at all?

It was quite apparent that he was not to make a noise.

He had patience—the kind of patience that grows with a diet of thrice-used tea bags and soggy crackers. He waited.

It wasn't the middle of the night after all, he perceived, though it was still utterly dark except for the moving blobs. He could hear sounds in the hotel corridor outside—faintly, though: the sound of a vacuum cleaner, and it might have been a city block away; the tiniest whisper of someone laughing.

He remembered one of his drunken fantasies of the night before—little robot mice, or so they seemed, spinning a curtain across the window; and he shuddered, because that had been no fantasy. The window was curtained. And it was mid-morning, at the earliest, because the chambermaids were cleaning the halls.

Why couldn't he move? He flexed the muscles of his arms and legs, but nothing happened. He could feel the muscles straining, he could feel his toes and fingers twitch, but he was restrained by what seemed a web of Gulliver's cords . . .

There was a tap at the door. A pause, the scratching of a key, and the room was flooded with light from the hall.

Out of the straining corner of his eye, Mooney saw a woman in a gray cotton uniform, carrying fresh sheets, standing in the doorway, and her mouth was hanging slack. No wonder, for in the light from the hall Mooney could see the room festooned with silver, with darting silvery shapes moving about. Mooney himself wore a cocoon of silver, and on the bed next to him, where Harse slept, there was a fantastic silver hood, like the basketwork of a baby's bassinet, surrounding his head.

It was a fairyland scene and it lasted only a second. For Harse cried out and leaped to his feet. Quick as an adder, he scooped up something from the table beside his bed and gestured with it at the door. It was, Mooney half perceived, the silvery, jointed thing he had used in the truck; and he used it again.

Pale blue light streamed out.

It faded and the chambermaid, popping eyes and all, was gone.

It didn't hurt as much the second time.

Mooney finally attracted Harse's attention, and Harse, with a Masonic pass over one of the little silvery things, set it to loosening and removing the silver bonds. The things were like little toy tanks with jointed legs; as they spun the silver webs, they could also suck them in. In moments, the webs that held Mooney down were gone.

He got up, aching in his tired muscles and his head, but this time the panic that had filled him in the truck was gone. Well, one victim more or less—what did it matter? And besides, he clung to the fact that Harse had not exactly said the victims were dead.

So it didn't hurt as much the second time.

Mooney planned. He shut the door and sat on the edge of the bed. "Shut up—you put us in a lousy fix and I have to think a way out of it," he rasped at Harse when Harse started to speak; and the man from the future looked at him with opaque pale eyes, and silently opened one of the flat canisters and began to eat.

"All right," said Mooney at last. "Harse, get rid of all this stuff."

"This. Stuff?"

"The stuff on the walls. What your little spiders have been spinning, understand? Can't you get it off the walls?"

Harse leaned forward and touched the kit. The little spider-things that had been aimlessly roving now began to digest what they had created, as the ones that had held Mooney had already done. It was quick—Mooney hoped it would be quick enough. There were over a dozen of the things, more than Mooney would have believed the little kit could hold; and he had seen no sign of them before.

The silvery silk on the walls, in aimless tracing, disappeared. The thick silvery coat over the window disappeared. Harse's bassinet-hood disappeared. A construction that haloed the door disappeared—and as it dwindled, the noises from the corridor grew louder; some sort of sound-absorbing contrivance, Mooney thought, wondering.

There was an elaborate silvery erector-set affair on the floor between the beds; it whirled and spun silently and the little machines took it apart again and swallowed it. Mooney had no notion of its purpose. When it was gone, he could see no change, but Harse shuddered and shifted his position uncomfortably.

"All right," said Mooney when everything was back in the kit. "Now you just keep your mouth shut. I won't ask you to lie—they'll have enough trouble understanding you if you tell the truth. Hear me?"

Harse merely stared, but that was good enough. Mooney put his hand on the phone. He took a deep breath and held it until his head began to tingle and his face turned red. Then the picked up the phone and, when he spoke, there was authentic rage and distress in his voice.

"Operator," he snarled, "give me the manager. And hurry up—I want to report a thief!"

▼

When the manager had gone—along with the assistant manager, the house detective and the ancient shrew-faced head housekeeper—Mooney extracted a promise from Harse and left him. He carefully hung a "Do Not Disturb" card from the doorknob, crossed his fingers and took the elevator downstairs.

The fact seemed to be that Harse didn't care about aboriginals. Mooney had arranged a system of taps on the door which, he thought, Harse would abide by, so that Mooney could get back in. Just the same, Mooney vowed to be extremely careful about how he opened that door. Whatever the pale blue light was, Mooney wanted no part of it directed at him.

The elevator operator greeted him respectfully—a part of the management's policy of making amends, no doubt. Mooney returned the greeting with a barely civil nod. Sure, it had worked; he'd told the manager that he'd caught the chambermaid trying to steal something valuable that belonged to that celebrated proprietor of valuable secrets, Mr. Harse; the chambermaid had fled; how dared they employ a person like that?

And he had made very sure that the manager and the house dick and all the rest had plenty of opportunity to snoops apologetically in every closet and under the beds, just so there would be no suspicion in their minds that a dismembered chambermaid-torso was littering some dark corner of the room. What could they do but accept the story? The chambermaid wasn't there to defend herself, and though they might wonder how she had got out of the hotel without being noticed, it was their problem to figure it out, not Mooney's to explain it.

They had even been grateful when Mooney offered handsomely to refrain from notifying the police.

"Lobby, sir," sang out the elevator operator, and Mooney stepped out, nodded to the manager, stared down the house detective and walked out into the street.

So far, so good.

Now that the animal necessities of clothes and food and a place were taken care of, Mooney had a chance to operate. It was a field in which he had always had a good deal of talent—the making of deals, the locating of contacts, the arranging of transactions that were better conducted in private.

And he had a good deal of business to transact. Harse had accepted without question his statement that they would have to raise more money.

"Try heroin or. Platinum?" he had suggested, and gone back to his viewer.

"I will," Mooney assured him, and he did; he tried them both, and more besides.

Not only was it good that he had such valuable commodities to vend, but it was a useful item in his total of knowledge concerning Harse that the man from the future seemed to have no idea of the value of money in the 20th Century, *chez* U.S.A.

Mooney found a buyer for the drugs; and there was a few thousand dollars there, which helped, for although the quantity was not large, the drugs were chemically pure. He found a fence to handle the jewels and precious metals; and he unloaded all the ones of moderate value—not the other diamond, not the rubies, not the star sapphire.

He arranged to keep those without mentioning it to Harse. No point in selling them now, not when they had several thousand dollars above any conceivable expenses, not when some future date would do as well, just in case Harse should get away with the balance of the kit.

Having concluded his business, Mooney undertook a brief but expensive shopping tour of his own and found a reasonably satisfactory place to eat. After a pleasantly stimulating cocktail and the best meal he had had in some years—doubly good, for there was no reek from Harse's nauseating concoctions to spoil it—he called for coffee, for brandy, for the day's papers.

The disappearance of the truck driver made hardly a ripple. There were a couple of stories, but small and far in the back—amnesia, said one; an underworld kidnapping, suggested another; but the story had nothing to feed on and it would die.

Good enough, thought Mooney, waving for another glass of that enjoyable brandy; and then he turned back to the front page and saw his own face.

There was the hotel lobby of the previous day, and a pillar of churning black smoke that Mooney knew was Harse, and there in the background, mouth agape, expression worried, was Howard Mooney himself.

He read it all very, very carefully.

Well, he thought, at least they didn't get our names. The story was all about the Loyal and Beneficent Order of Exalted Eagles, and the only reference to the picture was a brief line about a disturbance outside the meeting hall. Nonetheless, the second glass of brandy tasted nowhere near as good as the first.

▼

Time passed. Mooney found a man who explained what was meant by the Vale of Cashmere. In Brooklyn, there is a very large park—the name is Prospect Park—and in it is a little planted valley, with a brook and a pool; and the name of it on the maps of Prospect Park is the Vale of Cashmere. Mooney sent out for a map, memorized it; and that was that.

However, Mooney didn't really want to go to the Vale of Cashmere with Harse. What he wanted was that survival kit. Wonders kept popping out of it, and each day's supply made Mooney covet the huger store that was still inside. There had been, he guessed, something like a hundred separate items that had somehow come out of that tiny box. There simply was no room for them all; but that was not a matter that Mooney concerned himself with. They *were* there, possible or not, because he had seen them.

Mooney laid traps.

The trouble was that Harse did not care for conversation. He spent endless hours with his film viewer, and when he said anything at all to Mooney, it was to complain. All he wanted was to exist for four days—nothing else.

Mooney laid conversational traps, tried to draw him out, and there was no luck. Harse would turn his blank, pale stare on him, and refuse to be drawn.

At night, however hard Mooney tried, Harse was always awake past him; and in his sleep, always and always, the little metal guardians strapped Mooney tight. Survival kit? But how did the little metal things know that Mooney was a threat?

It was maddening and time was passing. There were four days, then only three, then only two. Mooney made arrangements of his own.

He found two girls—lovely girls, the best that money could buy, and he brought them to the suite with a wink and a snigger. "A little relaxation, eh, Harse? The red-haired one is named Ginger and she's partial to men with light-colored eyes."

Ginger smiled a rehearsed and lovely smile. "I certainly *am*, Mr. Harse. Say, want to dance?"

But it came to nothing, though the house detective knocked deferentially on the door to ask if they could be a little more quiet, please. It wasn't the sound of celebration the at the neighbors were objecting to. It was the shrill, violent noise of Harse's laughter. First he had seemed not to understand, and then he looked as astonished as Mooney had ever seen him. And then laughter.

Girls didn't work. Mooney got rid of the girls.

All right, Mooney was a man of infinite resource and sagacity—hadn't he proved that many a time? He excused himself to Harse, made sure his fat new pigskin wallet was in his pocket, and took a cab to a place on Brooklyn's waterfront where cabs seldom go. The bartender had arms like beer kegs and a blue chin.

"Beer," said Mooney, and made sure he paid for it with a twenty-dollar bill—thumbing through a thick wad of fifties and hundreds to find the smallest. He retired to a booth and nursed his beer.

After about ten minutes, a man stood beside him, blue-chinned and muscular enough to be the bartender's brother—which, Mooney found, he was.

"Well," said Mooney, "it took you long enough. Sit down. You don't have to roll me; you can earn this."

Girls didn't work? Okay, if not girls, then try boys . . . well, not boys exactly. Hoodlums. Try hoodlums and see what Harse might do against the toughest inhabitants of the area around the Gowanus Canal.

▼

Harse, sloshing heedlessly through melted snow, spattering Mooney, grumbled: "I do not see why we. Must? Wander endlessly across the face of this wretched slum."

Mooney said soothingly: "We have to make *sure*, Harse. We have to be sure it's the right place."

"Huff," said Harse, but he went along. They were in Prospect Park and it was nearly dark.

"Hey, look," said Mooney desperately, "look at those kids on sleds!"

Harse glanced angrily at the kids on sleds and even more angrily at Mooney. Still, he wasn't refusing to come and that was something. It had been possible that Harse would sit tight in the hotel room and it had taken all of the persuasive powers Mooney prided himself on to get him out. But Mooney was able to paint a horrible picture of getting to the wrong place, missing the Nexus Point, seventeen long years of waiting for the next one.

They crossed the Sheep Meadow, crossed the walk, crossed an old covered bridge; and they were at the head of a flight of shallow steps.

"The Vale of Cashmere!" cried Mooney, as though he were announcing a miracle.

Harse said nothing.

Mooney licked his lips, glancing at the kit Harse carried under an arm, glancing around. No one was in sight.

Mooney coughed. "Uh. You're sure this is the place you mean?"

"If it is the Vale of Cashmere." Harse looked once more down the steps, then turned.

"No, wait!" said Mooney frantically. "I mean—well, *where* in the Vale of Cashmere is the Nexus Point? This is a big place!"

Harse's pale eyes stared at him for a moment. "No. Not big."

"Oh, *fairly* big. After all—"

Harse said positively: "Come."

Mooney swore under his breath and vowed never to trust anyone again, especially a bartender's brother; but just then it happened. Out of the snowy bushes stepped a man in a red bandanna, holding a gun. "This is a stickup! Gimme that bag!"

Mooney exulted.

There was no chance for Harse now. The man was leaping toward him; there would be no time for him to open the bag, take out the weapon . . .

But he didn't have to. There was a thin, singing, whining sound from the bag. It leaped out of Harse's hand, leaped free as though it had invisible wings, and flew at the man in the red bandanna. The man stumbled and jumped aside, the eyes incredulous over the mask. The silvery flat metal kit spun round him, whining. It circled him once, spiraled up. Behind it, like a smoke trail from a destroyer, a pale blue mist streamed backward. It surrounded the man and hid him.

The bag flew back into Harse's hand.

The violet mist thinned and disappeared.

And the man was gone, as utterly and as finally as any chambermaid or driver of a truck.

There was a moment of silence. Mooney stared without belief at the snow sifting down from the bushes that the man had hid in.

Harse looked opaquely at Mooney. "It seems," he said, "that in these slums are many. Dangers?"

Mooney was very quiet on the way back to the hotel. Harse, for once, was not gazing into his viewer. He sat erect and silent beside

Mooney, glancing at him from time to time. Mooney did not relish the attention.

The situation had deteriorated.

It deteriorated even more when they entered the lobby of the hotel. The desk clerk called to Mooney.

Mooney hesitated, then said to Harse: "You go ahead. I'll be up in a minute. And listen—don't forget my knock."

Harse inclined his head and strode into the elevator. Mooney sighed.

"There's a gentleman here to see you, Mr. Mooney," the desk clerk said civilly.

Mooney swallowed. "A—a gentleman? To see me?"

The clerk nodded toward the writing room. "In there, sir. A gentleman who says he knows you."

Mooney pursed his lips.

In the writing room? Well, that was an advantage. The writing room was off the main lobby; it would give Mooney a chance to peek in before whoever it was could see him. He approached the entrance cautiously . . .

"Howard!" cried an accusing familiar voice behind him.

Mooney turned. A small man with curly red hair was coming out of a door marked "Men."

"Why—why, Uncle Lester!" said Mooney. "What a p-pleasant surprise!"

Lester, all of five feet tall, wispy red hair surrounding his red plump face, looked up at him belligerently.

"No doubt!" he snapped. "I've been waiting all day, Howard. Took the afternoon off from work to come here. And I wouldn't have been here at all if I hadn't seen *this.*"

He was holding a copy of the paper with Mooney's picture, behind the pillar of black fog. "Your aunt wrapped my lunch in it, Howard. Otherwise I might have missed it. Went right to the hotel. You weren't there. The doorman helped, though. Found a cab driver. Told me where he'd taken you. Here I am."

"That's nice," lied Mooney.

"No, it isn't. Howard, what in the world are you up to? Do you know the Monmouth County police are looking for you? Said there was somebody missing. Want to talk to you." The little man shook his head angrily. "Knew I shouldn't let you stay at my place. Your aunt warned me, too. Why do you make trouble for me?"

"Police?" Mooney asked faintly.

"At my age! Police coming to the house. Who was that fella who's missing, Howard? Where did he go? Why doesn't he go home? His wife's half crazy. He shouldn't worry her like that."

Mooney clutched his uncle's shoulder. "Do the police know where I am? You didn't tell them?"

"Tell them? How could I tell them? Only I saw your picture while I was eating my sandwich, so I went to the hotel and—"

"Uncle Lester, listen. What did they come to see you for?"

"Because I was stupid enough to let you stay in my house, that's what for," Lester said bitterly. "Two days ago. Knocking on my door, hardly eight o'clock in the morning. They said there's a man missing, driving a truck, found the truck empty. Man from the Coast Guard station knows him, saw him picking up a couple of hitchhikers at a bridge someplace, recognized one of the hitchhikers. Said the hitchhiker'd been staying at my house. That's you, Howard. Don't lie; he described you. Pudgy, kind of a squinty look in the eyes, dressed like a bum—oh, it was you, all right."

"Wait a minute. Nobody knows you've come here, right? Not even Auntie?"

"No, course not. She didn't see the picture, so how would she know? Would've said something if she had. Now come on, Howard, we've got to go to the police and—"

"Uncle Lester!"

The little man paused and looked at him suspiciously. But that was all right; Mooney began to feel confidence flow back into him. It wasn't all over yet, not by a long shot.

"Uncle Lester," he said, his voice low-pitched and persuasive, "I have to ask you a very important question. Think before you answer, please. This is the question: Have you ever belonged to any Communist organization?"

The old man blinked. After a moment, he exploded. "Now what are you up to, Howard? *You* know I never—"

"Think, Uncle Lester! Please. Way back when you were a boy—anything like that?"

"Of course not!"

"You're sure? Because I'm warning you, Uncle Lester, you're going to have to take the strictest security check anybody ever took. You've stumbled onto something important. You'll have to prove you can be trusted—or well, I can't answer for the consequences. You see, this involves—" he looked around him furtively— "Schenectady Project."

"Schenec—"

"Schenectady Project." Mooney nodded. "You've heard of the atom bomb? Uncle Lester, this is bigger!"

"Bigger than the at—"

"Bigger. It's the *molecule* bomb. There aren't seventy-five men in the country that know what that so-called driver in the truck was up to, and now you're one of them."

Mooney nodded soberly, feeling his power. The old man was hooked, tied and delivered. He could tell by the look in the eyes, by the quivering of the lips. Now was the time to slip the contract in his hand; or, in the present instance, to—

"I'll tell you what to do," whispered Mooney. "Here's my key. You go up to my room. Don't knock—we don't want to attract attention. Walk right in. You'll see a man there and he'll explain everything. Understand?"

"Why—why, sure, Howard. But why don't you come with me?"

Mooney raised a hand warningly. "You might be followed. I'll have to keep a lookout."

Five minutes later, when Mooney tapped on the door of the room—three taps, pause, three taps—and cautiously pushed it open, the pale blue mist was just disappearing. Harse was standing angrily in the center of the room with the jointed metal thing out ominously before him.

And of Uncle Lester, there was no trace at all.

Time passed; and then the time was all gone, and it was midnight, nearly the Nexus Point.

In front of the hotel, a drowsy cab-driver gave them an argument. "The Public Liberry? Listen, the Liberry ain't open this time of night. I ought to—Oh, thanks. Hop in." He folded the five-dollar bill and put the cab in gear.

Harse said ominously: "Liberry, Mooney? Why do you instruct him to take us to the Liberry?"

Mooney whispered: "There's a law against being in the Park at night. We'll have to sneak in. The Library's right across the street."

Harse stared, with his luminous pale eyes. But it was true; there was such a law, for the parks of the city lately had become fields of honor where rival gangs contended with bottle shards and zip guns, where a passerby was odds-on to be mugged.

"High Command must know this," Harse grumbled. "Must proceed, they say, to Nexus Point. But then one finds the aboriginals have made laws! Oh, I shall make a report!"

"Sure you will," Mooney soothed; but in his heart, he was prepared to bet heavily against it.

Because he had a new strategy. Clearly he couldn't get the survival kit from Harse. He had tried that and there was no luck; his arm still tingled as the bellboy's had, from having seemingly absent-mindedly taken the handle to help Harse. But there was a way.

Get rid of this clown from the future, he thought contentedly; meet the Nexus Point instead of Harse and there was the future, ripe for the taking! He knew where the rescuers would be and, above all, he knew how to talk. Every man has one talent and Mooney's was salesmanship.

All the years wasted on peddling dime-store schemes like frozen-food plans! But this was the big time at last, so maybe the years of seasoning were not wasted, after all.

"That for you, Uncle Lester," he muttered. Harse looked up from his viewer angrily and Mooney cleared his throat. "I said," he explained hastily, "we're almost at the—the Nexus Point."

▼

Snow was drifting down. The cab-driver glanced at the black, quiet library, shook his head and pulled away, leaving black, wet tracks in the thin snow.

The pale-eyed man looked about him irritably. "You!" he cried, waking Mooney from a dream of possessing the next ten years of stock-market reports. "You! Where is this Vale of Cashmere?"

"Right this way, Harse, right this way," said Mooney placatingly.

There was a wide sort of traffic circle—grand Army Plaza was the name of it—and there were a few cars going around it. But not many, and none of them looked like police cars. Mooney looked up and down the broad, quiet streets.

"Across here," he ordered, and led the time traveler toward the edge of the park. "We can't go in the main entrance. There might be cops."

"Cops?"

"Policemen. Law-enforcement officers. We'll just walk down here a way and then hop over the wall. Trust me," said Mooney, in the voice that had put frozen-food lockers into so many suburban homes.

The look from those pale eyes was anything but a look of trust, but Harse didn't say anything. He stared about with an expression of detached horror, like an Alabama gentlewoman condemned to walk through Harlem.

"Now!" whispered Mooney urgently.

And over the wall they went.

They were in a thicket of shrubs and brush, snow-laden, the snow sifting down into Mooney's neck every time he touched a branch, which was always; he couldn't avoid it. They crossed a path and then a road—long, curving, broad, white, empty. Down a hill, onto another path. Mooney paused, glancing around.

"You know where you are. Going?"

"I think so. I'm looking for cops." None in sight. Mooney frowned. What the devil did police think they were up to? They passed laws; why weren't they around to enforce them?

Mooney had his landmarks well in mind. There was the Drive, and there was the fork he was supposed to be looking for. It wouldn't be hard to find the path to the Vale. The only thing was, it was kind of important to Mooney's hope of future prosperity that he find a policeman first. And time was running out.

He glanced at the luminous dial of his watch—self-winding, shockproof, non-magnetic; the man in the hotel's jewelry shop had assured him only yesterday that he could depend on its time-keeping as on the beating of his heart. It was nearly a quarter of one.

"Come along, come along!" grumbled Harse.

Mooney stalled: "I—I think we'd better go along this way. It *ought* to be down there—"

He cursed himself. Why hadn't he gone in the main entrance, where there was sure to be a cop? Harse would never have known the difference. But there was the artist in him that wanted the thing done perfectly, and so he had held to the pretense of avoiding police, had skulked and hidden. And now—

"Look!" he whispered, pointing.

Harse spat soundlessly and turned his eyes where Mooney was pointing.

Yes. Under a distant light, a moving figure, swinging a night-stick.

Mooney took a deep breath and planted a hand between Harse's shoulder blades.

"Run!" he yelled at the top of his voice, and shoved. He sounded so real, he almost convinced himself. "We'll have to split up—I'll meet you there. Now run!"

Oh, clever Mooney! He crouched under a snowy tree, watching the man from the future speed effortlessly away . . . in the wrong direction.

The cop was hailing him; clever cop! All it had taken was a couple of full-throated yells and at once the cop had perceived that someone was in the park. But cleverer than any cop was Mooney.

Men from the future. Why, thought Mooney contentedly, no Mrs. Meyerhauser of the suburbs would have let me get away with a trick like that to sell her a freezer. There's going to be no problem at all. I don't have to worry about a thing. Mooney can take care of himself!

By then, he had caught his breath—and time was passing, passing.

He heard a distant confused yelling. Harse and the cop? But it didn't matter. The only thing that mattered was getting to the Nexus Point at one minute past one.

He took a deep breath and began to trot. Slipping in the snow, panting heavily, he went down the path, around the little glade, across the covered bridge.

He found the shallow steps that led down to the Vale.

And there it was below him: a broad space where walks joined, and in the space a thing shaped like a dinosaur egg, rounded and huge. It glowed with a silvery sheen.

Confidently, Mooney started down the steps toward the egg and the moving figures that flitted soundlessly around it. Harse was not the only time traveler, Mooney saw. Good! That might make it all the simpler. Should he change his plan and feign amnesia, pass himself off as one of their own men?

Or—

A movement made him look over his shoulder.

Somebody was standing at the top of the steps. "Hell's fire," whispered Mooney. He'd forgotten all about that aboriginal law; and here above him stood a man in a policeman's uniform, staring down with pale eyes.

No, not a policeman. The face was—Harse's.

Mooney swallowed and stood rooted.

"You!" Harse's savage voice came growling. "You are to stand. Still?"

Mooney didn't need the order; he couldn't move. No twentieth-century cop was a match for Harse, that was clear; Harse had bested him, taken his uniform away from him for camouflage—and here he was.

Unfortunately, so was Howard Mooney.

The figures below were looking up, pointing and talking; Harse from above was coming down. Mooney could only stand, and wish—wish that he were back in Sea Bright, living on cookies and stale tea, wish he had planned things with more intelligence, more skill—perhaps even with more honesty. But it was too late for wishing.

Harse came down the steps, paused a yard from Mooney, scowled a withering scowl—and passed on.

He reached the bottom of the steps and joined the others waiting about the egg. They all went inside.

The glowing silvery colors winked and went out. The egg flamed purple, faded, turned transparent and disappeared.

Mooney stared and, yelling a demand for payment, ran stumbling down the steps to where it had been. There was a round thawed spot, a trampled patch—nothing else.

They were gone . . .

Almost gone. Because there was a sudden bright wash of flame from overhead—cold silvery flame. He looked up, dazzled. Over him, the egg was visible as thin smoke, hovering. A smoky, half-transparent hand reached out of a port. A thin, reedy voice cried: "I promised you. Pay?"

And the silvery dispatch-case sort of thing, the survival kit, dropped soundlessly to the snow beside Mooney.

When he looked up again, the egg was gone for good.

He was clear back to the hotel before he got a grip on himself—and then he was drunk with delight. Honest Harse! Splendidly trustable Harse! Why, all this time, Mooney had been so worried, had worked so hard—and the whole survival kit was his, after all!

He had touched it gingerly before picking it up but it didn't shock him; clearly the protective devices, whatever they were, were off.

He sweated over it for an hour and a half, looking for levers, buttons, a slit that he might pry wider with the blade of a knife. At last he kicked it and yelled, past endurance: "Open up damn you!"

It opened wide on the floor before him.

"Oh, bless your heart!" cried Mooney, falling to his knees to drag out the string of wampum, the little mechanical mice, the viewing-machine sort of thing. Treasures like those were beyond price; each one might fetch a fortune, if only in the wondrous new inventions he could patent if he could discover just how they worked.

But where were they?

Gone! The wampum was gone. The goggles were gone. Everything was gone—the little flat canisters, the map instruments, everything but one thing.

There was, in a corner of the case, a squarish, sharp-edged thing that Mooney stared at blindly for a long moment before he recognized it. It was a part—only a part—of the jointed construction that Harse had used to rid himself of undesirables by bathing them in blue light.

What a filthy trick! Mooney all but sobbed to himself.

He picked up the squarish thing bitterly. Probably it wouldn't even work, he thought, the world a ruin around him. It wasn't even the whole complete weapon.

Still—

There was a grooved, saddle-shaped affair that was clearly a sort of trigger; it could move forward or it could move back. Mooney thought deeply for a while.

Then he sat up, held the thing carefully away from him with the pointed part toward the wall and pressed, ever so gently pressed forward on the saddle-shaped thumb-trigger.

The pale blue haze leaped out, swirled around and, not finding anything alive in its range, dwindled and died.

▼

Aha, thought Mooney, not everything is lost yet! Surely a bright young man could find some use for a weapon like this which removed, if it did not kill, which prevented any nastiness about a corpse turning up, or a messy job of disposal.

Why not see what happened if the thumb-piece was moved backward?

Well, why not? Mooney held the thing away from him, hesitated, and slid it back.

There was a sudden shivering tingle in his thumb, in the gadget he was holding, running all up and down his arm. A violet haze, very unlike the blue one, licked soundlessly forth—not burning, but destroying as surely as flame ever destroyed; for where the haze touched the gadget itself, the kit, everything that had to do with the man from the future, it seared and shattered. The gadget fell into white crystalline powder in Mooney's hand and the case itself became a rectangular shape traced in white powder ridges on the rug.

Oh, no! thought Mooney, even before the haze had gone. It can't be!

The flame danced away like a cloud, spreading and rising. While Mooney stared, it faded away, but not without leaving something behind.

Mooney threw his taut body backward; almost under the bed. What he saw, he didn't believe; what he believed filled him with panic.

No wonder Harse had laughed so when Mooney asked if its victims were dead. For there they were, all of them. Like djinn out of a jar, human figures jelled and solidified where the cloud of violet flame had not at all diffidently rolled.

They were alive, as big as life, and beginning to move—and so many of them! Three—five—six:

The truck-driver, yes, and a man in a long flannel underwear who must have been the policeman, and Uncle Lester, and the bartender's brother, and the chambermaid, and a man Mooney didn't know.

They were there, all of them, and they came toward him, and oh! but they were angry!

This Life and Later Ones

George Zebrowski

It's not unusual for a horror tale to threaten the protagonist with death. In George Zebrowski's tale, however, death might be welcomed. There have been a number of different scenarios for alternatives to the pain of old age, but the chilling, twisted tale that follows might make you yearn for the pain of quick death.

This story, first published in 1987, takes the notion of the afterlife to a terrible extreme, but not in any way that you might expect. It's not horrific at first glance, but if you think about the implications of this melancholy tale . . .

Zebrowski, author of a number of SF novels, most notably *Macro-life,* and several dozen short stories, has himself edited or co-edited a number of anthologies, and will have a new one out shortly, *Skylife* (with Gregory Benford), featuring tales of habitats in space.

> "Some people want to achieve immortality through their works or descendants. I prefer to achieve immorality by not dying."
>
> Woody Allen

Most people knew, by the turn of that first decade, that their lives would come to three choices: death with nothing after; death with the religious or mystical hope of a new existence; or translation into a manufactured afterlife. This last choice, which had to be acted upon well in advance of clinical death, was a service offered by AFTERLIVES UNLIMITED, a group of creative associates working out of Atlantic City since the end of the last century.

The first beyonds on the market were blank, limbo-like holding spaces where the dead waited, often crying out on the monitors to be erased, as they sat in what seemed to be gray pastures, or on flat plains and jagged mountainsides, under empty skies. Electronic souls massed in the afterworlds to decide how to live, and to test how much say they still had over their existence.

But as the programmers applied their ingenuity to the problems of world-creation, better interactive backgrounds were brought into play for the waiting departed. Things seemed to have improved somewhat by the time my father began to think of being placed, but I was worried about more than the technology.

"You disapprove, don't you son?"

I shrugged. He was past ninety. Who was I to deny him further life of any kind? "I don't know what I can say."

"Go ahead, there's not much I haven't thought myself."

"It's just that it seems to show, well, a lack of character on your part. Here you are, trembling at the edge of your grave, and you want this. If you had any convictions about life-after-death, you wouldn't hedge." I felt cruel.

He smiled and scratched his nose. "We haven't talked lately. I don't have any religious convictions left. This is the only remaining road for me, this or the dark. I suppose the technology isn't great, but I won't last long enough for the improvements to come in. Gotta go while I can still make the transfer without complications."

He went that same week. They used the actual atoms of his brain to form the transfer pattern, for metaphysical reasons of conserving identity, they said; otherwise we might consider him only a copy of himself. I went to the warehouse and saw row upon row of solid-state modules housing the electronic dead in what amounted to old age homes beyond the grave.

Visitors were allowed a week after transfer. I arrived in a bad mood, feeling guilty, expecting the worst. They ushered me into a small private room with a three-dee tank monitor on one wall.

I sat down and peered into the next world.

"Pop, are you there?" I asked, straining to see into the tank.

A shadow moved across a barren landscape, and suddenly a face gazed out at me. Its eyes seemed blind, but it was Pop.

"Pop, it's me! Can you hear?" My heart was pounding.

"Stop shouting! Do you know what you sound and look like in here? A big cloud with a nasty voice. Can't you do anything about that?"

"I'll try to talk lower. Is that better?"

"Not much. You still look awful."

"Is there anything you need?" I asked stupidly.

"Well, you could ask them to program some shaving utensils. Beards keep growing in here, don't ask me why."

"I'll ask, but what do the, uh, programmers say?"

"The dummies don't know how to do that very well yet, and they claim it's not in their budget! They surmise that there's some deep mental reason why the beard detail persists. Something to do with the method they used to transfer us. I'm glad your mother didn't live long enough to get in here, thank God."

"You wanted this . . . "

"I know, I know, there was no choice. But tell them that they have to make improvements!"

"What kind of improvements, Pop?" I asked, thinking he couldn't just cut off payments from his Afterlife Trust.

"This place just isn't real enough. It's like living on a bare stage set. Worse—even that seems phony!"

I looked into his eyes, but he seemed to be looking inward, as if into a hidden mirror. He appeared defeated, resigned, despite his protests. After a moment the face turned away from me, and I saw a small shadow creep away across the dark landscape.

"Shit," I muttered as my stomach turned over and tried to fall out. My own face stared back at me from an abyss.

I got up and went in search of the administration office.

"You must realize," the local manager said, "that these facilities were pressed into service before the technology was fully developed. People forced us to open. The funding pressures were enormous—open or lose it to a competitor."

"I know, but can't you do something about provisions—about, well, landscaping, putting a bit more reality into these places?"

He shook his head and smiled, forming two dimples and a second chin. "Let me introduce you to our ace programmer. He'll explain better than I can."

We came to an open door. Inside the room, a wiry man sat at a giant screen, staring at some mathematical symbols.

"Felix, this is Mr. Canetti. He has a relative inside."

"Please," Felix motioned me to a chair as he swiveled around from the screen. "What is it you wish to know?" he asked as I sat down.

I explained my father's complaints.

"There's not much we can do right now."

"But why not?" I demanded.

He sighed. "I'm sorry, but we can't do better on the scenery right now. I know it's not much better than cut-outs pasted onto cardboard, but we're working on it." He sounded weary, but still interested in his work.

"What about provisions?"

"They don't need them. In fact, they don't need anything, not even food. All we have to do is keep their matrix support power steady, maybe boost it once in a while."

"But they also have mental needs, aesthetic needs."

He shook his head. "We've tried sketching in details, but it's dangerous. Can't seem to put inanimate things in with any degree of accuracy, where they would be needed. There's a basic uncertainty built into dealing with these worlds, involving our ways of measuring energy inputs. I don't fully understand it myself. I'm a programmer, not a physicist."

"But you'll solve it, won't you?" The sound of hope in my voice was pathetic.

"In time we might be able to land provisions in a kind of storybook fashion. You know, program a phantom ship filled with luxuries, have it approach from the sea, dock and unload. They could come to it in safety, you see, by stages, without the danger of differing energy levels that we can't measure, and take what they need. We'd bypass the danger of erasing people or disfiguring them with arriving informational artifacts."

"How long before you can do it?" I asked impatiently.

"Depends on subscriptions, on grants, funding from the government, the number of researchers we can recruit. Not many are being trained for this kind of work. It's too new. It'll take years, Mr. Canetti. Would you rather we just erased him?"

I thought he was making a bad joke, but one look at his face convinced me he was serious and had meant no offense.

"Can you?" I asked.

"We're not even sure of that, since we've never tried it. We could probably do it. But don't mention it to—it's your father, isn't it?"

I nodded. "Why not?"

"He might demand it, and that might start something if others joined him. They might think they could die and pass on to still some other afterlife. Some of these people have gotten religion since they died."

I almost laughed, except that I felt like crying. "No one filled us in on any of these problems before I signed him up."

He looked at me sternly. "What choice did you have? Would you have let him die?"

"No," I said helplessly, feeling useless.

"There is one other choice, for now. Want to hear it?"

"Sure. Why not?"

"We could store him until the worlds are improved. But it's very expensive. Only the very wealthy have taken that option." Are you wealthy, Mr. Canetti, his eyes asked me.

"Yeah," I said, "the rich knew these worlds were bad. Who tipped them? Don't tell me, they bought the info."

"Quite right. This is a cutthroat business. But you can console yourself with the hope that it won't be more than a few years before better worlds come on the market. It has to happen."

"Only a few years?"

"Five at the outside. We'll perform miracles by then. People in the prime of life will want to live inside. It'll be better than life."

"Oh?"

His eyes lit up. "Well, as one possibility, you'll be able to visit people inside."

"Sure—I could sail in on the phantom schooner you mentioned and land smuggled supplies on my father's dream island."

"Why not! It's not impossible, in principle." He seemed a bit hurt by my remarks. "Of course he could come out in a cyber-body and spend time with you right now, or even permanently." But I knew that cyber-bodies were ruinously expensive, available only on a custom-made basis, and that the service contracts were ridiculous. "We do have a sub-contracting agreement for this option that we're still negotiating, if you're really interested. In your case we would need various guarantees and a financial statement."

"You sound as if you don't place much faith in the technique," I said.

He nodded. "Too many fatal malfunctions. Prosthetic embodiments can't ever be better than our environments. Consider the choice—the real world *again* or anything you can wish for!"

His company was clearly hedging its bets. "Send me some literature on the hardbodies anyway," I said, standing up to leave. It was no use trying to sound decisive; he had made me feel utterly naive.

▼

"There's nothing I can do right now, Pop," I said at the next visit. "You'll just have to wait. Things will improve."

"You've marooned me here!"

"Don't you have any friends in there? Haven't you met anyone?" I bit my tongue, not daring to ask about what sexual opportunities existed for him now, if any.

"Yeah, *in here* is right. Even you know it's just a damn box."

Flashes of light appeared behind him as I tried to explain what I had learned—what the difficulties were in the various technologies, the costs involved, the dangers of malfunction, the lack of an effective repair and service network—but it did no good. I decided not to mention what Felix had told me about the legal problems of identity transfer. Waivers of dubious legal value were being signed all over the place to circumvent inheritance laws. There was talk of limiting the rights of hardbody recipients; periodic sanity tests might be required. No one was sure nowadays when they had been born, how long they lived, or when they were dead. I felt drained by guilt when Pop finally turned away from me.

I watched his shadow move off into what seemed to be low black hills. The sky was made of red lead. Other shadows were moving around inside the tank. I strained to see, punishing myself with the hellish sight, then got up and went home.

▼

I suppose most people have collaborated with the enemy where death is concerned. Dying can't be helped, so accept it as best you can, rationalize it as necessary and inevitable; above all, don't poison what time you have by worrying about the coming end. In with the new and out with the old. Just imagine how terrible it would be if people you hated or had done you harm could live forever. There's solace in knowing for sure that one day they'll rot, even if you will, too.

It could have been worse. I thought of all those people who had invested in freezer immortality, going for the grim hope of gross preservation when electronic survival was just around the corner. Attempts were being made to transfer the mental patterns of some corpsicles, but without much success to date.

I became a brochure and prospectus hound, hungrily searching for some way to improve Pop's lot. But it all came down to one conclusion: he had gone too early; the technology was only just getting started. To make matters worse, there are few psychologists in the field of identity transfer—you died and woke up in another place, where your experience of a well-made world told you that this was no world at all. It had been made by an idiot god, or a devil attempting to mimic reality. And you couldn't even be sure that you were yourself. I was afraid of what I would learn each time I went to visit.

▼

"How's it going, Pop? Made any more friends?"

He'd been in for six weeks. This time, he didn't speak to me at all. He wouldn't even come forward so I could see him.

"It *is* a big change," Felix, the ace programmer, explained to me. "We didn't quite understand how big until we pulled in a few psycho-biologists. It seems that the loss of the body's emotion-producing systems begins to show up. The brain tries to go on as before, out of habit and memory, but then the coldness sets in. No glands for anger, love, hate, just remembrances of what those feels were."

"Can't you adjust inputs to make those emotions possible for them?" I asked, struggling with my own feelings.

"We're working on it. It takes endless details to create the experience of a world. Too many details for anyone to handle. Reality goes on, layer after layer of structure, both in the environments and in the human mind. Maybe it just can't be faked, ever. At least not in the way reality fakes it." He smiled.

"What about their sex lives?" I asked.

"Uh, we don't know. We don't watch to see, I mean." He sounded nervous.

"But you're telling me all this is failing!" I shouted.

He nodded. "Could be, could be."

"Then what's going to happen to all your . . . tenants?"

He shrugged. "Any number of things. We don't know yet, exactly. There's a chance we could give the subs—I mean subscribers—exactly *what* they want, by linking their minds to the modeling processors, so that they would just conjure up whatever they wish. Connect their output to their input, so to speak. The closed loop would give them the sense of omnipotence, actually." He paused. "But then again, the lack of limits might be bad for the human mind, some of the psychs are saying. God knows what hells of torment and degradation might appear in the tanks."

"What are you saying?" I shouted. "You're playing with people!"

He smiled at my mistake.

"People? Lives? They're all dead, electronic ghosts, shadows, Mr. Canetti. Don't insult me with your show of ethical indignation. We're doing the best we know how, and within the law."

"Yeah, sure," I said, "I know."

"Take it easy, buddy. You may need us yourself someday."

His words sent a chill down my spine.

I made a pest of myself after that, arriving three or four times a week, even if I didn't see my father. I questioned the flaccid director as often as I did Felix.

I worried about omnipotence.

What would it do to Pop to be able to have whatever he wanted? Anything was possible in the mental space of his new life. What would such power, however illusory, do to a human being? Would it only bring out the worst in human nature? It probably would.

"Don't worry," Felix said to me the following week. "It's still a long way off. He'd probably start out by calling back everything he'd lost in life, like his wife, for example, if she died in the old way. She'd appear to him just as he would want her, exacto. Good or bad—I don't know. He'd stop complaining, that's for sure."

I sat down before the tank and looked inside. The view was breathtaking this week. Green mountains, yellow sunlight, flowers—millions of flowers.

"Damn picture postcard," Pop said to me. "Beautiful little houses for us to live in, with rose bushes, and ivy on the walls."

"Well, what's wrong with that?"

"It isn't real. Looks good to you, but I can tell. Not what I remember. Too regular, too clean. There's no grime, no dust, no insects. Just another stage set."

"It's state-of-the-art, Pop."

"Look, kid, I know that. But it's not a world, no matter what they do to it. A world has a *history*. It *grew* to be the way it is. That took billions of years. There's a sense of something else, of things hidden, something you can't ever get a handle on, an unconscious part of reality, that's missing. It's not just me. Everyone here feels the same way. We can't help noticing. We talk about it, we compare. We're the only reality in this place, but there's no life to live, no gain or loss."

He still seemed emotional and argumentative. That much of his old self seemed to be surviving well enough.

"Pop, do you *care* for any of us out here, for me?" The question seemed to be the best way to confront my fears and suspicions.

He looked straight at me. "Not really—except that you guys have some power over us, so I have to talk to you. But I can't seem to feel the same way I did. How can I? You're no longer my only hope of immortality. You're your own man, and have been for some time. It's a relief, I suppose, remembering how often I got no relief from anything. We've both grown up."

"Do you want to get out of there, Pop?" I asked impatiently.

"I don't know—what do you have in mind?"

"I've been reading about the new cyber-bodies. We could put you in one. You'd be able to resume your life, walk around, do things."

"Sounds good. Probably has as many things wrong with it as this place. Maybe I should wait for when you can afford a blank clone to put me in?"

"No, Pop, I'll never be able to afford that. They take years to grow, and it's your biological twin you'll be invading, after you've killed its mental development. Do you want to deal with that, wondering all the time?"

"That's not a problem for me. Maybe I can get out and earn the money."

"And it's a hit-or-miss technique," I added, "making impressions in blank brains. They lose people, I'm told."

He looked straight at me. "I can't stay here son. I'll have to try a hardbody."

▼

It looked like him at thirty, but it was only foam over a metal frame. We got a good price on it. A twenty-year mortgage, with all my savings as a down payment, twenty per cent forfeit if he didn't like it and went back into the tank.

I read upon the aesthetics of prosthetic embodiment. Some people liked the overt Cartesian mind-body dualism. They could drive their new bodies from the head. I suppose it reminded them of their cars. Sex was also pretty straightforward.

On the day of Pop's resurrection, I went to the afterlives warehouse and watched nervously as they transmitted his identity pattern into a small solid-state unit; then they just plugged it into the head of the cyber-body.

He sat up. "Hello, son," he said coldly.

Then he got up and walked back and forth, signed a few papers, and went out the door, ignoring us all.

"No glands at all, now," Felix said, shaking his head. "But you should be glad. He'll be his own person and won't lean on you emotionally so much."

I turned to leave, feeling hopeless and defeated.

"Just one more detail, Mr. Canetti," the local manager said.

"What's that?"

"Well, you do know that we can't erase completely. There are echoes left in the tank."

My stomach jumped. "No—I don't know any such thing. What are you talking about?"

"It's not your responsibility, of course, but I thought you would like to know."

"What!" I shouted. "What is there to know?"

"Please calm down. You needn't trouble yourself."

"What do you mean? That it's him? It is, isn't it?"

"Well, yes, in a purely formal sense, but—"

"And you can't erase him completely?"

"Well, we could destroy the tank physically, but there are other tenants in there to consider. You do see our difficulty?"

I glared at Felix. The coward had left it to his boss to spring the complications on me.

▼

I'm back every week to visit. I think of him as Pop's ghost. He's very faint, but still there, and himself; more so than the hardbody that's walking around outside. He seems to need me.

"When are they going to improve this place?" he asks. "Maybe you should get me out?"

I don't know what to say. Getting him out will always be impossible, no matter how often I do it.

The Veldt

Ray Bradbury

Although he has worked in a number of genres—including mysteries, poetry, fantasy, and suspense—and in multiple media, including films and television, Ray Bradbury is known best as a science fiction writer. Many consider him to be something of a "poet of the future" because his work, while often dealing with events that are yet to come, is at its best framed in limpid, clean prose that seems completely contemporary and familiar even while describing something utterly new or even impossible. Bradbury is especially adept at re-creating small-town American life, depicting in deceptively sunny colors treacherous situations that seem entirely too plausible.

Of course, he has also written chilling cautionary tales, such as his novel *Fahrenheit 451*, which still carries a dark and dire message.

"The Veldt," a 1950 story about the "house of the future" is a tale that sneaks up on the reader, first bringing the premise of that "future house" to life, then striking with a terrible swiftness.

George, I wish you'd look at the nursery."

"What's wrong with it?"

"I don't know."

"Well, then."

"I just want you to look at it, is all, or call a psychologist in to look at it."

"What would a psychologist want with a nursery?"

"You know very well what he'd want." His wife paused in the middle of the kitchen and watched the stove busy humming to itself, making supper for four.

"It's just that the nursery is different now than it was."

"All right, let's have a look."

They walked down the hall of their soundproofed, Happylife Home, which had cost them thirty thousand dollars installed, this house which clothed and fed and rocked them to sleep and played and sang and was good to them. Their approach sensitized a switch somewhere and the nursery light flicked on when they came within ten feet of it. Similarly, behind them, in the halls, lights went on and off as they left them behind, with a soft automaticity.

"Well," said George Hadley.

They stood on the thatched floor of the nursery. It was forty feet across by forty feet long and thirty feet high; it had cost half again as much as the rest of the house. "But nothing's too good for our children," George had said.

The nursery was silent. It was empty as a jungle glade at hot high noon. The walls were blank and two dimensional. Now, as George and Lydia Hadley stood in the center of the room, the walls began to purr and recede into crystalline distance, it seemed, and presently an African veldt appeared, in three dimensions, on all sides, in color, reproduced to the final pebble and bit of straw. The ceiling above them became a deep sky with a hot yellow sun.

George Hadley felt the perspiration start on his brow.

"Let's get out of this sun," he said. "This is a little too real. But I don't see anything wrong."

"Wait a moment, you'll see," said his wife.

Now the hidden odorophonics were beginning to blow a wind of odor at the two people in the middle of the baked veldtland. The hot straw smell of lion grass, the cool green smell of the hidden water hole, the great rusty smell of animals, the smell of dust like a red paprika in the hot air. And now the sounds: the thump of distant antelope feet on grassy sod, the papery rustling of vultures. A shadow passed through the sky. The shadow flickered on George Hadley's upturned, sweating face.

"Filthy creatures," he heard his wife say.

"The vultures."

"You see, there are the lions, far over, that way. Now they're on their way to the water hole. They've just been eating," said Lydia. "I don't know what."

"Some animal." George Hadley put his hand up to shield off the burning light from his squinted eyes. "A zebra or a baby giraffe, maybe."

"Are you sure?" His wife sounded peculiarly tense.

"No, it's a little late to be *sure,*" he said, amused. "Nothing over there I can see but cleaned bone, and the vultures dropping for what's left."

"Did you hear that scream?" she asked.

"No."

"About a minute ago?"

"Sorry, no."

The lions were coming. And again George Hadley was filled with admiration for the mechanical genius who had conceived this room. A miracle of efficiency selling for an absurdly low price. Every home should have one. Oh, occasionally they frightened you with their clinical accuracy, they startled you, gave you a twinge, but most of the time what fun for everyone, not only your own son and daughter, but for yourself when you felt like a quick jaunt to a foreign land, a quick change of scenery. Well, here it was!

And here were the lions now, fifteen feet away, so real, so feverishly and startlingly real that you could feel the prickling fur on your hand, and your mouth was stuffed with the dusty upholstery smell of their heated pelts, and the yellow of them was in your eyes like the yellow of an exquisite French tapestry, the yellows of lions and summer grass, and the sound of the matted lion lungs exhaling on the silent noontide, and the smell of meat from the panting, dripping mouths.

The lions stood looking at George and Lydia Hadley with terrible green-yellow eyes.

"Watch out!" screamed Lydia.

The lions came running at them.

Lydia bolted and ran. Instinctively, George sprang after her. Outside, in the hall, with the door slammed, he was laughing and she was crying, and they both stood appalled at the other's reaction.

"George!"

"Lydia! Oh, my dear poor sweet Lydia!"

"They almost got us!"

"Walls, Lydia, remember; crystal walls, that's all they are. Oh, they look real, I must admit—Africa in your parlor—but it's all dimensional superreactionary, supersensitive color film and mental tape film behind glass screens. It's all odorophonics and sonics, Lydia. Here's my handkerchief."

"I'm afraid." She came to him and put her body against him and cried steadily. "Did you see: did you *feel?* It's too real."

"Now, Lydia . . . "

"You've got to tell Wendy and Peter not to read any more on Africa."

"Of course—of course." He patted her.

"Promise?"

"Sure."

"And lock the nursery for a few days until I get my nerves settled."

"You know how difficult Peter is about that. When I punished him a month ago by locking the nursery for even a few hours—the tantrum he threw! And Wendy too. They *live* for the nursery."

"It's got to be locked, that's all there is to it."

"All right." Reluctantly he locked the huge door. "You've been working too hard. You need a rest."

"I don't know—I don't know," she said, blowing her nose, sitting down in a chair that immediately began to rock and comfort her. "Maybe I don't have enough to do. Maybe I have time to think too much. Why don't we shut the whole house off for a few days and take a vacation?"

"You mean you want to fry my eggs for me?"

"Yes." She nodded.

"And darn my socks?"

"Yes." A frantic, watery-eyed nodding.

"And sweep the house?"

"Yes, yes—oh, yes!"

"But I thought that's why we bought this house, so we wouldn't have to do anything?"

"That's just it. I feel like I don't belong here. The house is wife and mother now and nursemaid. Can I compete with an African veldt? Can I give a bath and scrub the children as efficiently or quickly as the automatic scrub bath can? I cannot. And it isn't just me. It's you. You've been awfully nervous lately."

"I suppose I have been smoking too much."

"You look as if you didn't know what to do with yourself in this house, either. You smoke a little more every morning and drink a little more every afternoon and need a little more sedative every night. You're beginning to feel unnecessary too."

"Am I?" He paused and tried to feel into himself to see what was really there.

"Oh, George! She looked beyond him, at the nursery door. "Those lions can't get out of there, can they?"

He looked at the door and saw it tremble as if something had jumped against it from the other side.

"Of course not," he said.

▼

At dinner they ate alone, for Wendy and Peter were at a special plastic carnival across town and had televised home to say they'd be late, to go ahead eating. So George Hadley, bemused, sat watching the dining-room table produce warm dishes of food from its mechanical interior.

"We forgot the ketchup," he said.

"Sorry," said a small voice within the table, and ketchup appeared.

As for the nursery, thought George Hadley, it won't hurt for the children to be locked out of it awhile. Too much of anything isn't good for anyone. And it was clearly indicated that the children had been spending a little too much time on Africa. That *sun*. He could feel it on his neck, still, like a hot paw. And the *lions*. And the smell of blood. Remarkable how the nursery caught the telepathic emanations of the children's minds and created life to fill their every desire.

The children thought lions, and there were lions. The children thought zebras, and there were zebras. Sun—sun. Giraffes—giraffes. Death and death.

That *last.* He chewed tastelessly on the meat that the table had cut for him. Death thoughts. They were awfully young, Wendy and Peter, for death thoughts. Or, no, you were never too young, really. Long before you knew what death was you were wishing it on someone else. When you were two years old you were shooting people with cap pistols.

But this—the long, hot African veldt—the awful death in the jaws of a lion. And repeated again and again.

"Where are you going?"

He didn't answer Lydia. Preoccupied, he let the lights glow softly on ahead of him, extinguish behind him as he padded to the nursery door. He listed against it. Far away, a lion roared.

He unlocked the door and opened it. Just before he stepped inside, he heard a faraway scream. And then another roar from the lions, which subsided quickly.

He stepped into Africa. How many times in the last year had he opened this door and found Wonderland, Alice, the Mock Turtle, or Aladdin and his Magical Lamp, or Jack Pumpkinhead of Oz, or Dr. Doolittle, or the cow jumping over a very real-appearing moon—all the delightful contraptions of a make-believe world. How often had he seen Pegasus flying in the sky ceiling, or seen fountains of red fireworks, or heard angel voices singing. But now, this yellow hot Africa, this bake oven with murder in the heat. Perhaps Lydia was right. Perhaps they needed a little vacation from the fantasy which was growing a bit too real for ten-year-old children. It was all right to exercise one's mind with gymnastic fantasies, but when the lively child mind settled on *one* pattern . . . ? It seemed that, at a distance, for the past month, he had heard lions roaring, and smelled their strong odor seeping as far away as his study door. But, being busy, he had paid it no attention.

George Hadley stood on the African grassland alone. The lions looked up from their feeding, watching him. The only flaw to the illusion was the open door through which he could see his wife, far down the dark hall, like a framed picture, eating her dinner abstractedly.

"Go away," he said to the lions.

They did not go.

He knew the principle of the room exactly. You sent out your thoughts. Whatever you thought would appear.

"Let's have Aladdin and his lamp," he snapped.

The veldtland remained; the lions remained.

"Come on, room! I demand Aladdin!" he said.

Nothing happened. The lions mumbled in their baked pelts.

"Aladdin!"

He went back to dinner. "The fool room's out of order," he said. "It won't respond."

"Or—"

"Or what?"

"Or it *can't* respond," said Lydia, "because the children have thought about Africa and lions and killing so many days that the room's in a rut."

"Could be."

"Or Peter's set it to remain that way."

"*Set* it?"

"He may have got into the machinery and fixed something."

"Peter doesn't know machinery."

"He's a wise one for ten. That I.Q. of his—"

"Nevertheless—"

"Hello, Mom. Hello, Dad."

The Hadleys turned. Wendy and Peter were coming in the front door, cheeks like peppermint candy, eyes like bright blue agate marbles, smell of ozone on their jumpers from their trip in the helicopter.

"You're just in time for supper," said both parents.

"We're full of strawberry ice cream and hot dogs," said the children, holding hands. "But we'll sit and watch."

"Yes, come tell us about the nursery," said George Hadley.

The brother and sister blinked at him and then at each other. "Nursery?"

"All about Africa and everything," said the father with false joviality.

"I don't understand," said Peter.

"Your mother and I were just traveling through Africa with rod and reel; Tom Swift and his Electric Lion," said George Hadley.

"There's no Africa in the nursery," said Peter simply.

"Oh, come now, Peter. We know better."

"I don't remember any Africa," said Peter to Wendy. "Do you?"

"No."

"Run see and come tell."

She obeyed.

"Wendy, come back here!" said George Hadley, but she was gone. The house lights followed her like a flock of fireflies. Too late, he realized he had forgotten to lock the nursery door after his last inspection.

"Wendy'll look and come tell us," said Peter.

"She doesn't have to tell *me*. I've seen it."

"I'm sure you're mistaken, Father."

"I'm not, Peter. Come along now."

But Wendy was back. "It's not Africa," she said breathlessly.

"We'll see about this," said George Hadley, and they all walked down the hall together and opened the nursery door.

There was a green, lovely forest, a lovely river, a purple mountain, high voices singing, and Rima, lovely and mysterious, lurking in the trees with colorful flights of butterflies, like animated bouquets, lingering in her long hair. The African veldtland was gone. The lions were gone. Only Rima was here now, singing a song so beautiful that it brought tears to your eyes.

George Hadley looked in at the changed scene. "Go to bed," he said to the children.

They opened their mouths.

"You heard me," he said.

They went off to the air closet, where a wind sucked them like brown leaves up the flue to their slumber rooms.

George Hadley walked through the singing glade and picked up something that lay in the corner near where the lions had been. He walked slowly back to his wife.

"What is that?" she asked.

"An old wallet of mine," he said.

He showed it to her. The smell of hot grass was on it and the smell of a lion. There were drops of saliva on it, it had been chewed and there were blood smears on both sides.

He closed the nursery door and locked it, tight.

In the middle of the night he was still awake and he knew his wife was awake. "Do you think Wendy changed it?" she said at last, in the dark room.

"Of course."

"Made it from a veldt into a forest and put Rima there instead of lions?"

"Yes."

"Why?"

"I don't know. But it's staying locked until I find out."

"How did your wallet get there?"

"I don't know anything," he said, "except that I'm beginning to be sorry we bought that room for the children. If children are neurotic at all, a room like that—"

"It's supposed to help them work off their neuroses in a healthful way."

"I'm starting to wonder." He stared at the ceiling.

"We've given the children everything they ever wanted. Is this our reward—secrecy, disobedience?"

"Who was it said, 'Children are carpets, they should be stepped on occasionally'? We've never lifted a hand. They're insufferable—let's admit it. They come and go when they like; they treat us as if we were offspring. They're spoiled and we're spoiled."

"They've been acting funny ever since you forbade them to take the rocket to New York a few months ago."

"They're not old enough to do that alone, I explained."

"Nevertheless, I've noticed they've been decidedly cool toward us since."

"I think I'll have David McClean come tomorrow morning to have a look at Africa."

"But it's not Africa now, it's Green Mansions country and Rima."

"I have a feeling it'll be Africa again before then."

A moment later they heard the screams.

Two screams. Two people screaming from downstairs. And then a roar of lions.

"Wendy and Peter aren't in their rooms," said his wife.

He lay in his bed with his beating heart. "No," he said. "They've broken into the nursery."

"Those screams—they sound familiar."

"Do they?"

"Yes, awfully."

And although their beds tried very hard, the two adults couldn't be rocked to sleep for another hour. A smell of cats was in the night air.

▼

"Father?" said Peter.

"Yes."

Peter looked at his shoes. He never looked at his father any more, nor at his mother. "You aren't going to lock up the nursery for good, are you?"

"That all depends."

"On what?" snapped Peter.

"On you and your sister. If you intersperse this Africa with a little variety oh, Sweden perhaps, or Denmark or China—"

"I thought we were free to play as we wished."

"You are, within reasonable bounds."

"What's wrong with Africa, Father?"

"Oh, so now you admit you have been conjuring up Africa, do you?

"I wouldn't want the nursery locked up," said Peter coldly. "Ever."

"Matter of fact, we're thinking of turning the whole house off for about a month. Live sort of a carefree one-for-all existence."

"That sounds dreadful! Would I have to tie my own shoes instead of letting the shoe tier do it? And brush my own teeth and comb my hair and give myself a bath?"

"It would be fun for a change, don't you think?"

"No, it would be horrid. I didn't like it when you took out the picture painter last month."

"That's because I wanted you to learn to paint all by yourself, son."

"I don't want to do anything but look and listen and smell; what else is there to do?"

"All right, go play in Africa."

"Will you shut off the house sometime soon?"

"We're considering it."

"I don't think you'd better consider it any more, Father."

"I won't have any threats from my son!"

"Very well." And Peter strolled off to the nursery.

▼

"Am I on time?" said David McClean.

"Breakfast?" asked George Hadley.

"Thanks, had some. What's the trouble?"

"David, you're a psychologist."

"I should hope so."

"Well, then, have a look at our nursery. You saw it a year ago when you dropped by; did you notice anything peculiar about it then?"

"Can't say I did; the usual violences, a tendency toward a slight paranoia here or there, usual in children because they feel persecuted by parents constantly, but, oh, really nothing."

They walked down the hall. "I locked the nursery up," explained the father, "and the children broke back into it during the night. I let them stay so they could form the patterns for you to see."

There was a terrible screaming from the nursery.

"There it is," said George Hadley. "See what you make of it."

They walked in on the children without rapping.

The screams had faded. The lions were feeding.

"Run outside a moment, children," said George Hadley. "No, don't change the mental combination. Leave the walls as they are. Get!"

With the children gone, the two men stood studying the lions clustered at a distance, eating with great relish whatever it was they had caught.

"I wish I knew what it was," said George Hadley. "Sometimes I can almost see. Do you think if I brought high-powered binoculars here and—"

David McClean laughed dryly. "Hardly." He turned to study all four walls. "How long has this been going on?"

"A little over a month."

"It certainly doesn't *feel* good."

"I want facts, not feelings."

"My dear George, a psychologist never saw a fact in his life. He only hears about feelings; vague things. This doesn't feel good, I tell you. Trust my hunches and my instincts. I have a nose for something bad. This is very bad. My advice to you is to have the whole damn room torn down and your children brought to me every day during the next year for treatment."

"Is it that bad?"

"I'm afraid so. One of the original uses of these nurseries was so that we could study the patterns left on the walls by the child's mind, study at our leisure, and help the child. In this case, however, the room as become a channel toward—destructive thoughts, instead of a release away from them."

"Didn't you sense this before?"

"I sensed only that you had spoiled your children more than most. And now you're letting them down in some way. What way?"

"I wouldn't let them go to New York."

"What else?"

"I've taken a few machines from the house and threatened them, a month ago, with closing up the nursery unless they did their homework. I did close it for a few days to show I meant business."

"Ah, ha!"

"Does that mean anything?"

"Everything. Where before they had a Santa Claus now they have a Scrooge. Children prefer Santas. You've let this room and this house replace you and your wife in your children's affections. This room is their mother and father, far more important in their lives than their real parents. And now you come along and want to shut it off. No wonder there's hatred here. You can feel it coming out of the sky. Feel that sun. George, you'll have to change your life. Like too many others, you've built it around creature comforts. Why, you'd starve tomorrow if something went wrong in your kitchen. You wouldn't know how to tap an egg. Nevertheless, turn everything off. Start new. It'll take time. But we'll make good children out of bad in a year, wait and see."

"But won't the shock be too much for the children, shutting the room up abruptly, for good?"

"I don't want them going any deeper into this, that's all."

The lions were finished with their red feast.

The lions were standing on the edge of the clearing watching the two men.

"Now *I'm* feeling persecuted," said McClean. "Let's get out of here. I never have cared for these damned rooms. Makes me nervous."

"The lions look real, don't they?" said George Hadley. "I don't suppose there's any way—"

"What?"

"—that they could *become* real?"

"Not that I know."

"Some flaw in the machinery, a tampering or something?"

"No."

They went to the door.

"I don't imagine the room will like being turned off," said the father.

"Nothing ever likes to die—even a room."

"I wonder if it hates me for wanting to switch it off?"

"Paranoia is thick around here today," said David McClean. "You can follow it like a spoor. Hello." He bent and picked up a bloody scarf. "This yours?"

"No." George Hadley's face was rigid. "It belongs to Lydia."

They went to the fuse box together and threw the switch that killed the nursery.

The two children were in hysterics. They screamed and pranced and threw things. They yelled and sobbed and swore and jumped at the furniture.

"You can't do that to the nursery, you can't!"

"Now, children."

The children flung themselves onto a couch, weeping.

"George," said Lydia Hadley, "turn on the nursery, just for a few moments. You can't be so abrupt."

"No."

"You can't be so cruel."

"Lydia, it's off, and it stays off. And the whole damn house dies as of here and now. The more I see of the mess we've put ourselves in, the more it sickens me. We've been contemplating our mechanical, electronic navels for too long. My God, how we need a breath of honest air!"

And he marched about the house turning off the voice clocks, the stoves, the heaters, the shoe shiners, the shoe lacers, the body scrubbers and swabbers and massagers, and every other machine he could put his hand to.

The house was full of dead bodies, it seemed. It felt like a mechanical cemetery. So silent. None of the humming hidden energy of machines waiting to function at the tap of a button.

"Don't let them do it!" wailed Peter at the ceiling, as if he was talking to the house, the nursery. "Don't let Father kill everything." He turned to his father. "Oh, I hate you!"

"Insults won't get you anywhere."

"I wish you were dead!"

"We were, for a long while. Now we're going to really start living. Instead of being handled and massaged, we're going to *live.*"

Wendy was still crying and Peter joined her again. "Just a moment, just one moment, just another moment of nursery," they wailed.

"Oh, George," said the wife, "it can't hurt."

"All right—all right, if they'll only just shut up. One minute, mind you, and then off forever."

"Daddy, Daddy, Daddy!" sang the children, smiling with wet faces.

"And then we're going on a vacation. David McClean is coming back in half an hour to help us move out and get to the airport. I'm going to dress. You turn the nursery on for a minute, Lydia, just a minute, mind you."

And the three of them went babbling off while he let himself be vacuumed upstairs through the air flue and set about dressing himself. A minute later Lydia appeared.

"I'll be glad when we get away," she sighed.

"Did you leave them in the nursery?"

"I wanted to dress too. Oh, that horrid Africa. What can they see in it?"

"Well, in five minutes we'll be on our way to Iowa. Lord, how did we ever get in this house? What prompted us to buy a nightmare?"

"Pride, money, foolishness."

"I think we'd better get downstairs before those kids get engrossed with those damned beasts again."

Just then they heard the children calling, "Daddy, Mommy, come quick—quick!"

They went downstairs in the air flue and ran down the hall. The children were nowhere in sight. "Wendy? Peter!"

They ran into the nursery. The veldtland was empty save for the lions waiting, looking at them. "Peter, Wendy?"

The door slammed.

"Wendy, Peter!"

George Hadley and his wife whirled and ran back to the door.

"Open the door!" cried George Hadley, trying the knob. "Why, they've locked it from the outside! Peter!" He beat at the door. "Open up!"

He heard Peter's voice outside, against the door.

"Don't let them switch off the nursery and the house," he was saying.

Mr. and Mrs. George Hadley beat at the door. "Now, don't be ridiculous, children. It's time to go. Mr. McClean'll be here in a minute and . . ."

And then they heard the sounds.

The lions on three sides of them, in the yellow veldt grass, padding through the dry straw, rumbling and roaring in their throats.

The lions.

Mr. Hadley looked at his wife and they turned and looked back at the beasts edging slowly forward, crouching, tails stiff.

Mr. and Mrs. Hadley screamed.

And suddenly they realized why those other screams had sounded familiar.

▼

"Well, here I am," said David McClean in the nursery doorway. "Oh, hello." He stared at the two children seated in the center of the open glade eating a little picnic lunch. Beyond them was the water hole and the yellow veldtland; above was the hot sun. He began to perspire. "Where are your father and mother?"

The children looked up and smiled. "Oh, they'll be here directly."

"Good, we must get going." At a distance Mr. McClean saw the lions fighting and clawing and then quieting down to feed in silence under the shady trees.

He squinted at the lions with his hand up to his eyes.

Now the lions were done feeding. They moved to the water hole to drink.

A shadow flickered over Mr. McClean's hot face. Many shadows flickered. The vultures were dropping down the blazing sky.

"A cup of tea?" asked Wendy in the silence.

Little Man

Ramsey Campbell

Among the horror writers of the past thirty years, I can't think of one who has written more finely crafted and eerily frightening stories than British author Ramsey Campbell. The author of more than a dozen highly effective chilling novels, Campbell is blessed with the ability to turn an ordinary-seeming situation into something threatening or downright dangerous.

Winner of the World Fantasy Award and the Bram Stoker Award for his fiction, Campbell seems never to tire of creating an endlessly inventive string of tales that make one not want to turn out the light lest sleep—or dreams—invade.

"Little Man," published in 1986, is Campbell at his best. Often he writes about people who aren't terribly confident, or who have some kind of problem which they feel makes them vulnerable. In this story of a boy who is preyed upon by bullies, vengeance seems somehow necessary. The means fits our definition of technohorror all too well.

Despite all his frustrations, Neal didn't go straight to the murder machine. First he played the pinballs, old friends he could make allowances for: Lady Luck and her costive straining to produce a ball, King Pin with his buzzing spastic flipper, Lucky Fruit who tricked you into thinking that your ball had reached the replay lane, until a kink in the wire rail let it slip out of play. He lost on all of them, and was glad he'd left the murder machine until last; it always calmed him.

It was December. A wind shrill as gulls swept up from the beach, along the stubby Bed & Breakfast terraces, and rattled the windows of The Mint. The fairground was closed for the winter; the rides huddled beneath canvas, enormous doughnuts, giant spiders; the track of the roller coaster might have been the skeleton of a dinosaur which had crawled up from the beach to die. All summer Neal had ridden the dragon of the coaster, which had let him look down on people for once. They'd looked as small as the figures in the murder machine.

He pushed his coin into the rusty slot and gripped the sides of the machine. The miniature street—little more than a strip of plywood on which house-fronts were cartooned—was on a level with his face. As he leaned closer to the glass, the machine rocked forward on its lame front leg. Neither the movement nor his coin brought the performers out of hiding. Sometimes they arrived halfway through the show, like actors who'd sneaked out for a drink.

Here came a woman, juddering out of a hole in the left-hand end of the plywood, painted to resemble the mouth of an alley. She was daubed like a tin soldier—red cheeks, orange flesh, staring eyes; the buttons of her red coat were blurred dabs of white paint. A metal stalk protruded between her feet and jerked her along a track.

She was halfway down the street when a door popped open and the man with the knife pounced, dragging her inside. The door twitched shut. Beyond the polythene window a light glared red, and the squealing began, something like a siren, something like a mouse. Neal couldn't see what was happening beyond the crimsoned window, even when he pressed his face against the glass.

The light blinked out, the squealing ran down. That was all: no policeman today. No two performances were the same, which was why the machine fascinated him—but when would it repeat the performance he was sure he'd once seen?

He stood back, rubbing the rusty stains from his hands. The sounds of the arcade came flooding back: the giggles of a little girl who was riding a mechanical turtle, the worn-out gunfire of an electronic rifle range, the unsteady tape of rock music, doggedly repeating itself. Again the world was bigger than he was—and it included school.

This year school was worse than ever. Half the masters seemed to delight in humiliating him, pretending they couldn't see him when he was standing up. "Where's that wild guess coming from? Oh, *there* you are." Some were cruel without meaning to be: the English master who'd persuaded him to appear in the end-of-term play, and even Neal's best friend Jim. "Come on, Conan," Jim said. "It's about time you came to the disco."

The disco was beside the promenade. Gulls swooped over the dark beach, their cries sharp as splintered ice, sharp as the creases of Neal's trousers. He wondered why he'd bothered to dress carefully, for the interior of the disco was chaotic with lights and darkness. When the girls approached he wondered why he'd bothered to come at all.

"Brought your little brother?" one shouted at Jim above the bombardment of music.

"Don't be funny, Di. This is my friend Neal. Karen, this is Neal."

"Hello down there," Karen said.

When the girls danced away Neal said, "I'm going."

▼

Jim persuaded him to stay and found a partner whose friend let Neal buy her a Coke, then another, while he put off the moment when they would have to dance. Eventually they did, her lit chin hovering above him like a UFO, and he could tell that she'd taken pity on him. He left as soon as he could, hating himself.

If The Mint hadn't been closed for the night he would have gone straight to the machine. As he stalked home his surroundings looked like shrunken cartoons of themselves, hardly convincing: the locked fairground and Crazy Golf, the terraces that claimed to be full of hotels. Whenever he felt like this he seemed to be viewing the world through glass, a barrier that walled him into himself, and now that he'd reached puberty the barrier was more difficult to break.

It was no wonder. Apart from everything else, each rehearsal increased his dread of the end-of-term play. Why had he let himself be roped in? So that the English master would be on his side? He would pretend to be ill, except that his parents would know he was faking. They had enough to worry about now that two of the families who always stayed in the guest house were going abroad next summer. "You show them," his mother had cried when he'd told her about the play. All he was likely to show the audience, he thought bitterly as he slammed the ball into Lady Luck, was how much of a fool he was.

At least the murder machine distracted him. He couldn't time the performances, since he had no watch, but often the arcade seemed to recede, leaving him alone with the machine, for hours. Sometimes a policeman dragged the man in black into a doorway beneath a sketch of a police station's lamp. He was only pretending to drag him—his hand wasn't even touching the murderer's collar—and Neal imagined that as soon as they vanished beyond the door, the man in black dealt with him.

But what did the man in black do? Once, seconds after the scarlet woman had veered into his room, his door twitched ajar. Neal pressed his forehead against the glass. Murderer and victim were standing absolutely still—the man's eggshell face was turned toward Neal, the lifeless pinprick eyes and the mouth like a cut just starting to bleed—yet Neal had the impression that he'd stopped whatever he'd been doing. As the door snapped shut, he glimpsed red notches deep in the back of the woman's neck and in her left wrist.

That reminded him of something someone had once told him. Had it been his grandfather? What exactly had he said? He was no longer alive to be asked. Neal found himself trying to remember in class, the masters' voices receding, calling him back with questions he couldn't answer. "Use your little head," one master told him. Even the sarcasm couldn't reach him; the looming memory preoccupied him—until the end of term, until the play.

As soon as he emerged onto the stage, among the heaps of polystyrene and tinsel that were meant to look like snow, his heart sank. "There you are, Imp," said the pantomime magician, who was two years older than Neal. Neal's parents were sitting in the front row—his mother emitting small dismayed cries at any risqué jokes, his father frowning down at his fingernails—and so Neal had to scurry about squeaking and pretend he was enjoying it, while he was thinking: scuttle, scuttle, like a rat. He was sure the audience was laughing at him, not with him.

"You were the best," his mother cried afterward. His father nodded gruffly, not looking at him. Neal was glad to get away from them, but before he reached the dressing room he came face to face with Roger. Roger, who bad a patchy mustache which failed to hide his pimples, often bullied Neal. "Hello, imp," he sneered.

"Sod off." Roger's pasty face reddened and began to quiver. "Don't you tell me to sod off," he said, grabbing Neal with hands like bunches of raw sausage. Neal kicked him viciously on the shin, leaving him howling. "I'll get you for that after Christmas, you little bastard."

Lashing out had relieved Neal's tension, but not enough. He was ready for the murder machine, too much on edge to dawdle over the pinballs. All along the main street, shops were for sale; the circus posters that patched their windows shivered in the wind from the beach. Even the survivors—gift shops full of plastic and cardboard, fish and chip shops called The Chef's, Maxim's, Café de Paris—were dark. The dusty window of the Midland Café was sown with dozens of dead flies.

Neal reached The Mint and halted, his fists and feet clenching. A little girl and her parents were at his machine. Slamming open the glass doors of The Mint didn't scare them off. He flounced over to King Pin and stood muttering, too impatient to catch the balls with the flippers. No doubt the family thought he was cursing the pinball, not the girl. She seemed to embody all his frustrations; his resentment was scraping his nerves, resentment harsh as the miserly clicking of the fruit machines, the clicking that grew vicious in his ears, and louder. When she screamed, his first reaction was to smile.

She shrank away from the machine and held up her hands, which were smeared red. Behind her, Neal saw, the murderer's door was wide open. Before he could glimpse what was happening beyond, it snapped shut. If her parents hadn't been there he would have demanded to know what she'd seen, but they were ushering her out. "It's only paint," her mother said, which seemed further to upset the little girl. "Damned disgusting way to run a business," said the father, wondering perhaps where the paint had come from.

Though he hadn't had time to see into the murderer's room, Neal didn't resent the machine, it had got rid of the little girl, after all. The man's blank face with its pinhole eyes seemed friendly, the face of a beloved old toy. When the scarlet woman jerked into view, Neal observed that there were no red grooves in her neck or her wrist. He didn't understand, but he was prepared to wait for understanding.

Soon it was Christmas. His gifts came from The Money Spinner, one of the gift shops—a jigsaw, some pencils that changed color halfway through. His parents could afford only a dwarfish turkey, and his mother stiffened when he helped himself to a second mince pie. VACANCY said the sign in their front window, which was how the house felt for the rest of the holidays. Perhaps one day he would live somewhere that didn't make him feel so small.

He went for walks along the coast road. At low tide, sea and sand and clouds were bare elongated strips. Splinters of pale green sky were set into the clouds. The miles of flat narrow road were deserted except for gulls, some of which perched like vultures on the wastebins above the beach. He could almost see a figure in black in the distance, dodging along the road from bin to concrete bin, where litter writhed feebly in the wind. His grandfather had described something like that figure once, but why should Neal think he needed to visualize it clearly? For nights he was unable to sleep until he tired himself out with his efforts. Once, at the start of a dream, the figure jerked toward him, and he would have seen its face if the shrieks of gulls, disturbed by something on the coast road, hadn't wakened him. He was still trying to grasp it, no longer even wondering why he should, when the spring term began by confronting him with Roger.

Roger was gripping the rusty railings of the schoolyard as if they were spears. "Imp, imp, imp," he sputtered, like an engine trying to start. "I've been waiting for you, Imp. I've got something to give you tonight, behind the sheds."

"Leave him alone," Jim said. "Pick on someone your own size."

In some ways Neal was glad he'd intervened, for if it came to a fight between himself and Roger he knew he had no chance. But Roger sneered, "What are you afraid of, little boy? Afraid you won't be able to grow up?"

"Come on, Conan. Don't let him rile you."

"Just stop calling me that," Neal shouted. Suddenly he hated both of them. He stalked into the school, where Roger could do nothing.

All day Neal's mind and body felt as though they were seething. Every few minutes he had to wipe his hands down the sides of his desk. Yes, he would fight Roger; he'd kick him in the groin, as Jim had told him they did in the films. Suppose he missed? Roger would grab his leg and break it, he'd throw him down and kick his ribs in, stamp on his face—

"Wake up, Imp. didn't you hear the question?" The master looked bored, unaware of any sarcasm; Neal was the Imp and that was all there was to it. At four o'clock, almost blind with self-disgust, Neal walked away from the school so quickly he might as well have been running.

▼

The streets were cartoons, hardly even two-dimensional. Nothing was real except him and his thoughts. The sounds of The Mint fell away, leaving him alone with his friend. Murderer and victim disappeared into the room. Was there a shadow on the polythene window, a shadow that looked to be slicing and sawing? When the lights in the machine went out Neal lingered, imagining the tiny black-eyed face waiting in the dark, though it didn't seem so tiny once the dark grew as large as his feelings.

He had no idea how long he stood in front of the machine, nor what he was thinking. One thing was sure: that night he didn't think of Roger. He slept soundly, free of dreams. Next morning Jim told him that Roger had been knocked down on the coast road. He'd stepped in front of the car without looking, though he should have seen it coming hundreds of yards away; nobody could tell what had distracted him. Jim stared, then walked away, as Neal grinned.

Let him go: Neal didn't need him. Everyone had better watch out now, even Jim, if that was his attitude. The sarcasm of the masters no longer bothered Neal; the more they taunted him, he felt, the worse it would be for them, though he didn't examine why he thought so.

His sense of security lasted until the night he went to see John Travolta in *Carrie*.

The Grand, which stood at the far end of the promenade, hadn't lived up to its name for years. Its ocher frontage looked built of sand, and ready to crumble. Ghosts of pre-war prices clung to the glass of the paybox. The manager stood at the top of the steps to the foyer; the knees and elbows of his dress suit were shiny as his toecaps. "About turn," he said to Neal. "This isn't for kids."

Neal's lips felt stiff and swollen, almost paralyzed. "I was eighteen last month."

"Aye, and I'm John Travolting. Scuttle away now, scuttle away." What made it worse was that he'd just let in two girls who Neal knew were barely fourteen, younger than himself. Worse yet, they were with Roger, who was hobbling boastfully on crutches. Crowing at Neal, the three vanished into the cinema.

Long before he reached The Mint he could see the shadow on the murderer's window, could hear the manager squealing in the tiny room. The shops on the main street were closed and dark, the bare road was the colour of ice on a pond; worn patches of light lay beneath the streetlamps. He was too deep in himself to wonder at first why there were new dummies in a shop that had been closed for months.

They weren't dummies, nor were they inside the window. They were four youths, absolutely still and silent except for the leathery creaking of their motorcycle gear. Were they waiting for him to turn his back before they pounced? Sweat stung him like lit matches.

As soon as he'd walked past, his neck and his limbs feeling stiff as china, they began to follow him. They still made no sound except for the creaking leather. He didn't dare to run, for they could certainly outrun him, but if a single shop had been unlocked he might have dodged aside. Here at last was The Mint, but even that was no refuge. One stopped the door from closing with the metal toecap of his boot, and they crowded in after Neal.

"At least something's open in this frigging town," one said loudly. They must have driven along the coast, expecting the fairground to be open. They quickly grew intolerant of the eccentricities of the pinballs; one kicked Lady Luck as though that would tame her. Neal stood guarding the murder machine, which he didn't want to play while they were there, in case they came to watch.

The tallest of them sauntered over. "Go on, kid, put your money in if you're going to." Neal could say nothing, and the youth shoved him aside. "Let someone else have a go, then."

Neal tried to push him away from the machine. Blood rushed to his head, which felt in danger of bursting. His lips were huge and parched. "It's mine," he spluttered.

"Hey, look at this. He wants a fight." The youth picked Neal up easily, and holding him like a ventriloquist's dummy, talked for him in a shrill mechanical voice. "It's mine! It's mine!"

"That's enough." It was Mr. Old, who ran The Mint. "Put him down and get out, the four of you, or I'll call the police."

"Go on then," the leader said, dropping Neal so as to menace Mr. Old, "call the bloody police."

"That's exactly what I intend to do. You get away while you can, Neal. Run along now, go *on!*"

Neal could scarcely walk; his limbs were spastic with rage. He jerked along the street, looking for something to smash. Why couldn't it be the leader of the motorcylists? When he saw the four emerging from The Mint, without a police car in sight, he fled. That night he lay sleepless for hours, punching the pillow in blind fury, clawing convulsively at the blankets.

In the morning he managed to control his rage, telling himself that tonight he would be alone with the machine. He'd play it until it showed him what he wanted to see, he vowed to himself, what had been troubling him since before Christmas.

Perhaps it was the vow that let him remember at last.

That afternoon one master was discussing local history: how the town had been built as a seaside resort for the Lancashire industrial towns, how it was dying of cheap Spanish holidays. Who could tell him about the history of the town? Suddenly Neal could, and blurted it out as it came to him. "There was the man who started killing people when he came home from the first world war. He used to cut them up and leave the bits along the coast road. When the police caught him finally he tried to pretend he just had his hands in his pockets, only they weren't *his* hands."

"No need to sound so pleased about it. I should try to put it out of your mind if I were you," the master said, and called on someone else, leaving Neal feeling guilty and furious because he did. He'd been pleased about remembering, he told himself, and then he wondered if it would make a difference to the machine. Perhaps he would be able to make out what happened in the reddened room, now that he knew what he was looking for.

No, it would not. That was clear as soon as he came in sight of The Mint and saw the pavement outside, littered with broken glass. Every machine was wrecked. The murder machine was a tangle of metal and plywood and jagged glass, amid which he could see no figures at all. He didn't need to ask who had done all this: he could hear their motorcycles roaring along the beach.

He trudged down to the promenade, with not the least idea of what he meant to do. Again he felt crippled by rage. Above the sea the moon hung, a plate whose pattern looked worn and blurred. At the distant edge of the sea, against the dim glittering of the waves, the motorcycles raced back and forth. "You bastards," Neal screamed.

The riders heard him. Now it was fear that crippled his legs. The cycles roared like animals which knew they had trapped their prey. The cycle with the tallest rider reared up and came for Neal. He watched helplessly as it raced toward him, leaving a track pale as a snail's on the sand. The way the cycle grew as it sped closer seemed unreal as a dream, from which he wouldn't waken until it crashed into him. Even if he ran now, the rider would catch him long before he reached the houses. Nevertheless he tried to run, struggled to move his feet—just one and he'd be running. He was still fighting his paralysis when the rider leapt from the motorcycle.

For a moment Neal thought that he'd flung the cycle aside so as to grab him, then that the cycle had collided with a piece of driftwood lying on the beach, driftwood which had sprung up from the collision. But no, the dark shape wasn't wood, for it bounded over to the fallen rider, its movements stiff and jerky against the glittering of the waves. Confused, Neal thought it might be another of the cyclists—surely it must be a helmet, not the head, that looked pale as the moon—but only until it stooped to the groaning youth. Its movements were more assured now, the sawing of its right hand back and forth. Though the scene looked like a pantomime performed by dolls beside a toy motorcycle, the screams were appallingly human.

Neal ran from the coast road, afraid to look back. The streets were unreal, aloof from him, isolating him with his panic. The terraces of houses locked him out. Only the moon was menacingly vivid, a pale sketch of a face playing hide and seek with him among the houses.

By the time he reached home he was wheezing. He slammed the rusty gate behind him and stumbled along the few yards of path. He struggled to turn the key in the front door. Whatever had happened on the beach, it was nothing to do with him. He was home now, safe. The white face behind him was only the moon.

But there was a rusty movement, which might have been the gate—and a scraping voice, small but growing. "What shall we do next?" it said.

Screens

JOHN SHIRLEY

In the late 1970s, John Shirley leaped into the science fiction scene, writing stories that challenged the established limits of the field. Shirley considered himself "punk" at the time, and backed up his claims with a number of high-octane stories and his first novel, *City Come A-Walking,* a science-fantasy that many feel was a precursor to the "cyberpunk" movement of the early 1980s.

"Screens," from 1989, is a complex tale that takes one of the original new-age ideas—space colonies—and uses it as a taking-off point for a suspenseful story that deals simultaneously with a number of hot-button issues of the last quarter-century: pollution, mind control, television, cults. Despite this broad agenda, "Screens" works very effectively as technohorror, though the way in which it is horrific might not be immediately apparent. With elements reminiscent of films such as *Logan's Run, Silent Running,* and *Mad Max,* "Screens" is still completely original, and ultimately a powerfully dramatic story of human survival against terrible odds.

Out there the air is toxic; the land is nearly barren. The sky, even at noon, is the bruised color of mud at a city dump. The oozing plain has the sheen of a puddle coated with gasoline: a slick of diseased rainbows. It would eat away my skin if I were to step into it unprotected.

In here, it's safe, stainless, warm, shaded in amicable colors, with clean air and plenty of food and room to stroll.

I'm leaving here forever, and I'm going out there.

Into the murk that twitches, from time to time, with the clumsy movement of the subhumans. I'm going out there when I conclude this log. This is the final entry, my last tape record, my assessment of conditions on Earth at the date of my return.

I was born about 250 years ago, in Austin, Texas. I should have died around, I suppose, 140 years ago. I wish I had. If I hadn't married Freda, I would have.

▼

I met Freda Gunderson at Solarsong Farm, in New Mexico. It was winter when we met. More than two centuries ago. In the spring of that year, she asked me to marry her.

The desert, unfolding beyond the adobe walls of the Hackman hacienda grounds, was stippled soft orange and blue with cactus flowers. Near the balcony a mellow wind stirred one of the palms that Hackman had transplanted, so that it nodded like a drunk musician over a piano.

In nightgown and bathrobe, Freda and I were sitting at the second-floor terrace, overlooking the thoroughly irrigated garden, listening to the shuss of the sprinklers, the chatter of some desert bird who'd happened on this oasis and couldn't believe his luck.

Freda's red-gold hair and fair skin and blue eyes seemed an extension of the garden, to me; the arc of her full breasts in the filmy blue negligee was in thematic concordance with the great arc of the planet around us. We held hands and sipped tea, and all the trivial things we said seemed to brim over with the significance of intimacy. OK, sure: I was in love.

And I was impressed with her. Freda was an arcological scientist, with master's degrees in botany, zoology, and climatology. Most people are lucky to have one master's. Freda, at thirty-four, had three. But then, she'd graduated from high school at thirteen years old.

"It's good to see you happy this morning, Ricky," she said. "You're moody, most of the time." Her English was perfect, but her faint Swedish accent clung to her talk like some intoxicating ethnic perfume.

"I'm moody? I guess it's this place. It's a little too perfect here. Maybe a little too civilized for me. And Glass's people—" I glanced down at the glinting lozenge of the huge greenhouse, a hundred yards away, on the far side of the mansion's grounds. "—watch us all the time." You could see out from the greenhouse, but you couldn't see in. They had long-range surveillance cameras there, I knew. And they set watches on us when we walked about the grounds or went into town. "Daniel Glass is security paranoid."

"I know what you mean," she said diplomatically. "But I think you and Glass have more in common than you like to admit. You both love the Gaia. The natural world. Glass is a poet, too."

I winced, remembering Glass's poetry, recited after one of his Vibratory Sermons. Some ghastly Castaneda-ish number about the Cactus Spirits Holding Up The Sky. Mawkish stuff. My analytical left-brained Freda wouldn't know good poetry if it nibbled her earlobe.

"Glass is a poet *technically,*" I said. "But mostly what he is—" I hesitated, conscious that we were probably being recorded, and then plunged recklessly on, "—is a despot. A puppeteer. He's got Hackman in his pocket. He makes us sit on those New Age cushions while he preaches his New Age drivel—not only drivel but fifteen years out-dated—about merging into a new society of 'vibratory harmony.' Preaching self-denial and screwing half the women in the project—The guy is a classic *cult leader.* Going to lead us all to the promised land in the sky."

"The Starsong colony is not Glass's idea. It was Dr. Branheimer's. And Papa's."

"That's the point, Freda." I let go of her hand and brushed my hair out of my eyes. My thick black hair had grown long and unruly, and I'd let my beard grow. Freda's father, Dr. Gunderson, didn't approve of my style. He wasn't enthusiastic about Freda's romance with a liberal arts major, anyway. "Glass has co-opted your father's ideas." I glanced to the east, where the sun had just risen over the big geodesic dome that was the Arcology Model, the self-sustaining ecological unit that the project wanted to replicate in the L-5 orbit. I could see one of the guards from the Glass family crossing the lawns between the dome and the hacienda-styled mansion that Hackman had given over to the project personnel. The guard was a long way off, but I could make out the glint of his tacky golden-sun medallion, with its green-glass center; I could imagine his tightly beatific smile, which never wavered as he checked in with the other guards on his 'fone, using code names like Laser and Aurora and Icemelt. Every one of them a former junkie or acidhead or near schizophrenic basket case that Glass had put back together in his own preferred reconstruction; making them utterly dedicated to the American-born guru.

"It's useless to complain about Glass. Hackman adores him. And the project is all Hackman's money and the money of Hackman's business associates. Half a billion dollars of it. Glass is part of the project to stay." She stood up, came around the table to sit by me, to take my hands. Something about the thought-out formalism of the act rang a warning bell in my head. "Ricky . . . while you were in Santa Fe, they made a decision. Glass has convinced them to move up the date of the final launch. We're going to the colony—I mean, the project is going. Soon. Next July. A little over a year." Stricken by the implications, I stared at her. She went on hastily, "You can go with us, Ricky."

"Come off it. I'd be dead weight. I'm a literary academic. Useless! Just another guy pawing through the Lake poets, and Whitman, Jeffers, Blake—and Yeats and Byron when they were feeling close to nature. *Those* are my people. I don't belong on a space colony. I'm not technophilic enough. And Glass would never tolerate me—he knows how I feel about him."

"You've helped this project a lot," she said earnestly, looking me in the eyes. "You wrote the best promotional material; it helped us get a lot of backers. You know a bit about environmental science, you're willing to work in the land—Dr. Branheimer said you were a lot of help in the greenhouse—and if you were to marry me, that would make it definite. They would *have* to let you come."

"Me. Sure . . . Freda, I don't *want* to go. I like the idea of the arcology in the sky. I like the chance to preserve a lot of plant species and animal species, away from the acid rains. But I don't want to *live* there. There's another way—you can stay here on Earth and work to save it. With me."

"I can't, darling. I just cannot. It would break my father's heart. And I have given my life to this. It is what my father and I always planned for. I have to go. If you love me, you'll go with me. We can come back sometime, Ricky . . . "

But we never did.

We were married two days later. And two *years* later—it took them a year longer than they expected—we took the shuttle to the low-orbit station, and then took one of Hackman's new freighters to the Starsong colony in the L-5 orbit. The colony was, as I knew it would be, cramped, malodorous, gravitationally inconsistent, and an endless prescription for work that was never quite filled.

It was growing, though. Module by module, it expanded into the void. And after a year and a half of murderously tedious work, of enduring the claustrophobic stink of pressure suits, and after losing two men and a woman to faulty sealants in the EVA units . . . it was beginning to pay off. The colony's garden in space was thriving and we were starting to manufacture the zero-g gimcracks that Hackman had hoped would make his money back for him. The pressure was easing. We decided to give ourselves a holiday . . .

Glass didn't share our optimism. Glass, in fact, didn't share anything with us but what he had to. The rest of the time he holed up in his dorm section with his toadies. He hadn't found paradise on the colony, and he sure as hell hadn't converted any new followers; worse, he'd had to actually *work*. And he was convinced the U.S. government—which had in fact tried to stop the project, claiming it was "uncontrollable and dangerous" —was out to get him. So when Hackman announced that he'd authorized a couple of senators to come up and check us out, Glass decided they were spies for the Pentagon. "The Pentagon wants to take us over so it can launch a first strike against the PanArabic Republic from here!" Glass raved. "They'll make the colony into an orbital missile base! They'll start World War III!"

We laughed at him.

So Glass simply appeared on the colony's TV monitors one morning, announcing that we had to make "the ultimate sacrifice" in order to "prevent the fascists from destroying life on Earth!"

Glass—forgive me—had cracked. To be fair, Earth was experiencing a vigorous political upheaval just then because of the Famine . . . What was going on below us was enough to make anyone believe the end of the world was coming. Because it was.

You know about the Famine? Maybe you don't—no telling when anyone's going to hear this. The Famine came because . . .

It came because in the twentieth century we thought we had plenty of time to deal with the air pollution problem. The atmosphere was vast, and we were cutting back on pollution. A little. But that thinking reckoned without synergistic reactions. It assumed that the wild variety of random chemicals released into the atmosphere would just sort of float around harmlessly. Stupid thinking. Some of them reacted with one another, and with other environmental factors. We should have seen it coming in the 1980s, when sulfur dioxide and other chemicals combined to form acid rain, began gnawing at the biosphere . . .

But it was in the year 2018 that the sky fell apart.

The phenomenon hit the news media a week after Freda and I moved to the colony. It started with the catalyst. Terranoxin was a compound released into the air by a variety of industrial polluters. By itself, Terranoxin was not found to have a negative environmental impact; but a dissolution of the ozone layer had radically increased ultraviolet radiation. And Terranoxin, exposed to UV radiation, experienced a synergistic reaction that boosted it into a catalytic compound capable of runaway instability. It formed a slick on plant surfaces, which forged a long chain of inert molecules binding oxygen and nitrogen into itself. Essentially, it ate the oxygen and nitrogen produced by living things. Carbon dioxide continued to be produced, but oxygen and nitrogen weren't. The reaction *began* small—but a catalyst will work through its medium and survive; a catalyst is capable of expanding exponentially. We had succeeded in making pollution that made pollution. Pollution that reproduced. The atmosphere's ability to absorb and filter pollution was overwhelmed and quickly became irrelevant.

Oxygen and nitrogen were rapidly diminishing; the air was becoming unbreathable. Animals died; the food chain was shattered. People moved into narrower and narrower enclaves of breathable air. Great hurricanes of poisonous air swept over the land, smothering whole cities. The disruption turned cropland into dust bowls. Oxidation of ocean-dumped organic wastes and the pernicious action of pesticides worked with Terranoxin to destroy the oxygen-production capability of the seas.

The world moved indoors. The urban domes were hastily thrown up—and many were almost as quickly torn down in the riots. Only the wealthy could afford a healthy diet, even in the U.S. And the consequent stress on the planet's social systems generated massive political strife. Sure, Glass: it was easy to be paranoid.

Glass—with his pinpoint pupils, his shaven head, his anorexia—had always been a paranoid, manipulating his followers with a masterful paternalism to close ranks around him. To be an extension of him, a buffer against the world.

So I can't say I was surprised when Glass opened the air locks, and sabotaged the life-support seals.

I was doing a systems check on the escape pods when it happened. I was the only one near enough to use them. I heard the others screaming through the intercom. It was more horrible hearing it filtered. It was like they had a big mechanical hand clamped over their mouths. I thought: *Get into a pressure suit; find Freda.*

That's when I saw the suits. Slashed. Glass had been ready for this for a while.

The air was going. Understand that. *The air was going.* Freda was on the other side of the colony, working in the agribubble. The instruments told me it was one of the first sections to become a vacuum. She was a goner.

There was nothing I could do. I tell myself that all the time.

I was numb. Mechanically, I got into the escape pod. I set it for ejection, and I hit the switch that would put me in suspended animation until I was picked up and rescued.

As the gas put me under, I realized that the pod's ejection system had been sabotaged. It should have launched immediately. Eventually, the suspended animation would reach its limits . . . So I was going to die, too. The guilt that had frozen my nerves melted away. I was flooded with relief. I was going to die with Freda, after all.

That was all right with me.

▼

The suspension gas is supposed to preserve you for about three hundred years. Theoretically. Some people claim it'd work for only a few decades. No one had had a chance to test it out. I've got news for the skeptics.

I don't know why the pod ejected from the dead hulk of the colony, after more than two hundred years. Maybe a meteor strike, jarring some damaged mechanism into action. Or a long-term effect of radiation on the pod's launch systems. I don't know. But . . .

After two hundred years the escape pod launched itself.

▼

Their orbital drones, maintaining the city's solar-power transmission stations, picked up the pod's signal and brought it down. More or less automatically. Nothing humane about it. They put me down a few miles outside the city, where the airport used to be.

I didn't stir from the pod for a couple of days. I'd used almost no measurable oxygen in suspension, so there was a few days' worth left. I spent them feeling like a warmed-over corpse, which was maybe what I was. I *looked* OK—but I had mental images of old horror movies I'd seen as a kid. George Romero stuff about walking corpses. Rotting faces. That was my self image for those two days.

Still, I sucked down the electrolytic solution, I ate the mash, and when I could make myself work, I repaired the pressure suits. Looking out the ports, I saw the acid ooze, the nightmare sky; could see that the atmosphere was pitting the pod's window glass. Maybe it wasn't Earth.

But when the weather cleared, I saw the pale, familiar face of the moon, like the dying face of a sick old man. And I saw the curving gleam of the dome, rising smudged and segmented, at the horizon. Big as a mountain.

Kansas City.

A grief. A terrible grief that could not be encompassed by any poetry I could fashion. Beyond the sick grief and horror of a mother who has missed her child for days, and finds his body broken and rotted in her own well, and wonders how long he'd suffered down there . . . Past the grief of a man who realizes that, through his own bumbling, self-indulgence, he has infected his wife and newborn baby with AIDS. Even more than grief for Freda. Grief for a planet.

They hadn't found a way to contain or reverse the catalyst. Or if they did, it came too late.

Protected, for a while, by the pressure suit, I slogged through the bogs toward the dome. The sky was a ceiling of cobwebs. I remembered some lines from Gerard Manley Hopkins:

Generations have trod, have trod, have trod;
And all is seared with trade; bleared, smeared with toil,
And wears man's smudge and shares man's smell: the soil
is bare now, nor can foot feel, being shod.

And for all this, nature is never spent;
There lives the dearest freshness deep down things;
And though the last lights off the black West went
Oh, morning at the brown brink eastward springs—

But that was the bitterest drink at the wake: Hopkins was wrong. There would be no morning at the brown brink eastward. They had killed the world, finally. Or the world as I knew it. There was life here, of a sort, in the poisonous ooze. But it was life the way obscene doggerel on a bathroom wall is poetry.

And Freda was dead. I wanted to be dead, too.

Maybe it was curiosity. Maybe it was the faint hope that they might have preserved something green and something feathered under the dome. There might be many such areas of preservation; they might be, ironically, terraforming the Earth somewhere.

I used to have a fair torch for hope in me. It was down to a pilot light on a grimy gas oven now. But it still burned.

The air lock was a man-high square panel flush with the dome. I cleaned away some of the gunk that clung to the lower part of the dome; read the blocky, flaking lettering: KANSAS CITY: ARLK 56.

I had radioed to them, and received no reply. Perhaps my radio was faulty, or they weren't monitoring those frequencies anymore. Or perhaps they didn't care if I died out there.

But the air lock opened, sliding creakily aside. I stepped into a featureless chamber of milky plastic walls. Startlingly pristine, after the bogs. The lock sealed behind me. Poisonous air drained away; breathable air hissed in. A green arrow flashed overhead. I unscrewed the helmet. Brassy smells. Plastic. Detergent.

A ball of warmth expanded in me. I was going to see someone alive! Maybe there'd be a welcoming committee and a big to-do. Fine. Let them paw me, gape at me, tear my clothing for souvenirs. It was all human contact. It was healthy life. It was a stinging reply to the flat gray hopelessness I'd crossed through on my way here. I needed human contact.

The smooth, waxy wall dilated an opening. Beyond was a long, empty hallway. They had to decontaminate me. I followed the hallway to its end: a shower room where a gray uniform hung on a peg.

I stripped and showered. I could smell a disinfectant in the water. Germ-killing ultraviolet lights came on in the ceiling as I dried. I dressed in the uniform: soft, durable paper of some kind. I felt it contract to conform to my shape as I zipped it up.

Padding down the hall in my soft gray slippers, I came to an elevator. The doors parted. Something within was examining me. It was a dull chrome sphere about two feet in diameter, with two knobs at opposite poles, either side. It rolled toward me like a beach ball. I had the distinct impression it was observing me.

Was this all that was left? The automatons of the place? Had the inhabitants died and left their robots to eternally maintain the empty city as a pointless monument to them?

I took a deep breath to calm myself. "I'm Richard Gale Mazursky. From the Starsong colony. I've been in suspended animation—according to the suspension computer in the escape unit, it was, uh, for more than two centuries. Look—can you take me to a . . . a person?

It rolled back into the elevator. I accompanied it, and we rode silently down many, many levels.

We arrived at another bland corridor, pale blue walls, the ceiling faintly glowing, plush white synthetic rug. Muzak was playing from somewhere; so homogenized I couldn't make out any definite tune. I accompanied the machine through an archway into a simple apartment. A room, fifteen paces to a side, containing soft dun rectangular couches, slots in one wall, and a toilet. A large screen on the wall was lit, and on it, waiting, was a ?. A question mark. A big black one. Followed by an old photo of myself. It had been taken not long before I went up to the Starsong colony. It was a blowup of my small corner of a group photo, a publicity shot of the project planners. My expression was rueful, faintly impatient; beside me, all that was visible of Freda was her shoulder. My gut contracted, and I looked at the floor. "Yeah, that's me. Or was me."

I looked up at the screen as a picture of the colony appeared. Then an X was marked over it. And a question mark.

"Yeah. It's gone. I'm pretty sure I'm the only survivor. Was I right? Is it a couple of centuries since I went under?"

A + appeared on the screen. A plus. Positive. Meaning affirmative.

A picture of a food tube appeared on the screen, and then a question mark.

I wasn't hungry. Moths with razor wings jittered in my stomach. "No, thanks. Look, I mean it this time—*I want to see some people."*

The silver ball rolled out the door behind me. There was no way to shut the door. It was only a slice out of the wall.

▼

There they were. People. And a big luminous gray-white screen. The screen filled half the wall and dominated the room. The other three walls were gentle pastels of blue, green, and yellow; everything I was to see was done in the same reductionistic simplicity. No decor, a few cushions. On these were four people with their backs to me.

They were dressed in bright colors, and their clothing was jump-suit-style like mine, but with no two cut precisely alike. The primary colors of their clothes bled as if tie-dyed, spreading out from the centerline of the body. It reminded me of a fad that had been going before Freda and I left Earth. Kirlian clothing. It responded to your bioelectric field, and changed colors, eventually set in color patterns that were supposed to be distinctive to you. Their hairstyles were similar—sort of pixie-ish, sort of pageboy-ish, but each was faintly distinct.

Their eyes were fixed on the screen, rapt but placid, as if listening with great respect, though the image was soundless.

I was afraid to speak at first, to break the pervading sense of rapport. The ambience was fragile with it. I felt as if I were intruding on a church service.

What was I doing here? Maybe I was a bad memory, to these people.

But I needed them. The hunger in my hands made my fingers tremble for human touch; the hunger in my lips burned for conversation. "Uh—hi. I'm . . . excuse me, the robot brought me here . . . I'm Richard Mazursky."

No reaction. The chrome ball rolled out of the room, and I had the odd feeling I was left alone. The people on the couches hadn't moved, hadn't acknowledged my speech. Were they deaf? Were they—

I saw the girl blink. The young man with silky blond hair shifted his pose slightly.

Maybe I was being snubbed because I had violated some arcane rule of etiquette.

I looked at the screen. It was the only light source. A soft silvery light. For the first time I took in the image. Four rubbery gray cubes marching on a naked, gelatinous gray plain, one after the other. The cubes weren't exactly alike. One had a notch. Another had a crater in it. Another had a knob and a notch . . . Approaching from the horizon's vanishing point, a procession of white rubber cones slid over the ground, five of them to the cube's four. The procession of cubes intersected the path of the cones. The cubes stopped as if pitched up against a brick wall; then the cones stopped. The cubes turned red, the cones green.

"They win," the woman said, in a pleasant voice. Not too toneless, not too expressive.

"Yes, I said, clearing my throat. "Evidently the, ah, cones have won. I think. Anyone care to instruct me in the significance of this? Is it, um, religious?"

I'd spoken extra loudly. No one so much as twitched.

I was shaking. "You people have a visitor from two centuries in the past every day? I mean, didn't your systems inform you? I just heard you speak English, and this is Kansas, Toto . . . You wouldn't get that, I don't suppose . . . Look—just direct me to the nearest park. Or greenhouse. Something. I want to know that something green survived. I *need* to know that . . . "

No response. I looked at the screen. The image had changed. I saw something that looked like a pincushion, waving its pins frantically. Nearby it, three spindles amoebically merged to become a larger spindle, birthing a sphere—it made my eyes hurt. When I looked away, I could still see the images for a moment, tenuous as flashbulb blurs.

I knelt beside the girl. "Can you hear me?" I whispered. No reaction. Chin propped in hands, she lay on her stomach, her legs closed and straight out behind her. A slightly Asiatic cast to her skin and eyes, the shape of her face. There was a flush in her cheeks, and her brown eyes were shining. She seemed healthy, alert. I wanted to touch her. Just to feel the life in her. To know that the world wasn't dead.

No, I told myself. You'd probably commit a solecism if you touched her. This could be a religious ritual of some kind.

She blinked, because it was time for her to blink. Her eyes followed the jockeying procession of cones, spheres, cusps, the shifts in color on the screen. The digital images were reflected in perfect miniature in her eyes.

I reached out a hand to her cheek, my fingers trembling so near I could feel her body heat on the tips. I snatched the hand back.

Wait. I sat back, arms around upraised knees, and waited. Sometimes I watched the screen or the roiling shadows it threw on the bare walls. But the images, though simplistic, were disturbing. Their tenacity in repeated patterns of mobility, their gelatinous activity—something about it suggested living beings. I pressed my face into my knees, and waited.

Hours sifted by. When I became aware that the room was darkening, I looked up. The screen was blank except for four shivering green patterns running the width of the screen. Wavelength patterns. Up and down, up and down. EEGs, I supposed. The four strangers were asleep, lying on their cushions.

Swallowing my frustration, I stretched out on a cushion. After a while I slept. My dreams were blank.

▼

The increased light from the screen woke me. The screen showed four snaking cylinders—each slightly distinct from the others—circling the rubbery gray-white pincushion, with its mass of out-thrust prickles. It seemed alien to the other objects. A departure in style.

A blue squeeze tube was lying on the rug beneath my couch. Without appetite, I sucked the faintly spicy mash, watching the others. They were eating, too, watching the screen. I disposed of my tube and sucked water from a hose in the wall, used the chemtoilet, and returned to my cushion. One of the cylinders was bending, wrinkling at the middle near the spiny button. As I watched, it pressed one of the pincushion's spines—which vanished. I felt a chill in my gut corresponding with the instant of the spine's disappearance.

OK. The pincushion was me.

I moved to a corner of the room. The pincushion moved away from the cylinders. The people in the room hadn't moved, but their images had. So they controlled their images some other way. A group of eight-sided polyhedrons marched from the horizon toward the cylinders . . .

I looked away from the screen. Reluctantly this time.

Hours passed. More games, if that's what they were, were played out on the screen. Someone said, "Entropy check" once. Otherwise the day was like the one before. And it passed. And I slept. And the next morning, it started again. Just the same.

I went for a walk. I found more rooms with more people in them, identically occupied. More or less like the others. Distinct from one another, but distinct as people who work in a shopping mall are: variations of a theme. They are generally of the same physical type—the type who used to sell deodorants and wine coolers and Diet Coke on TV.

It was the same in the other buildings. The streets were empty. I saw no children, no old people. The occupants of the apartments ignored me. Sometimes they did a little light maintenance, assisted by small robots like metal and plastic crustaceans; the little robots cleaned the dome, vacuumed floors, expunged fungi. Sometimes I caught the town's inhabitants doing light calisthenics, eating, using the toilets, even copulating in a mechanical sort of way. They didn't kiss when they did it. And they never took their eyes from the screen during all these activities.

I followed a young man as he trotted purposefully through the halls as he watched a projection of a rubbery spiral followed by a pincushion. We rode the elevator to the roof. It was crowded with naked watchers sunning themselves, in silence, lying on their backs, eyes staring upward. The young man stripped and lay on his back with the others, soaking up the sunlight and staring at the trapped sky. Overhead, gigantically magnified, projected holographically onto the air under the dome, were several dozen geometric forms circling one pincushion, performing the same shimmying stately minuets of meaninglessness.

Sickened by claustrophobia, I looked away from the projection. The city stretched out as far as I could see on three sides. The great geodesic was lost in the faint blue mist of distance. The buildings were shaped like cones, like blocks, like spheres. Far away was one white pyramid. There were no trees, no birds, nothing growing. Nothing green anywhere, except on me: my uniform had begun to change color.

It had to be somewhere. They must have preserved *something.*

I went back down to the first inhabited room I'd seen. Things were unchanged there. I sat down, thinking, glancing at the screen now and then. Egg shapes, faintly distinct, circling a pincushion. One of them advanced toward the pincushion. "Fuck off," I muttered. It backed away. The encircling went on. The fuses of my patience were burning out.

After three hours of it, I advanced, physically, toward one of the women—the one with the vaguely Oriental features. I was distantly aware that on the screen the pincushion was advancing on one of the egg shapes. I stepped in between the woman and the screen, blocking her view.

"Look at me," I hissed. "I'm afraid I have to insist. I'm sorry if I'm screwing up a sacred ritual, but my sanity's at stake." She just stared. Looking toward me, not seeing me. I could see the screen images reproduced in her eyes, tiny and perfect. I looked down at myself. The picture was there, projected on the front of my jumpsuit. The pincushion was waving its spines at one of the egg shapes . . .

I split. Fuming, I sprinted through the halls. I ran into apartments, shouting. I did everything short of violence to attract their attention. I shouted, "Fire! Earthquake!" Nothing. No reaction. I tugged their clothing, rearranged their bodies. They resisted a little, but not much. And when I forcibly turned their heads, a projection of the screen would follow their line of sight. If I woke them from sleep, a screen projection appeared instantly.

I shouted in their ears, I beat my chest; I bit through my skin and dripped blood on them. They cleaned away the blood, but they kept their eyes on the screen. I caressed them, embraced them, wept on them—I'm ashamed to admit I even considered rape. I was that angry. But I wasn't that far gone.

▼

I walked out, headed for the street. And this time I found the monument at the very center of the city. It was in a city square, atop a three-hundred-foot pyramid, one seamless chunk composed of something like milk glass. I climbed a slippery stairway. At the five-foot-square space on top of the pyramid was an ancient Zenith color TV set, protected by a bubble of glass, plugged into an old-fashioned socket on the glassy floor. The tube faced me, and there was a single picture on the screen . . . I watched for a while, and the picture on the old wooden-cased Zenith remained the same. A man's head and shoulders, a fixed image; he was smiling coyly, his gray-haired head tilted to the right, one eye closed in a wink. Across his chest were letters, yawing in a weakness of the horizontal hold, spelling out: BREWSTER REGINALD PHILBIN, MD, BSP, PHD.

It was a monument. "Must be hard to get parts," I muttered. Overhead, the enormous screen image in the concave interior face of the dome showed a pincushion approaching a ∞. A zero.

Zero. One, two, and three of the spines on the pincushion vanished. I was left with a sinking feeling. When another spine vanished, I retreated.

I turned and fled down the stairs, skidding the last twenty.

———▼———

It had to be fast. The others knew what was happening via the screens. Maybe via something else, too. I had to do it before they could stop me.

I picked her up. The woman I'd tried to talk to, the almost Oriental one. I slung her over my shoulder in a fireman's carry and turned to carry her away from the room. The others—never taking their eyes from the screen—moved as if to block me. But they were too slow. I darted out of the door, down the hall, grimacing at the effort. She wasn't heavy, until you tried to run with her. She wriggled silently on my shoulder; her eyes were locked on the projected miniature of the screen that followed us down the hall.

I heard no one in pursuit. I took the elevator down to the lowest level it would take me.

I carried her to a room I'd found the day before. It contained what I guessed was a heating and air-conditioning mechanism, a leviathan of metal pipes and chrome blocks and glass, humming and shooshing with the internal passage of air and power. The light was indirect, too sharp in some parts of the room, dim in others. A chain-link fence guarded the mechanism; but the lock had been left open. People still made mistakes. I went through the gate, and carried the wriggling girl to a dusty area enclosed by pipes fanning out from the machine like the arms of a Hindu god. I sat her down on the floor.

It worked. The projected image vanished. The metal leviathan—maybe its electric field—had blocked out the projection. The girl made a long, low wail of panicky disorientation. I was afraid she'd run for it, and I'd have to knock her down. And I didn't know if I could bring myself to do that. But she sat frozen, her head moving herky-jerky around, looking for guidance.

I took her face between my hands and turned her to look me in the eyes. "Can you see me now?"

She stared—then, like a wounded dog, she turned and snapped her jaws at my hand. Sank her teeth into the meat of my palm.

Jerking my hand away, swearing, I backed off. She looked at the floor, wild-eyed, a little blood running from the corner of her pretty mouth.

"I apologize to both of you," Dr. Philbin said.

He stepped from behind, smiling sadly. Looking almost exactly like his TV image. Same suit. I couldn't see him clearly because of the dimness in this enclosure. But I thought he had the same expression as the face on the TV. I hadn't heard him, I supposed, because of the noise of the machine.

He was looking right *at* me. He was talking right *to* me.

I sagged back against a pipe. Something in my stomach drew in its claws, curled up, and went to sleep. *Someone was talking to me.*

"Why'd you make me go through all this before you showed up?" I asked.

"I overestimated you. Thought you would socialize more easily. I don't like to interfere personally . . . I suppose it's the researcher in me. It was something of an experiment. A bad one. I let this young woman down, and all the others, in making that estimation of you."

"I wasn't going to hurt the girl. I wanted to force her to communicate with me. To talk. Just talk. She was the lightest to carry . . ."

"Force her is the operative phrase here. Imposing your social imperatives on our society by main force."

"Look—suppose you explain this place to me. And then we'll talk about morality."

▼

He talked for a while, and I asked questions, and I got the gist of it.

▼

Motivation, Philbin said, was ruled by the manipulation of archetypes in the subconscious. Something psychologists knew about analytically and Madison Avenue knew instinctively. The operation of the various substructures of the mind—the ego, the id, et al.—involved the use of a lexicon of symbols. Those symbols, and the archetypes they comprised, could be simplified and abstracted, purified for external concretization, and presented to the brain's centers of initiative directly—normally we react to symbols indirectly, through a long, slow process of filtering and selection. Before Philbin, conditioning was indirect, related to the use of experimental stereotypes: visual dramatizations of people enmeshed in desires for sex, success, recognition, approval. The conditioning dramatization sometimes came through television programming. The brain received and translated the imagery from social symbology to cerebral symbology. Social symbols became mathematic by way of the brain's eidetic translations.

Philbin cut out the middle man. He taught computer-controlled TV the language of the inner mind. "A language it took me forty years and the aid of dozens of researchers to learn." When applied with a totality of stimulus the same style of imagery imposed from birth to death—absolute rapport was established. And absolute rapport meant absolute control.

"Television is mesmerizing," Philbin said. "People will turn and look at a TV even during an argument. I knew that there was something special going on there, something more than the eye being drawn to light and movement—and that it could be used constructively." He just stood there as he talked, in the same voice, motionless. I looked at the girl. She was staring at him. Twitching. The wound in my hand throbbed. Philbin went on, "I saw a new Dark

Ages coming with the fall of the ecosystem, the destruction of the food chain. We needed an orderly society to survive. A method for training people, for teaching them to be part of a harmonious social environment . . . When the atmosphere began its transformation, and the anaerobic organisms became the dominant life-forms, and the acid winds stripped the Earth . . . only Kansas City survived; it was the only *completely* environmentally shielded city at the time of the collapse. Home of the Philbin Institute. I was, ah, influential in the city—and when the emergency called for a new order, my system was implemented. We spent most of the first century refining the system—and developing our survival technologies, our artificial food and air systems. There simply was no room for any extraneous organisms, Mr. Mazursky. We had to give human beings priority . . . In the second century our application of my social system was further refined, and evolved to . . . what you have seen. No materialized conflicts. All conflicts, all competition, all ego games and striving and desires, are acted out on the screen. We've trained our people to identify so thoroughly with the screen imagery that it's quite satisfying to them. They direct the screen with the output of their bioelectric fields, which the city's central computers are equipped to receive and interpret. There is individuality here—true individuality. They are aware of one another, of their little distinctions, in a peripheral sort of way. They gravitate together and apart very, very slowly, and react to one another physically as well as on the screen—but of course the screen imagery is uppermost. It is what they identify with, finally . . . " He smiled. "You have that you-have-made-a-society-of-mindless-conformists look on your face, sir. Not at all: The city is maintained by the people, for the people, of the people, and every day everyone casts their vote. On the screens. A consensus is evolved and steps are taken. That's why we added roof-sunning last year. It was voted in."

"Come on. You're telling me they have free will? You don't use this system to control them?"

"They are influenced to accept certain fundamentals. Any society expects the same. And they're happy with it—these people don't have to suffer the hassles of reproducing, raising children. Or dying. Their consciousnesses do not die. When they begin to age, we clone them; their minds are cybernetically downloaded into the new brain, when the clone has matured."

"Rebirth in sterility. But they're—"

"Don't tell me they're not experiencing the joys and passions of life. They are. But they're trained to experience their feelings eidetically. On the screen. Ever seen two professional chess players go at it? They are motionless, concentrating—but don't imagine they aren't boiling with excitement inside . . . "

"It's still stasis. Deciding on a new sunroof isn't progress. You could be cloning plants, animals—there must be samples somewhere, maybe in deep freeze, or . . . "

"It would be hopeless. The planet, *has* an ecology, sir. The new one, based on new systems of chemical interaction with organic molecules. Anaerobic systems. It has overtaken the planet. Hopeless to try and reverse it. Anyway, why bother? If we succeeded, we'd generate disturbing social interference patterns—as you yourself have. 'If it ain't broken, don't fix it,' Mr. Mazursky."

"I see. The urban-village paradise is achieved, so don't disturb it. Look, Philbin—we were all on our way somewhere. We blew it, and derailed the train. But there was someplace we were intended to get to. You're stopping the last people who have the chance. And this kind of living just isn't intense enough to really satisfy anyone, Philbin . . ."

"You sound like those quaint fellows from my childhood. Punk rockers, they were called."

"Punks?" I scowled. Nasty thought. I was a scholar of naturalist poetry. But then I shrugged. "Maybe it's sort of punk. Maybe a little punk is necessary from time to time."

"You're a fascist, Mazursky." He had dropped the "Mister." "You want to supplant our tribalism with your own. And to you, *I'm* a fascist."

He was right. It was relative. But . . .

"I'm going to go with what used to be called poetic intuition," I said. "And fight you."

I decided I'd take him with us. With the girl and me. By force. I might need him as a hostage. I stepped in, and sliced an uppercut at the point of his jaw.

My fist sailed through his head. The image shimmied.

He was a hologram. "You don't think I'd risk myself here, do you, Mr. Mazursky?"

"An image. A TV image." I shook my head, feeling heavy and stupid. "I guess I wanted to believe you were there so badly I didn't really look very close . . . Christ, you probably don't even look like that anymore. Cloned a few times yourself . . . " I trembled with frustration. I'd wanted that contact. Wanted to see him *react* as I hit him.

"Now it's time for you to make a decision, Mr. Mazursky. You can give yourself over to retraining. Or you can go out there. And die."

"I'm going back to the escape pod. There's some air left. There are people out there . . . sort of . . . I caught a glimpse yesterday, through the glass . . . "

"They're not people as you know them, Mr. Mazursky. We haven't seen them up close. But we're quite sure they're subhuman. They're not oxygen breathers, certainly . . . "

"If I give in, I'll be seeing projections everywhere I go."

"Eventually. But everything you see has always been a projection—on the visual cortex. Your mind edits and distorts things. You see nothing really directly. This way we give you the symbols of the social world more directly."

"And I lose the bulk of my perceptions. I prefer the living world to your social world, Philbin. I have made up my mind: I'm going. And I want to take the girl with me. You send some of your athletic couch potatoes to stop me—I'll kick in a few heads before they get me. It'll be a bad trade."

"Very well. She's already traumatized beyond recovery. Take her. Her designation is Curl. Go back out the way you came in."

And he blinked out.

Something tore loose in me, and it began to howl. "Come back here, Philbin! I'm not through with you! Listen, asshole—it was things like . . . like *this place* that put the goddamn planet into a doze till it fell apart! It was television; it was malls—it was the brain death of your urban villages, turning people inward, into videogames and away from the outer world—that's how it got poisoned and died and no one knew! It was like we were watching TV while the baby was poisoning itself in the kitchen! We got lost in our idiotic little distractions, and we projected all our problems onto little television dramatizations . . . and nothing seemed real! And when we realized it was real, it was too goddamn late, Philbin! *It was television that killed the world, you smug bastard!"*

I had shouted myself hoarse. Fugued, drained, my voice echoed in the dull industrial spaces of the room, and was swallowed up, and lost. And Philbin didn't come back.

▼

I had to drag Curl along at first. But after a few minutes she stopped yammering wordlessly, stopped gnashing her teeth and whimpering. She sank into a sort of ambulatory catatonia. Philbin didn't try to reclaim her. No screen projection followed us. We reached air lock 56. My suit was there, and in it was the tape-log I've been using to make this record. There was also a rather antique pressure suit for Curl—a crude sled with a big tubular device that synthesized oxygen from carbon dioxide and carbon monoxide. A miniature of what the city used for its own air. And there was a supply of "Food." Philbin was curious about me, it seemed, and what I might do out there if I survived awhile. He was still a scientist—perhaps more bored than he would admit.

The crossing to the pod was hard, because I got no help from Curl in pulling the sled. But the hardest part was getting her into the extra pressure suit. She came out of the catatonia, and bit me again.

▼

Three days since the last entry. Things have happened. I'm not recording this in the escape pod. Oh, it was workable enough. I got the oxymix mechanism working in it.

I was thinking last night that maybe—almost certainly—it was wrong to drag Curl out here. She'd probably die out here with me. Die young. Like Freda. Who was I to say that death was better for Curl than life in the dome?

But it was hard to think about taking Curl back. Sometimes she looked me in the eye, seemed to try to understand me. And I managed to get her to take some food on the second day. And she bit me only once yesterday.

She can talk, when she wants to. Remembering speech from an earlier clone-sequence, probably. This morning she said some things. Starting with: "Are they alive?"

She was looking out the window. I stared at her—and then looked out the window and saw them. At first the way they looked made me sick.

The stuff was crawling over them with a life of its own. I assumed it was their skin. Slick, gray-purple oily gunk. Bubbles for their eyes.

I just stared, and waited, as they came in through the hatch. Two of them. They took off their heads. Peeled them off.

They were humans, under the oily stuff. Protective suits of some kind. Living suits, maybe. Bred for this. Creatures that live anaerobically, producing oxygen for the host who wears them . . .

"When you first got here, we tried to catch up with you," the taller of the two men said, "to warn you away from that dome. They're complete assholes in there. But you moved too fast for us. We can't move very well in these scavenger suits."

"You coming back to the farm with us?" the shorter one said. He had mossy teeth and greasy, matted hair, and he was grimy. "Except for the Kansas City dome, we're pretty sure we're all there is. We got only a hundred square miles terraformed, but it's comin'. Long as our bubble holds . . . You coming with us? You hurry, you can make dinner. Corn on the cob. Fresh!" He grinned at us.

"Are we going to go with them?" Curl asked me. She was sweating with the effort at this kind of communication. Squinting as if she had a headache. But sane.

"Yeah," I said. I took her hand. "I think we will."

She raised my hand to her lips. She didn't bite me.

Mammy Morgan Played the Organ; Her Daddy Beat the Drum

MICHAEL FLYNN

If you were wondering whether you'd find a ghost story among these technohorrors, you can stop your speculation now. Michael Flynn, best known for his hard science fiction, has produced a truly classic tale of spirits invading the realm of human habitation.

Set in a library in Philadelphia, "Mammy Morgan . . ." could be said to have been a story that would sooner or later be fated to get written, since libraries are in a way already haunted by the souls of the authors of all the books on their shelves. But as is true of any good ghost story, the characters' lives fuel the tension that is the core of this tense, exciting tale.

This 1990 story is based upon certain actual circumstances, but the story itself employs a blend of atmosphere, technology, and intertwined private lives to create a highly charged tale with roots more than a century old and a heart-stopping climax that is set firmly in the here and now.

I

An idle breeze was all it was. It was all it could have been.

Hilda Schenckweiler raised her head and looked around the business office. A sound? The old library building creaked at night, as its century-old foundation snuggled deeper into the soil. It popped and groaned with voices that went unnoticed during the bustle of the day, but which caught the attention during the still evenings. And the other librarians told certain stories, absurd stories on the face of them, that became more uncertain and less absurd as the night deepened. She laid aside the correspondence she had been answering and sat very still.

Yes, definitely a sound. But what? A soft, sliding sound, like the breath of a sleeping child. Familiar, but that nagging sort of familiarity that defied recognition. A shuddery feeling crawled like spiders up the back of her head, and she brushed instinctively at her hair.

The sound seemed to come from behind her. She rose from her seat, hesitated a moment, then walked to the doorway that led to Interlibrary Loan. The illumination spilling from the business office spread a fan of light into the darkened work areas, teasing the dim shapes of tables and arching doorways from the shadows. Her own shadow, elongated and angular, was a spear thrusting into the shrouded gloom. Open doorways were cave mouths along the left-hand wall. Directly ahead, across the workroom, the entrance to Acquisitions & Processing was a blacker rectangle, barely discernible in the stray light from the desk behind her.

She held her breath and listened. It was a quiet, almost casual sound. It seemed somehow idle, diffident.

The clock in the boardroom next door began to chime. Seven notes spaced in slow cadence. She caught her lower lip between her teeth and backed away from the yawning mouths of the dark doorways. When she bumped into the desk her heart froze for an instant. Without taking her eyes off the open workroom door, she probed behind herself with her right hand.

And knocked over the pencil cup. Pencils, pens, and paper clips clattered to the floor, and Hilda watched as, in slow motion, a gum eraser bounced soundlessly out the door and into the workroom, where it lay neatly centered in the wedge of light.

Her heart timed the long seconds that followed. With every beat she became more certain that someone—something—would emerge from one of the doorways.

But no on came to pick up the eraser. No shadow fell across the doorway. And, after another minute had passed, she realized that the sounds had stopped.

Slowly, she untensed, releasing a breath she hadn't known she was holding. Alone at night in a large building . . . It was easy to get spooked. She had been warned about it when she had volunteered for the overtime. The building was too dark. There were no windows in the business office to admit the streetlights or the moonlight or the comforting sounds of evening traffic.

She stepped boldly into the darkened workroom. Darker shadows limned huge and silent shapes that she knew—*she knew!*—were book racks and furniture. Yet, behind the veils of darkness she could imagine—things.

She turned left and glanced inside the boardroom. Shadows of tree branches played black lightning across the window. A reflected streetlamp glimmered in the surface of the broad, polished conference table, like the moon on a midnight pond. The Empress Maria Theresa stared back primly from her portrait on the wall.

Hilda left the boardroom, closing the door carefully behind her, and continued across the Interlibrary Loan workroom. The floorboards complained beneath the carpeting. As she passed the entrance to Cataloguing, a blue-green flash teased the corner of her eye. A flashbulb? An electrical short? She stood in the entrance peering at the dim shapes looming in the darkness.

Nothing.

No flash. No sparks. Yet, she had seen something. She was sure of it. She groped for the wall switch and the overhead fluorescents flickered on. Squinting her eyes against the sudden illumination, Hilda took a careful step into the room. To her right was the huge, incongruous brick fireplace, a reminder of a time long ago when this had been a public reading room. (Reading in those days had been a serious business, conducted in comfortable, quiet surroundings.) To her left was the long worktable with the scissors and the paste and the Dewey reference books. Backed against the far wall stood the row of five-foot-high wooden catalogues. She saw nothing out of place.

But, when she turned to go, she froze. The fireplace was flanked by two doors: the one she had just come in and another on the farther side. Between the other door and the fireplace itself stood two, small, nine-drawer cabinets, one atop the other. The center drawer of the top cabinet hung halfway out.

She approached it with tentative steps, circling around to her left. That was what the sound had been. The familiar sound of card drawers opening and closing. That was all it had been.

Except that she was alone in the building.

A damp cold enveloped her, and her breath was mist in the suddenly frigid air. Hilda wrapped her body tightly in her arms, and the sigh of an old wind ran up her spine. Someone was watching her. Someone behind her. She felt it. She could feel the eyes on the back of her head; twin spots like the pressure of two fingertips where her neck joined her skull. It was not a menacing feeling, exactly. She felt no menace, but a cold disinterest that was far more chilling than any threat could be. Her breathing was loud and hoarse in her ears. She did *not* want to turn around. She did not want to turn around. She . . .

Felt a hand run through her hair.

And screamed.

And when she did turn, she saw there was no one behind her, after all. Nobody.

So it must have been a breeze. What else could it have been?

II

"What else?" Leo Reissman asked. "A hysterical reaction," he told her, "brought on by the isolation and the dark. The human mind is a strange and wonderful thing. The neural impulses that we interpret as sights or sounds can be triggered without any external input. By a migraine, for example." He folded his vest and beamed at the two women. He wondered if this might be the case that would make his reputation; restore his respectability in the department. Odd—to chase over half a country in search of the bizarre, then to find it, almost literally, in his own backyard. More likely, though, it was nothing. Another false alarm. Night fears of the sort he was already too familiar with.

"I saw what I saw," Hilda Schenckweiler insisted, twisting her hands together. "The drawer was open. That was no hallucination. I shoved it closed myself. The rest of it. The sound. The light. The cold. I don't know. But that drawer was open."

"Ah, but what was the significance of its being open?" he asked. "Perhaps it had been hanging open the whole while."

The director was sitting behind her desk, turning Leo's business card over and over in her hands. She looked up at him. "Everything is properly put away when the library closes."

Leo shrugged. "Carelessness does happen," he reminded them.

"It's not the first time," said Hilda suddenly. Leo looked at her with surprise; the director, with annoyance. She flushed. "I mean odd things happening at night, not carelessness."

Leo raised his eyebrows. "Indeed?"

"It is very eerie sitting in the old building at night," the director told him, and Leo wondered briefly why she insisted on answering for her librarian. "We've all gotten 'the willies' at one time or another. Dr. . . . " She glanced briefly at the business card she was twisting in her hand. "Dr. Reissman. That doesn't mean there is anything, well, supernatural taking place."

Leo blinked and lifted his head. "Oh, dear. I should think not!" he said.

The director seemed confused. She looked at Hilda. "But the patrolman said that he would send around a man who . . . Hilda, how did he put it?

"A man who has had experience with this sort of phenomenon," Hilda quoted carefully.

"He said that?" Leo chuckled. "Oh, Sam was just being mysterious. That's his nature. I helped him out once with a little problem he had, but there was nothing supernatural about it. I don't believe in the supernatural."

"But . . . " The director flicked her finger against his business card. "aren't you a psychic?"

"What? Oh *that's* why you're confused." He gestured toward the business card. "If you would read it again?" he suggested.

The director frowned at him, frowned at the card "Physicist," she read. She looked up at Leo. "Physicist?"

Leo smiled at them again. "Certainly. Nothing supernatural about physics, I assure you."

▼

"I don't understand," Hilda said to him as they stood together at the entrance to the Cataloguing Room. "Why would a physicist be interested in ghosts?"

Leo studied the layout of the room from the doorway. Yes, there was the catalogue, nestled between the fireplace and the other doorway. The accused looked innocent enough. Hardly the sort of thing to frighten a librarian.

Yet, hardly the sort of thing to open and close of itself on a dark, lonely night.

Probably just a case of nerves, he told himself. Nerves and fright accounted for more apparitions than anything physical. That was the problem with this sort of thing. It was often a struggle to establish whether anything had happened at all. And most often of all, he knew with a glum satisfaction, nothing had happened. That would explain so much. It was an answer he hungered for with an intensity that sometimes frightened him. If it *were* true, then he was most assuredly alone; but he would know, at last, why he was alone.

"Ghosts?" he answered her at last, though with more force than he had intended. "There are no such things as ghosts." Something harsh must have come out in his voice, because Hilda backed away from him.

"Then, do you think I'm crazy? That I imagined it all?"

"I didn't say that," he assured her. "Perhaps you did see something. But if you did, then it was something real, made of matter and energy, not a ghost." He shrugged his shoulders and pushed his hands into his pants pockets. "No, I don't believe in ghosts," he continued. "But I don't believe that the edge of the universe or the inside of the nucleus are the only frontiers of physics, either. There are still discoveries to be made in the odd nooks and crannies of the workaday world." He turned his mouth up. "Other physicists study quarks. I study quirks."

She smiled tentatively at his joke.

"I think," he continued, "that what you saw was a natural phenomenon that has never been properly studied. Like *Kugelblitz.* That was once dismissed as folklore, too." He realized abruptly that they were both still standing in the doorway, like two kids afraid to enter a haunted house. "Well," he said, rubbing his hands, "shall we get started?"

He crossed the room and began examining the card catalogue. It was a very old, dark wood cabinet about three feet by three feet, and it sat atop a second, similar cabinet. The dark wood shone from decades of rubbing hands. Leo touched the little brass fingerhook on the front of one of the drawers and it slid easily in and out. "Was this the drawer?" He wondered if the drawers could slide by themselves. From traffic vibrations, perhaps. Unlikely, but . . . Experimentally, he shook the heavy, wooden unit, but it did not budge and the drawers stayed put.

"No," he heard her say. "The one I saw was the center drawer, second row, but I heard the sounds for several minutes. More than the one drawer might have moved."

Or none, Leo thought. He turned and saw with surprise that Hilda was still standing in the doorway. "aren't you coming in?" he asked.

She hugged herself and shook her head. "I'm frightened."

"There's no need to be frightened."

He had meant to comfort her; but—unexpectedly—she flared up at him. "What do you know about it? You weren't there!"

"I—" Memories bubbled beneath his thoughts. The birds blackening the sky. The half-heard fragment of a word. Lying awake sweat-soaked in the heart of the night. He pressed his teeth into his lower lip. "I've studied a fair number of snugs," he said finally.

"Snugs?"

"SNGs. Standard Nighttime Ghosts." He found quick refuge in the jargon. "The acronym is less semantically loaded. If you use the word 'ghost,' you make assumptions about what the phenomenon is."

She turned up her mouth. "And if you use the acronym, you make assumptions about what it *isn't.*"

"I'm sorry," he told her. "I never meant to sound patronizing. Whether your snug was a real phenomenon or not, your fright certainly was."

"Don't trivialize it!" She hunched over her folded arms. "My fright was more than just a 'real phenomenon.' It was something I *felt*. That I still feel."

"Would it help," he asked quietly after a moment, "if I told you that I know exactly how you felt?"

Hilda raised her head and studied him for a few moments. Her mouth parted slightly, and Leo was afraid that she would ask him how he knew how she felt; but she said nothing. Finally, she unfolded her arms and stepped into the room. As she approached the catalogue, she sidestepped to her left and pointed to a file drawer. "That's the one I saw open."

Leo sucked in his breath. She had walked *desail*. . . . The Dundrum Effect? If so, how to test it? As casually as he could, he walked to the fireplace and pretended to look up the flue. He pulled his head out. "Ms. Schenckweiler," he said, "would you come over here a moment?"

She gave him a frown. "What is it?" He watched her turn and take a step . . .

"There! You're doing it again!"

She stopped and looked around herself with a bewildered expression. "What?"

"Just now, and earlier, when you walked toward the catalogue, you turned—right about there." He pointed to a spot half a meter in front of the catalogue. "As if you were stepping around an obstacle."

Hilda stared at the empty air, then she turned wide eyes on him. "Obstacle?" she said. Her voice rose in pitch, and she took a hasty step backward away from The Spot. "Do you mean the ghost is still there?" Her hand sought her mouth.

Dammit, now I've frightened her. Leo raised his hands, palms out. "Now don't—" He stopped himself. He had almost said *don't be frightened*. "It's a common experience. I call it the Dundrum Effect, after the Irish village where Conway first described it. I believe that it is due to a sort of 'peripheral vision' that some especially sensitive people possess. Perhaps a sense much as the blind develop, when they can 'feel' the presence of a wall or of another person."

She lowered her hand slowly. "It does help a little."

"Eh? What does?"

"Your dry-as-dust explanations. You make it sound so ordinary. That . . . takes the edge off." She kept staring at The Spot.

Dry-as-dust? Leo grunted. He took a tape measure and a small notebook from his jacket pocket and measured The Spot's location from several benchmarks around the room. He entered the figures in the notebook. "SNGs," he told her as he worked, "generally recur within well-defined loci. So, it is always there, even if it is not always manifest."

"What do you mean?" Hilda responded. "They don't move"

Leo was kneeling on the floor. He released the button on the tape measure and the steel strip snaked back into the spool. He rocked back on his heels and considered her question. "Well, not exactly," he said. "Some are mobile. . . . That is, some do move. But they move along well-defined trajectories; always repeating the same actions."

"I see," she said. "Like an obsessive-compulsive personality disorder."

He cocked his head. "Actually, more like a stuck record. Don't jump to the conclusion that snugs have a personality to be 'compelled'; or that they are even 'conscious,' in some sense. Those are some of the assumptions we make when we say 'ghosts.' When you think about it, the ocean tides show the same sort of 'compulsive' behavior."

"How do you *know* that your 'snugs' don't have self-awareness? aren't they the spirits of the dead?"

Leo hesitated a moment. He rubbed his left hand absently with his right. *The flutter of birds blackening the sky. The faint echo of an unheard voice.* He took a deep breath and buried the memories that threatened to break surface. "I don't know that they are. Carpenter's Conjecture is that souls and ghosts are equivalent entities; but that has never been proven. Back in 1906, a Boston physician named MacDougall weighed six people on platform scales as they were dying, and recorded a weight loss of ten to forty grams at the moment of death. So it would seem that *something* physical leaves the body at death. However, no one has ever repeated the experiment under proper controls, so we cannot be sure. The weights MacDougall recorded are about the same as for the snugs I've measured; but the similarity of mass may be coincidence. There may be snugs that are not souls; and souls that are not snugs. And even if there is a connection of some sort, the snug may be nothing more than a . . . a holographic recording of the soul, lacking volition or awareness."

Hilda leaned forward and waved her hand tentatively through the air above The Spot. "I . . . don't feel anything."

Leo rose and brushed at his pants. "No, you wouldn't. Snugs have extremely low density. About a tenth of a milligram per cubic centimeter. You could walk right through them and never notice. Go ahead. Take a step forward."

She looked at him and hesitated. "Go ahead," he urged her. "It can't hurt you."

She closed her eyes and took three abrupt steps. Then she opened her eyes and slowly unclenched her fists. "Nothing." She looked at him. "No feeling of avoidance."

"Exactly. The Dundrum Effect only occurs when you don't consciously think about where you're walking."

"I didn't feel a thing," she said.

"I told you snugs have low density."

Hilda laughed a short, high-pitched laugh that caused Leo to give her an uncertain look.

"What is it?"

"The old proof that ghosts are invisible. You've never seen one, have you? Then that proves that they're invisible!"

III

The director stopped him as he passed through the business office on his way out.

"May I see you for a moment?" She stood in the doorway to the secretary's office. Leo shifted the overcoat draped across his arm and glanced toward the hall door where Hilda Schenckweiler waited for him.

"Certainly," he said.

"Hilda, you may wait for Dr. Reissman downstairs."

Leo followed the director through the secretary's office and left into the librarian's office. He noticed a fireplace in the corner, the twin to the one in the Cataloguing Room, and surmised that these two offices had been built from a second reading room, a mirror image of the one on the other side of the building. The director sat behind her desk, leaning forward in her chair, elbows planted on the desktop. Leo waited for her to say what she intended to say.

"This 'investigation' of yours needn't last long."

He was not sure if she was making a forecast, expressing an opinion, or giving an order. Leo had heard the quotation marks in her voice. "I will try to be expeditious," he said.

She picked up a pencil from her desk and twisted it in her fingers. "I doubt that there is any more to this incident than simple hysteria."

"Most of the cases that I have examined," he said carefully, "have turned out to be nothing more than wild imagination. A few have been deliberate hoaxes."

The director tapped the eraser end of the pencil on her desk blotter. "I don't believe Hilda would deliberately hoax anyone."

Something about her voice pricked Leo's curiosity. "But . . ." he probed.

The woman sat back and brushed a hand at her hair. "It is really not my place to say. . . ."

But you'll say it anyway.

"Hilda *has* had a few problems in her life recently. Her mother, you understand. She had to put her in a home. She has been seeing a psychiatrist about it."

"Seeing a psychiatrist is not—"

She broke him off with a flip of her hand. "I know that, Doctor. I know that. These days it is almost a status symbol. But—" She paused in thought. "What I am trying to say is that the Library Ghost is an old tradition with the staff here. Every time a new girl is scheduled to work evenings, she is told all sorts of stories. You know the kind I mean. Well, the old building is genuinely creepy at night, and you do hear sounds and feel light drafts. Someone with, well, with an uncertain imagination, may magnify them into—who knows what?" She laid the pencil down; picked it up again.

Leo nodded curtly. "I understand Ms. Schenckweiler may not have seen anything. That is certainly a possibility that I will keep in mind." He straightened his overcoat and turned to go.

The director's voice stopped him at the door. "It will all turn out to be a hyperactive imagination. You'll see."

He turned and looked at her. Her fingers were twisting and turning the pencil. Leo locked eyes with her for a moment. Then he nodded. "More than likely," he told her.

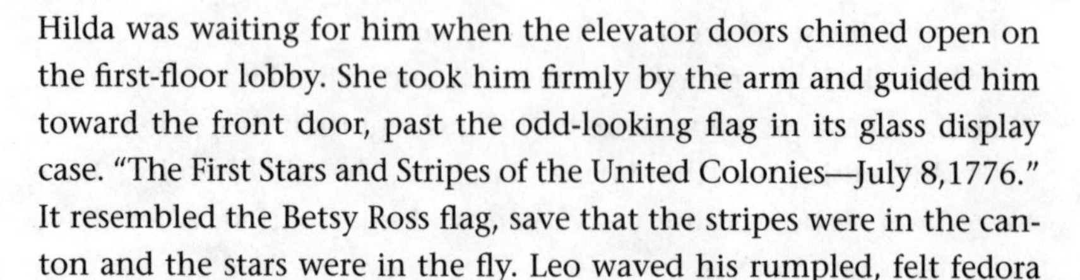

Hilda was waiting for him when the elevator doors chimed open on the first-floor lobby. She took him firmly by the arm and guided him toward the front door, past the odd-looking flag in its glass display case. "The First Stars and Stripes of the United Colonies—July 8,1776." It resembled the Betsy Ross flag, save that the stripes were in the canton and the stars were in the fly. Leo waved his rumpled, felt fedora toward the rear door. "But, my car . . . " he started to say.

"I thought you told me you wanted a tour of the grounds outside."

Leo didn't remember saying that at all. He looked at her and opened his mouth, but then thought better of it. There was a crease on her forehead, above her nose, and her face has a tight, closed-in expression. He shrugged. Whatever it was she wanted to tell him, he would learn in due time. So, he followed her lead. Outside was a bracing October afternoon, and a walk around the building would do him no harm.

They stepped out into a swirl of wind; red and gold leaves chattered in their faces. Leo clamped his hand firmly to his head to keep his hat from flying off. The sidewalk was bounded on the left by the "new" annex and on the right by a brick wall retaining the bank of a grassy knoll. The wind, trapped in the pocket, struggled to escape.

Leo strode briskly forward, out of the whirlwind. At the point where the sidewalk cascaded down flights of steps to Church Street, he turned and faced the building. The library grounds occupied the entire block of Church Street between Fifth and Sixth. The original building, a dark brick Carnegie-style structure, sat atop the crest of the knoll in the center of the block. Attached to its east face and extending to the corner of Fifth, was the annex that now housed the Circulating Collection. Behind the two loomed the massive, tree-shrouded, stone knob of Mount Jefferson.

A side path branched off the sidewalk and wound west toward the old building. *The original entrance,* Leo surmised, studying the arched portal with its decorative scrollwork. *They don't make 'em like that anymore.* It was sealed up now; the old, grand staircase was a platform for shrubbery planters. *Too bad.* The old building *looked* like a library. Its facade was distinctive; not like the anonymous structures they put up nowadays. Stone benches were spotted here and there about the grounds. Leo wondered if anyone ever used them.

Hilda was waiting for him at the point where the sidewalk forked. Beside her, atop the grassy knoll, was an odd-looking stone structure. It was flat, like a table or a bench; but it was too low for the one and too wide for the other. And it was surrounded by a wrought-iron fence. Leo frowned at it. He felt he should know what it was: that, in another setting, it would be instantly recognizable. "What is that?" he asked her.

Hilda turned her head. "What, this? Why, it's only Billy."

The surprise in her voice was overdone. *She wanted me to see this,* he thought. *It's why she led me out this way.* Leo hunched his shoulders against the wind and walked up the side path and around on the grass to look down on the object.

It was a flattopped sepulcher. A grave.

Of course. Instantly recognizable; but not something that one would expect to find sitting beside the town library's main entrance. Leo knelt and brushed away the dirt that obscured the horizontal slab. *William M. Parsons, Esq.,* he read. *Born May 6, 1701. Died December 22, 1752. He rocked Easton in her cradle and watched of her infant footsteps with paternal solicitude.* He ran his fingers across the slab. The stone was cold and rough. Old. It was strange to think that this grave was nearly a quarter century old when certain men had pledged their lives and fortunes at Philadelphia.

He looked up and saw that Hilda had joined him. "This is a grave," he said, which was stupid because she knew it was a grave. "A grave on the library grounds. Why did no one mention this earlier?"

Hilda rubbed her palms together against the chill. She glanced briefly at the windows overlooking them. "The director thought it would be best not to bring it up."

"Why ever not?" He stood and brushed at his trousers.

"Because she doesn't want any sensationalism attached to the library. She doesn't want us on the cover of the *National Enquirer.*"

He grunted. *Then why did you insist on leading me right to it?* He wanted to ask her straight out, but something in her face made him hesitate. Some deep-seated worry that gnawed within her. Best to approach the issue sideways. If at all. What did Hilda Schenckweiler's state of mind have to do with his investigation? Perhaps nothing. Perhaps everything. He remembered what the director had told him just before he left. Then he wondered if Hilda might have waited outside the office and overheard the comments. Showing him the grave might be nothing more than an act of defiance on her part. "I can appreciate her fears; but I really do need all the facts of your case."

"My case." She gestured toward the sepulcher. "Parsons was the city's founder. He did the surveying and laid out the plots for Thomas Penn." She gazed toward the far corner of the building; at the Cataloguing Room windows. "Do you think that he was doing late-night research or something?"

Leo laughed. "No, I don't know that he has anything to do with what happened last night; but, then I don't know that he hasn't, either. Unless I have all the data, I cannot decide what is important and what is not."

Hilda glanced again at the oversize windows of the Librarian's Office, and Leo turned and saw the slat of a venetian blind flick closed.

"Is there anything else you haven't told me?"

Hilda took a deep breath. "Follow me."

The second grave was less elaborate. It was little more than a rock surrounded by an iron rail situated in the little park on the west side of the driveway. The rock was about two feet high and was worn and pitted. Leo thought it looked a bit like a meteor. A large concavity on its top had collected a pool of stagnant rainwater, in which floated a brown, curled leaf.

Elizabeth Bell Morgan, stated the small plaque. *"Mammy Morgan" Died October 16, 1839. Aged about 79 years.* Leo grunted. He squinted at the plaque. "Mammy Morgan. Is that the same Mammy Morgan—"

"That the hill was named after? Of course. How many Mammy Morgans do you suppose there were?"

"Just asking." He shaded his eyes and looked south across the rooftops. From Mount Jefferson, Mammy Morgan's Hill was a motley of orange and gold and red in the October-lit distance. "Who was she? When I moved out here, Magruder took me around and showed me all the sights; but they're only names to me."

Hilda folded her arms against the chill. "I suppose you could call her a foundress of our library. Her donations of money and law books helped get the library started back in 1811."

"Law books? She was a lawyer? wasn't that unusual for a woman back then?"

Hilda shook her head. "She wasn't a lawyer, but she was probably better educated than most of the lawyers in town. She was born and raised a Quaker in Philadelphia, but her parents sent her to school in Europe. She had fallen in love with a soldier boy and they hoped to 'cure' her. That was before the Revolution. She came here later, in 1793, when the yellow fever epidemic swept Philadelphia. Her husband set her and the children up in a hotel on the hill" —she gestured toward the south "then he went back to Philadelphia, and wound up in a mass grave."

"What? Why on earth would he go back?"

"Why? He was a doctor. That's what doctors do during epidemics. History is full of forgotten, everyday heroes like Abel Morgan. Afterward, the Widow Morgan bought the hotel and ran it for fifty years. She had a fine collection of books from her European studies and her favorite pastime was reading law."

Leo chuckled. "Light reading, eh?"

Hilda scowled. "It beats soap operas. She kept her law books on a bench in the hotel's public room. Her neighbors kept asking for her opinions on disputes, so she began to dispense law,' as she put it."

"Like Judge Roy Bean," said Leo. "The Law South of the Lehigh."

She turned her mouth up. "Without the arbitrary hangings. She was a woman. She ruled so wisely that people seldom appealed their cases to the regular courts. The Germans began to call her *Die Mommie.* When she died, the funeral procession stretched over two miles, from here all the way to Lachenour Heights. The Indian corn mill"—she gestured toward the tombstone—"was added later."

"One of your folk heroes, I see. But there's more to the story," he prodded. "Isn't there?"

Hilda rubbed her arms and looked at the stone. "You know how people are. An educated woman, living alone, supporting herself. Especially in those days. The local bar tried especially hard to discredit her, spreading malicious stories about her character and about goings-on in her hotel. Some people said . . . Well, they said she was a witch."

He looked at her. "A witch."

She looked back. "Nonsense of course. But people love to spread malicious rumors. There was a children's rhyme: *'Mammy Morgan played the organ/Her daddy beat the drum.'* It was no more than rhyme play on her name; but some tried to make it sound as if she was involved in powwow magic."

Leo pursed his lips. "So, there are two graves on the library grounds, then."

Hilda cocked her head. "Follow me," she said.

▼

Leo stared at the indentation in the northeast section of the library's driveway. "Eighty-eight?" he asked incredulously.

"There's a vault under there," Hilda told him.

"Eighty-eight bodies?" He still couldn't believe it. He looked around: at the buildings, the parking lot. There was an old man sitting on one of the park benches, reading a book. Children were playing in the dead-end of Sixth Street. The rocky knob behind him rose steeply into a whispering shroud of trees. "What is this, a cemetery?"

"Yes."

He gave her a sharp glance. "Are you serious?"

"Quite serious," she replied tartly. "You might as well know it all. When they started construction on the library in 1901, the cheapest land available was the old German Reformed Cemetery, on this hill-top. There were 514 bodies in it then, and they exhumed them all."

Leo's breath caught in his throat. Digging up hundreds of rotted corpses . . . The gaping skulls; the bones fleshed out in tatters . . . What was it like to turn over the earth and find . . . No, he was letting his imagination get the better of him. The bodies the—"remains"—would have been in coffins, and the coffins would have been largely intact. Most of them, anyway. He took a deep breath and glanced at Hilda. "What . . . What did they do with them all?" he asked huskily.

She gave him a quizzical look. "Reusing old cemeteries was fairly common around the turn of the last century. People weren't as uptight about 'disturbing the dead' as they are now. The city wrote letters to all the relatives and descendants they could locate, asking them to come and claim the remains. Most of them were reburied elsewhere." Her eyes dropped to the concavity in the asphalt. "All but these eighty-eight. They were put in new wooden caskets and buried together in a large underground cavern."

"I see. And were there any, ah, unusual events reported during the construction?"

"She said I shouldn't tell you."

Leo looked at her. "The director."

"Yes. But . . . " She shrugged heavily. "What's the point? You can look it up in our own archives. It was never kept secret. There were even newspaper features about it over the years." She pointed toward the end of the driveway. "The people who lived along North Fifth claimed they saw moving lights at night; and—" She paused and made a face. "A headless woman."

Leo stifled a sudden laugh. The lights were a possibility; but the headless woman was too much. Too Gothic. Although, he reminded himself, this part of Pennsylvania had been heavily settled by Germans, so Gothic images might be expected. He studied the row houses along North Fifth Street at the end of the driveway. The site of the vault would have been clearly visible back then. "You're not pulling my leg, are you?" Some people thought it was great fun to try to fool him with tall tales. Hilda didn't seem the type, but you never knew.

"Of course I'm not," she said. "But I can't answer for the local residents a hundred years ago. *They* may have been pulling every leg in sight. You know the German sense of humor. The next night, people came from all over town, hoping to see 'die shpooken'; but nothing happened. Then, after everyone left, the locals claimed the ghosts came back."

Leo smiled. "You're right. It sounds like they were having some fun."

"I'm sure they were; because no one reported anything unusual in the mid-sixties."

"Oh? What happened then?"

"That's when the annex was built." She gestured toward the newer building. "The weight of the construction equipment broke the vault open. Caskets disintegrated and there were bones and skulls rolling all over."

It took him by surprise. Death images clawed their way to the surface of his mind. Whitened skeletons robed in rotted, worm-eaten flesh. Hanks of colorless hairs: eyeless sockets. *Gonna roll them bones.* He sucked in his breath. "My God! That's terrible!"

"Yes, it sounds like a scene from a bad horror movie, doesn't it?"

Leo mopped his brow against the chill autumn air. "But for one difference."

"What's that?"

"In the movies, that sort of scene is always a prelude to something grisly and horrible. But in the real world, when you 'disturb the dead,' nothing supernatural happens."

▼

One side of the parking lot opened onto the park by Sixth Street; the other was bounded by the wooded knob of rock—private property, Hilda told him. A castellated stone wall marched along the backside of the grounds, from the stone knob all the way across the dead end of Sixth. Gravel crunched beneath their feet as they walked together toward his car.

They stopped beside his car and Leo fished in his pocket for his keys. Hilda glanced toward the library building. "Do you think you can explain what happened to me last night?"

There was an odd tightness to her voice, and Leo studied her as he juggled the car keys in his hand. "I don't know," he replied honestly. "We don't have all the answers. We never will."

"Oh," she said, and fell silent.

He paused with his keys out and gazed across the roof of his car. Leafy branches reached up and over the stone wall. In the distance he could see the trees and houses covering the slopes of College Hill. He frowned. There was something wrong with the vista. Foreground and background; but no middle ground. "What's on the other side of that wall," he asked.

"Nothing."

"Eh?" He froze, dreading what she would say next.

"Unless you could 120 feet of air as something."

Leo glanced from her to the wall and back. There was a sudden void in his chest. He knew what she meant. He knew. He pocketed his keys and walked slowly to the back end of the lot. Every step was torture, but he had to see for himself. When he reached the wall, he craned his neck and looked down without leaning over.

A heavily shrubbed, rocky cliff dropped in a near vertical line to the black asphalt ribbon of Bushkill Street. Toy cars hummed below across his field of vision. Farther west, the slope was more gentle and ribbed with trees growing out of the side of the hill; but here, at the east edge of the parking lot, it was a straight drop. *A stumble, Falling, falling. Leo! Hands grabbing. Bushes torn out by their roots.* The scene below seemed to turn slowly counterclockwise. He backed away and stared at the comforting solidity of the rocky knob that capped Mount Jefferson. It added, he judged, another thirty feet; and the drop-off was just as sheer. The high-dive platform.

Hilda joined him. "It's a long way to fall, isn't it?"

Leo started. What macabre impulse had prompted her to say that?" "Not really," he said. "It would only take about three seconds to reach the bottom. It would be over with quickly."

"Three seconds?" she said. "Long enough to realize what was happening to you." She braced her hands on the top of the wall and leaned over. Leo gasped and grabbed her by the arm.

"Hey!"

"Don't do that!" She pulled her arm from his grasp. "What's the matter with you?"

"I . . . don't like heights," he said. His heart was pumping heavily. *Long enough to know.*

She gave him an odd look; but stepped away from the wall and folded her arms. "It's getting cold. I'd better get back inside."

"All right."

"I'm sorry. Did I make you nervous, leaning out like that?"

"No. Yes." Some people had no grasp of physics; no conception of the forces that could kill them. Their knowledge of force and motion came from Hollywood movies and television shows.

Not more than a few meters away, the planetary mass was waiting to smash her like a bug onto a windshield; and she leaned out over the wall and dared it.

They walked together back to his car, and Leo fumbled again with his keys. A cliff. He hadn't known that the library backed so close to the cliff.

"Do you think anyone could survive?"

"What?" He looked at Hilda. "Survive what?"

She was gazing toward the back end of the parking lot. "A fall. Off the cliff. You said it would only take three seconds to reach the bottom."

Good Lord! He refused to turn and look with her. "It's not how long you fall that matters," he told her. "It's how fast you're moving when you hit. Free-falling one hundred twenty feet, under gravitational acceleration . . . " He thought it through, doing the calculations in traditional units so she would understand. Numbers were a comforting abstraction, hiding the reality of the drop; the terror of the fall. "You would hit the ground traveling eighty-eight feet per second. That's roughly sixty miles an hour."

She looked at the wall. "Oh." She thought for a moment. "It would be horrible to die like that, to *watch* it happening to you.

Can you imagine what it would be like to know that you were going to die?"

Branches snapping; shrubs uprooted; stones clattering loose beneath flailing hands. Leo gave a backward glance at the wall. "But it would be so much worse to remember afterward."

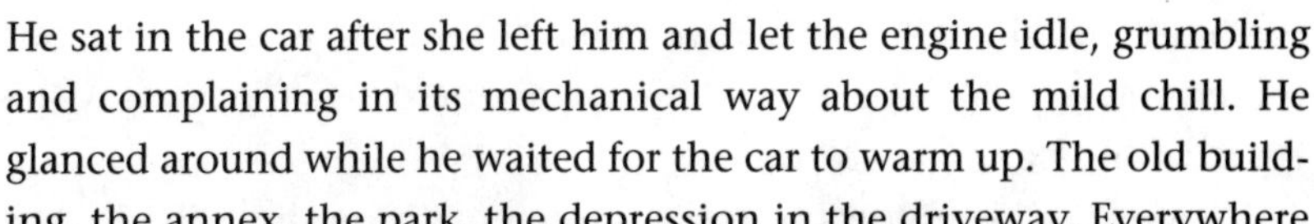

He sat in the car after she left him and let the engine idle, grumbling and complaining in its mechanical way about the mild chill. He glanced around while he waited for the car to warm up. The old building, the annex, the park, the depression in the driveway. Everywhere but that awful drop behind him. Hilda's remarks. So thoughtless; so callous. Gallows humor. He fought to expel it from his mind. He concentrated on the problem at hand. The haunt. If it was a haunt.

So, the library was built on deconsecrated ground. And there's the body of the town's founder, who watched over it all his life—and maybe longer. And the body of a woman who was certainly not a witch, but who loved to read books. And the bodies of eighty-eight poor souls thrown into a common grave and later spilled all over like a game of pick-up sticks.

Yes, this could be an interesting case. If only there hadn't been a cliff.

IV

Hilda felt the director watching over her shoulder as she wound the roll of graph paper into a tube. She wished the other woman would not stand so close and hunched her shoulders as she strapped a rubber band around the tube.

"What is all that?" asked the director.

"I told you. It's a strip recorder for the thermocouples. Leo . . . Dr. Reissman asked me to bring the tracings in today." She put the graph paper into her purse and snapped it shut.

"Does that mean he's finished?" The director's lips pressed together as she surveyed the equipment set up around the room. "I don't like my library cluttered up this way."

"I don't know. I'll ask him."

The director muttered something.

"What did you say?"

"I said he was a crazy old coot. Wasting his time—and ours—on this foolishness."

"He isn't that old."

The director looked at her. "Nor that crazy, I suppose."

"He's nice," Hilda told her. "A gentleman. Maybe a little stuffy. And shy because he's stuffy. And he's afraid of heights." She hefted the purse and slung it over her shoulder. "I think he is very sad about something, an old hurt. Sometimes, when he doesn't know anyone is watching, he forgets to smile."

"Does he." The director made a moue with her lips. "Well, he's kept this business out of the newspapers. I'll grant him that. But what has he discovered after two weeks? People have been seeing and hearing and feeling things in this library for years. You weren't the first to hear card drawers sliding. Or the first to feel a hand in your hair." The director's hand made a half-conscious move toward her own coiffure.

"I know. I've talked to Andy, Barbara, and Lynn and some of the others who used to work here. They would tell each other ghost stories whenever any of them had to work late."

The director cracked a smile. "I imagine half the nighttime experiences here have been because of those stories."

"And the other half?" Hilda asked.

The director's face went hard. "It was just a manner of speaking."

Leaving the library, Hilda felt her car bounce through the depression in the driveway. She had driven over that spot hundreds of times before. Now, every time she did so, she remembered what lay under it. Restlessly, perhaps?

She thought for a moment about the thermocouples that Leo had installed around the Cataloguing Room. Physical evidence, he had told her. *Our first priority is to establish whether the phenomenon is internal or external.* A fancy way he had of hinting that it might have all been in her mind. It was easier to believe that than to believe that ghosts might be real. . . . *From ghosties and ghoulies and long-legged beasties and things that go bump in the night, Good Lord, deliver us.* If ghosts were real, what else might be? What horrors might lurk in the shadows around us?

Yet, what if it *had* all been in her mind? In many ways, that was even more frightening, because that would mean it was herself and not reality that was cracking. *The breakdown of the universe I can deal with.* The other was a road she had no desire to travel. She had already seen what lay at the end of it.

She tightened her grip on the steering wheel; and, when she turned right onto Fifth, she cut much harder than she needed to.

▼

The college had perched atop the hill overlooking a bend of the Bushkill Creek since 1826, and its older buildings had had ample time to acquire the customary mantle of ivy. Cliffs dropped to the Bushkill on two sides of the campus, while city streets and residential housing hemmed it in on the east and north. Hilda found herself a parking place on McCartney, close by the campus gate. When she entered, she encountered the marquis, himself.

"Lafayette, I am here," she told the statue.

A passing student showed her the way to the physics building, where the department secretary told her which office was Dr. Reissman's and said she could go inside and wait. "It isn't as if there were anything worth stealing in there," she said with a sniff.

▼

Hilda found Leo's office cluttered, but neat. One entire wall was taken up by shelves stuffed with books and technical journals arranged according to some obscure logic. On one shelf sat a black box with a set of funny-looking lenses. A cable connected it to a computer on a side table. A plain wooden desk facing the far wall was stacked high with papers, each stack held in place by machinists' blocks of various shapes.

She lifted the paperweight from one of the stacks and saw that on top was a typewritten manuscript: "On Possible Mechanisms for a Thermophotonic Effect," by Leo M. Reissman, Ph.D. Paper-clipped to it was a handwritten note: *Sorry, Leo, but the referees just couldn't buy it.* Beneath that paper she found another: "Frequency and Duration of SNG Sightings, with Reference to Boltzmann Statistics." This time the attached note read: *Is this a joke?*

Hilda replaced the papers and paperweight and wandered idly around the office. A small, framed snapshot sat on the right-hand corner of the desk. She picked it up and looked at it. Two teenage boys—identical twins—dressed in scout uniforms smiled back at her. They had their arms around each other's shoulders and they looked like younger versions of the physicist. Leo's sons? The twin smiles frozen in time gave her no answer.

She set the snapshot down and peered into the corner between the bookshelves and the desk. A dollhouse? She bent over and lifted it. Yes, a dollhouse. The plastic kind, made with snap-together panels. Cheap. Not like the one her grandfather had built for her in his workshop. (Sometimes she wondered what had ever happened to it. Why did the adult always yearn for the treasures that the teenager spurned?) She studied the dollhouse she held. Each room was filled with a clear, gelatin-like plastic. Now what—?

"What would a grown man want with a dollhouse in his office, right?"

The voice behind her made her jump, and she nearly dropped the toy. She turned and saw Leo standing in the doorway. "L—Dr. Reissman. You startled me."

"I'm sorry." He waved a hand toward the chair beside the desk. "Have a seat, Ms. Schenckweiler. I hadn't expected you so soon."

Hilda sat holding the dollhouse in her lap. She looked at it dumbly for a moment, then she made an exasperated sound in her throat and started to get up; but Leo took it from her.

"Never mind. I'll put it back." He gave the toy an affectionate glance. "This is my main claim to fame, you know."

"A dollhouse?"

He cocked his head at her. "Oh, yes. You wouldn't know, would you? It's why the college keeps me around in my dotage. They're hoping for another apple to rap me on the head and reflect credit on them—presumably for granting me a spot under their tree. You see, I once devised a reliable and inexpensive method for projecting holographs. That was my field of specialization before I took up more arcane realms. Lasers and holography." He placed the dollhouse on the desk, with the open back facing Hilda. "Lasers and holography," he repeated to himself. He opened and closed the front door of the dollhouse. "Watch this."

He stepped to the bookcase, where he pressed something on the black box. Ghostly shapes flickered inside the rooms. Near-solid images of furniture and wallpaper appeared. Hilda leaned forward. Why, that was marvelous! He was projecting three-dimensional pictures of the furnishings into each room.

Leo tapped some buttons on the computer console, and the furniture in the living room changed style and color. The phantom wallpaper became a new shape and pattern. Hilda gasped.

He turned the unit off and the furnishings winked out. "What do you think of it?"

"I think it's very clever. Delightful. I wish I had known about this before I redecorated my house. I've always found it difficult to visualize an entire room from a sample swatch of wallpaper or carpeting. Decorators and architects must love this."

"They do, but that is just one application. I understand that some enterprising individuals in California are attempting a holographic motion picture." Leo lifted the dollhouse from the table. "Patent royalties and tenure," he said. "Those are what grant me the freedom to pursue my somewhat unorthodox investigations. Well . . . " He returned the dollhouse to its cranny. "Enough of my checkered past. What do you have for me?"

Crackpots, Hilda told herself, did not invent clever and useful gadgets. Leo thought that ghosts were real—or, at least, that there was a reality that people called "ghosts"—and Leo was a serious and practical scientist. She took the rolls of graph paper from her purse. "I put fresh rolls into the recorders and reset the timers the way you showed me. Was that all right?"

"Oh, certainly. Certainly." He rubbed his hands together briskly. "Now, which one is the chart for The Spot?"

She handed it to him and he pulled off the rubber band and unrolled it like a papyrus scroll. He studied it silently for a few minutes; then he chuckled to himself. "Yes. Yes." He rapped the paper with his fingernail. "Excellent."

"What is it?"

He spread the sheet across the table. "Look here," he pointed. "And here." Hilda bent over the chart and stared at the wriggling pen line.

"There's your snug," he told her. "See those jogs in the plot? Those are temperature drops."

She shook her head. The wriggling line was just a wriggling line. The jog his finger pointed to looked no different to her than any of the other random ups and downs; only a trifle deeper. "I don't see anything. Why is that so important?"

He looked at her and blinked his eyes. "Why, it proves that there is something physical happening at that location. Something that caused the temperature to fall abruptly. It wasn't in your head."

"I never thought it was." *Liar.* The untightening she felt deep within herself belied that. *Oh, Mother* . . . She ran her finger along the graph. The sharp spikes were icicles, sudden bursts of cold. Real, physical cold; measured not by a shivering librarian, but by an inanimate instrument. *Not crazy. Not crazy.* Who ever said that objectivity was dehumanizing?

"I don't understand. What does the temperature have to do with the gh— ah, 'snug.'"

Leo pulled a small rule from his shirt pocket and measured the slopes of the lines. "When a snug lights up," he said, "it uses energy. My guess is that it converts the thermal energy in the air directly to photons, somehow tapping the 'high-energy tail' of the Maxwell-Boltzmann thermal distribution. The only spirit involved is Maxwell's Demon. Ah . . ." He looked up at her and flushed. "I'm doing it again. Lecturing. You see, air molecules are not all the same. . . . Well, let's say that they are not all the same 'temperature.' That's close enough. There is a random distribution of temperatures. Some air molecules are 'warmer'; and—"

"Wait a minute! Are you trying to tell me that ghosts are a lot of hot air?"

His flush deepened. "No, I am trying *not* to tell you that, because I have heard it too often from my colleagues here." He hung his head and entered the numbers into a small desk calculator. "A thermocouple converts heat energy into electricity. Why can there not be a similar mechanism—a natural mechanism—that converts heat into light? It needn't be too energetic. The brightest snug I've ever measured has had an output of less than twenty watts. Regardless . . . " He raised his head again and looked at her. "If a snug uses the high end of the thermal energy curve to energize itself, the temperature of the surrounding air will naturally drop. When the dew point is reached, the moisture in the air will condense, so you would feel 'cold and clammy' and the snug will be shrouded in fog. So, you see . . . " He spread his hands, "the traditional descriptions of ghosts match physical theory quite well. Even to the extent that 'shrouded ghosts' are more commonly seen in the British Isles, where the dew point is high."

Leo blinked at the calculator display. "The temperature drops in the library averaged about 3.4°C per minute. That would make your snug's power output . . . " His fingers danced on the keypad. ". . .around five watts. Durations ranged from a few seconds to five minutes."

Hilda ran her finger along the plot trace. "It was real. That's all that matters."

He hunched over the rule, measuring the distances between icicles. "Mean recurrence rate . . . 2,460 minutes, plus or minus a trivial amount that could be instrument error. Let's see . . . Forty-one hours. Hunh." He put the end of the rule in his mouth and chewed on it. "Diurnally out of synch. That's interesting."

Hilda raised her head and looked at him. "What? You mean the ghost reappears every two days? I don't believe it! More people would have seen it."

Not every two days. Forty-one hours. That would be . . . Got it! It's a harmonic of the lunar month! One-sixteenth. So, each appearance would be seven hours earlier in the day than the previous one." He stopped and blinked at her. "Oh. Why haven't more people seen it? Think. Most of the nighttime events would take place on weekends or holidays or in the wee hours of the morning, when no one was around to see them. And more than half the occurrences would be during daylight or early evening when the building lights would be on. A five-watt snug doesn't make much of a flash and the vast majority of the events would be too brief to notice. You were lucky that night, to have experienced such a long-lasting event."

Lucky? She supposed that, from Leo's viewpoint, she had been. But he hadn't been there. He hadn't experienced that horrid feeling. "What about the cold?" she asked, to avoid thinking about it. "Or the fog? People would notice that, even during the day. Especially in the summer."

"Would they? In an air-conditioned building? Or would they think it was a draft? Most thermoluminescent events would be very short—a few seconds, perhaps. Boltzmann statistics. The longer the event, the less frequently it occurs. Now, a 'bright' twenty-watt snug would trigger a drop of, say, ten degrees celsius per minute. That's a maximum, without convection or anything. So if the snug 'lit up' for two seconds, you would experience a local temperature drop of at most one-third of a degree. Who would notice? And the Library Snug is much dimmer than that. It only shows up on my trace because of the sensitivity of the instruments."

"Then it probably won't happen to me again," she said.

Leo sighed. "Probably not," he said with regret. "Reproducibility is such a problem in this field. Oh." He looked into her eyes and, surprised, she turned her face away. "It was a frightening experience, wasn't it?" His eyes grew distant. "Frightening," he repeated to himself. "I could prepare a schedule for you of the snug's expected reappearance. There is no way of telling beforehand whether an event will fall in the longer-lived tail of the distribution: but you can schedule your late-night work to avoid them."

"That would be nice. Thank you."

"Meanwhile . . . " He pulled a calendar appointment book from his shirt pocket and flipped quickly through the pages. "You first sensed the snug, when? The ninth, wasn't it?"

"Yes. It was seven at night." She shivered. "I still remember the chimes."

"Uh-huh. And the last event on the strip recorder was, hmm . . ." He ran his eye down the chart on his desk. "Six P.M. on the twenty-first."

"Hey!" she said. "That means there was one today, doesn't it?" She closed her eyes and counted the hours on the clockface. "At eleven A.M.!" She gasped. "I was in the room then!"

Leo was still studying his calendar. "didn't notice anything, right?"

"I—No."

He waved a pencil at the graph. "Daytime. Short duration. If you weren't looking straight at it, you wouldn't know anything had happened. Even if you were, the overhead lights would probably have masked it. Here we go. The next one is at four A.M. the day after tomorrow." He shook his head. "Too soon. We won't be ready in time. It'll have to be nine P.M. on the twenty-sixth." He penciled a notation on his calendar and put it back in his shirt pocket. He reached behind himself to the desk, where he found a small booklet, which he opened.

"Ready? Ready for what?"

He picked up his telephone and flipped through the booklet. "I have a friend in aerospace engineering who doesn't think I'm too crazy," he told her. "He has some computer-imaging equipment he will let me borrow, if I'm not too explicit about why I want it. I'll tell him it's for a holographic experiment. He'll know I'm lying, but that will cover him with his chairman.

"You want to take its picture. The ghost."

"The snug. Of course. More than just a visual picture. With modern image-enhancement techniques I can study the snug at virtually every wavelength and obtain a pretty thorough electromagnetic footprint."

"You want to set up all this equipment in the Cataloguing Room? The director won't be happy about that."

"She won't care," Leo predicted. "Not too much, anyway. The twenty-sixth is a Sunday. No one will be around to be scandalized."

"Well, I'll ask her," she said uncertainly.

Leo smiled. "Tell her I will continue to pester her if she does not let us do this experiment."

Hilda looked at her watch. "Look at the time!" she said. "I've got to be going. I suppose your wife will be waiting supper for you."

"My wife?" Leo seemed puzzled, as if wondering whether he had forgotten if he had one. Then he blinked and said, "Oh, no. I am not married. I never have been."

"Oh." She pointed toward the desk. "I thought those were your sons."

"Sons?" He twisted his head to see where she was pointing. "Ah." He gazed at the picture for a long time before answering. "That picture was taken many years ago," he said finally. "A great many years ago. I am the one on the left." He stared at the snapshot a while longer before adding, "Harry and I did everything together. Read the same books, saw the same movies, earned the same merit badges." He smiled slightly, his head cocked in reminiscence. "Dated the same girl. You never saw one of us without the other. We dressed alike. We even thought alike. Sometimes he would answer a question before I even asked it."

"Where is he now?"

Leo sighed and turned his back on the picture. "Dead."

"Oh. I'm sorry."

Leo shrugged. "It was a long time ago." He made a ball of his hands, twisted his fingers together.

"I'm sorry," she repeated, unable to think of anything else worth saying.

Leo studied his hands. "It was the only thing we never did together."

V

He hadn't thought about Harry in a long time. Leo rinsed his mouth and spat into the sink. He put his toothbrush back in the rack: then he leaned forward and studied his own face in the mirror. It would have been Harry's face too, he decided. They would never have grown too different. He tried not to think about reality; about what Harry's face must look like now, after all these years below the ground. Decay. Rot. Worms. He shuddered and turned out the bathroom light and went to bed.

And lay there unable to sleep. It was too hot with the covers on, too cold with them off. The dark and the quiet blanketed him. Far away, he could hear a faint, intermittent knocking. Only his own pulse in his ears. He had established that long ago, after innumerable and futile trips to his apartment door, peering through the spyhole at empty hallways. Only his own pulse, audible now that the world was hushed. He closed his eyes and tried to empty his mind.

As he relaxed into the borderland of sleep, the voices began.

Fragments. Soft, random syllables, chopped off, with long pauses in between. Seldom a complete word. Never anything that made sense. *Wonder-*, whispered a voice. And *Waysdi-*. Leo strained to hear the message, knowing there was none. *Beewith-* and *Verythi-*. The voices were without tone or inflection—not masculine, not feminine—bursting like shells in the silence of his mind.

Insensibly he drifted out of the borderland and the popcorn voices were stilled. As he lay there in the quiet he became gradually aware that some one was watching him. He was lying on his side and behind him was the wall and between the bed and the wall stood . . . something.

It watched him as he lay there. He could feel its height. It was black and featureless, with not even eyes to break its seamless shadow. Utterly silent, with no whisper of breath—its gaze neither threatening nor benevolent, but an implacable dispassion. It watched without feeling or interest.

Leo knew he had to see it, to confront it. He gathered his will from a dozen scattered points and rolled over on his back and opened his eyes . . .

And awoke lying on his side in the darkness.

He contemplated the fact that he had dreamed about dreaming, and wondered if, even now, he was awake; because, if so, he had awoken into his dream, into the same dark bedroom, curled into the same position.

With the same monstrous feeling of being watched.

He twisted around and stared into the darkness between the bed and the wall, and there was nothing there save the darkness itself. Unless . . . was there, within the darkness, a deeper shadow, somehow solid? He could feel its inexorable presence pressing on his skin, brushing the small hairs of his neck and arms.

Leo opened his mouth to speak, but the words came out as a flaccid cry, a low-pitched moan that lacked the will to scream. He woke with a gasp and groped for the bedside lamp and turned it on, fearful that, this once, there would be a shadow its light would not dispel.

But, of course, there was not.

He sat up in his bed, with his back braced against his pillows, and listened to the hammer of his heart. Resolutely, his eyes sought out the familiar landmarks of his room. The chest. The hairbrush. The tie thrown across the chairback. Simple, ordinary objects. Anchors to reality. Comforting in their everyday intimacy. Slowly, his pulse stilled, and he lay back down again. There was no need to check the thermocouple. He had disconnected it a long time ago. In all the years, there had never been a quiver on it.

He went to sleep with the light on—something he had not done since he was a boy.

▼

The next morning, Leo's nightmare faded while he installed the equipment in the library. That was the best therapy. Concentrate on the task at hand. Lose yourself in the details of a routine task; let the mind idle in neutral while the subconscious sorts things out. He started to hum.

Hilda picked up the loose end of a cable. "Where do you want this?"

"Here, give it to me. It goes in the computer port."

A complete physical record, he thought. At last, he would have a complete physical record. Electromagnetic, sound, temperature, and relative humidity. Everything. Let Magruder argue with that, if he could!

Leo stopped humming and grimaced. He probably would. What did physical evidence mean? There had been too many photographs of "flying saucers" and "Martian faces" and "Loch Ness monsters."

Mistaken identity. Wishful thinking. Even outright hoaxes. Magruder wouldn't accuse him of hoaxing the department. At least, not aloud.

He set his jaw. This would be no blurred, half-focused snapshot. This was the best equipment NASA could buy.

"What's wrong?"

"Eh?" He looked up from his wiring and saw Hilda watching him. "What do you mean?"

"Well, you looked so happy there for a while. Then, all of a sudden, you were the face of gloom."

He twisted his smile. "I was just thinking about some of my colleagues, how they won't accept my findings, in spite of everything."

"I don't understand. They're scientists. They'll have to believe you if you show them the evidence."

Leo wiped his hands on a rag. He set the camera atop its tripod and screwed it in place. "You don't know scientists. If they already believe a thing is impossible, they'll refuse even to look at the evidence. If I had Magruder here and he saw the snug for himself, he would still refuse to believe it. A trick, he'd say. An illusion. He might even find a stage magician who could duplicate everything that happened. As if any phenomenon that *could* be duplicated by hoax must therefore *be* a hoax." He smiled sadly and looked into the distance. "I am an embarrassment to them. They think I am so far around the bend, that I cannot even see the bend anymore." He picked up a screwdriver. "They took away my freshman classes this year. I'm professor emeritus, now. E-meritus. That means 'without merit.'" He laughed at his own joke.

"And can you see it?" she asked.

"Can I what?"

"See the bend."

He paused and looked at her with raised eyebrows. Hilda had her hands half-raised and clenched at waist level. "As clearly as anyone else," he told her. He bent again over his work. Why was Hilda so concerned with *his* mental health? "You see, I don't have a problem with snugs—hell, with 'ghosts.' There is a class of phenomenon that needs explaining, that's all. I have no vested interest in the nature of the explanation. The problem with unbelievers is their dogmatism."

"What do you mean?"

He grunted. "They can't just disbelieve. They've got to disbelieve in a certain way: Orthodox disbelief! Talk with an atheist some time; you'll never get a clearer vision of the fundamentalist God. God, they'll tell you, wouldn't play games with fossils or light waves just to trick us into thinking that the universe was older than six thousand years. Now, *Loki* might very well do that, or *Raven;* but those aren't the gods that they disbelieve in."

"You don't really believe that—"

"That the physical universe was created in 4004 B.C.?" He made a face. "Of course not. Although the date does approximate the creation of our *cultural* universe. No. I was merely using it as an example, to show how even unbelievers hold certain unquestionable beliefs. My colleagues have a mental image of the *sort* of ghosts they do not believe in, and if someone like me comes along with a different paradigm—a materialistic one, unconnected with magic or superstition . . . Why, they'll denounce it as rank heresy! I try to talk about a mechanism for the thermophotonic effect, and they'll argue that spells and pentagrams violate conservation of energy. I try to describe the frequency and duration of certain odd events, and they'll point out that mediums and spiritualists are frauds. I wonder if there might not be *something* that needs explaining, and they'll bring up crystals and pyramid power." He tossed the screwdriver to the table. It banged and rolled and dropped to the floor. Leo made a face. "Sorry," he said. "Even if we nutcases can grow exasperated with the stupidity of others."

"'What am I doing in here with all these crazy people?'"

Leo chucked. "Yes, exactly." But he looked at her and saw she wasn't smiling. "What's wrong?"

She folded her arms under her breasts and hunched over. She studied the equipment on the table. "I wasn't making a joke," she told the oscilloscope.

Leo stood quietly with the cable in his hand and waited.

Hilda unfolded her arms and lightly touched the knobs on the scope. "You would think that when a person's mind goes, she wouldn't recognize mental illness in others. But it isn't like that at all." She turned and looked him in the eye. "My mother and I were very close." She said it as a challenge. "Especially after Father died. We were the kind of mother and daughter who dressed alike and went places together. I look like her—I mean, I look like she did when she was younger. There isn't a trace of my father anywhere in my face. Even after I was grown, we did things together. I thought she was just so wonderful, and I wanted to be just like her."

"Then . . . ?"

She looked away, at the card catalogue, at the racks of books. "Then something happened inside her head. I don't know what it was. The doctors didn't know what it was. They talked about strokes and lithium imbalance and I don't know what else. But they didn't know anything, really. What it all came down to was that she wasn't my mother anymore. She was a stranger who saw things, who heard things. Sometimes the voices talked to her; and she talked back. Twice, she left my apartment while I was at work and wandered around the neighborhood. After a while, I couldn't deal with it anymore and I—" Her hands clenched again. "I had her committed. When I went back the first time to visit her, she gave me the most heartbreaking and bewildered look and asked me why she was in there with all those crazy people."

Leo saw a tear in the corner of her eye. "It was probably the best thing you could have done," he said slowly. "I mean, the professionals would know how to—"

"You don't understand." She shook her head slowly. "When I visit the place where she lives now . . . when I look at her, I see myself, only older. *I wanted to grow up to be just like her!"*

"Oh." Leo bent over and plugged the cable into the computer.

"So I've got to know, Dr. Reissman. I've got to know, am I starting to see things, too?"

He straightened and looked at her. Hilda's lower lip was almost white from the pressure of her teeth. "I told you you weren't. I showed you the traces on the temperature records. You saw something real."

She shook her head. "You showed me some lines on a chart. They could have meant anything. I don't understand things like that. I'm not a technical person. I just want to know if I can believe you. Or are you a nutcase, too?"

Leo wiped his palms on his pants legs. *What can I tell her? That I hear voices? That things visit me in the night?* He touched the computer with his forefinger, rubbing it along the top of the case. "The mind can see and hear things that aren't real. I'll grant you that. I think it happens to everyone at some time or another. The signals are blocked or scrambled or misinterpreted. But it doesn't matter what I am. Because this—" He rapped the computer with his knuckles. "This will only see a picture if there are photons; it will only record a voice if there are sound waves."

Hilda flexed her fingers, brushed at the sleeves of her blouse. "Then let the machines tell us if were sane," she said; but Leo pretended he hadn't heard.

VI

The ticking of the clock in the boardroom next door was a steady, distant metronome. *Funny*, Hilda thought. She had never realized how loud it was; unless its sound was magnified by the evening stillness, or by her imagination. She glanced to her right, where Leo sat quietly in the other chair studying the instruments that he had racked on the table before him. *How can he wait so calmly?* she wondered. He reached out to the oscilloscope and turned one of its knobs an infinitesimal fraction to the right. Hilda thought he had turned it to the left just a short while ago; so perhaps he was not as calm as he appeared. That made her feel fractionally better.

"How much longer?" she asked.

Leo pushed his sleeve up. "Five minutes. That is one minute less than the last time you asked."

Hilda blushed. She was acting like a fidgety schoolgirl. Yet the waiting was, in many ways, worse than the unexpected apparition of a fortnight or so past. Surprise could be numbing; but anticipation amplified everything, until the nerve endings stuck out a foot beyond the skin, and the least little event exploded on the senses.

In five—no, four—minutes, a ghost would appear. Or not. And she was afraid of either outcome, though in different ways. The unknown; or the known-too-well. Unless it was not fear, but another emotion entirely, that trembled in her body.

Leo rose and walked to the doorway, where he turned off the overhead lights. The room went dark, except for the dim green glow of his instruments and scopes. "We will be better able to see it with our own eyes," he said, "if the room is darkened."

Hilda turned from him and hunched herself in her chair. She clenched and unclenched her hands. The glow from Leo's instruments teased the corners of her eyes. She stared into the darkness, toward The Spot, waiting. "How much—"

"Sh!"

Dim shapes emerged from the black as her vision adjusted to the room. There was the work bench, the fireplace, and, yes, the old card catalogue. The only sounds were her own breath and the faint electrical hum of the equipment.

It seemed as if an endless time went by. Then a light winked in the air, as brief as a firefly on a summer's eve; a spark that was gone before it was ever seen. Leo rose and walked toward the light switch. Hilda expelled her breath. "Was that it?"

Leo turned the lights back on. He returned to the instrument table and leaned over the scope. He pressed a button. "Yes," he said.

"Why, that was hardly anything at all." She felt peeved; as if the ghost had let her down. All that anticipation. All that buildup. It seemed anticlimactic. Only a fleeting glimmer in the dark. No sliding drawers. No hand in her hair. No piercing cold. She clasped her hands together. Had she imagined everything, after all?

She watched over Leo's shoulder as he replayed the apparition on his computer screen. She saw the spark flash again—a digitized memory of it. Leo froze the display and the screen showed a featureless smear of white. Not what she had ever imagined a ghost should look like. Yet, the instruments *had* recorded something.

Leo scowled and advanced the record one frame at a time. Forward. Backward. Forward, again. Hilda could not decide what he was looking for. The whiteness wasn't there, then it was, then it wasn't. Like a light that had turned on and off.

When she leaned forward to see better, she placed her hand on his shoulder, and he jerked as if electrocuted. Hilda backed away from him. He gave her a distant, preoccupied look and turned back to the screen without speaking. His fingers made clacking sounds on the keyboard.

Finally, he signed. "Here, look at this," he said.

Hilda stepped cautiously to his side. She did not know why he was so edgy, but she did not want to disturb him. "What is it?"

"I have enhanced the signal to show greater detail."

The freeze frame showed the same featureless blob she had seen before. She shook her head. "I don't see anything."

Leo made a sound in his throat. "Look more carefully. See the way it narrows into a head? And those dark spots near the top. Those must be eyes, wouldn't you say.?

"No. It's just a white smear."

"It's not only white. The spectral analysis shows some blue with some overtones of green. Auroral effects from the excitation of diatomic nitrogen and monatomic oxygen."

"If you say so," she said doubtfully.

"I have had more practice than you at image interpretation. Let me refine the image further." He again bent over the keyboard and the NASA equipment did whatever it was that it did. The image on the screen changed colors. Vertical wipes passed through it, changed it. The edges became sharper. The suggestion of contour emerged.

"There is a face there. I know it." Leo hit the keys several more times and features solidified out of the smoky shape. "There! There! Do you see it now?"

"I see a woman in a billowy gown," she said slowly. The balloon shape could be a hoop skirt. The halo could be a bonnet. And, yet, if she concentrated on it long enough, she could see the pits of eyes and the shadow of a long straight nose. She looked at Leo. Had the image been there in the shape all the time, waiting to be evoked by the computer; or had Leo, for some reason of his own, imposed an image upon it—an electronic Michelangelo creating a digital *Madonna?* She couldn't know. She couldn't. If you worried at it long enough, could your heart not find any form at all buried in formlessness? weren't there bestiaries in inkblots; menageries in the clouds?

Leo straightened with a satisfied look on his face. "That proves it, wouldn't you say?" Hilda started to answer, but realized that he was not talking to her. "A human face couldn't be a coincidence. There must be a connection between ghosts and the souls of the dead." He folded his arms and studied the woman on the screen. "I wonder who she was? One of the women in the vault? Or Mammy Morgan herself?" He pulled out a chair and sat down and began scratching rapidly in his notebook. "I should be able to excite the ghost artificially. Increase its brightness and duration. With a laser, perhaps. The matrix appears to be a hologram of some sort; the light is naturally coherent. Yes. With a laser, I can amplify the signal; make contact." The point of his pencil snapped against the notebook page and he looked at it dumbly.

Ghost. He had said "ghost." Hilda wondered what had become of snugs. She realized suddenly that Leo was never going to settle the reality of her ghost or the stability of her mind. Everything he said or did could be colored by his own yearnings for . . . . What? Vindication? Respectability? Something else? She had been foolish to rely on this old man and his facade of scientific objectivity. No amount of gadgetry could ever quiet her doubts, because the doubts had grown inside herself, where no instrument could reach.

"I could bring my own laser over. The projector. Create an excited state directly in the heart of the ghost." He flipped the pages of his notebook. "Damn!" He ran his finger down a column of figures. "The next two apparitions will be during the daylight on weekdays. Well, I've waited this long; I can wait a short while longer." He drummed his fingers on the table. Then he looked at her as if he had suddenly recalled her presence.

"Your director would be very upset if this equipment were still sitting here tomorrow morning. We must break it down and store it for a few days. Is there a room here in the library I can use?"

"Yes," she said. "There's a place in back of the closed stacks."

"Good. Good." He nodded. "Would you help me set it up again on Friday after the library closes? The next nighttime appearance is twelve o'clock that night."

"Midnight," she said without checking the calendar. "All Hallows' Eve."

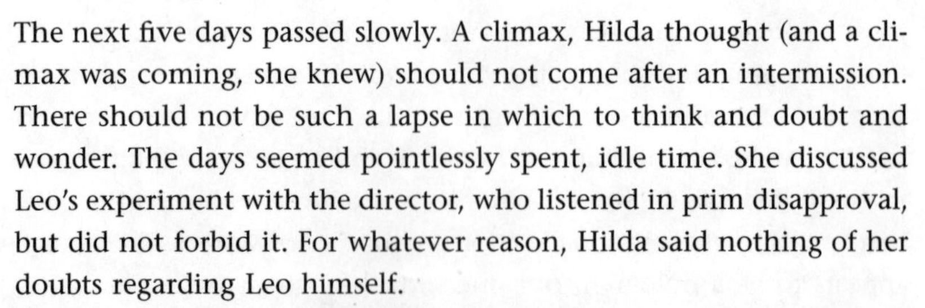

The next five days passed slowly. A climax, Hilda thought (and a climax was coming, she knew) should not come after an intermission. There should not be such a lapse in which to think and doubt and wonder. The days seemed pointlessly spent, idle time. She discussed Leo's experiment with the director, who listened in prim disapproval, but did not forbid it. For whatever reason, Hilda said nothing of her doubts regarding Leo himself.

She read all she could about ghosts. Not the sensational things, the kinds of reports that smacked of showmanship and the need to be noticed; but the quietly understated tales of casual, everyday haunts. Most haunts, she discovered, did not involve grisly and horrible events. Instead, they were almost matter-of-fact. The sound of a ball bouncing down the hallway, when there was no such ball. A shadow on a wall, when there was nothing to cast it. They were almost comforting in their ordinariness. The Irish ghost scholar, Dr. Michael MacLiammoir, wrote that "it is the unbeliever who feels the greatest fear of ghosts; for the believer knows that they are harmless."

She made it a point to be in the Cataloguing Room on the occasion of both the predicted daytime events. She was not sure why, or what she expected to see—which was nothing in the first case and (maybe) a brief spark in the second—but she could not wait out the days doing nothing.

Then, finally, it was the night of Leo's experiment. Hilda drove to the library at ten P.M. Midnight, he had said; but of course, he would need time to set up his equipment. The downtown was empty when she drove though; her tires hissed on abandoned streets. Stone veterans of Antietam and Gettysburg gazed down from their monument in

Centre Square. It was a ghostlit night. Black clouds streaked a silver-dollar moon. The wind shivered naked tree branches against the sky.

She turned onto Church and drove past the darkened library. A single light broke the black facade; the director's office, she noted with surprise. Why tonight, of all nights, had the director stayed to watch? Hilda turned into the driveway and drove all the way to the rear parking lot. Her headlight beams cut across the night, picking out the colorless shapes of two other cars and, briefly, a solitary figure standing by the back wall.

When she cut her engine, she could hear the muted rush of the wind through the trees. She shivered. It was a cold sound, a lonely sound. Autumn was, in many ways, a colder time than winter. She unbuckled herself and got out of the car. The slam of the door closing behind her echoed in the nighttime silence. She peered toward the wall, where she had seen the figure, and saw Leo already approaching. His overcoat, unbuttoned, flapped in the breeze; and he held his hat in place with his left hand. The smile that cut his face tightened his skin like a drum.

"Well," he said. "Tonight is the night."

And that simply had to be true, because it could mean anything.

"All Hallows' Eve," she told Leo as they reconnected the monitors, "was the old Celtic New Year. New Year's Day began at sunset on the last day of October. The Celts believed that spirits of those who had died during the year would roam the night, trying to occupy the bodies of the living. People dressed themselves in frightening costumes to scare the spirits off."

Leo grunted as he strung the cables. "I know that. It's all myth, though. Superstition. The dead go walking all year round, not just tonight."

There was no possible reply to a remark like that. And he had said it in so reasonable a tone. Still, if he was right that the recurrent, spontaneous light flashes were the souls of the dead, they did indeed go a-walking all year round. Every two days in the library workroom.

If there was any connection at all. She thought it was remarkable that, as she had come to think of the flashes as simple, physical events, Leo had gone the other way. Rather suddenly, it seemed to her. Between her visit to his office and their first test on the twenty-sixth. Something had happened to him over that weekend. Make contact, he had said after that first test. Contact with what? A flashbulb? A holographic recording? Leo was not setting up an experiment, she suddenly realized; he was conducting a séance. Not with trumpets or tambourines, though; there would be no holding hands in the dark. This was a modern séance, with all the modern, electronic conveniences.

She watched him hunched over his work. His lips were drawn tight against his teeth, and his hand trembled very slightly. *What was he thinking?* she wondered. She was not sure she wanted to know.

▼

Everything was ready by eleven-forty, and the last few minutes seemed to drag by as slowly as they had five days before. Leo had rigged his laser to a photoelectric cell so that it would fire the instant the ghost appeared. The idea, he explained, was not to destroy the entity, but to amplify it through a kind of supercharging. Hilda did not understand what he said about energy levels and transitions and the like. She assumed that, in this one arena, at least, he was a competent gladiator.

She was not concerned with whether the ghost would appear. It would, and that was all there was to it. The sun rose and set; thiamin ran through her phases; and the library ghost would make its regular appearance. As simply and predictably as that. And didn't that predictability argue against its being a 'person'? People always took you by surprise. Consider her mother, or even Leo. Things happened; people changed. Only the natural world ran forever in a predictable rut. "The stars in their courses . . . " So, it might not be a ghost as she had always thought of ghosts, as hauntings by the unquiet dead. It might be, as Leo had once told her, a stuck, holographic record. But that did not bother her. It wasn't *what* it was that mattered, but only *that* it was. It was that knowledge that made her safe within her own skull.

The director appeared in the doorway, bearing a tray. She carried it to the worktable against the east wall and set it down. "I thought you might want some coffee," she said.

Leo raised his head. "What? Who . . . " Oh. No. No, coffee. Thank you." He ducked back to his work.

"I'll have a cup," Hilda said quietly.

The director poured from a portable electric poet into two china cups and handed one to Hilda.

"Thank you." Hilda sipped from the hot liquid. "Why are you here?" she asked bluntly.

The director shrugged. "Who can resist putting her beliefs to the test? Tonight is the denouement, isn't it? Tonight will settle things once and for all."

Hilda glanced at Leo. "Some things."

The director followed her glance. She raised her own cup to her lips. "Yes. Well."

Leo turned out the lights and they waited quietly in the dark while the clock crept toward midnight. Hilda could hear the hushed sounds of breathing and, occasionally, the sharp tink of a cup against its saucer. The director had said nothing more after the first brief sentences. She stood in the shadows beside Hilda, thin and proper and faintly disapproving, and asked no questions. Hilda resisted the urge to cross the room and sit beside Leo. Instead, she leaned back against the worktable. "Soon, now," Leo's voice announced from the gloom.

When the clock in the boardroom struck, Hilda jerked and leaned forward, peering into the dark. She held her breath as the soft chimes rang a slow, leaking drip of sound.

It happened suddenly on the tenth ring. A brightness flickered on the far side of the room and, simultaneously, a ruby red beam of light, straight as a steel rod, pierced its heart. In an instant, a phosphorescent sphere bloomed in the darkened room. It was white with a tinge of blue around its edges. It throbbed like a soap-bubble heart.

Hilda shivered in the sudden cold. Her breath made puffs of steam that glowed in the pale light emanating from the ghost.

Campfire–shadows writhed on the walls. Hilda heard the director's coffee cup shatter on the floor; she saw Leo stand and lean across his table.

"Can you hear me?" Leo asked.

The pearly ball of light stretched and twisted like an amoeba.

"Can you take a message? For Harry? I must speak with him!"

The ghost pulsated and danced in the air.

The director grabbed her by the sleeve. "Do you see it?" she demanded. "Do you see it?"

Hilda disengaged her sleeve from the curled fingers. "Of course, I see it."

"Oh, it's wonderful! It's so wonderful!"

She turned and looked at the woman. The director's face was a crescent moon in the ghostly light. "Why?" she asked her. "Why is it so wonderful?"

"Don't you see? It means we go on. It means we don't end when we die!"

Across the room, Leo shouted questions at the light. Hilda backed away from her companions. Were they both mad? The apparition was an iridescent soap bubble floating in the air. A strange thing, yes, a beautiful thing; but only a thing, as incapable of silent witness as it was of answering questions. Was she the only one who saw nothing more? Were they blind; or she?

The world was an enigma, a conundrum that everyone solved to their own contentment; and in the end, each person's world was as impenetrably individual as her mother's. The ghost was a perfect mirror, reflecting whatever images each imagination could project. The director saw eternal life glowing in the room. Harry saw a channel to his dead brother. She saw . . .

A light. Only a light. Mystery, but no image.

Leo gave a shout and twisted something on his control panel. The instruments hummed louder and the ruby light brightened. The ghost waxed, shimmering with a thousand colors. Streamers of azure and crimson roiled through it. Silver bubbles drifted from the center toward the edge and fell back inward. The surface twitched and spasmed. Frost appeared on the windowpanes of the room, on the worktables. The cold bit into Hilda and her teeth chattered.

Then the ghost fell in on itself like a collapsing star. For just an instant, Hilda thought she saw it coalesce into a slim, fine-featured woman; then it shattered into a billion twinkling lights that exploded soundlessly into the corners of the room, dying like fireworks in the nighttime sky.

The room fell dark.

Hilda sucked in a breath. Beside her, she heard the director's soft "Amen." The hum of the equipment was the only other sound. The cold slowly faded; the frost dripped from the windows. The laser cast a small, red spot on the card catalogue. Abruptly, it, too, vanished. Across the room she heard Leo sob.

Hilda hit the light switch and saw Leo slumped in his chair with his face in his hands. She went to him and put a gentle hand on his shoulder. "Leo?"

He turned a face toward her. "He'll never come back," he said. "He'll never come back." He pushed her hand away, rose, and staggered from the room.

"Who?" That was the director. The question was flat, unemotional. Hilda turned around and saw the same hard face she had always known. There was no trace of her earlier exaltation. "Who will never come back?"

Hilda sighed and hugged herself. Who? Everyone. Anyone. Leo's brother. Her mother. All the strangers we once thought we knew. "Harry," she said aloud. "Leo's twin brother, Harry."

The director pressed her lips together. "Of course, he won't. His brother is dead. I talked to his chairman. He told me that Dr. Reissman's brother had died while they were on a Boy Scout hike. He stumbled off a cliff in the dark." She shook her head. "Tragic. I imagine twins are very close."

Hilda felt the blood drain from her.

"Off a cliff? Oh, God!" And she turned and bolted from the room.

When she burst from the library's back door into the cold of the night, the wind bit through her blouse like a knife. It tore her hair loose and sent it streaming. It sucked the breath from her open mouth. She remembered what she had said to Leo that first day. *A long way to fall. Time enough to know.* How cruel her words must have been! But she hadn't known. How could she have known?

Time enough for a gulping breath; then she turned and ran to the parking lot. Halfway across the flat asphalt surface, she skidded to a halt. Leo was standing atop the stone wall at the east end, where the drop was nearly sheer. She did not want to startle him; so she walked slowly to his side and waited for him to notice her.

He was staring down into the black depths. Above, the moon glowed cold behind racing clouds. Hilda shivered in the icy wind.

"You should go back inside," he said after a moment. "You'll catch pneumonia."

"You will, too."

He shook his head. "I won't be standing here long enough for that to matter."

"Please, Leo. Harry can't want that."

He turned his head and looked at her. His cheeks drooped, pulling his mouth down. "He must."

"Why?" She forced her voice to remain as quiet and as reasonable as his. She wanted to shout, to scream at him. *Calm,* she told herself. *Stay calm.*

"Why? So we can be together, like we always were. Like we were meant to be."

She knew then that there was a third sort of fear. She knew that Leo would die unless she saved him, and she did not know if she could do it. Caring was not enough. She had not been able to save her own mother.

"You can't mean that." Did you argue with the suicidal? Did logic convince them? If not logic, what?

"I knew it the moment it happened." He spoke in a quiet, distant voice. "I woke up in the middle of the night, and I knew that something had happened to him. I roused the scoutmaster and told him that Harry was gone, that he needed help." He sighed and studied the cloud-shrouded sky. "It was just growing light when we found him. He was at the bottom of a hundred-foot cliff. He had gone off to take a leak away from the camp, turned the wrong way in the dark, and walked off the edge. When I closed my eyes I could picture every step he had taken. I could remember his hands flailing wildly, grasping vainly for handholds as he fell. Fingers breaking against the rocks." He looked again at the rocks below him.

"He was still alive," he continued. "If he had been dead already, it might not have hurt so much. But he was still alive. I saw him move an arm. It took an hour for them to find another way to the bottom. I sat at the top of the cliff and watched. Harry opened his eyes and he saw me up there looking down; and, for an instant, I saw myself seeing him. Then he closed his eyes and he didn't move again. A few minutes later, every bird in the forest took wing and circled above, blackening the sky, screeching. I knew that Harry had died. There was always a link of some sort, a channel that joined us; and someone had just . . . hung up the extension. That's as clearly as I can explain it. I could call out, but no one would ever answer again. I have never been happy since that moment."

"It must have been terrible." She thought her words were shallow, inadequate; but it did not matter. He continued as if she had not spoken at all.

"A few years later, I thought I heard a whisper over our private line. A few words spoken in the darkness as I fell asleep. I thought Harry was trying to reach me. To tell me something important. I tried to listen; but the harder I concentrated, the more elusive the words were. They were . . . 'peripheral' sounds. Every night, before I went to bed, I prayed that Harry would come back. But I had read 'The Monkey's Paw' and sometimes I was afraid that my prayers would be answered. Teenage boys don't like to cry; but I cried. I cried. Then, one night, while I was in college; he did come back. Or he tried to."

Hilda took a deep breath and hunched over. She knew, she shouldn't try to grab him. If she did, he would pull away and fall; and she would never be able to hang on to him. "What happened?" Behind her, she could hear the library door open and footsteps clicking on the asphalt. She knew that the director had followed them—after first stopping sensibly for her overcoat. Without turning, Hilda gestured with her hand, and she heard the other woman leave, to—sensibly—call the rescue squad.

"I was asleep," Leo said. "I was in my dormitory room asleep when I felt him standing beside my bed. The prickling at the back of my head woke me up and, for a moment, I thought I had dreamed it. Then, I realized that I could still feel the presence beside me. I stared toward it, but I could see nothing. I tried to raise my arm to reach out, but I was paralyzed. I felt nothing over the channel Harry and I had shared—only a vast indifference—so I knew that, though he was trying to come back to me, he was unable to make it through all the way."

"Did it . . . Did you . . . " She let her breath out. "I know the feeling." He nodded slowly. "Yes, so you told me. That was when I knew that ghosts were souls. When you told me that you had felt the same thing. That could not have been coincidence."

"But that mightn't mean that at all. You told me so yourself."

"I did. I *wanted* apparitions to be false, or that they not be souls. I needed to believe that."

"You never were objective about it."

He shook his head and studied the darkness below him. "If ghosts were real and they were souls, then why had Harry never come back to me?"

There was nothing she could answer to that. "What changed your mind?"

"Last Friday night, my haunt returned. I knew it wasn't real—I had settled that years ago—but I knew your library ghost was real. And that didn't make any sense. Why the library ghost and not Harry? I had to know."

How paper-thin was the barrier between thought and unreality. The slightest thing—a stroke, a psychic trauma—rips it through. She recalled that Leo used his laser to project images. What had they really seen in the workroom tonight? Did even Leo know? "I was close to my mother, too," she told him. "We could have been twins, too; except for the age."

He looked at her. "Your mother is still alive."

She avoided his gaze. "But I treated her as if she were dead. Your brother dead, but you treat him as if he were alive. You won't let him go."

He turned and faced the drop once more. "I can't."

"How many years has it been?"

"A great many."

"It's too long ago to matter anymore."

He turned a tear-stained face to her. He looked older than at any other time she had seen him. "It will always matter. If I had gotten up with him, he would never have died."

So, that was it. Hilda felt like crying herself. "Or you might both have died. You can't torture yourself over things that might have been."

"Can't I? My brother is dead, and it was my fault. Now, my career is finished; my colleagues laugh at me. Why should I not take this one last step? It is such a small one."

"Because *I* don't want you to!" She cried it, shouted it into the night.

"Eh?" He gave her an astonished look.

She was angry with him, for what he had done to her and to her life; and for what he had done to himself. "Do you think I want to go through the rest of my life with the same load of guilt you've been carrying: always rerunning this night and asking myself what I could have done differently? Blaming myself?"

He looked stricken. "But . . . But you mustn't blame yourself," he said. "You can not be responsible for what I do."

She held her breath, willing him to see the connection. She could not tell him; he had to tell himself. He stood there for two long breaths, studying her. The seconds seemed to stretch out forever. Then he nodded. "Yes. I see." He glanced once more at the abyss below him; then he stepped down onto the solidity of the parking lot. He began to shake. Hilda closed her eyes briefly and said a prayer of thanks. She opened her arms and he stepped into them and laid his head on her shoulder and wept. "There,' she said. "It's all right now." She patted him on the back. "It's all right."

"I would have jumped," he said. "I would have."

"I know. It's all right, now."

"No, it is not all right," he said after a long silence. "I'm frightened of what I yet might do." He shook his head. "I'm not happy. I won't be anytime soon; but I think, perhaps, I can see happiness from here."

After a few moments, he disengaged himself. He rubbed his hand over his face and turned back to the wall. Hilda held one hand out to him, but he only approached the wall and gazed over its edge. The tears still coated his checks. Hilda watched him, her arms half-raised toward him, her hands clenched. The wind was bitterly cold. Winter was coming. All tears were ice; and winter must be brave.

Masks

DAMON KNIGHT

Some people leave a bigger footprint than others. Damon Knight, writing science fiction since the 1940s, has written some wonderful short stories, as well as a number of novels, including the extraordinary *The Man in the Tree.* In the 1960s he had stories adapted for television, and has long been famous for a particularly scary episode of *The Twilight Zone* adapted from his 1950 short story "To Serve Man."

But perhaps Knight will be remembered more for editing the twenty-one volumes of *Orbit,* widely regarded as the most important source of short science fiction from 1966 until its demise in the late 1980s. In addition, he was a founder of the Milford Writers Workshop and was the major force behind the founding of the Science Fiction Writers of America.

"Masks," written in 1958, is one of the most unusual and chilling of the technohorrors in this book. As he does in much of his work, Knight takes a common science fiction idea—replacement of the human body entirely by mechanical parts—and gives it a macabre but realistic twist.

The eight pens danced against the moving strip of paper, like the nervous claws of some mechanical lobster. Roberts, the technician, frowned over the tracings while the other two watched.

"Here's the wake-up impulse," he said, pointing with a skinny finger. "Then here, look, seventeen seconds more, still dreaming."

"Delayed response," said Babcock, the project director. His heavy face was flushed and he was sweating. "Nothing to worry about."

"Okay, delayed response, but look at the difference in the tracings. Still dreaming, after the wake-up impulse, but the peaks are closer together. Not the same dream. More anxiety, more motor pulses."

"Why does he have to sleep at all?" asked Sinescu, the man from Washington. He was dark, narrow-faced. "You flush the fatigue poisons out, don't you? So what is it, something psychological?"

"He needs to dream," said Babcock. "It's true he has no physiological need for sleep, but he's got to dream. If he didn't, he'd start to hallucinate, maybe go psychotic."

"Psychotic," said Sinescu. "Well—that's the question, isn't it? How long has he been doing this?"

"About six months."

"In other words, about the time he got his new body—and started wearing a mask?"

"About that. Look, let me tell you something, he's rational. Every test—"

"Yes, okay, I know about tests. Well—so he's wake now?"

The technician glanced at the monitor board. "He's up. Sam and Irma are with him." He hunched his shoulders, staring at the EEG tracings again. "I don't know why it should bother me. It stands to reason, if he has dream needs of his own that we're not satisfying with the programmed stuff, this is where he gets them in." His face hardened. "I don't know. Something about those peaks I don't like."

Sinescu raised his eyebrows. "You program his dreams?"

"Not program," said Babcock impatiently. "A routine suggestion to dream the sort of thing we tell him to. Somatic stuff, sex, exercise, sport."

"And whose idea was that?"

"Psych section. He was doing fine neurologically, every other way, but he was withdrawing. Psych decided he needed that somatic input in some form, we had to keep him in touch. He's alive, he's functioning, everything works. But don't forget, he spent forty-three years in a normal human body."

▼

In the hush of the elevator, Sinescu said, ". . . Washington."

Swaying, Babcock said, "I'm sorry, what?"

"You look a little rocky. Getting any sleep?"

"Not lately. What did you say before?"

"I said they're not happy with your reports in Washington."

"Goddamn it, I know that." The elevator door silently opened. A tiny foyer, green carpet, gray walls. There were three doors, one metal, two heavy glass. Cool, stale air. "This way."

Sinescu paused at the glass door, glanced through: a gray-carpeted living room, empty. "I don't see him."

"Around the ell. Getting his morning checkup."

The door opened against slight pressure; a battery of ceiling lights went on as they entered. "Don't look up," said Babcock. "Ultraviolet." A faint hissing sound stopped when the door closed.

"And positive pressure in here? To keep out germs? Whose idea was that?"

"His." Babcock opened a chrome box on the wall and took out two surgical masks. "Here, put this on."

Voices came muffled from around the bend of the room. Sinescu looked with distaste at the white mask, then slowly put it over his head.

They stared it each other. "Germs," said Sinescu through the mask. "Is that rational?"

"All right, he can't catch a cold or what have you, but think about it a minute. There are just two things now that could kill him. One is a prosthetic failure, and we guard against that; we've got five hundred people here, we check him out like an airplane. That leaves a cerebrospinal infection. Don't go in there with a closed mind."

The room was large, part living room, part library, part workshop. Here was a cluster of Swedish-modern chairs, a sofa, coffee table; here a workbench with a metal lathe, electric crucible, drill press, parts bins, tools on wallboards; here a drafting table; here a free-standing wall of book- shelves that Sinescu fingered curiously as they passed. Bound volumes of project reports, technical journals, reference books; no fiction except for *Fire* and *Storm* by George Stewart, and *The Wizard of Oz* in a worn blue binding. Behind the bookshelves, set into a little alcove, was a glass door through which they glimpsed another living room, differently furnished: upholstered chairs, a tall philodendron in a ceramic pot. "There's Sam," Babcock said.

A man had appeared in the other room. He saw them, turned to call to someone they could not see, then came forward, smiling. He was bald and stocky, deeply tanned. Behind him, a small, pretty woman hurried up. She crowded through after her husband, leaving the door open. Neither of them wore a mask.

"Sam and Irma have the next suite," Babcock said. "Company for him; he's got to have somebody around. Sam is an old air-force buddy of his, and besides, he's got a tin arm."

The stocky man shook hands, grinning. His grip was firm and warm. "Want to guess which one?" He wore a flowered sport shirt. Both arms were brown, muscular and hairy, but when Sinescu looked more closely, he saw that the right one was a slightly different color, not quite authentic.

Embarrassed, he said, "The left, I guess."

"Nope." Grinning wider, the stocky man pulled back his right sleeve to show the straps.

"One of the spin-offs from the project," said Babcock. "Myoelectric, servo-controlled, weighs the same as the other one. Sam, they about through in there?"

"Maybe so. Let's take a peek. Honey, you think you could rustle up some coffee for the gentlemen?"

"Oh, why, sure." The little woman turned and darted back through the open doorway.

The far wall was glass, covered by a translucent white curtain. They turned the corner. The next bay was full of medical and electronic equipment, some built into the walls, some in tall black cabinets on wheels. Four men in white coats were gathered around what looked like an astronaut's couch. Sinescu could see someone lying on it: feet in Mexican woven-leather shoes, dark socks, gray slacks. A mutter of voices.

"Not through yet," Babcock said. "Must have found something else they didn't like. Let's go out onto the patio a minute."

"Thought they checked him at night—when they exchange his blood, and so on . . .?"

"They do," Babcock said. "And in the morning, too." He turned and pushed open the heavy glass door. Outside, the roof was paved with cut stone, enclosed by a green plastic canopy and tinted-glass walls. Here and there were concrete basins, empty. "Idea was to have a roof garden out here, something green, but he didn't want it. We had to take all the plants out, glass the whole thing in."

Sam pulled out metal chairs around a white table and they all sat down. "How is he, Sam?" asked Babcock.

He grinned and ducked his head. "Mean in the mornings."

"Talk to you much? Play any chess?"

"Not too much. Works, mostly. Reads some, watches the box a little." His smile was forced; his heavy fingers were clasped together and Sinescu saw now that the fingertips of one hand had turned darker, the others not. He looked away.

"You're from Washington, that right?" Sam asked politely. "First time here? Hold on." He was out of his chair. Vague upright shapes were passing behind the curtained glass door. "Looks like they're through. If you gentlemen would just wait here a minute, till I see." He strode across the roof. The two men sat in silence. Babcock had pulled down his surgical mask; Sinescu noticed and did the same.

"Sam's wife is a problem," Babcock said, leaning nearer. "It seemed like a good idea at the time, but she's lonely here, doesn't like it—no kids—"

The door opened again and Sam appeared. He had a mask on, but it was hanging under his chin. "If you gentlemen would come in now."

In the living area, the little woman, also with a mask hanging around her neck, was pouring coffee from a flowered ceramic jug. She was smiling brightly but looked unhappy. Opposite her sat someone tall, in gray shirt and slacks, leaning back, legs out, arms on the arms of his chair, motionless. Something was wrong with his face.

"Well, now," said Sam heartily. His wife looked up at him with an agonized smile.

The tall figure turned its head and Sinescu saw with an icy shock that its face was silver, a mask of metal with oblong slits for eyes, no nose or mouth, only curves that were faired into each other. ". . . project." said an inhuman voice.

Sinescu found himself half bent over a chair. He sat down. They were all looking at him. The voice resumed, "I said, are you here to pull the plug on the project." It was unaccented, indifferent.

"Have some coffee." The woman pushed a cup toward him.

Sinescu reached for it, but his hand was trembling and he drew it back. "Just a fact-finding expedition," he said.

"Bull. Who sent you—Senator Hinkel."

"That's right."

"Bull. He's been here himself; why send you? If you are going to pull the plug, might as well tell me." The face behind the mask did not move when he spoke; the voice did not seem to come from it.

"He's just looking around, Jim," said Babcock.

"Two hundred million a year," said the voice, "to keep one man alive. doesn't make much sense, does it. Go on, drink your coffee."

Sinescu realized that Sam and his wife had already finished theirs and that they had pulled up their masks. He reached for his cup hastily.

"Hundred percent disability in my grade is thirty thousand a year. I could get along on that easy. For almost an hour and a half."

"There's no intention of terminating the project," Sinescu said.

"Phasing it out, though. Would you say phasing it out."

"Manners, Jim," said Babcock.

"Okay. My worst fault. What do you want to know." Sinescu sipped his coffee. His hands were still trembling. "That mask you're wearing," he started.

"Not for discussion. No comment, no comment. Sorry about that, don't mean to be rude; a personal matter. Ask me something—" Without warning, he stood up, blaring, "Get that damn thing out of here!" Sam's wife's cup smashed, coffee brown across the table. A fawn-colored puppy was sitting in the middle of the carpet, cocking its head, bright-eyed, tongue out.

The table tipped, Sam's wife struggled up behind it. Her face was pink, dripping with tears. She scooped up the puppy without pausing and ran out. "I better go with her," Sam said, getting up. "Go on; and, Sam, take a holiday. Drive her into Winnemucca, see a movie."

"Yeah, guess I will." He disappeared behind the bookshelf wall.

The tall figure sat down again, moving like a man; it leaned back in the same posture, arms on the arms of the chair. It was still. The hands gripping the wood were shapely and perfect but unreal: there was something wrong about the fingernails. The brown, well-combed hair above the mask was a wig; the ears were wax. Sinescu nervously fumbled his surgical mask up over his mouth and nose. "Might as well get along," he said, and stood up.

"That's right, I want to take you over to Engineering and R and D," said Babcock. "Jim, I'll be back in a little while. Want to talk to you."

"Sure," said the motionless figure.

▼

Babcock had had a shower, but sweat was soaking through the armpits of his shirt again. The silent elevator, the green carpet, a little blurred. The air cool, stale. Seven years, blood and money, five hundred good men. Psych section, Cosmetic, Engineering, R and D, Medical, Immunology, Supply, Serology, Administration. The glass doors. Sam's apartment empty, gone to Winnemucca with Irma. Psych. Good men, but were they the best? Three of the best had turned it down. Buried in the files. *Not like an ordinary amputation, this man has had everything cut off.*

The tall figure had not moved. Babcock sat down. The silver mask looked back at him.

"Jim, let's level with each other."

"Bad, huh."

"Sure it's bad. I left him in his room with a bottle. I'll see him again before he leaves, but God knows what he'll say in Washington. Listen, do me a favor, take that thing off."

"Sure." The hand rose, plucked at edge of the silver mask, lifted it away. Under it, the tan-pink face, sculptured nose and lips, eyebrows, eyelashes, not handsome but good-looking, normal-looking. Only the eyes wrong, pupils too big. And the lips that did not open or move when it spoke. "I can take anything off. What does that prove."

"Jim. Cosmetic spent eight and a half months on that model and the first thing you do is slap a mask over it. We've asked you what's wrong, offered to make any changes you want."

"No comment."

"You talked about phasing out the project. Did you think you were kidding?"

A pause. "Not kidding."

"All right, then open up, Jim, tell me; I have to know. They won't shut the project down; they'll keep you alive but that's all. There are seven hundred on the volunteer list, including two U.S. senators. Suppose one of them gets pulled out of an auto wreck tomorrow. We can't wait till then to decide; we've got to know now. Whether to let the next one die or put him into a TP body like yours. So talk to me."

"Suppose I tell you something but it isn't the truth."

"Why would you lie?"

"Why do you lie to a cancer patient."

"I don't get it. Come on, Jim."

"Okay, try this. Do I look like a man to you."

"Sure."

"Bull. Look at this face." Calm and perfect. Beyond the fake irises, a wink of metal. "Suppose we had all the other problems solved and I could go into Winnemucca tomorrow; can you see me walking down the street, going into a bar, taking a taxi."

"Is that all it is?" Babcock drew a deep breath. "Jim, sure there's a difference, but for Christ's sake, it's like any other prosthesis—people get used to it. Like that arm of Sam's. You see it, but after a while you forget it, you don't notice."

"Bull. You pretend not to notice. Because it would embarrass the cripple."

Babcock looked down at his clasped hands. "Sorry for yourself?"

"Don't give me that," the voice blared. The tall figure was standing. The hands slowly came up, the fists clenched. "I'm in this thing. I've been in it for two years. I'm in it when I go to sleep, and when I wake up, I'm still in it."

Babcock looked up at him. "What do you want, facial mobility? Give us twenty years, maybe ten, we'll lick it."

"No. No."

"Then what?"

"I want you to close down Cosmetic."

"But that's—"

"Just listen. The first model looked like a tailor's dummy, so you spent eight months and came up with this one, and it looks like a corpse. The whole idea was to make me look like a man, the first model pretty good, the second model better, until you've got something that can smoke cigars and joke with women and go bowling and nobody will know the difference. You can't do it, and if you could, what for."

"I don't—Let me think about this. What do you mean, a metal—"

"Metal, sure, but what difference does that make. I'm talking about shape. Function. Wait a minute." The tall figure strode across the room, unlocked a cabinet, came back with rolled sheets of paper. "Look at this."

The drawing showed an oblong metal box on four jointed legs. From one end protruded a tiny mushroom-shaped head on a jointed stem and a cluster of arms ending in probes, drills, grapples. "For moon prospecting."

"Too many limbs," said Babcock after a moment. "How would you—"

"With the facial nerves. Plenty of them left over. Or here." Another drawing. "A module plugged into the control system of a spaceship. That's where I belong, in space. Sterile environment, low grav, I can go where a man can't go and do what a man can't do. I can be an asset, not a goddam billion-dollar liability."

Babcock rubbed his eyes. "Why didn't you say anything before?"

"You were all hipped on prosthetics. You would have told me to tend my knitting."

Babcock's hands were shaking as he rolled up the drawings. "Well, by God, this just may do it. It just might." He stood up and turned toward the door. "Keep your—" he cleared his throat. "I mean, hang tight, Jim."

"I'll do that."

When he was alone, he put on his mask again and stood motionless a moment, eye shutters closed. Inside, he was running clean and cool; he could feel the faint reassuring hum of pumps, click of valves and relays. They had given him that: cleaned out all the offal, replaced it with machinery that did not bleed, ooze or suppurate. He thought of the lie he had told Babcock. *Why do you lie to a cancer patient?* But they would never get it, never understand.

He sat down at the drafting table, clipped a sheet of paper to it and with a pencil began to sketch a rendering of the moon-prospector design. When he had blocked in the prospector itself, he began to draw the background of craters. His pencil moved more slowly and stopped; he put it down with a click.

No more adrenal glands to pump adrenaline into his blood, so he could not feel fright or rage. They had released him from all that—love, hate, the whole sloppy mess—but they had forgotten there was still one emotion he could feel.

Sinescu, with the black bristles of his beard sprouting through his oily skin. A whitehead ripe in the crease beside his nostril.

Moon landscape, clean and cold. He picked up the pencil again.

Babcock, with his broad pink nose shining with grease, crusts of white matter in the corners of his eyes. Food mortar between his teeth.

Sam's wife, with raspberry-colored paste on her mouth. Face smeared with tears, a bright bubble in one nostril. And the damn dog, shiny nose, wet eyes . . .

He turned. The dog was there, sitting on the carpet, wet red tongue out—*left the door open again*—dripping, wagged its tail twice, then started to get up. He reached for the metal T square, leaned back, swinging it like an ax, and the dog yelped once as metal sheared bone, one eye spouting red, writhing on its back, dark stain of piss across the carpet, and he hit it again, hit it again.

The body lay twisted on the carpet, fouled with blood, ragged black lips drawn back from teeth. He wiped off the T square with a paper towel, then scrubbed it in the sink with soap and steel wool, dried it and hung it up. He got a sheet of drafting paper, laid it on the floor, rolled the body over onto it without spilling any blood on the carpet. He lifted the body in the paper, carried it out onto the patio, then onto the unroofed section, opening the doors with his shoulder. He looked over the wall. Two stories down, concrete roof, vents sticking out of it, nobody watching. He held the dog out, let it slide off the paper, twisting as it fell. It struck one of the vents, bounced, a red smear. He carried the paper back inside, poured the blood down the drain, then put the paper into the incinerator chute.

Splashes of blood were on the carpet, the feet of the drafting table, the cabinet, his trouser legs. He sponged them all up with paper towels and warm water. He took off his clothing, examined it minutely, scrubbed it in the sink, then put it in the washer. He washed the sink, rubbed himself down with disinfectant and dressed again. He walked through into Sam's silent apartment, closing the glass door behind him. Past the potted philodendron, over-stuffed furniture, red-and-yellow painting on the wall, out onto the roof, leaving the door ajar. Then back through the patio, closing doors.

Too bad. How about some goldfish.

He sat down at the drafting table. He was running clean and cool. The dream this morning came back to his mind, the last one, as he was struggling up out of sleep: *slithery kidneys burst gray lungs blood and hair ropes of guts covered with yellow fat oozing and sliding and oh god the stink like the breath of an outmouth no sound nowhere he was putting a stream down the slide of the dunghole and*

He began to ink in the drawing, first with a fine steel pen, then with a nylon brush. *his heel slid and he was falling could not stop himself falling into slimy bulging softness higher than his chin, higher and he could not move paralyzed and he tried to scream tried to scream tried to scream*

The prospector was climbing a crater slope with its handling members retracted and its head tilted up. Behind it the distant ringwall and the horizon, the black sky, the pinpoint stars. And he was there, and it was not far enough, not yet, for the earth hung overhead like a rotten fruit, blue with mold, crawling, wrinkling, purulent and alive.

But Smile No More

STEPHEN DEDMAN

Although he's been publishing short fiction for less than a decade, Stephen Dedman has made a tangible impact on the field of speculative fiction. This Australian writer has written stories with powerful impact in a variety of narrative voices. His first novel, *The Art of Arrow Cutting,* was published in 1997, and was nominated for the Bram Stoker Award for Best First Horror Novel.

"But Smile No More" takes place in a bar, but don't let that fool you. The source of the horror in this quietly scary story isn't immediately obvious, and once it is apparent it becomes clear that it's a danger of which we all should be aware.

Written in 1990, this tale might have sprung from the headlines of newspapers over the last twenty years. Genetic engineering is no longer science fiction, and we can only hope that no one is attempting what is done in this story of cold-blooded calculation and its human consequences. Sometimes horror's face is deceptively calm, but no less frightening than if it was screaming.

1

I'm a bartender, not a biochemist, so I've never really understood why booze gets people drunk, or happy, or maudlin; I just make a living out of it. Booze, I mean: my customers don't get very drunk. Around here is mostly fancy offices, so I get the tie and briefcase crowd in for business lunches, and then I send the girls home at eight: this end of town is pretty dead at night, anyway. A few professional drinkers pass through, on their way down, but they don't talk much. All these new skyscrapers have stockbroker-proof windows, so the would-be jumpers take to the elevators and drift down here. They don't understand sums of money below a million dollars, so I can charge what I like for cocktails: I made a fortune in the Crash of '87, enough to keep the wife happy and send my son to Yale, and if '99 is as bad as the lunchtime crowd predicts, I'll sell the place and retire early.

But this guy came in one Tuesday night, after nine; said he was a biochemist and asked to try every bottle on the shelf. He looked Asian, probably Vietnamese, and I have the devil of a time trying to guess *their* ages, but he had a thin little beard, so he wasn't a kid. And his eyes . . . well, I'm pretty good with eyes: I guessed he was under thirty, only got drunk when he needed to and he needed to now.

I just nodded, and asked, 'Left to right?' I keep the ouzo in the middle for guys like this—and make sure they pay in advance.

'Left to right is fine,' he replied, and I knew from his voice that he was sober, and he wasn't happy, and he wasn't much of a drinker, not in terms of experience—the way he grimaced when he tasted the tequila confirmed *that*. His eyebrows hinted that he might have smiled, once, but a man should not be held responsible for his eyebrows. Then he toasted me and said, 'To lemmings.'

At least, that's what I thought he said; it didn't sound like 'two lemons', which would've made more sense . . . and, like I said, he was sober. 'Lemmings?' I asked.

He nodded, 'You know anything about lemmings?'

'I know they're little furry creatures from Scandinavia that go crazy every three or four years and think they're stockbrokers.'

He blinked, then smiled politely and unconvincingly. 'Oh, they're not that crazy. Nor, whatever the creationists might say, are they a new type of Gadarene swine, throwing themselves over cliffs to drown our demons.' He drained his tequila like he was drowning a demon himself, then pushed the glass towards me.

I've never met a drunk who could say 'creationist'. My son, who's studying paleontology, can't even say it when he's sober, not without a few qualifying adjectives.

'You know any biology?' he asked, as I poured him a Southern Comfort.

'Just enough to extrapolate you're going to have a hell of a headache tomorrow.'

The smile didn't change. 'You know how you can take a spider and remove all of its silk, and it'll try to spin a web anyway? It's on a sort of autopilot, all instinct and no independent thought. Or how a wombat will always follow a set route, even if you build a fence in its way?'

I'd heard about the trick with the spider, so I nodded. 'You mean that lemmings used to migrate, but the sea wasn't always there?'

'He thought of that, but . . . ' He swallowed the Southern Comfort like it was medicine, then gave me the empty glass and another ten-dollar coin. 'Did you ever hear of a biologist called Peter Ericsson?'

'No.' Danny, my son, may have mentioned him—he likes to talk, and I just nod a lot (it's a trick bartenders learn early)—but the name didn't ring any bells.

'Or Iain Bourne?'

I shook my head.

'Okay.' He relaxed slightly, as much as a man can on a bar stool, and began. 'Ericsson was just an associate professor at one of the smaller, less prestigious state universities. He might've done better for himself if he'd specialised . . . but he was a great believer in "basic research". And, one night back in '67 or '68, he got to thinking about lemmings. I think he was looking for the ancestor of the dolphin . . . All the marine mammals, you know, are descended from a land species, after all, and no land mammal particularly resembles dolphins or whales . . . The lemming's a generic shape for a mammal—rather like the African hyrax, which is the closest living relative of the elephant which it scarcely resembles . . . '

He sipped at his vodka; he had me intrigued now, and I resolved to pour his drinks slowly, hoping to hear the end of this. I've known my share of happy drunks, and maudlin drunks, and violent drunks, and incoherent drunks, but this guy was a pleasantly garrulous drunk, and I'm partial to the breed.

'But that wasn't an explanation,' he continued. 'Even seals don't try to travel over land for distances like that. So, he thought, like you, what if there was once a suitable environment, where there was now only ocean?' Continental drift was too slow, but . . . could there have been a glacier, forming a land bridge, during the Ice Age? There could've, but apparently there wasn't. Or . . . glaciers elevated lands in the south, depressing lands in the north, reversing the procedure when they retreated . . . Nice idea, but again, the geologists said there wasn't any evidence for it.

'Okay, what if the lemmings' sense of direction had gone somehow haywire? No one was sure whether lemmings *had* a sense of direction, so it seemed a sensible place to start. Basic research, after all.

'The research was difficult—lemmings are, not surprisingly, hard to obtain, and the University wasn't generous with its equipment. The lemmings were also uncooperative when it came to running mazes, and not particularly eager to learn. A researcher in a more prestigious college might have given up there, but Ericsson, after all, was used to unenthusiastic students. After half year of persistence, he managed to obtain results suitable for a control group. He then set about confusing them with random periods of light and dark, wet and dry, temperate and cold—even false starscapes. No pattern.

'The next experiment required a bottle of thirty-two-year-old Scotch whisky, or so I'm told.'

'For the lemmings?' I gasped.

'No, for the Dean of Physics. Eventually, with his help, Ericsson was able to demonstrate that lemmings were dependent on a magnetic sense—an internal compass. And since it was proven that Earth's magnetic poles periodically inverted, instincts, evolved when the magnetic north pole was somewhere in Antarctica, resulted in mass suicide.'

I shook my head admiringly. 'Wow.'

'Oh, that was nothing. It would have earned Ericsson a Size 10 footnote in the history of science, and it earned him the hatred of the Creationists, which should have been enough for any educated man. It also took him out of the college and into a well-funded government research lab.'

He fell silent, and I wondered whether he'd finished; the ending didn't seem to justify the meanings. He sipped slowly at his vodka, rolling it around his mouth like a wine taster, then asked, 'Did you ever think there were some things man wasn't meant to know?'

I shrugged. 'I know there are a lot of things a man doesn't *want* to know.'

He looked around the bar at the dark, empty chairs and shiny half-full bottles, and asked, 'You think that's why they drink?'

'Yeah, sometimes.'

He nodded. 'Well, Ericsson set out to find the physical location of this magnetic sense. He figured it required a concentration of iron, and that it was probably in the brain . . . and if it wasn't near the surface, it was going to be hard to isolate surgically. But hell, lysergic acid blocks the serotonin pathways, preventing rational thought, and alcohol (as you may have noticed) shows a preference for the reticular formation, so why not an iron-based molecule that zooms in on a magnetic sense centre?

'Unfortunately, biochemistry still relies largely on trial and error, even when your theory is perfectly sound. *Vide* thalidomide, or Agent Orange . . . '

'You don't have to tell me about Agent Orange,' I replied, sourly. 'My brother Terry was marinated in the stuff. Died of cancer without getting a cent.'

He nodded, his face blank. 'Yeah, I heard about that. Sorry.'

I shrugged, wondering *how* he'd heard; I don't usually talk about Terry when I'm sober, and I don't drink on the job. A lot of my clientele still think Vietnam was good business and that chemical warfare has been given a bad press—and they don't come here to argue. If there was any one person more guilty than all the others, I could . . . well, do *something*, but as it is . . . 'You were saying?'

'One of the molecules that Ericsson chanced upon accumulated in the pleasure centre, the "rivers of reward". And stayed there, isolating it from the rest of the brain. And it didn't *just* work in lemmings.

'Ericsson died in '71, never realising that he'd discovered a cure for happiness . . . and if he had, I doubt he would have tried it on humans. But by that time, it was in Bourne's hands.'

He stared into his vodka, then downed it in two godalmighty gulps and handed me the empty glass. I poured him a Bacardi and waited.

'I don't have to tell you what things were like in the Nixon days; you probably know all about the CIA SNAFUS like MKULTRA and using

LSD on their own informers.' I nodded. 'Bourne tried it out on prisoners on Death Row the ultimate chemical castration.

'The prisoners reported feeling calmer, more resigned to their fate, less irascible and violent . . . but they were hardly a representative group. Bourne had Ericsson's work classified, which is why Ericsson never became famous. It was a lot of balls because there wasn't a one-in-a-million chance that it would've led anyone to developing the same drug but classified work pays better.

'Bourne gave the drug to students next, but the results of *that* were classified too . . . which meant that it was a failure, and possibly a nightmare. At best, the long-term results were just too hard to follow up. A few of his subjects were drafted, sent to Nam; and strangely, *none* of them came back. The others . . . well, either nothing happened, or there's been a cover-up, or maybe both. But, anyway, that wasn't what Bourne wanted. He wanted to give the drug to *very* young babies, so they would *never* know pleasure.'

I shuddered involuntarily, almost spilling my Coke. 'Why?'

He shrugged, 'His hypothesis was that happy people did not make the great discoveries; why should they want to? They were already happy. And the Chinese used to use eunuchs' (*you* try saying that after four stiff drinks) 'for their civil servants, because they didn't get distracted or ambitious. Of course, the relationship between pleasure and happiness isn't entirely understood, and there was no better way of finding out. Analysis requires destruction; it *means* destruction. Taking apart . . . '

'Even if you don't know how to put it together again.'

'Exactly. Can you *un*-mix a drink? But that didn't matter to Bourne. I'm not even sure that the project was approved because of his high-flown nonsense; the CIA probably thought of it as just another mind drug, a depressant that could pacify prisoners . . . or draftees, maybe. Or maybe make perfect soldiers who couldn't be seduced or get sentimental. But that's by the way—Bourne was given his subjects. Abortions were still illegal, you remember, and orphans are a buyer's market in wartime. Mostly black, of course, or Hispanic, but some of us were refugees, and Bourne insisted on a few white babies too; a mix of races, and a nearly even mix of boys and girls—'

'Some of *us?'*

'Yes,' he said quietly and sipped at his Bacardi. 'I was one of the Throng—that's what we called ourselves, later. Lydia suggested it; she was interested in languages, and in poetry, in emotions—in a purely theoretical sense, of course. It's from a poem by Edgar Allan Poe, a man with no great gift for happiness himself: *A hideous throng rush out forever/And laugh—but smile no more.*

'We didn't all rush out together: a few of us were adopted, and Bourne helped us get scholarships . . . I suppose we studied harder than the Irash, but we weren't all brilliant—Irash, by the way, was our name for the rest of you. Short for Irrationals. Nothing personal.'

He drained his Bacardi, pushed the glass towards me, glanced at his watch, and shook his head. 'Gotta go,' he said, a little thickly. 'Be back next week.'

2

I don't call Danny as often as I should, I guess, and I felt a little silly phoning him—but I've forgiven him for a lot of strange behaviour over the past twenty-seven years, and he owes me.

'Ericsson?'

'Yeah.'

'Doesn't ring any bells, Dad—but I'm not a biochemist.'

'What about that work you did last year?'

There was a rather expensive silence. Maybe he hadn't expected me to remember, or he probably thought I was only pretending to listen. Actually, I do listen; I learnt to do it when his mother walked out seventeen years ago. I don't always *understand,* is all.

'I just found the fossils; Linda did the chem lab work . . . Can I get back to you on this?'

I remembered, too late, that he and Linda had had a wonderful working relationship, followed very recently by a brief and cataclysmic romance. 'Yeah, please . . . and Danny?'

'Yeah, Dad?'

'Did you ever tell anyone about your Uncle Terry?'

'I don't think so . . . ' he replied, uncertainly. 'The chem labs here do a lot of defence research work, and I may have let it slip . . . why?'

'It doesn't matter,' I said, and hoped it didn't.

3

The biochemist came back on the Friday with a young woman. The place was busy; one of the girls served them, and I didn't see them until they were leaving. The woman had dark hair and very dark eyes; she looked about twenty-two from the eyes down, but she didn't smile. I waited for him Tuesday night, but he didn't show.

The Tuesday after, about quarter to ten, the place was empty again when the door opened, and the biochemist hurried in as though it were freezing outside. 'Hi.'

'Hi.' He looked at the row of bottles and asked, 'Where was I ?'

I poured him a Johnny Walker. 'The Irash.'

'Yeah. No offence.'

'None taken,' I assured him. 'How many are there of you?'

'Fifteen. There were twenty-one, but—' He shrugged and sipped at the whisky. 'I suppose it could be worse. We don't get depressed, I guess; we don't get down, because we were never up. We don't feel that we've lost anything, because we never had it to lose. I wonder how much worse it would feel if you *could* remember having been happy, without being able to recreate it. . . . '

His eyes became slightly misty and his voice very soft, and I almost expected him to fall over . . . but he recovered in an instant. 'Bourne wanted us to become scientists, of course,' he continued, his voice as crisp as new banknotes, 'and some of us did. And some of us settled for being technicians and engineers. Vanessa is studying Medicine, and Julio set a college record for low grades in Political Science, though I understand he did quite well at Psych. Two of the girls had kids of their own—none of *us* could—and held on to them long enough to see if it was hereditary . . . and apparently it isn't.'

He looked into his glass and shook his head. 'Babies have this secret weapon: they smile. It makes their mothers feel happy and maternal. Sometimes I wonder how *any* of us were adopted.' I shrugged. 'The experiment is over now, and I suppose we should be happy, if happiness were ever logical—which I wouldn't know.' He took a mouthful of his Scotch, grimaced, and asked for a Bloody Mary.

'What about Bourne?'

'What about him?'

'Is he still alive?'

'Oh, yes. He left the Project in '88, after the defense contracts scandal, and took a job with Condor Pharmaceuticals. Works near here, as a matter of fact.'

He took the Bloody Mary unsteadily in his left hand, holding it like a chess piece instead of like a glass, then moved it over to stand before the stool at his left. 'Good evening, Dr. Bourne,' he said loudly.

I looked up, startled. A man in his early fifties who knew how to wear an expensive suit was standing in the doorway. He spared me a glance, then walked slowly towards my customer. 'Good evening, Paul. How's the science fiction?'

Paul showed his teeth in an insincere grin. I stared at both of them, wondering who was lying.

'I see you've started without me,' said Bourne. 'Am I late?'

'No.'

'Is this mine, or have you become ambidextrous?'

'It's yours. On me.'

'Thank you.' He sat and tasted the drink. 'So, how is everyone?'

'Bradley quit,' replied Paul. 'He decided he didn't want to make bombs any more. Lydia's lecturing in semiotics.' Bourne shook his head in mock disgust, then took another mouthful of the Bloody Mary. 'Vanessa's in town. She gave her baby up for adoption last month, and I haven't heard from the others in more than a year. Have you?'

'Michael's been made a junior partner,' he replied. 'Apart from that, everyone's still where they were: no real news.'

'No weddings? No kids?' Paul's voice was softly mocking. Bourne ignored him.

'And what've you been doing?'

'Following in your footsteps,' said Paul. 'I've improved on the formula.'

Bourne dropped his glass; fortunately, it was nearly empty and it hadn't far to fall before it hit the bar. Suddenly, I believed everything Paul had told me.

'You can reverse the process?' asked Bourne, with forced casualness.

Paul continued to grin, leaving both of us in suspense for nearly half a minute. 'No,' he said finally. 'I'm still working on *that*, but I think the damage is irreversible. Like brain cells killed by alcohol; nothing can regenerate them. No, this was just a slight modification, but a serendipitous and useful one. It has the same effects as the original, but it's water soluble, and you don't have to inject it; it can be administered orally. It tastes like hell, but you only need a drop—and it's nearly colourless . . . '

And so was Bourne's face as he stared at the dregs in his glass. Paul stood, a little unsteadily, and reached into his pocket. I shook my head.

'That's okay,' I told him. 'No charge. Not for a friend of Terry's.'

Paul stared at me, and then he laughed. It wasn't a happy laugh, but it was a laugh all the same. And then he walked out.

4

That should've been the end, and maybe it was . . . but four nights later, on my way home, I saw cops and an ambulance clustered outside Arnheim House. The pavement was cracked and bloody. Obviously someone had jumped from the roof—and Arnheim House is twelve storeys tall. The top four contain the offices for Condor Pharmaceuticals.

But I didn't stop to see who it had been. I haven't seen Paul since, or Bourne, or heard anything of either of them, and sometimes I wonder . . . but never for very long. Maybe it isn't logical, but like I'd told Paul, there are some things a man doesn't want to know . . .

But they haunted me, the Throng, and I look for them everywhere. Sometimes I wonder if they've come here, to celebrate or mourn, never smiling, and I haven't recognised them amid the laughing lemmings . . .

I smile a lot, and I wait for people to smile back . . . I know you're out there. And some days, God help me, I think I know how you feel.

The Dead

Michael Swanwick

Michael Swanwick has become an overnight success in the past few years, though it took considerably longer than that for him to reach the point of ignition. He's won various awards, including the Nebula for his novel *Stations of the Tide,* and the World Fantasy Award for his novel *Iron Dragon's Daughter.*

Although he hasn't written a great number of stories, those he has produced have been of uncommonly high quality. No exception is the following truly creepy story, penned in 1996, which you could say is about zombies. This is not at all a funny story, but if you appreciate a macabre joke you might find something to chuckle about. On the other hand, you might just find this to be one of the most horrifying tales in the book. However it strikes you, I promise it will make an indelible impression.

Three boy zombies in matching red jackets bussed our table, bringing water, lighting candles, brushing away the crumbs between courses. Their eyes were dark, attentive, lifeless; their hands and faces so white as to be faintly luminous in the hushed light. I thought it in bad taste, but "This is Manhattan," Courtney said. "A certain studied offensiveness is fashionable here."

The blond brought menus and waited for our order.

We both ordered pheasant. "An excellent choice," the boy said in a clear, emotionless voice. He went away and came back a minute later with the freshly strangled birds, holding them up for our approval. He couldn't have been more than eleven when he died and his skin was of that sort connoisseurs call "milk-glass," smooth, without blemish, and all but translucent. He must have cost a fortune.

As the boy was turning away, I impulsively touched his shoulder. He turned back. "What's you name, son?" I asked.

"Timothy." He might have been telling me the *specialité de maison*. The boy waited a breath to see if more was expected of him, then left.

Courtney gazed after him. "How lovely he would look," she murmured, "nude. Standing in the moonlight by a cliff. Definitely a cliff. Perhaps the very one where he met his death."

"He wouldn't look very lovely if he'd fallen off a cliff."

"Oh, don't be unpleasant."

The wine steward brought our bottle. "Château Latour '17." I raised an eyebrow. The steward had the sort of old and complex face that Rembrandt would have enjoyed painting. He poured with pulseless ease and then dissolved into the gloom. "Good lord Courtney, you *seduced* me on cheaper."

She flushed, not happily. Courtney had a better career going than I. She outpowered me. We both knew who was smarter, better connected, more likely to end up in a corner office with the historically significant antique desk. The only edge I had was that I was a male in a seller's market. It was enough.

"This is a business dinner, Donald," she said, "nothing more."

I favored her with an expression of polite disbelief I knew from experience she'd find infuriating. And, digging into my pheasant, murmured, "Of course." We didn't say much of consequence until dessert, when I finally asked, "So what's Loeb-Soffner up to these days?"

"Structuring a corporate expansion. Jim's putting together the financial side of the package, and I'm doing personnel. You're being headhunted, Donald." She favored me with that feral little flash of teeth she made when she saw something she wanted. Courtney wasn't a beautiful woman, far from it. But there was that fierceness to her, that sense of something primal being held under tight and precarious control that made her hot as hot to me. "You're talented, you're thuggish, and you're not too tightly nailed to your present position. Those are all qualities we're looking for."

She dumped her purse on the table, took out a single-folded sheet of paper. "These are the terms I'm offering." She placed it by my plate, attacked her torte with gusto.

I unfolded the paper. "This is a lateral transfer."

"Unlimited opportunity for advancement," she said with her mouth full, "if you've got the stuff."

"Mmm." I did a line-by-line of the benefits, all comparable to what I was getting now. My current salary to the dollar—Ms. Soffner was showing off. And the stock options. "This can't be right. Not for a lateral."

There was that grin again, like a glimpse of shark in murky waters. "I knew you'd like it. We're going over the top with the options because we need your answer right away—tonight preferably. Tomorrow at the latest. No negotiations. We have to put the package together fast. There's going to be a shitstorm of publicity when this comes out. We want to have everything nailed down, present the fundies and bleeding hearts with a *fait accompli.*"

"My God, Courtney, what kind of monster do you have hold of now?"

"The biggest one in the world. Bigger than Apple. Bigger than Home Virtual. Bigger than HIVac-IV," she said with relish. "Have you ever heard of Koestler Biological?"

I put my fork down.

"Koestler? You're peddling corpses now?"

"Please. Postanthropic biological resources." She said it lightly, with just the right touch of irony. Still, I thought I detected a certain discomfort with the nature of her client's product.

"There's no money in it." I waved a hand toward our attentive waitstaff. "These guys must be—what?—maybe two percent of the annual turnover? Zombies are luxury goods: servants, reactor cleanups, Hollywood stunt deaths, exotic services" —we both knew what I meant— "a few hundred a year, maybe, tops. There's not the demand. The revulsion factor is too great."

"There's been a technological breakthrough." Courtney leaned forward. "They can install the infrasystem and controllers and offer the product for the factory-floor cost of a new subcompact. That's way below the economic threshold for blue-collar labor.

"Look at it from the viewpoint of a typical factory owner. He's already downsized to the bone and labor costs are bleeding him dry. How can he compete in a dwindling consumer market? Now let's imagine he buys into the program." She took out her Mont Blanc and began scribbling figures on the tablecloth. "No benefits. No liability suits. No sick pay. No pilferage. We're talking about cutting labor costs by at least two thirds. Minimum! That's irresistible, I don't care how big your revulsion factor is. We project we can move five hundred thousand units in the first year."

"Five hundred thousand," I said. "That's crazy. Where the hell are you going to get the raw material for—"

"Africa."

"Oh, God, Courtney." I was struck wordless by the cynicism it took to even consider turning the sub-Saharan tragedy to a profit, by the sheer, raw evil of channeling hard currency to the pocket Hitlers who ran the camps. Courtney only smiled and gave that quick little flip of her head that meant she was accessing the time on an optic chip.

"I think you're ready," she said, "to talk with Koestler."

At her gesture, the zombie boys erected projector lamps about us, fussed with the settings, turned them on. Interference patterns moiréd, clashed, meshed. Walls of darkness erected themselves about us. Courtney took out her flat and set it up on the table. Three taps of her nailed fingers and the round and hairless face of Marvin Koestler appeared on the screen. "Ah, Courtney!" he said in a pleased voice. "You're in—New York, yes? The San Moritz. With Donald." The slightest pause with each accessed bit of information. "Did you have the antelope medallions?" When we shook our heads, he kissed his fingertips. "Magnificent! They're ever so slightly braised and then smothered in buffalo mozzarella. Nobody makes them better. I had the same dish in Florence the other day, and there was simply no comparison."

I cleared my throat. "Is that where you are? Italy?"

"Let's leave out where I am." He made a dismissive gesture, as if it were a trifle. But Courtney's face darkened. Corporate kidnapping being the growth industry it is, I'd gaffed badly. "The question is—what do you think of my offer?"

"It's . . . interesting. For a lateral."

"It's the start-up costs. We're leveraged up to our asses as it is. You'll make out better this way in the long run." He favored me with a sudden grin that went mean around the edges. Very much the financial buccaneer. Then he leaned forward, lowered his voice, maintained firm eye-contact. Classic people-handling techniques. "You're not sold. You know you can trust Courtney to have checked out the finances. Still, you think: It won't work. To work the product has to be irresistible, and it's not. It can't be."

"Yes, sir," I said. "Succinctly put."

He nodded to Courtney. "Let's sell this young man." And to me, "My stretch is downstairs."

He winked out.

Koestler was waiting for us in the limo, a ghostly pink presence. His holo, rather, a genial if somewhat coarse-grained ghost afloat in golden light. He waved an expansive and insubstantial arm to take in the interior of the car and said, "Make yourselves at home."

The chauffeur wore combat-grade photomultipliers. They have him a buggish, inhuman look. I wasn't sure if he was dead or not. "Take us to Heaven," Koestler said.

The doorman stepped out into the street, looked both ways, nodded to the chauffeur. Robot guns tracked our progress down the block.

"Courtney tells me you're getting the raw materials from Africa."

"Distasteful, but necessary. To begin with. We have to sell the idea first—no reason to make things rough on ourselves. Down the line, though, I don't see why we can't go domestic. Something along the lines of a reverse mortgage, perhaps, life insurance that pays off while you're still alive. It'd be a step toward getting a goddamn free ride for too long; the least they can do is to die and provide us with servants."

I was pretty sure Koestler was joking. But I smiled and ducked my head, so I'd be covered in either case. "What's Heaven?" I asked, to move the conversation onto safer territory.

"A proving ground," Koestler said with great satisfaction, "for the future. Have you ever witnessed bare-knuckles fisticuffs?"

"No."

"Ah, now there's a sport for gentlemen! The sweet science at its sweetest. No rounds, no rules, no holds barred. It gives you the real measure of a man—not just of his strength but his character. How he handles himself, whether he keeps cool under pressure—how he stands up to pain. Security won't let me go to the clubs in person, but I've made arrangements."

▼

Heaven was a converted movie theater in a rundown neighborhood in Queens. The chauffeur got out, disappeared briefly around the back, and returned with two zombie bodyguards. It was like a conjurer's trick. "You had these guys stashed in the *trunk?"* I asked as he opened the door for us.

"It's a new world," Courtney said. "Get used to it."

The place was mobbed. Two, maybe three hundred seats, standing room only. A mixed crowd, black and Irish and Koreans mostly, but with a smattering of uptown customers as well. You didn't have to be poor to need the occasional taste of vicarious potency. Nobody paid us any particular notice. We'd come in just as the fighters were being presented.

"Weighing two-five-oh, in black trunks with a red stripe," the ref was bawling, "tha gang-bang *gang*sta, the bare-knuckle *brawla*, the man with tha—"

Courtney and I went up a scummy set of back stairs. Bodyguard-us-bodyguard, as if we were a combat patrol out of some twentieth-century jungle war. A scrawny, potbellied old geezer with a damp cigar in his mouth unlocked the door to our box. Sticky floor, bad seats, a good view down on the ring. Gray plastic matting, billowing smoke.

Koestler was there, in a shiny new hologram shell. It reminded me of those plaster Madonnas in painted bathtubs that Catholics set out in their yards. "Your permanent box?" I asked.

"All of this is for your sake, Donald—you and a few others. We're pitting our product one-on-one against some of the local talent. By arrangement with the management. What you're going to see will settle your doubts once and for all."

"You'll like this," Courtney said. "I've been here five nights straight. Counting tonight." The bell rang, starting the fight. She leaned forward avidly, hooking her elbows on the railing.

The zombie was gray-skinned and modestly muscled, for a fighter. But it held up its hands alertly, was light on its feet, and had strangely calm knowing eyes.

Its opponent was a real bruiser, a big black guy with classic African features twisted slightly out of true so that his mouth curled up in a kind of sneer on one side. He had gang scars on his chest and even uglier marks on his back that didn't look deliberate but like something he'd earned on the streets. His eyes burned with an intensity just this side of madness.

He came forward cautiously but not fearfully, and made a couple of quick jabs to get the measure of his opponent. They were blocked and countered.

They circled each other, looking for an opening.

For a minute or so, nothing much happened. Then the gangster feinted at the zombie's head, drawing up its guard. He drove through that opening with a slam to the zombie's nuts that made me wince.

No reaction.

The dead fighter responded with a flurry of punches, and got in a glancing blow to its opponent's cheek. They separated, engaged, circled around.

Then the big guy exploded in a combination of killer blows, connecting so solidly it seemed they would splinter every rib in the dead fighter's body. It brought the crowd to their feet, roaring their approval.

The zombie didn't even stagger.

A strange look came into the gangster's eyes, then, as the zombie counterattacked, driving him back into the ropes. I could only imagine what it must be like for a man who had always lived by his strength and his ability to absorb punishment to realize that he was facing an opponent to whom pain meant nothing. Fights were lost and won by flinches and hesitations. You won by keeping your head. You lost by getting rattled.

Despite his best blows, the zombie stayed methodical, serene, calm, relentless. That was its nature.

It must have been devastating.

The fight went on and on. It was a strange and alienating experience for me. After a while I couldn't stay focused on it. My thoughts kept slipping into a zone where I found myself studying the line of Courtney's jaw, thinking about later tonight. She liked her sex just a little bit sick. There was always a feeling, fucking her, that there was something truly repulsive that she *really* wanted to do but lacked the courage to bring up on her own.

So there was always this urge to get her to do something she didn't like. She was resistant; I never dared try more than one new thing per date. But I could always talk her into that one thing. Because when she was aroused, she got pliant. She could be talked into anything. She could be made to beg for it.

Courtney would've been amazed to learn that I was not proud of what I did with her—quite the opposite, in fact. But I was obsessed with her as she was with whatever it was that obsessed her.

Suddenly Courtney was on her feet, yelling. The hologram showed Koestler on his feet as well. The big guy was on the ropes being pummeled. Blood and spittle flew from his face with each blow. Then he was down; he'd never even had a chance. He must've known early on that it was hopeless, that he wasn't going to win, but he'd refused to take a fall. He had to be pounded into the ground. He went down raging, proud and uncomplaining. I had to admire that.

But he lost anyway.

That, I realized, was the message I was meant to take away from this. Not just that the product was robust. But that only those who backed it were going to win. I could see, even if the audience couldn't, that it was the end of an era. A man's body wasn't worth a damn anymore. There wasn't anything it could do that technology couldn't handle better. The number of losers in the world had just doubled, tripled, reached maximum. What the fools below were cheering for was the death of their futures.

I got up and cheered too.

In the stretch afterward, Koestler said, "You've seen the light. You're a believer now."

"I haven't necessarily decided yet."

"Don't bullshit me," Koestler said. "I've done my homework, Mr. Nichols. Your current position is not exactly secure. Morton-Western is going down the tubes. The entire service sector is going down the tubes. Face it, the old economic order is as good as fucking gone. Of course you're going to take my offer. You don't have any other choice."

The fax outed sets of contracts. "A Certain Product," it said here and there. Corpses were never mentioned.

But when I opened my jacket to get a pen Koestler said, "Wait. I've got a factory. Three thousand positions under me. I've got a motivated workforce. They'd walk through fire to keep their jobs. Pilferage is at zero. Sick time practically the same. Give me one advantage your product has over my current workforce. Sell me on it. I'll give you thirty seconds."

I wasn't in sales and the job had been explicitly promised me already. But by reaching for the pen, I had admitted I wanted the position. And we all knew whose hand carried the whip.

"They can be catheterized," I said—"no toilet breaks."

For a long instant Koestler just stared at me blankly. Then he exploded with laughter. "By God, that's a new one! You have a great future ahead of you, Donald. Welcome aboard."

He winked out.

We drove on in silence for a while, aimless, directionless. At last Courtney leaned forward and touched the chauffeur's shoulder.

"Take me home," she said.

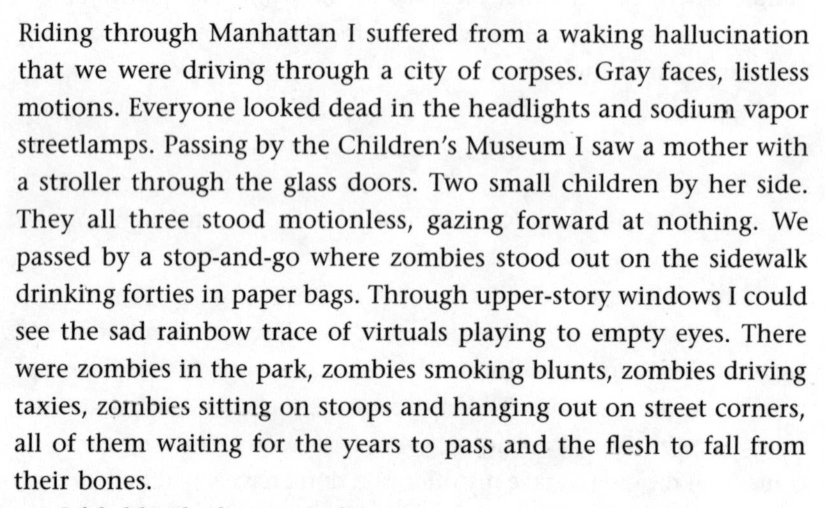

Riding through Manhattan I suffered from a waking hallucination that we were driving through a city of corpses. Gray faces, listless motions. Everyone looked dead in the headlights and sodium vapor streetlamps. Passing by the Children's Museum I saw a mother with a stroller through the glass doors. Two small children by her side. They all three stood motionless, gazing forward at nothing. We passed by a stop-and-go where zombies stood out on the sidewalk drinking forties in paper bags. Through upper-story windows I could see the sad rainbow trace of virtuals playing to empty eyes. There were zombies in the park, zombies smoking blunts, zombies driving taxies, zombies sitting on stoops and hanging out on street corners, all of them waiting for the years to pass and the flesh to fall from their bones.

I felt like the last man alive.

Courtney was still wired and sweaty from the fight. The pheromones came off her in great waves as I followed her down the hall to her apartment. She stank of lust. I found myself thinking of how she got just before orgasm, so desperate, so desirable. It was different after she came, she would fall into a state of calm assurance; the same sort of calm assurance she showed in her business life, the aplomb she sought so wildly during the act itself.

And when that desperation left her, so would I. Because even I could recognize that it was her desperation that drew me to her, that made me do the things she needed me to do. In all the years I'd known her, we'd never once had breakfast together.

I wished there was some way I could deal her out of the equation. I wished that her desperation were a liquid that I could drink down to the dregs. I wished I could drop her in a wine press and squeeze her dry.

At her apartment, Courtney unlocked her door and in one complicated movement twisted through and stood facing me from the inside. "Well," she said. "All in all, a productive evening. Good night, Donald."

"Good night? aren't you going to invite me inside?"

"No."

"What do you mean, no?" She was beginning to piss me off. A blind man could've told she was in heat from across the street. A chimpanzee could've talked his way into her pants. "What kind of idiot game are you playing now?"

"You know what no means, Donald. You're not stupid."

"No I'm not, and neither are you. We both know the score. Now let me in, goddamnit."

"Enjoy your present," she said, and closed the door.

I found Courtney's present back in my suite. I was still seething from her treatment of me and stalked into the room, letting the door slam behind me so that I was standing in near-total darkness. The only light was what little seeped through the draped windows at the far end of the room. I was just reaching for the light switch when there was a motion in the darkness.

Jackers! I thought, and all in panic lurched for the light switch, hoping to achieve I don't know what. Credit-jackers always work in trios, one to torture the security codes out of you, one to phone the numbers out of your accounts and into a fiscal trapdoor, a third to stand guard. Was turning on the lights supposed to make them scurry for darkness, like roaches? Nevertheless, I almost tripped over my own feet in my haste to reach the switch. But of course it was nothing like what I'd feared.

It was a woman.

She stood by the window in a white silk dress that could neither compete with nor distract from her ethereal beauty, her porcelain skin.

When the lights came on, she turned toward me, eyes widening, lips parting slightly. Her breasts swayed ever so slightly as she gracefully raised a bare arm to offer me a lily. "Hello, Donald," she said huskily. "I'm yours for the night." She was absolutely beautiful.

And dead, of course.

▼

Not twenty minutes later I was hammering on Courtney's door. She came to the door in a Pierre Cardin dressing gown and from the way she was still cinching the sash and the disarray of her hair I gathered she hadn't been expecting me.

"I'm not alone," she said.

"I didn't come here for the dubious pleasures of your fair white body." I pushed my way into the room. (But couldn't help remembering that beautiful body of hers, not so exquisite as the dead whore's, and now the thoughts were inextricably mingled in my head: death and Courtney, sex and corpses, a Gordian knot I might never be able to untangle.)

"You didn't like my surprise?" She was smiling openly now, amused.

"No, I fucking did not!"

I took a step toward her, I was shaking. I couldn't stop fisting and unfisting my hands.

She fell back a step. But that confident, oddly expectant look didn't leave her face. "Bruno," she said lightly. "Would you come in here?"

A motion at the periphery of vision. Bruno stepped out of the shadows of her bedroom. He was a muscular brute, pumped, ripped, and as black as the fighter I'd seen go down earlier that night. He stood behind Courtney, totally naked, with slim hips and wide shoulders and the finest skin I'd ever seen.

And dead.

I saw it all in a flash.

"Oh, for God's sake, Courtney!" I said, disgusted. "I can't believe you. That you'd actually . . . That thing's just an obedient body.

There's nothing there—no passion, no connection, just . . . physical presence."

Courtney made a kind of chewing motion through her smile, weighing the implications of what she was about to say. Nastiness won.

"We have equity now," she said.

I lost it then. I stepped forward, raising a hand, and I swear to God I intended to bounce the bitch's head off the back wall. But she didn't flinch—she didn't even look afraid. She merely moved aside, saying, "In the body, Bruno. He has to look good in a business suit."

A dead fist smashed into my ribs so hard I thought for an instant my heart had stopped. Then Bruno punched me in my stomach. I doubled over, gasping. Two, three, four more blows. I was on the ground now, rolling over, helpless and weeping with rage.

"That's enough, baby. Now put out the trash."

Bruno dumped me in the hallway.

I glared up at Courtney through my tears. She was not at all beautiful now. Not in the least. You're getting older, I wanted to tell her. But instead I heard my voice, angry and astonished, saying, "You . . . you goddamn, fucking necrophile!"

"Cultivate a taste for it," Courtney said. Oh, she was purring! I doubted she'd ever find life quite this good again. "Half a million Brunos are about to come on the market. You're going to find it a lot more difficult to pick up *living* women in not so very long."

▼

I sent away the dead whore. Then I took a long shower that didn't really make me feel any better. Naked, I walked into my unlit suite and opened the curtains. For a long time I stared out over the glory and darkness that was Manhattan.

I was afraid, more afraid than I'd ever been in my life.

The slums below me stretched to infinity. They were a vast necropolis, a neverending city of the dead. I thought of the millions out there who were never going to hold down a job again. I thought of how they must hate me—me and my kind—and how helpless they were before us. And yet. There were so many of them and so few of us. If they were to all rise up at once, they'd be like a tsunami, irresistible. And if there was so much as a spark of life left in them, then that was exactly what they would do.

That was one possibility. There was one other, and that was that nothing would happen. Nothing at all.

God help me, but I didn't know which one scared me more.

Patterns

Pat Cadigan

To those who think women can't write tough: You obviously haven't read the works of Pat Cadigan. In dozens of short stories and a few novels over the last fifteen years, Cadigan has established herself as one of the most tough-minded writers of speculative fiction.

In "Patterns," from 1987, she writes about television, violence, and the interface of the two. What she's really writing about is how the fabric of society is frayed and torn by television, how our definitions of reality and fantasy have blurred under the constant assault of the video god.

Is this story violent? Yes. Though the violence of this tale is subject to interpretation by each reader, it's safe to say that there is a high quotient of fear and tension generated by Cadigan's finely drawn portrait of video violence. Perhaps more than any other story in the book, "Patterns" challenges you to decide where the line between fantasy and reality is drawn. And in this story, where that line is drawn is a matter of life and death.

I have this continuing fantasy of assassinating the President. Any President.

To step forward within a crowd, raising my weapon and aiming it at the President's head. Sometimes in the movie unreeling in my mind, my hand comes up holding a Luger Parabellum PO8 with the ridiculously long 190mm barrel. Other times I am holding a more likely Mauser Military Pistol. Twice I have found myself clutching an Uzi with the stock detached, three or four times I held a .357 Smith & Wesson Magnum. Once—only once—I stared down the length of a crossbow at the chief executive.

In the fantasy, I am not scared or angry. I don't think about the fact that I am taking a human life—the President, after all, is not so much human as manufactured, a product made flesh by the bipartisan system and the media in accidental conjugation. Is it wrong to fire at the dot pattern on a TV screen? I feel nothing beyond a mild nervousness, the slight (very slight) stage-fright I used to experience during my acting days. That my stage-fright was never acute enough to give me the cold sweats or send me vomiting into the handiest receptacle probably contributed to my lack of success in the theatre. In a one-person show, I could have been overlooked.

I know what you're thinking. I dream of assassination as a way to become visible at last. You are wrong. There is far more power in invisibility than in fame.

In fact, my fantasy movie has never proceeded beyond the point at which I raise my weapon and train it on the President. The action freezes when the President's gaze rests on the instrument of his/her destruction. But I know the rest of it:

I brace myself and fire. The President falls backwards, face a red ruin, body jerking in every direction. He/she is caught by aides and Secret Service agents and lowered to the ground. The crowd is completely silent. They are neither frightened nor in shock, just passive as the dot pattern rearranges itself. I lower the weapon to my side, then turn and walk away without hurry. Nobody looks at me. I walk some unmeasured distance to a car I recognize as mine, parked at an innocuous curb. I get in, twist the key waiting in the ignition and drive off.

In the days to come, there will be no mention of what happened to the President, ever, nor will there be any news about the government again. With one shot, I have obliterated not just the President but both Houses of Congress, the Supreme Court, Social Security, the National Endowment for the Arts, the Government Printing Office, the Gross National Product, the FTC, the CIA, the HEW and the Immigration and Naturalization Service, among others, as well as postponing forever the next election year. But life goes on anyway. I drive an endless highway across the United States and through the windshield I observe the permanent status quo I have visited on the American people. They don't know what has happened and they don't find it odd that they keep living in the same homes, working the same jobs, hearing the same music on the radio, watching the same dot patterns. Like me, they travel without destination. The days melt into each other with no distinguishing characteristics. The seasons come in and go out as they were meant to do in textbooks, but no one grows older. The treadmill has achieved a state of being both in motion and at rest simultaneously. Test pattern. Entropy.

All because I shot the President's dot pattern.

▼

Seen in close-up, the dot pattern could almost be taken for a collection of organisms, very cooperative organisms which have discovered a choreography that will produce patterns pleasing to the eyes of much larger and much less cooperative organisms.

Quotation from Chairman Busby Berkeley and Miss Amy Lowell: *Christ! What are patterns for?*

I'll tell you.

▼

The screen crackles when I put my finger on it. Static electricity; the dots warning me off their pattern. I pull my finger back and make it a pistol barrel pointing at the President, who is giving the State of the Union address. The President looks directly at "me" and hesitates. The dots at work on his pattern burble and boil and show me the red ruin that could be the result of my gun hand. Then the President's head re-forms and he goes on with his speech. We are in great need of reform in this country, he says, but even so, the State of the Union in general is most hope-inspiring.

Now. While there's still hope.

I cover the President's face with my finger. Loud crackling, followed by a close-up which put my finger absurdly on the President's moving mouth. He doesn't bite, but there is some mild electricity running up my arm.

▼

"It was all them cop shows," his mother said. "All that violence, they oughta get it off the tube." She said it on television, at his televised trial. Christ! What are patterns for? First-degree murder.

▼

"Always such a good kid," my mother would say. "Never a moment's trouble. Helped around the house and never answered back, either. Good-natured, you know. And when all the other kids were hanging out on the streets or chasing each other around and getting into trouble, *my* kid was studying. *My* kid always wanted to be somebody."

How true. I could have had my own show, in fact. If the technology had been good enough in those days, I might have lived in a suburban dot pattern, walked to school to my own theme music, mouthed dialog to my own laugh track. And achieved endless childhood in syndication. I could have been syndicated; I could have been a contender. Instead of a COMMERCIAL INTERRUPT FOR STATION IDENTIFICATION. It is often necessary to amputate a frame or two for the sake of format. So sorry, apparently the program director spliced this one a little early. But since it happened anyway, you have sixty seconds to contemplate your mantra. *Now* how much would you pay?

▼

Late at night, the patterns change and rearrange. I can't sleep. Two, three, four in the morning, the dots perform before my dry eyes. Slices, dices, juliennes. How much would you pay? Don't answer yet . . . stainless steel never needs sharpening. Now how much would you pay? Don't answer yet . . . act now and we'll throw in the fabulous Kalashnikov rifle, the most successful automatic rifle ever made! Gas operated, simultaneous bolt action and cocking, with a handy selector lever for single shot or automatic at a rate of 100 rpm, that's 100 rpm! *Isn't that amazing?* A mere 8 pounds with a folding metal stock, perfect for the murder of the head of state of your choice! Call now, operators are standing by!

I blink. When you awake, you will remember everything.

I want to call friends to ask if they have just seen this, too. Then I remember, all my friends are electric.

In living color.

A Famous Actor has shot himself. When they found him, the television in his townhouse was still on, murmuring merrily to itself as it played one of his old movies. I see it on the six o'clock news. Dot pattern of a dot pattern.

Now how much would you pay?

I have taken to dreaming in dots. Reruns. I raise my arm. I am holding a Browning GP35. I know nothing about guns. Its rate of fire is 25 rpm with a muzzle velocity of 1110 feet per second and it is going to make cheap chuck of the President's face. I know nothing about guns. The dot pattern knows. Point-blank range is that distance at which the bullet achieves its highest velocity, the distance the President is from me now. And it's on every channel, even cable.

Cable?

When I awake, I remember everything, in dot patterns, in living color.

A soap opera actress reports being assaulted in a restaurant by an irate woman wielding a Totes umbrella, shouting, "You leave that nice lady's husband alone, you slut! hasn't that poor woman had enough trouble without you trying to steal her man?" The actress's companions manage to pull the woman away. The rest of the people in the restaurant—diners, waiters, waitresses, busboys, maitre d'—all watch. They are neither frightened nor in shock.

And now, what will I do?

I consult the schedule. It is not time to run all the drug dealers out of Florida. Last night, the score was evened for the right-thinking on the mean streets of New York, it won't have to be done again for another week. I think I will defend my heavyweight title against the challenger in Las Vegas. I double up my fists and inspect the knuckles. Yes, these can go fifteen rounds, piece of Duncan Hines cake.

I press my knuckles against the screen. Wild crackling. The dots swarm in liquid patterns around each point of contact. Electricity is flowing up both arms, dancing through the nerve endings which sizzle into life and join the pattern.

My hands are being taped as I hold them out. I got to keep my fuckin hands up, do I hear, just keep my fuckin hands up and let him dance himself out and then jab his motherfuckin head off. The dots pulse, live from Caesar's Palace, more live than life. Fitted out with this dot pattern to wear, I could strike sparks in the moving, living air.

Now I know it can be done. The fight goes by in a swirl of dot pattern light. I keep my fuckin hands up and let him dance himself out and then jab his motherfuckin head off. The fight is not important. Now I know it can be done.

But I have to wait until the swelling goes down and the black eye fades. Never mind. You should see the other dot pattern.

More on that story from our correspondent in Washington.

Dot-pattern Washington snaps under the scanning line. The White House looks a little fuzzy. So does our correspondent. I touch her microphone; the dots leap in frenzy as I reshape their pattern into a 127mm barrel version of the Gyrojet pistol and then back into a microphone. Not yet. Tonight there is a press conference.

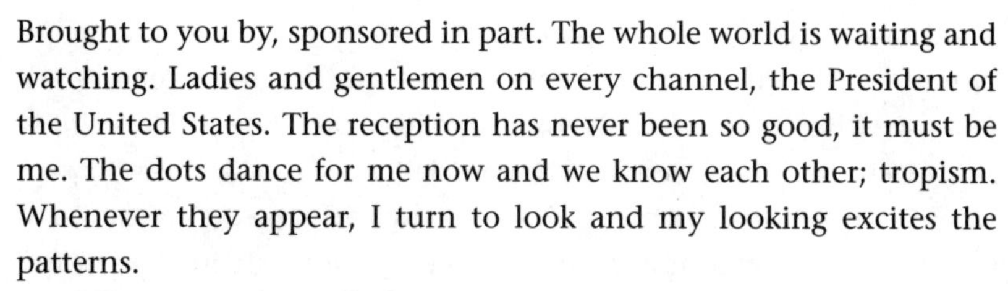

Brought to you by, sponsored in part. The whole world is waiting and watching. Ladies and gentlemen on every channel, the President of the United States. The reception has never been so good, it must be me. The dots dance for me now and we know each other; tropism. Whenever they appear, I turn to look and my looking excites the patterns.

What are patterns for?

I'll show you. I'll . . . *show* . . . you. As I show myself.

The dots sparkle around my hands in the continuing fantasy shown live on every channel. I run my fingers through them like a helping of stardust and reshape the pattern. They know what I need here. The Colt Commando with telescopic butt fully extended for shoulder firing, as used by the Green Berets, who have also been on this channel. The dots remember the pattern and here it is.

I step forward in the crowd of reporters demanding to be called on. The President's dot pattern scans the room, looking for a likely questioner. Then he sees "me" and hesitates. I have raised the Colt to my shoulder. Everyone is watching.

I touch my finger to the screen. The President's head disappears in a red mist, dot patterns gone insane. The room is completely silent, neither frightened nor shocked. Behind the podium, the Great Seal, the curtains, the President's aides, and Secret Service agents begin to unravel from the hole where the President's head was.

Embarrassed, puzzled anchorman. We are sorry for the interruption in transmission. Apparently we are having technical difficulties. We'll have more information for you after this.

No, we won't. That is all the information we are ever going to have, ever.

Fade to commercial. Dogs pounce on bowls of food. I sit on the couch, nodding. It's all over now. It wasn't quite how I expected it to go but it was, after all, adapted for television.

The commercial is followed by another commercial and then the embarrassed, puzzled anchorman. Apparently we are permanently cut off from our hook-up in the nation's capital. We will try to have some news on the rest of the press conference as soon as possible.

A fast recap of the statements and questions up until the moment I murdered the President's dot pattern, when things unraveled like celluloid melting away, a promise of an update soon. They patch the foreshortened evening schedule with a made-for-TV movie. Time to go.

I leave my apartment, go down to my car parked at an innocuous curb. The key is not waiting in the ignition but in my pocket. Such a good kid, never a moment's trouble. We can live in the same homes, work at the same jobs, hear the same music on the radio, watch the same dot patterns. We travel without destination. What are patterns for?

Nothing, any more.

▼

There used to be too much violence on TV. But not now.

The Mangler

Stephen King

When they hear the name Stephen King most people think immediately of horror. Even though King has written a number of novels that have nothing to do with horror, it's the genre in which he first gained his great fame. Known worldwide, subject of his own bookclub, sought avidly by Hollywood producers, Stephen King is possibly the most popular author of the last quarter century.

While he also has some very severe critics, King deserves his fame. A masterful storyteller possessed of a sure sense of plot and a gift for creating believable and sympathetic characters, he has written more than thirty best-selling novels and several dozen powerful short stories. The man can flat-out write!

"The Mangler," written in 1972, is classic King, and wonderfully entertaining. I won't spoil anything for you by telling you that the mangler of the title is a machine that irons clothing—and it kills people. And it must somehow be stopped. Given Stephen King's touch, the result is a story you'll remember for years to come.

Officer Hunton got to the laundry just as the ambulance was leaving—slowly, with no siren or flashing lights. Ominous. Inside, the office was stuffed with milling, silent people, some of them weeping. The plant itself was empty; the big automatic washers at the far end had not even been shut down. It made Hunton very wary. The crowd should be at the scene of the accident, not in the office. It was the way things worked—the human animal had a built-in urge to view the remains. A very bad one, then. Hunton felt his stomach tighten as it always did when the accident was very bad.

Fourteen years of cleaning human litter from highways and streets and the sidewalks at the bases of very tall buildings had not been able to erase that little hitch in the belly, as if something evil had clotted there.

A man in a white shirt saw Hunton and walked toward him reluctantly. He was a buffalo of a man with head thrust forward between shoulders, nose and cheeks vein-broken either from high blood pressure or too many conversations with the brown bottle. He was trying to frame words, but after two tries Hunton cut him off briskly:

"Are you the owner? Mr. Gartley?"

"No . . . no. I'm Stanner. The foreman. God, this—"

Hunton got out his notebook. "Please show me the scene of the accident, Mr. Stanner, and tell me what happened."

Stanner seemed to grow even more white; the blotches on his nose and cheeks stood out like birthmarks. "D-do I have to?"

Hunton raised his eyebrows. "I'm afraid you do. The call I got said it was serious."

"Serious—" Stanner seemed to be battling with his gorge; for a moment his Adam's apple went up and down like a monkey on a stick. "Mrs. Frawley is dead. Jesus, I wish Bill Gartley *was* here."

"What happened?"

Stanner said, "You better come over here."

He led Hunton past a row of hand presses, a shirt-folding unit, and then stopped by a laundry-marking machine. He passed a shaky hand across his forehead. "You'll have to go over by yourself, Officer. I can't look at it again. It makes me . . . I can't. I'm sorry."

Hunton walked around the marking machine with a mild feeling of contempt for the man. They run a loose shop, cut corners, run live steam through home-welded pipes, they work with dangerous cleaning chemicals without the proper protection, and finally, someone gets hurt. Or gets dead. Then they can't look. They can't—

Hunton saw it.

The machine was still running. No one had shut it off. The machine he later came to know intimately: the Hadley-Watson Model-6 Speed Ironer and Folder. A long and clumsy name. The people who worked here in the steam and the wet had a better name for it. The mangler.

Hunton took a long, frozen look, and then he performed a first in his fourteen years as a law-enforcement officer: he turned around, put a convulsive hand to his mouth, and threw up.

▼

"You didn't eat much," Jackson said.

The women were inside, doing dishes and talking babies while John Hunton and Mark Jackson sat in lawn chairs near the aromatic barbecue. Hunton smiled slightly at the understatement. He had eaten nothing.

"There was a bad one today," he said. "The worst."

"Car crash?"

"No. Industrial."

"Messy?"

Hunton did not reply immediately, but his face made an involuntary, writhing grimace. He got a beer out of the cooler between them, opened it, and emptied half of it. "I suppose you college profs don't know anything about industrial laundries?"

Jackson chuckled. "This one does. I spent a summer working in one as an undergraduate."

"Then you know the machine they call the speed ironer?"

Jackson nodded. "Sure. They run damp flatwork through them, mostly sheets and linen. A big, long machine."

"That's it," Hunton said. "A woman named Adelle Frawley got caught in it at the Blue Ribbon Laundry crosstown. It sucked her right in."

Jackson looked suddenly ill. "But . . . that can't happen, Johnny. There's a safety bar. If one of the women feeding the machine accidentally gets a hand under it, the bar snaps up and stops the machine. At least that's how I remember it."

Hunton nodded. "It's a state law. But it happened."

Hunton closed his eyes and in the darkness he could see the Hadley-Watson speed ironer again, as it had been that afternoon. It formed a long, rectangular box in shape, thirty feet by six. At the feeder end, a moving canvas belt moved under the safety bar, up at a slight angle, and then down. The belt carried the damp-dried, wrinkled sheets in continuous cycle over and under sixteen huge revolving cylinders that made up the main body of the machine. Over eight and under eight, pressed between them like thin ham between layers of superheated bread. Steam heat in the cylinders could be adjusted up to 300 degrees for maximum drying. The pressure on the sheets that rode the moving canvas belt was set at 800 pounds per square foot to get out every wrinkle.

And Mrs. Frawley, somehow, had been caught and dragged in. The steel, asbestos-jacketed pressing cylinders had been as red as barn paint, and the rising steam from the machine had carried the sickening stench of hot blood. Bits of her white blouse and blue slacks, even ripped segments of her bra and panties, had been torn free and ejected from the machine's far end thirty feet down, the bigger sections of cloth folded with grotesque and bloodstained neatness by the automatic folder. But not even that was the worst.

"It tried to fold everything," he said to Jackson, tasting bile in his throat. "But a person isn't a sheet, Mark. What I saw . . . what was left of her . . . " Like Stanner, the hapless foreman, he could not finish. "They took her out in a basket," he said softly.

Jackson whistled. "Who's going to get it in the neck? The laundry or the state inspectors?"

"Don't know yet," Hunton said. The malign image still hung behind his eyes, the image of the mangler wheezing and thumping and hissing, blood dripping down the green sides of the long cabinet in runnels, the burning *stink* of her . . . "It depends on who okayed that goddamn safety bar and under what circumstances."

"If it's the management, can they wiggle out of it?"

Hunton smiled without humor. "The woman died, Mark. If Gartley and Stanner were cutting corners on the speed ironer's maintenance, they'll go to jail. No matter who they know on the City Council."

"Do you think they were cutting corners?"

Hunton thought of the Blue Ribbon Laundry, badly lighted, floors wet and slippery, some of the machines incredibly ancient and creaking. "I think it's likely," he said quietly.

They got up to go in the house together. "Tell me how it comes out, Johnny," Jackson said. "I'm interested."

▼

Hunton was wrong about the mangler; it was clean as a whistle.

Six state inspectors went over it before the inquest, piece by piece. The net result was absolutely nothing. The inquest verdict was death by misadventure.

Hunton, dumbfounded, cornered Roger Martin, one of the inspectors, after the hearing. Martin was a tall drink of water with glasses as thick as the bottoms of shot glasses. He fidgeted with a ball-point pen under Hunton's questions.

"Nothing? Absolutely nothing doing with the machine?"

"Nothing," Martin said. "Of course, the safety bar was the guts of the matter. It's in perfect working order. You heard that Mrs. Gillian testify. Mrs. Frawley must have pushed her hand too far. No one saw that; they were watching their own work. She started screaming. Her hand was gone already, and the machine was taking her arm. They tried to pull her out instead of shutting it down—pure panic. Another woman, Mrs. Keene, said she *did* try to shut it off, but it's a fair assumption that she hit the start button rather than the stop in the confusion. By then it was too late."

"Then the safety bar malfunctioned," Hunton said flatly. "Unless she put her hand over it rather than under?"

"You can't. There's a stainless-steel facing above the safety bar. And the bar itself didn't malfunction. It's circuited into the machine itself. If the safety bar goes on the blink, the machine shuts down."

"Then how did it happen, for Christ's sake?"

"We don't know. My colleagues and I are of the opinion that the only way the speed ironer could have killed Mrs. Frawley was for her to have fallen into it from above. And she had both feet on the floor when it happened. A dozen witnesses can testify to that."

"You're describing an impossible accident," Hunton said.

"No. Only one we don't understand." He paused, hesitated, and then said: "I will tell you one thing, Hunton, since you seem to have taken this case to heart. If you mention it to anyone else, I'll deny I said it. But I didn't like that machine. It seemed . . . almost to be mocking us. I've inspected over a dozen speed ironers in the last five years on a regular basis. Some of them are in such bad shape that I wouldn't leave a dog unleashed around them—the state law is lamentably lax. But they were only machines for all that. But this one . . . it's a spook. I don't know why, but it is. I think if I'd found one thing, even a technicality, that was off whack, I would have ordered it shut down. Crazy, huh?"

"I felt the same way," Hunton said.

"Let me tell you about something that happened two years ago in Milton," the inspector said. He took off his glasses and began to polish them slowly on his vest. "Fella had parked an old icebox out in his backyard. The woman who called us said her dog had been caught in it and suffocated. We got the state policeman in the area to inform him it had to go to the town dump. Nice enough fella, sorry about the dog. He loaded it into his pickup and took it to the dump the next morning. That afternoon a woman in the neighborhood reported her son missing."

"God," Hunton said.

"The icebox was at the dump and the kid was in it, dead. A smart kid, according to his mother. She said he'd no more play in an empty icebox than he would take a ride with a strange man. Well, he did. We wrote it off. Case closed?"

"I guess," Hunton said.

"No. The dump caretaker went out next day to take the door off the thing. City Ordinance No. 58 on the maintenance of public dumping places." Martin looked at him expressionlessly. "He found six dead birds inside. Gulls, sparrows, a robin. And he said the door closed on his arm while he was brushing them out. Gave him a hell of a jump. That mangler at the Blue Ribbon strikes me like that, Hunton. I don't like it."

They looked at each other wordlessly in the empty inquest chamber, some six city blocks from where the Hadley-Watson Model-6 Speed Ironer and Folder sat in the busy laundry, steaming and fuming over its sheets.

▼

The case was driven out of his mind in the space of a week by the press of more prosaic police work. It was only brought back when he and his wife dropped over to Mark Jackson's house for an evening of bid whist and beer.

Jackson greeted him with: "Have you ever wondered if that laundry machine you told me about is haunted, Johnny?"

Hunton blinked, at a loss. "What?"

"The speed ironer at the Blue Ribbon Laundry, I guess you didn't catch the squeal this time."

"What squeal?" Hunton asked, interested.

Jackson passed him the evening paper and pointed to an item at the bottom of page two. The story said that a steam line had let go on the large speed ironer at the Blue Ribbon Laundry, burning three of the six women working at the feeder end. The accident had occurred at 3:45 P.M. and was attributed to a rise in steam pressure from the laundry's boiler. One of the women, Mrs. Annette Gillian, had been held at City Receiving Hospital with second-degree burns.

"Funny coincidence," he said, but the memory of Inspector Martin's words in the empty inquest chamber suddenly recurred: *It's a spook* . . . And the story about the dog and the boy and the birds caught in the discarded refrigerator.

He played cards very badly that night.

▼

Mrs. Gillian was propped up in bed reading *Screen Secrets* when Hunton came into the four-bed hospital room. A large bandage blanketed one arm and the side of her neck. The room's other occupant, a young woman with a pallid face, was sleeping.

Mrs. Gillian blinked at the blue uniform and then smiled tentatively. "If it was for Mrs. Cherinikov, you'll have to come back later. They just gave her medication."

"No, it's for you, Mrs. Gillian." Her smile faded a little. "I'm here unofficially—which means I'm curious about the accident at the laundry. John Hunton." He held out his hand.

It was the right move. Mrs. Gillian's smile became brilliant and she took his grip awkwardly with her unburnt hand. "Anything I can tell you, Mr. Hunton. God, I thought my Andy was in trouble at school again."

"What happened?"

"We was running sheets and the ironer just blew up—or it seemed that way. I was thinking about going home an' getting off my dogs when there's this great big bang, like a bomb. Steam is everywhere and this hissing noise . . . awful." Her smile trembled on the verge of extinction. "It was like the ironer was breathing. Like a dragon, it was. And Alberta—that's Alberta Keene—shouted that something was exploding and everyone was running and screaming and Ginny Jason started yelling she was burnt. I started to run away and I fell down. I didn't know I got it worst until then. God forbid it was no worse than it was. That live steam is three hundred degrees."

"The paper said a steam line let go. What does that mean?"

"The overhead pipe comes down into this kinda flexible line that feeds the machine. George—Mr. Stanner—said there must have been a surge from the boiler or something. The line split wide open."

Hunton could think of nothing else to ask. He was making ready to leave when she said reflectively:

"We never used to have these things on that machine. Only lately. The steam line breaking. That awful, awful accident with Mrs. Frawley, God rest her. And little things. Like the day Essie got her dress caught in one of the drive chains. That could have been dangerous if she hadn't ripped it right out. Bolts and things fall off. Oh, Herb Diment—he's the laundry repairman—has had an awful time with it. Sheets get caught in the folder. George says that's because they're using too much bleach in the washers, but it never used to happen. Now the girls hate to work on it. Essie even says there are still little bits of

Adelle Frawley caught in it and it's sacrilege or something. Like it had a curse. It's been that way ever since Sherry cut her hand on one of the clamps."

"Sherry?" Hunton asked.

"Sherry Ouelette. Pretty little thing, just out of high school. Good worker. But clumsy sometimes. You know how young girls are."

"She cut her hand on something?"

"Nothing strange about *that*. There are clamps to tighten down the feeder belt, see. Sherry was adjusting them so we could do a heavier load and probably dreaming about some boy. She cut her finger and bled all over everything." Mrs. Gillian looked puzzled. "It wasn't until after that the bolts started falling off. Adelle was . . . you know . . . about a week later. As if the machine had tasted blood and found it liked it. Don't women get funny ideas sometimes, Officer Hinton?"

"Hunton," he said absently, looking over her head and into space.

Ironically, he had met Mark Jackson in a washateria in the block that separated their houses, and it was there that the cop and the English professor still had their most interesting conversations.

Now they sat side by side in bland plastic chairs, their clothes going round and round behind the glass portholes of the coin-op washers. Jackson's paperback copy of Milton's collected works lay neglected beside him while he listened to Hunton tell Mrs. Gillian's story.

When Hunton had finished, Jackson said, "I asked you once if you thought the mangler might be haunted. I was only half joking. I'll ask you again now."

"No," Hunton said uneasily. "Don't be stupid."

Jackson watched the turning clothes reflectively. "Haunted is a bad word. Let's say possessed. There are almost as many spells for casting demons in as there are for casting them out. Frazier's *Golden Bough* is replete with them. Druidic and Aztec lore contain others. Even older ones, back to Egypt. Almost all of them can be reduced to startling common denominators. The most common, of course, is the blood of a virgin." He looked at Hunton. "Mrs. Gillian said the trouble started after this Sherry Ouelette accidentally cut herself."

"Oh, come on," Hunton said.

"You have to admit she sounds just the type," Jackson said.

"I'll run right over to her house," Hunton said with a small smile. "I can see it. 'Miss Ouelette, I'm Officer John Hunton. I'm investigating an ironer with a bad case of demon possession and would like to know if you're a virgin.' Do you think I'd get a chance to say good-bye to Sandra and the kids before they carted me off to the booby hatch?"

"I'd be willing to bet you'll end up saying something just like that," Jackson said without smiling. "I'm serious, Johnny. That machine scares the hell out of me and I've never seen it."

"For the sake of conversation," Hunton said, "what are some of the other so-called common denominators?"

Jackson shrugged. "Hard to say without study. Most Anglo-Saxon hex formulas specify graveyard dirt or the eye of a toad. European spells often mention the hand of glory, which can be interpreted as the actual hand of a dead man or one of the hallucinogenics used in connection with the Witches' Sabbath—usually belladonna or a psilocybin derivative. There could be others."

"And you think all those things got into the Blue Ribbon ironer? Christ, Mark, I'll bet there isn't any belladonna within a five-hundred-mile radius. Or do you think someone whacked off their Uncle Fred's hand and dropped it in the folder?"

"If seven hundred monkeys typed for seven hundred years—"

"One of them would turn out the works of Shakespeare," Hunton finished sourly. "Go to hell. Your turn to go across to the drugstore and get some dimes for the dryers."

It was very funny how George Stanner lost his arm in the mangler.

Seven o'clock Monday morning the laundry was deserted except for Stanner and Herb Diment, the maintenance man. They were performing the twice-yearly function of greasing the mangler's bearings before the laundry's regular day began at seven-thirty. Diment was at the far end, greasing the four secondaries and thinking of how unpleasant this machine made him feel lately, when the mangler suddenly roared into life.

He had been holding up four of the canvas exit belts to get at the motor beneath and suddenly the belts were running in his hands, ripping the flesh off his palms, dragging him along.

He pulled free with a convulsive jerk seconds before the belts would have carried his hands into the folder.

"What the Christ, George!" he yelled. "Shut the frigging thing *off!*"

George Stanner began to scream.

It was a high, wailing, blood-maddened sound that filled the laundry, echoing off the steel faces of the washers, the grinning mouths of the steam presses, the vacant eyes of the industrial dryers. Stanner drew in a great, whooping gasp of air and screamed again: *"Oh God of Christ I'm caught I'M CAUGHT—"*

The rollers began to produce rising steam. The folder gnashed and thumped. Bearings and motors seemed to cry out with a hidden life of their own.

Diment raced to the other end of the machine.

The first roller was already going a sinister red. Diment made a moaning, gobbling noise in his throat. The mangler howled and thumped and hissed.

A deaf observer might have thought at first that Stanner was merely bent over the machine at an odd angle. Then even a deaf man would have been the pallid, eye-bulging rictus of his face, mouth twisted open in a continuous scream. The arm was disappearing under the safety bar and beneath the first roller; the fabric of his shirt had torn away at the shoulder seam and his upper arm bulged grotesquely as the blood was pushed steadily backward.

"Turn it off!" Stanner screamed. There was a snap as his elbow broke.

Diment thumbed the off button.

The mangler continued to hum and growl and turn.

Unbelieving, he slammed the button again and again—nothing. The skin of Stanner's arm had grown shiny and taut. Soon it would split with the pressure the roll was putting on it; and still he was conscious and screaming. Diment had a nightmare cartoon image of a man flattened by a steamroller, leaving only a shadow.

"Fuses—" Stanner screeched. His head was being pulled down, down, as he was dragged forward.

Diment whirled and ran to the boiler room, Stanner's screams chasing him like lunatic ghosts. The mixed stench of blood and steam rose in the air.

On the left wall were three heavy gray boxes containing all the fuses for the laundry's electricity. Diment yanked them open and began to pull the long, cylindrical fuses like a crazy man, throwing them back over his shoulders. The overhead lights went out; then the air compressor; then the boiler itself, with a huge dying whine.

And still the mangler turned. Stanner's screams had been reduced to bubbly moans.

Diment's eye happened on the fire ax in its glassed-in box. He grabbed it with a small, gagging whimper and ran back. Stanner's arm was gone almost to the shoulder. Within seconds his bent and straining neck would be snapped against the safety bar.

"I can't," Diment blubbered, holding the ax. "Jesus, George, I can't, I can't, I—"

The machine was an abattoir now. The folder spat out pieces of shirt sleeve, scraps of flesh, a finger. Stanner gave a huge, whooping scream and Diment swung the ax up and brought it down in the laundry's shadowy lightlessness. Twice. Again.

Stanner fell away, unconscious and blue, blood jetting from the stump just below the shoulder. The mangler sucked what was left into itself . . . and shut down.

Weeping, Diment pulled his belt out of its loops and began to make a tourniquet.

▼

Hunton was talking on the phone with Roger Martin, the inspector. Jackson watched him while he patiently rolled a ball back and forth for three-year-old Patty Hunton to chase.

"He pulled *all* the fuses?" Hunton was asking. "And the off button just didn't function, huh? . . . Has the ironer been shut down?

. . . Good. Great. Huh? . . . No, not official." Hunton frowned, then looked sideways at Jackson. "Are you still reminded of that refrigerator, Roger? . . . Yes. Me too. Goodbye."

He hung up and looked at Jackson. "Let's go see the girl, Mark."

She had her own apartment (the hesitant yet proprietary way she showed them in after Hunton had flashed his buzzer made him suspect that she hadn't had it long), and she sat uncomfortably across from them in the carefully decorated, postage-stamp living room.

"I'm Officer Hunton and this is my associate, Mr. Jackson. It's about the accident at the laundry." He felt hugely uncomfortable with this dark, shyly pretty girl.

"Awful," Sherry Ouelette murmured. "It's the only place I've ever worked. Mr. Gartley is my uncle. I liked it because it let me have this place and my own friends. But now . . . it's so *spooky."*

"The State Board of Safety has shut the ironer down pending a full investigation," Hunton said. "Did you know that?"

"Sure." She sighed restlessly. "I don't know what I'm going to do—"

"Miss Ouelette," Jackson interrupted, "you had an accident with the ironer, didn't you? Cut your hand on a clamp, I believe?"

"Yes, I cut my finger." Suddenly her face clouded. "That was the first thing." She looked at them woefully. "Sometimes I feel like the girls don't like me so much anymore . . . as if I were to blame."

"I have to ask you a hard question," Jackson said slowly. "A question you won't like. It seems absurdly personal and off the subject, but I can only tell you it is not. Your answers won't ever be marked down in a file or record."

She looked frightened. "D-did I do something?"

Jackson smiled and shook his head; she melted. *Thank God for Mark,* Hunton thought.

"I'll add this, though: the answer may help you keep your nice little flat here, get your job back, and make things at the laundry the way they were before."

"I'd answer anything to have that," she said.

"Sherry, are you a virgin?"

She looked utterly flabbergasted, utterly shocked, as if a priest had given communion and then slapped her. Then she lifted her head, made a gesture at her neat efficiency apartment, as if asking them how they could believe it might be a place of assignation.

"I'm saving myself for my husband," she said simply.

Hunton and Jackson looked calmly at each other, and in that tick of a second, Hunton knew that it was all true: a devil had taken over the inanimate steel and cogs and gears of the mangler and had turned it into something with its own life.

"Thank you," Jackson said quietly.

▼

"What now?" Hunton asked bleakly as they rode back. "Find a priest to exorcise it?"

Jackson snorted. "You'd go a far piece to find one that wouldn't hand you a few tracts to read while he phoned the booby hatch. It has to be our play, Johnny."

"Can we do it?"

"Maybe. The problem is this: We know something is in the mangler. We don't know *what.*" Hunton felt cold, as if touched by a fleshless finger. "There are a great many demons. Is the one we're dealing with in the circle of Bubastis or Pan? Baal? Or the Christian deity we call Satan? We don't know. If the demon had been deliberately cast, we would have a better chance. But this seems to be a case of random possession."

Jackson ran his fingers through his hair. "The blood of a virgin, yes. But that narrows it down hardly at all. We have to be sure, very sure."

"Why?" Hunton asked bluntly. "Why not just get a bunch of exorcism formulas together and try them out?"

Jackson's face went cold. "This isn't cops 'n' robbers, Johnny. For Christ's sake, don't think it is. The rite of exorcism is horribly dangerous. It's like controlled nuclear fission, in a way. We could make a mistake and destroy ourselves. The demon is caught in that piece of machinery. But give it a chance and—"

"It could get out?"

"It would love to get out," Jackson said grimly. "And it likes to kill."

When Jackson came over the following evening, Hunton had sent his wife and daughter to a movie. They had the living room to themselves, and for this Hunton was relieved. He could still barely believe what he had become involved in.

"I canceled my classes," Jackson said, "and spent the day with some of the most god-awful books you can imagine. This afternoon I fed over thirty recipes for calling demons into the tech computer. I've got a number of common elements. Surprisingly few."

He showed Hunton the list: blood of a virgin, graveyard dirt, hand of glory, bat's blood, night moss, horse's hoof, eye of toad.

There were others, all marked secondary.

"Horse's hoof," Hunton said thoughtfully. "Funny—"

"Very common. In fact—"

"Could these things—any of them be—interpreted loosely?" Hunton interrupted.

"If lichens picked at night could be substituted for night moss, for instance?"

"Yes."

"It's very likely," Jackson said. "Magical formulas are often ambiguous and elastic. The black arts have always allowed plenty of room for creativity."

"Substitute Jell-O for horse's hoof," Hunton said. "Very popular in bag lunches. I noticed a little container of it sitting under the ironer's sheet platform on the day the Frawley woman died. Gelatin is made from horse's hooves."

Jackson nodded. "Anything else?"

"Bat's blood . . . well, it's a big place. Lots of unlighted nooks and crannies. Bats seem likely, although I doubt if the management would admit to it. One could conceivably have been trapped in the mangler."

Jackson tipped his head back and knuckled bloodshot eyes. "It fits . . . it all fits."

"It does?"

"Yes. we can safely rule out the hand of glory, I think. Certainly no one dropped a hand into the ironer *before* Mrs. Frawley's death, and belladonna is definitely not indigenous to the area."

"Graveyard dirt?"

"What do you think?"

"It would have to be a hell of a coincidence," Hunton said. "Nearest cemetery is Pleasant Hill, and that's five miles from the Blue Ribbon."

"Okay," Jackson said. "I got the computer operator—who thought I was getting ready for Halloween—to run a positive breakdown of all the primary and secondary elements on the list. Every possible combination. I threw out some two dozen which were completely meaningless. The others fall into fairly clear-cut categories. The elements we've isolated are in one of those."

"What is it?"

Jackson grinned. "An easy one. The mythos centers in South America with branches in the Caribbean. Related to voodoo. The literature I've got looks on the deities as strictly bush league, compared to some of the real heavies, like Saddath or He-Who-Cannot-Be-Named. The thing in that machine is going to slink away like the neighborhood bully."

"How do we do it?"

"Holy water and a smidgen of the Holy Eucharist ought to do it. And we can read some of the Leviticus to it. Strictly Christian white magic."

"You're sure it's not worse?"

"Don't see how it can be," Jackson said pensively. "I don't mind telling you I was worried about that hand of glory. That's very black juju. Strong magic."

"Holy water wouldn't stop it?"

"A demon called up in conjunction with the hand of glory could eat a stack of Bibles for breakfast. We would be in bad trouble messing with something like that at all. Better to pull the goddamn thing apart."

"Well, are you completely sure—"

"No, but fairly sure. It all fits too well."

"When?"

"The sooner, the better," Jackson said. "How do we get in? Break a window?"

Hunton smiled, reached into his pocket, and dangled a key in front of Jackson's nose.

"Where'd you get that? Gartley?"

"No," Hunton said. "From a state inspector named Martin."

"He know what we're doing?"

"I think he suspects. He told me a funny story a couple of weeks ago."

"About the mangler?"

"No," Hunton said. "About a refrigerator. Come on."

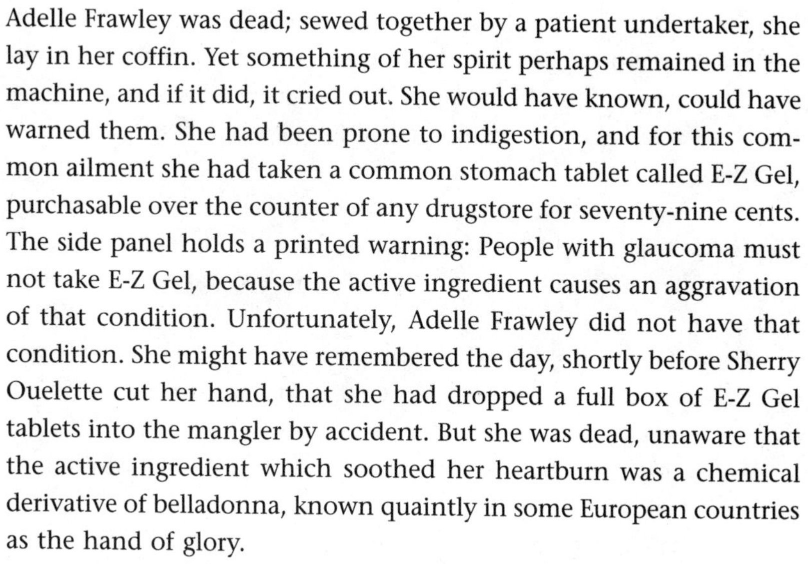

Adelle Frawley was dead; sewed together by a patient undertaker, she lay in her coffin. Yet something of her spirit perhaps remained in the machine, and if it did, it cried out. She would have known, could have warned them. She had been prone to indigestion, and for this common ailment she had taken a common stomach tablet called E-Z Gel, purchasable over the counter of any drugstore for seventy-nine cents. The side panel holds a printed warning: People with glaucoma must not take E-Z Gel, because the active ingredient causes an aggravation of that condition. Unfortunately, Adelle Frawley did not have that condition. She might have remembered the day, shortly before Sherry Ouelette cut her hand, that she had dropped a full box of E-Z Gel tablets into the mangler by accident. But she was dead, unaware that the active ingredient which soothed her heartburn was a chemical derivative of belladonna, known quaintly in some European countries as the hand of glory.

There was a sudden ghastly burping noise in the spectral silence of the Blue Ribbon Laundry—a bat fluttered madly for its hole in the insulation above the dryers where it had roosted, wrapping wings around its blind face.

It was a noise almost like a chuckle.

The mangler began to run with a sudden, lurching grind—belts hurrying through the darkness, cogs meeting and meshing and grinding, heavy pulverizing rollers rotating on and on.

It was ready for them.

When Hunton pulled into the parking lot it was shortly after midnight and the moon was hidden behind a raft of moving clouds. He jammed on the brakes and switched off the lights in the same motion; Jackson's forehead almost slammed against the padded dash.

He switched off the ignition and the steady thump-hiss-thump became louder. "It's the mangler," he said slowly. "It's the mangler. Running by itself. In the middle of the night."

They sat for a moment in silence, feeling the fear crawl up their legs.

Hunton said, "All right. Let's do it."

They got out and walked to the building, the sound of the mangler growing louder. As Hunton put the key into the lock of the service door, he thought that the machine *did* sound alive—as if it were breathing in great hot gasps and speaking to itself in hissing, sardonic whispers.

"All of a sudden I'm glad I'm with a cop," Jackson said. He shifted the brown bag he held from one arm to the other. Inside was a small jelly jar filled with holy water wrapped in waxed paper, and Gideon Bible.

They stepped inside and Hunton snapped up the light switches by the door. The fluorescents flickered into cold life. At the same instant the mangler shut off.

A membrane of steam hung over its rollers. It waited for them in its new ominous silence.

"God, it's an ugly thing," Jackson whispered.

"Come on," Hunton said. "Before we lose our nerve."

They walked over to it. The safety bar was in its down position over the belt which fed the machine.

Hunton put out a hand. "Close enough, Mark. Give me the stuff and tell me what to do."

"But—"

"No argument."

Jackson handed him the bag and Hunton put it on the sheet table in front of the machine. He gave Jackson the Bible.

"I'm going to read," Jackson said. "When I point at you, sprinkle the holy water on the machine with your fingers. You say: In the name of the Father, and of the Son, and of the Holy Ghost, get thee from this place, thou unclean. Got it?"

"Yes."

"The second time I point, break the wafer and repeat the incantation again."

"How will we know if it's working?"

"You'll know. The thing is apt to break every window in the place getting out. If it doesn't work the first time, we keep doing it until it does."

"I'm scared green," Hunton said.

"As a matter of fact, so am I."

"If we're wrong about the hand of glory—"

"We're not," Jackson said. "Here we go."

He began. His voice filled the empty laundry with spectral echoes. "Turnest not thou aside to idols, nor make molten gods for yourself. I am the Lord thy God . . . " The words fell like stones into a silence that had suddenly become filled with a creeping, tomblike cold. The mangler remained still and silent under the fluorescents, and to Hunton it still seemed to grin.

". . . and the land will vomit you out for having defiled it, as it vomited out nations before you." Jackson looked up, his face strained, and pointed.

Hunton sprinkled holy water across the feeder belt.

There was a sudden, gnashing scream of tortured metal. Smoke rose from the canvas belts where the holy water had touched and took on writhing, red-tinged shapes. The mangler suddenly jerked into life.

"We've got it!" Jackson cried above the rising clamor. "It's on the run!"

He began to read again, his voice rising over the sound of the machinery. He pointed to Hunton again, and Hunton sprinkled some of the host. As he did so he was suddenly swept with a bone-freezing terror, a sudden vivid feeling that it has gone wrong, that the machine had called their bluff—and was the stronger.

Jackson's voice was still rising, approaching climax.

Sparks began to jump across the arc between the main motor and the secondary; the smell of ozone filled the air, like the copper smell of hot blood. Now the main motor was smoking; the mangler was running at an insane, blurred speed: a finger touched to the central belt would have caused the whole body to be hauled in and turned to a bloody rag in the space of five seconds. The concrete beneath their feet trembled and thrummed.

A main bearing blew with a searing flash of purple light, filling the chill air with the smell of thunderstorms, and still the mangler ran, faster and faster, belts and rollers and cogs moving at a speed that made them seem to blend and merge, change, melt, transmute—

Hunton, who had been standing almost hypnotized, suddenly took a step backward. "Get away!" he screamed over the blaring racket.

"We've almost got it!" Jackson yelled back. "Why—"

There was a sudden indescribable ripping noise and a fissure in the concrete floor suddenly raced toward them and past, widening. Chips of ancient cement flew up in a starburst.

Jackson looked at the mangler and screamed.

It was trying to pull itself out of the concrete, like a dinosaur trying to escape a tar pit. And it wasn't precisely an ironer anymore. It was still changing, melting. The 550-volt cable fell, spitting blue fire, into the rollers and was chewed away. For a moment two fireballs glared at them like lambent eyes, eyes filled with a great and cold hunger.

Another fault line tore open. The mangler leaned toward them, within an ace of being free of the concrete moorings that held it. It leered at them; the safety bar had slammed up and what Hunton saw was a gaping, hungry mouth filled with steam.

They turned to run and another fissure opened at their feet. Behind them, a great screaming roar as the thing came free. Hunton leaped over, but Jackson stumbled and fell sprawling.

Hunton turned to help and a huge, amorphous shadow fell over him, blocking the fluorescents.

It stood over Jackson, who lay on his back, staring up in a silent rictus of terror—the perfect sacrifice. Hunton had only a confused impression of something black and moving that bulked to a tremendous height above them both, something with glaring electric eyes the size of footballs, an open mouth with a moving canvas tongue.

He ran; Jackson's dying scream followed him.

▼

When Roger Martin finally got out of bed to answer the doorbell, he was still only a third awake; but when Hunton reeled in, shock slapped him fully into the world with a rough hand.

Hunton's eyes bulged madly from his head, and his hands were claws as he scratched at the front of Martin's robe. There was a small oozing cut on his cheek and his face was splashed with dirty gray specks of powdered cement.

His hair had gone dead white.

"Help me . . . for Jesus' sake, help me. Mark is dead. Jackson is dead."

"Slow down," Martin said. "Come in the living room."

Hunton followed him, making a thick whining noise in his throat, like a dog.

Martin poured him a two-ounce knock of Jim Beam and Hunton held the glass in both hands, downing the raw liquor in a choked gulp. The glass fell unheeded to the carpet and his hands, like wandering ghosts, sought Martin's lapels again.

"The mangler killed Mark Jackson. It . . . it . . . oh God, it might get out! We can't let it get out! We can't . . . we . . . oh—" He began to scream, a crazy, whooping sound that rose and fell in jagged cycles.

Martin tried to hand him another drink but Hunton knocked it aside. "We have to burn it," he said. "Burn it before it can get out. Oh, what if it gets out? Oh Jesus, what if—" His eyes suddenly flickered, glazed, rolled up to show the whites, and he fell to the carpet in a stonelike faint.

Mrs. Martin was in the doorway, clutching her robe to her throat. "Who is he, Rog? Is he crazy? I thought—" She shuddered.

"I don't think he's crazy." She was suddenly frightened by the sick shadow of fear on her husband's face. "God, I hope he came quick enough."

He turned to the telephone, picked up the receiver, froze.

There was a faint, swelling noise from the east of the house, the way that Hunton had come. A steady, grinding clatter, growing louder. The living-room window stood half open and now Martin caught a dark smell on the breeze. An odor of ozone . . . or blood.

He stood with his hand on the useless telephone as it grew louder, louder, gnashing and fuming, something in the streets that was hot and steaming. The blood stench filled the room.

His hand dropped from the telephone.

It was already out.

About the Editor

James Frenkel has been editing books throughout the nineties. In stints with Dell/Delacorte; his own publishing company, Bluejay Books; and, for the past thirteen years, Tor Books, he has edited numerous best-selling and critically acclaimed books, particularly in the fields of science fiction, fantasy, and horror.

The packager of the award-winning *Year's Best Fantasy and Horror* series, Frenkel also works as a literary agent for many notable authors of fiction and nonfiction. A New York City native, he lives with his wife, author Joan D. Vinge, and their children in Madison, Wisconsin.